A NICOLLETTE BEVERLEY SPY NOVEL

A Dangerous Business

THE BATTLE CONTINUES

A.R. Goldsmith

FLARE BOOKS
El Paso, Texas

Publisher: Flare Books, an imprint of Catalyst Press
For further information, write info@catalystpress.org
You can find out more at catalystpress.org.
In North America, this book is distributed by
Consortium Book Sales & Distribution, a division of Ingram.
Phone: 612/746-2600
cbsdinfo@ingramcontent.com
www.cbsd.com

In South Africa, Namibia, and Botswana,
this book is distributed by Protea Distribution.
For information, email orders@proteadistribution.co.za
Library of Congress Control Number: 2025943670

To my wonderful wife, Pauline.

Special thanks to my family;
Elizabeth, Sharon, Adam, Danny, Nathan,
Zoe, Bailey, Charlotte, and Jacob.

With deep gratitude for their assistance:
Paul Fitzer, RAF retired
Jim Zamillo
Donald Henn
Jessica Powers

Table of Contents

A NICOLLETTE BEVERLEY SPY NOVEL

A Dangerous Business

THE BATTLE CONTINUES

A.R. Goldsmith

Escape

The only sounds were the soft muffles of twigs crunching under her feet and the occasional loud boom from thunder far away. The narrow muddy path twisted and turned through the seemingly endless jungle, illuminated only by individual small torches and the random distant lightning. Every now and then, the guide would whisper for the group to increase pace and keep quiet.

Nicollette Beverley's heart raced with a sense of urgency to reach the town of Chiang Rai as soon as possible. The only airport in this remote region of Thailand was located there. Then a flight to Bangkok and home to England.

The increasing rate of thunder was a sign that the monsoon rains would be coming again, making a difficult journey even more dangerous. And who knew if they were being followed. She trudged on, subconsciously reaching for the weapon holstered against her right thigh, making sure it was still there.

Just a few hours ago, Nicollette and her colleagues had been working inside a makeshift, clandestine communications hut in a remote area of northwestern Thailand. For the past month, the select group of analysts and intelligence officers from various countries had been monitoring the movement of drugs and military equipment in and out of the nearby "Golden Triangle," the place where Thailand, Laos, and Burma meet. There were seventeen members at the remote facility. It was a 24-hour, seven day a week operation. The group consisted of two Germans, two French, two Spaniards, two Americans and two Brits. There were five NATO soldiers as well as three Thai guides. Two of the NATO soldiers were from the Special Forces and they, along with a Thai guide, were planted deep in the jungle, reporting information back to the communications hut which was then forwarded to Bangkok. There were only two women in the group, a Spanish analyst and Nicollette.

The overall mission was to interdict the heroin and opium pipeline heading to Europe. "Stop it at the source and the whole bridge to Europe will collapse," Nicollette remembered from the initial briefing. Last year's air bombing of the area did little to stem the flow and the situation worsened when local drug lords resumed arming their militias with military equipment abandoned by the Americans in Vietnam. Although the equipment was old, it was still serviceable and formidable in this remote area of Southeast Asia. If action was not taken soon, the heavily armed drug lords could quickly overrun the local authorities and set up a nearly impenetrable fiefdom in the "Golden Triangle." Drug trafficking would be much harder to stem and certainly be more costly in manpower and money. Nicollette and the group's mission was simple: obtain definitive intelligence of the area, regarding the various trafficking routes and sources while maintaining communications with Bangkok. And most importantly, stay alive.

It had been over a fortnight since she had arrived from England. The day-long hike through the jungle to the remote communications site left her dehydrated, mosquito-bitten, and exhausted. Now, despite the darkness and the storm coming, the group had to evacuate back to Chaing Rai in half the time. The group took a quick break while the guides looked for a way to cross a large stream.

Nicollette remembered being summoned to a meeting with Major Blasingame when she was "asked" to volunteer for the mission. "In all of Group 228/157 with this part of the world Nicollette," she said. "You have been monitoring the communications from that area for some time now. I believe it started when you first came here after your training."

Her first days in Group 228/157 seemed like such a long time ago. She thought of those days of operation "Twist" and how it all seemed so surreal and far away, the strange communications coming across her screen from a distant land and the stress of coding and decoding accurately with speed. Nicollette had noted the information coming from Thailand about the movement of military hardware and asked her supervisor what to do. She was instructed to stand by. And now she was here.

The other Brit in the group was that supervisor, Mr. Peter Johnson, who now was the communications expert of the clandestine site. Nicollette had worked on various internal communication projects with him since her first days in Group 228/157. He was with Nicollette in Ash Sha' am during operation Abraham's Tent where he was wounded during the firefight on the Lesser Tunb Island. Nicollette felt comfortable around Mr. Johnson, even in such a dangerous assignment as this remote area of Thailand. He looked out for her, almost like an uncle, or a substitute father. Despite his status as a bachelor, she knew Peter Johnson would make a good father.

"Let's go," the guide commanded, bringing Nicollette back to reality. "We've still got a ways to go."

The mosquito bites on her legs itched. *Damn bugs!* She took a sip of water from her canteen and splashed a bit onto the red welts. She had grabbed the canteen as they were being rushed out of the communications hut. Everything else was left behind to make room for communications equipment in her backpack. What wasn't taken was disabled by Mr. Johnson.

The haste to leave had been caused by the sudden arrival of one of the Special Forces soldiers back from the field, out of breath and bleeding from a deep cut in his leg. The NATO officer in charge quickly intervened. The hut was small and Nicollette overheard the conversation. While being bandaged and gathering his breath, the soldier explained how he and the two others that were with him had made it to their assigned lookout position without any problem. "Nothing out of the ordinary and we took all the necessary precautions. We had just set up our radio and started our observation of the North Trail when we spotted a caravan of trucks about two kilometers away, heading towards our position. Our radioman, Ollie, I mean Olufsen, was reaching for the headset to report in when shots rang out. Our Thai guide, Charn Chai, was killed. We could tell we were outnumbered, so we set a grenade to the radio and crawled under the brush to escape. We must have crawled one hundred meters before we stood up. The area was quiet, but we decided to split up just in case. About ten minutes later, I heard automatic weapons fire. They must have been following Olufsen. I circled back to see what was happening. I proceeded with extra care, using all the precautions, and managed to get close enough to see ten gunmen with what looked like AKs circling a body. It looked to be Olufsen, not sure if he was alive or not. There were too many of them to make a stand, so I crawled down an embankment to a small creek and headed back here. I got caught up on some downed tree limbs and brush and my leg was severely cut. The damn mossies were having lunch on me. I don't know if I was followed or not, but these bandits sure mean business."

Having heard the story, the officer in charge brought the group together and ordered an immediate evacuation. He was taking no chances and made a final communication to Bangkok. Instructions were given and nothing of importance was to be left behind. The sun was setting as he ordered firearms for everyone qualified to use one. They had twenty minutes to move out.

The guides found a river crossing about a kilometer south of where the group was resting. The thunder and lightning continued, and a steady rain fell. Nicollette found it more difficult to navigate the uneven, muddy terrain while carrying her backpack. She was soaked, making everything feel much heavier, including her clothes. The only good news was the rain had chased off the relentless mossies, but the trail was becoming even more treacherous, the mud getting deeper, seemingly trying to suck Nicollette's boots right off her feet. She took each step with extreme caution.

The path started to incline and soon she found herself, along with the group, on some rocks overlooking a river. The guides had strung a line about twenty-five meters long across the river and Nicollette was escorted to the river's bank. The river was swollen and moving fast as the rain continued to fall.

Before she could get organized to cross, the soldier that was protecting the rear of the group came rushing down the path to the river's edge. He was carrying his automatic weapon in his arms and sought out the commanding officer. He pointed back to the path and had an animated conversation with the officer.

"Bad news, I'm afraid. We're being followed," the officer announced. "My guess is we have about a fifteen-minute head start, but we still have about ten kilometers to go. We need to get across quickly."

Not wanting to get caught at the river's edge with the civilians, the NATO Officer commanded, "NOW!"

Nicollette's heart raced. An almost numb feeling came over her as she recalled the firefight on the Lessor Tunb Island, and Lieutenant Amin yelling at her, *Fire the damn gun, Miss Beverley! Fire the damn gun!*

Would she hesitate again when faced with the same situation?

A soldier held out his hand and assisted her to the rope crossing the river. The rushing water quickly brought Nicollette back to the moment. Her heart continued to race, but the numbness and fatigue melted away, leaving her keenly aware of their perilous situation. The water was lapping at her knees as she slowly walked across the sandy bottom of the river. She gripped the rope tightly with her right hand, proceeding step by step through the rushing water. The sandy river bottom turned uneven and rocky as she approached the midpoint. Her grip on the rope tightened even further as defense against a river flow that seemed determined to knock her down. The water was now at her waist. Subconsciously, Nicollette reached across her body to feel for her weapon. *It's still there, Nicky,* she told herself, *it's still there.*

The rain fell relentlessly, and the river was becoming more insistent on making the crossing difficult. A small grin crossed her face as the river bottom's surface started to rise. She was almost across, just a few more meters. A sudden push on her back gave her additional encouragement. She glanced over her shoulder. Peter Johnson gave her a smile and a wink. "You're doing great, Nicollette. Almost there."

An outstretched hand was extended in her direction. Nicollette grabbed it and pulled herself from the thigh-high water onto the rocky riverbank. A soldier pointed her towards an opening a few meters above the river's edge. She climbed to a small clearing between several large trees and looked back at the last of her colleagues crossing the bloated, muddy river. Once the last soldier had made it across, the guide rope was cut. The NATO officer motioned for everyone to follow the Thai guide forward while he would take the rear, the last two soldiers following about one hundred meters behind.

The group hadn't walked very far when there was a bright flash and a loud boom just off to the right. Tree and plant debris flew everywhere, and a mud shower rained down on the weary group. The percussion from the blast knocked Nicollette to her knees. At first, she thought it was lightning, but word quickly spread through the group that it was a rocket-propelled grenade. A second and third blast sent Nicollette flat on the ground, her face buried in mud and the sound of distant automatic weapons fire permeating the air.

Peter Johnson grabbed Nicollette's arm and helped her to her feet. Her ears rang as she reached the leather band, unlocking her weapon from its holster. "Hopefully, we won't need that, Nicky," Mr. Johnson said as he nudged her to get going.

Just the same, I'm taking no chances, Nicollette thought.

The NATO officer checked to make sure everyone was good and urged the group to get moving quickly. The rain had slowed to a drizzle and finally stopped. The cloud cover slowly started to clear, allowing the full moon to shine light through the dense jungle canopy. The group walked heavily on as fatigue crept over Nicollette's body. She was absolutely soaked and the backpack felt like it weighed five stone. She reached for her canteen and drank the last bit of water. *One foot in front of the other, Nicky. You can do this,* she kept telling herself.

The sound of automatic weapons fire seemed to drift away as the group moved further away from the river crossing. Nicollette estimated that they had traveled about three kilometers when the forward Thai guide came running to the group. There was a quick conversation with the NATO officer and then the guide ran back ahead. The NATO officer gathered the group together and explained there was a clearing and a small dirt road ahead. The road went to Chaing Rai but the area was filled with bandits. "We will proceed with extra caution and stay to the side of the road. Those of you that can, please ease the burden of those that need relief. We need to be nimble. If you have a weapon, keep it at the ready."

Within minutes, the group started down the path towards the clearing.

Peter Johnson looked at Nicollette. "You good, Nicky?"

Nicollette smiled. "I'll be alright. Thanks."

She was dirty from head to toe. Her face, arms, and legs were splattered with mud and her hair wet and moulded to her head. She held one strap of the backpack with her left hand and her weapon with her right.

At the small road, the Thai guide signaled to advance. It

appeared they were heading in a southerly direction. To her right, there was about a fifty meter clearing. To her left, the deep forest. The moon was in full view now, illuminating the narrow dirt road. The footing was firmer, and the group seemed to be making better time. About one hundred meters ahead, the light given by the guide's torch illuminated his silhouette. At once, he turned back to the group and motioned with his torch. The NATO officer whispered and directed everyone to get off the road and duck into the forest. Nicollette ran several meters into the woods and crouched behind a tree as a pair of headlights moved slowly down the road. The noise from the motor gained intensity as the vehicle lumbered closer and closer. She pulled her weapon to shoulder height and aimed it at the approaching vehicle, thumb firmly on the safety. There were eight pairs of lights, now just fifty meters away. *Friend or foe?* Nicollette wondered.

The vehicles suddenly stopped and there were voices as doors opened to let out their human cargo. Nicollette could not make out their numbers, but she guessed it was at least thirty or so. She looked over at Mr. Johnson. He was lying belly on the ground with his weapon in a ready position. Silhouettes of people advanced up the road from the lorries. They were waving torches towards the clearing and into the forest. *My God! They're looking for someone, something…us!*

The silhouettes were now less than twenty meters away, and Nicollette could make out the shadows to be men carrying automatic weapons. She placed a finger to her pistol, checking to make sure the safety was released.

Now they were less than ten meters away. Nicollette lowered her head as a light beam from a torch glanced around her and over her head. Thoughts raced through her mind. *Is this it? In a jungle in some backwards forgotten place? What will they do with us? Me? I must try and remain calm!* Nicollette pushed against the wet vegetation on the muddy ground. Her breathing accelerated along with her racing heart. The lower part of her body was turning numb, all the energy focused on her arms and head.

She slowly, deliberately, raised her head. The armed men were on the road directly in front of her, less than five meters away. The armed men continued to walk past her and up the road. It felt like an eternity before the searchers and their lorries were finally past her and the group. She raised her head to see the dim red taillights of the last trailing lorry.

Peter Johnson whispered, "You ok, Nicky?"

Her mouth felt like it was full of cotton wool. All she could do was nod. He rolled over and the two of them raised to their knees.

The NATO officer slowly walked onto the dirt road and motioned for the group to join him. As Nicollette stood, her lower body felt numb. She stumbled forward and Peter Johnson caught her by the arm. The two of them walked gingerly towards the assembled group.

The NATO officer did a quick head count. "They're gone for now, but we must remain diligent. This is hostile territory so please remain alert. I believe Chaing Rai is this way." The officer pointed in the direction the armed men had come from. He looked around the area. "Where's that guide anyway?"

The group started down the road.

Nicollette lumbered along, fatigued. She had been walking for nearly three hours in relentless rain and on unstable ground. Her boots were filled with water, and they made a squishy sound with each step.

The group had only walked a short way when the guide and another person came running up the road. The guide was yelling and waving his hands for the group to stop. The NATO officer walked towards the two and an animated conversation ensued. Nicollette pulled her weapon from her side. She looked at Peter Johnson, his weapon firmly in his hand as the Thai guide and his companion raced up the road in the direction of the armed searching group.

The NATO officer called the group in a circle around him. "It appears that those armed men were friends, not bandits. They were looking to bring us to Chaing Rai! Just before we left our post, I sent a couple of messages and Bangkok must have alerted the local authorities. Our Thai guide was caught and quickly thought to be a bandit. A man from the same village as our guide was able to identify him as friendly, but the search party had already left. So good news, we are going to have a lift to Chaing Rai. Bad news though, this area is filled with bandits. We're not home yet."

Nicollette turned to look up the road. She could just make out some dim lights in the distance. The lights became brighter and soon there were four lorries in front of the group. The officer shook hands with the commander of the search party as the guide played interpreter. "Let's load up," commanded the officer, "five to a lorry. Let's go, people."

Peter Johnson helped Nicollette take off her backpack and handed it off to a man in the lorry. She felt relief as she climbed into the back and took a seat on the right-side bench. Peter Johnson sat next to her, and the lorry caravan proceeded slowly down the dirt road.

Nicollette looked at the two armed men sitting across from her. *We're not home yet. We're not home yet, Nicky!*

Chaing Rai

Nicollette glanced out of the open back of the lorry at the lights behind them. Several armed men ran alongside the slow moving lorries. *An armed escort.* The adrenaline rush she felt just thirty minutes ago had since subsided and her fatigued body had started demanding rest. Nicollette placed a hand on her holstered weapon as her eyes became too heavy to remain open.

A jolting stop and commotion outside the lorry brought her out of her brief slumber. Instinctively, she squeezed the hand that was still resting on top of her weapon. The men of the armed escort were quickly moving around the stopped caravan. She turned to Peter Johnson. "What do you think is happening?"

"I'm not sure, but my guess is we've run into a bit of trouble. Wait here while I find out what's going on." Peter climbed out of the lorry and into the pandemonium, while the two other men in the lorry followed.

The three men disappeared behind the truck. She was now alone. Instinctively, she pulled her gun from the holster and held it on her lap. The noise outside continued unabated. Curiosity taking over, Nicollette stood from the bench and gingerly climbed down off the truck. Her feet had just landed on the rough road when automatic weapon fire interrupted the noise. She dropped onto the wet dirt road. Tracer bullets flew through the air, visible as streaming lights. Gunfire rang out from the jungle and what appeared to be return fire came from the first two lorries in the caravan. A strong smell of sulphur followed by an even stronger smell of burning rubber nearly suffocated her. She crawled a bit further under the truck, straining to get a better look. She could just make out that the lead lorry of the caravan was on fire.

PING!

A tracer bullet hit the front of the truck she was under, quickly followed by three more.

PING! PING! PING!

Nicollette crawled backwards out from under the lorry and crouched behind a tire, pointing her gun towards the tracers coming from the jungle. *Should I fire back? It might give up my position. Maybe they were random shots. Stay calm, Nicky, stay calm!*

Her heart pounded as the gunfire continued in intensity. Her palms were sweaty, causing her grip on the gun to slip. She briefly revisited the firefight on the Lesser Tunb Island. *Fire the damn gun, Miss Beverley! Fire the damn gun!*

But this was different. The reinforcements were here, already engaging the enemy, and she was not alone. *Be calm, Nicky. Breathe.*

A sudden tap on her back caused Nicollette to flinch and turn around. She found herself pointing her gun at Peter Johnson. "Steady on! Easy! Nicollette, it's me," he responded.

She quickly lowered her weapon. "What's happening? What's going on?"

"We've been ambushed! The bandits must have followed the NATO men when they withdrew from the riverside. The lead lorry stopped when the soldiers were spotted on the side of the road. They jumped aboard and then all hell broke loose!"

"What are we going to do?" Nicollette responded.

Peter took a breath. "Here's what we are going to do. The security force is going to tie down the bandits whilst we drive the last two lorries out of here. It's a bit of a gamble, but we can't stay here!" Peter's normally strong and calm demeanour had changed to fear and angst. "It's all we've got, Nicollette."

The NATO Officer crawled to the back of the lorry followed

by four analysts. "You six into this lorry," he commanded, pointing at Nicollette, Peter, and four others. "I'll take the rest into the one behind. Start the engines. Hopefully, the gunfire will cover the noise. Leave the lights off, we'll be driving dark; no need to give them a target. When you see the red flare, take off. Stay to the right of the road and don't stop! The bandits are on the left. Now, who has weapons?"

Nicollette, Peter Johnson, and five others acknowledged the officer.

"Good, use them if you have too. Let's go and good luck!"

The officer directed his five passengers to stay low and load into the lorry behind. He entered the lorry on the driver's side as Peter announced that he would drive. He asked for two men with weapons to sit facing the rear opening.

Peter held his hand out to assist Nicollette into the lorry. An adrenaline rush swept through her body. Her heart was still pumping fast as she looked sternly at Peter Johnson.

"I'm driving, sir!"

"We don't have time to argue, Nicollette!"

"Good, it's settled then." She ran to the driver's door. "Are you coming?"

Peter shut the tailgate and rushed to the passenger door. As he entered the truck, the sound of gunfire erupted. The tracer bullets were flying in all directions just ahead of them. "There it is, the red flare," he announced as he pointed at the windshield. "Alright, Nicollette, let's go!"

Nicollette turned the key and the engine rattled to life. Placing her foot on the clutch, she put the lorry in gear and rolled forward, leaving about ten meters between her lorry and the two in front of them.

Ping, ping, ping. Tracer bullets bounced off the passenger side front fender as they moved down the dirt road.

Nicollette veered to the right and into a small water-filled gulley to pass the stalled vehicle in front of them. The cabin rocked and bumped. She kept a firm grip on the steering wheel and control of the gas and clutch as she steered through the mud and water. Smoke was streaming from the engine and filling the cabin of the heavily damaged stalled vehicle. Suddenly, there was an insistent knock on her window.

Nicollette turned to see a soldier running aside her door. His face was covered with a combination of gunfire residue, smoke, and mud. He motioned for her to roll down the window.

"Please, please!" he yelled at the window and motioned his hands for her to stop.

She had to decide. The officer's instructions were clear: "'Don't stop!'" *But maybe this is an emergency.* Nicollette slowed the vehicle and put her left hand on her weapon. She slowly rolled her window down.

"Please, miss. We have wounded that must get help right away. Please."

Nicollette strategically stopped her vehicle so that the smoking lorry next to them would provide a bit of protection, but the front end of their vehicle was exposed. Nicollette opened her door as the soldier rushed to the rear.

Peter followed her out through the driver's door. The sound of weapons fire intensified as the two of them reached the tailgate area.

"I'll tell the officer what's going on, Nicollette," Peter yelled at her. "You help here. Be quick!"

The trailing lorry slowed to a stop just a couple of meters behind. Nicollette looked at the men in the back of her truck. "We're picking up some wounded. Let's lend 'em a hand and make some room."

She opened the gate and the first wounded soldier was helped into the truck. Within seconds, there were three more wounded, including two on makeshift stretchers. The gunfire continued unabated as Nicollette shut the tailgate and ran back to the driver's side.

"Let's get the hell out of here, Nicollette!" Peter screamed.

Nicollette slammed the lorry in gear and released the clutch. It lurched forward. Ping, ping, ping.

The gunfire intensified, bullets hitting against its side as they passed the remains of the lead vehicle, nothing was left of it except its metal frame and smouldering tires.

Nicollette forced the lorry back onto the road and pounded the accelerator. They gained speed and she pushed it aggressively along the muddy road.

Peter rolled his window down and stuck his head out for a quick look. "I believe we're clear, and the trailing lorry is right behind us."

Just then there was a faint whistling sound and a dull thud. Nicollette looked over at Peter. He was holding his left shoulder and grimacing in pain.

"Peter!" Nicollette shouted. "You're hit!"

Ping, ping, ping.

Three more bullets hit the passenger door. Nicollette held Peter Johnson back against the seat. She fired her weapon through the open window into the dark forest, in between taking glances of the dirt road ahead of her. *Fire the damn gun, Miss Beverley! Show resistance!*

She emptied her chamber as additional gunfire came from the back of her lorry and the trailing lorry. Peter's eyes were now closed, his body bouncing up and down from the effects of the muddy dirt road. The lorry was now moving at nearly forty kilometers an hour, amplifying each bump. Nicollette's right hand maintained a vice-like grip on the steering wheel, ensuring the lorry would give no argument, her eyes shifting between the dirt road and her wounded friend sitting next to her.

Nicollette estimated they had traveled about a kilometer when there was an insistent knock on the rear window of the cabin. Peter was slumped forward, his head leaning heavily against her left arm. There was another round of knocking. Nicollette aimed the steering wheel dead center and quickly reached behind herself with her right hand, opening the curtain separating the cabin from the bed. "What is it?"

A voice from behind her responded in a thick German accent. "The vehicle behind us is flashing its lights. I think they want us to stop."

Peter opened his eyes and whispered, "I think the officer wants us to slow down. Pull over, Nicollette."

His right hand was now holding his left shoulder and blood was staining his shirt. The red liquid traveled through his fingers.

I must stop, he's badly hurt. Maybe there's a first aid kit somewhere in here, she thought.

She carefully pulled the lorry off to the side, allowing the vehicle behind them to come along broadside. From the driver's window of the adjoining lorry, the NATO officer looked at the two of them. "How come Mr. Johnson isn't driving, Miss Beverley?"

Nicollette was caught short. *Of all the things to ask after what we just went through!* She took a breath and responded, "Because I am, sir." The words seemed to come to her too fast for her mind to screen them. She continued, "We have four wounded in the back and Mr. Johnson has been hit as well. Do you have a first aid kit?"

"No, Miss Beverley, but we're only a few kilometers from the paved road that takes us to Chaing Rai. You follow me and stay close, we're still not clear yet."

Nicollette nodded as the officer's lorry pulled away. Peter's bloody right hand still covered his wounded shoulder.

Must do something! Nicollette pulled her partially tucked shirt from her shorts, found the third button, and ripped it. She balled up the cloth material. Gently, she moved Peter's hand from the wounded shoulder and placed the makeshift bandage under his shirt, covering the blood-soaked wound, then softly placing his hand back. He gave a quiet groan. "Let's go," she whispered, climbing back to the driver's seat.

The lorry lurched forward onto the rough road. Nicollette resumed her firm grip on the steering wheel, eyes focusing on the winding road ahead. The lead vehicle was now too far ahead to be seen. *Maybe it's due to the few minutes I spent attending to Peter or maybe to the NATO officer wanting to "show up" a woman driver. Never mind, just stay focused, Nicky,* she thought.

The road continued its winding path, its scaly skin still pronounced with each jolt of the cabin. Nicollette slowed its speed to relieve the effects of the bumpy ride on the lorries' passengers. She felt for the four wounded soldiers in the back and even more so for the friend sitting next to her.

As they approached a particularly sharp bend, Nicollette noticed shadows on the trees on the side of the road. *The sky is cloudy, so there is not much moonlight. I wonder...*

Her thoughts suddenly stopped, and her heart went into overdrive as she could just make out lights ahead of them pointing in their direction. She slowed the lorry to a halt and knocked on the cabin rear window. The German analyst reached in from the bed and pulled the curtain aside. "What is it, Miss Beverley?"

Nicollette pointed to the lights in the distance. "What do you think?"

"It's too far to see exactly, but I think I can just make out the outline of the lead lorry. What about you?"

"Could be," she responded. She remembered the officer's words, *We're not in the clear yet.* "I think we should proceed carefully; it could be a trap. How are the wounded?"

"I'm no doctor, but it looks like two of them are stable, and two are not so good. There is a lot of blood."

"How are we for weapons?"

"We have two guns and a little ammunition."

Nicollette thought about her pistol. She had emptied her rounds during the last firefight, her gun now useless. *Peter Johnson,* she thought.

Reaching over, she loosened the retaining strap of his holster and slowly removed his weapon. She checked the cartridges, eight rounds left. *At least it's something.* Turning back to the German analyst, she said, "Have your weapons ready, we'll take it slow. We must take the chance; we have the wounded to consider."

Nicollette rolled the lorry forward, advancing very cautiously towards the lights, the pistol resting between her legs. *Slowly, Nicky, very slowly.*

Closer and closer, the vehicle crawled to the source of the lights, now just about one hundred meters away. Two lorries directly ahead, side by side, blocked the road. Their headlights were bearing down on her vehicle. Her hands were wet from the tight grip on the wheel. She brought the lorry to a stop about twenty-five meters from the blocking vehicles, silhouettes of people moving about.

Nicollette brought the lorry to a stop and picked up her gun. Peter whispered, "We've stopped, Nicollette, what's going on?"

"Never mind. Just stay still."

"Be careful. For God's sake, please be careful."

Nicollette tapped on the rear window. The German analyst peered through the window. "I'm going out. Be ready," she announced.

The doorhandle pulled easily as she slowly exited the cabin. Not wanting to reveal she was armed, Nicollette kept the gun in her left hand, released the safety, and kept close to the hood of the lorry as she cautiously walked forward.

When she reached the front of the lorry, an intense blinding light hit her face. Someone yelled at her in Thai. Nicollette froze, trying to remain calm. Again, someone shouted in Thai. She shielded her eyes from the blinding white light. Her body reacted as each heartbeat hit her chest like a cricket bat striking a ball.

A third yell, then silence, the intense light still bearing down on her. Ten seconds passed, then twenty, then a minute. Silence. *Come and get me,* Nicollette thought as she confirmed her grip on the weapon. *I'm here, come and get me!*

The next words were yelled aloud at her from behind the bright lights. "Who goes there?" Like a bolt of lightning, the silence was shattered. A second time, "Who goes there?"

Nicollette gathered herself and responded in a calm voice, "Nicollette Beverley," as she slowly raised her weapon to her side.

"Louder please!" someone commanded.

"I'm Nicollette Beverley!"

"Please step forward where we can see you."

Nicollette slowly walked forward, gripping her gun tightly. *One foot at a time. This is it, Nicky, get ready, girl!*

Three more steps.

"Stop!" commanded the speaker.

Nicollette could detect people walking towards her, her right hand still shielding her eyes from the bright light. She raised her gun with her left hand as she tried to identify the approaching group. Closer and closer, the group moved quietly towards her, only the sounds of shoes shuffling on the muddy road breaking the silence. Then she heard the words that brought her to her knees. "It's alright, Miss Beverley, you can stand down now."

It was the voice of the NATO officer. *Such a voice, such a beautiful voice!* "Hurry, there are wounded," he commanded.

Nicollette looked down at the dirt road, activity pounding all around her. The officer extended his hand, inviting her to stand. He spoke softly, "We had to be sure, Miss. When we lost you behind us, we thought the worst. We had to be sure."

Medics helped Peter from the cabin and onto a stretcher. As they carried him past her, he held out his hand. "Brave girl," he whispered.

Nicollette stood frozen amid all the activity. She was safe. Her left arm hung limp at her side, still holding the gun. Her heart pounded and her breathing was heavy as the activity around her continued.

"We will be leaving in three minutes, Miss. The commander has asked me to assist you," a soldier announced as he extended his arm toward her.

Nicollette looked back at her lorry. Two soldiers entered the cabin as several others ran to the back. She looked at the extended arm in front of her. "Thank you, I'm ok," she responded.

She followed him, setting the safety on her gun and placing it back in her holster. Slowly, a deep feeling of relief warmed her.

The soldier led her to a vehicle parked behind a caravan of lorries. Nicollette watched from her window as several large lorries passed them heading towards the area of the earlier firefight. *Reinforcements, I bet.* Then she watched as three ambulances advanced in front of the car. She thought of the wounded and mostly she thought about Peter. *Get well, my friend!* she thought as the last ambulance passed them.

The car moved into line as the NATO officer looked at her from the front seat. "We are about an hour out of Chiang Rai, Miss Beverley, why don't you get a bit of kip?"

The early rays of the sun were visible as the car entered the paved road taking them to Chaing Rai. She had been awake for almost twenty-four hours and she felt like she had lived a lifetime in those hours. Her eyelids were quickly becoming heavy. "Chaing Rai," she whispered as she fell asleep.

Bangkok

"Miss Beverley." the woman's soft voice insisted. "Miss Beverley, we're here. We're in Chiang Rai."

Nicollette exited the car as the early morning sunlight peeked through the thick and ominous clouds. It was damp, very damp, and hot, very hot. Nicollette glanced at her watch. It was just a short time ago that they were picked up in the jungle. *A short cat nap,* she thought.

Nicollette looked around as her co-workers were being hurried into the building next to them. About a block away, she saw local street vendors setting up and, in the other direction, the rescue lorries parked along the side of the road. There was no activity on the block in front of the building. The escort grabbed Nicollette's elbow. "We must move along, Miss."

Nicollette was quickly directed to a room, passing several heavily armed Thai soldiers in the lobby. The NATO officer and most of her colleagues from the operation were already in the room. However, there were people in the room she didn't recognize. There was a tea cart off to the side and a large map was taped to the rear wall.

The door shut behind her as she poured tea into a paper cup. The NATO officer walked up to her. "Good morning, Miss Beverley, I trust you had a good nap."

Nicollette didn't know what to say, not wanting to embarrass herself because she had fallen asleep on the ride to Chiang Rai.

"A quick cat nap," she replied.

"Good," he replied and continued, "I want to speak with you after the briefing, Miss Beverley."

"Yes sir."

As the officer turned away, Nicollette thought of Peter Johnson. "Sir, any news about Mr. Johnson?"

With a stern expression, he replied, "Well talk about that later."

The NATO officer walked to the front of the room and asked for the group to be seated. Nicollette took a seat next to the Spanish analyst. Her co-worker was still upset over the events of the past night, complexion pale, eyes wide open. She was fidgeting in the seat, unable to calm herself.

She grabbed Nicollette's hand.

"Todo está bien. Está bien," Nicollette said.

A slight smile crossed the analyst's face. "Gracias."

"I know it's been a long night, so I'll make this briefing short," the NATO officer stated as he turned towards the map and pointed. "Our operation was located approximately here, and the observation point was about ten kilometers further north. Our surveillance discovered aggressive activity on the North Trail, located about here. We made the decision to evacuate our base. We quickly traveled to a branch of the Ping River. Our rear guard detected that we were being followed and a gunfight ensued after we crossed the river. Three of our team stayed to cover the group as we continued to a point here, where we were picked up by a rescue party, loaded into lorries, and continued on. Later, when the three rear guards caught up to us, they must have been followed. A heavy gunfight started and we sustained casualties and lost two vehicles. We were able to escape the fight and continued down the trail in the two remaining vehicles, encountering sporadic gunfire on the way. We were met further down the road by two more squads of troops and medical personnel. The wounded were given medical attention and placed into ambulances. Everyone else was put into transport for the trip to Chaing Rai. The two squads of troops continued on to support the initial rescue party. We arrived in Chaing Rai at 0616 hours."

The NATO officer paused and sipped from a paper cup. "It seems the weather will cooperate later this afternoon. We will be flying to Bangkok at about 1500 hours and staging here at 1400 hours. In the meantime, consider yourselves restricted to this building. You are only to leave your rooms with an escort."

The officer peered at the small group. "I want to be perfectly clear, in Chaing Rai, we do not know who is friend or foe, and that includes the area around this building. Stay in your room, get some rest and be safe. If you need anything, ask your escorts. Any questions? None? Good. We will assemble here at 1400 hours. Briefing adjourned."

As Nicollette poured a cup of tea, a hand touched her elbow. She turned to see her soldier escort.

"The officer in charge would like to speak with you, Miss. Please follow me."

Nicollette followed her escort to a door in the far corner of the room. She opened the door. "In here, Miss, please."

Nicollette walked into the small windowless room, not much bigger than a large closet. Two single light bulbs provided the only light. The NATO officer entered the room along with a Thai military officer.

"You may be excused," the officer commanded the escort.

The escort left the room and shut the door, leaving only Nicollette and the two men in the room.

"You may sit, Miss Beverley," the officer commanded.

Nicollette sat on a steel chair as the two men remained standing. Her heart was pounding, and her palms were becoming sweaty. *What's this all about? What am I doing here?* The officer continued his relentless stare as he slowly circled the seated Nicollette. The silence in the room was almost unbearable and Nicollette grew anxious from the tension. Finally, the officer spoke.

"Miss Beverley, I want to talk to you about events earlier this morning. First, as the officer in charge, let me say that I was not happy with your action in commandeering the escape lorry from a more senior person. Your action could have jeopardized the safety of the group and our chances to escape from a dangerous situation. Secondly, you took it upon yourself to stop your vehicle to assist the injured, placing the trailing lorry in direct gunfire and endangering the lives of those inside. This, despite my direct instructions not to stop on the road. Finally, you left your vehicle to encounter the unknown ahead of you on a dark road, unescorted or protected. The brashness you displayed could have cost you significantly, notwithstanding the success of the escape. May I remind you Miss Beverley, you are not a cowboy, excuse me, cowgirl!"

Nicollette had never been reprimanded before. She looked down at her folded hands, remembering the events of the last twenty-four hours. *Was I brazen or brave? Stupid or strong?*

She slowly raised her head. She was too tired to respond, too tired for any emotion, all of her strength just seemed to have been sucked out of her. Nicollette worked hard to gather herself and started to form words in order to respond, but before she could speak, the officer continued.

"Now Miss Beverley, Nicollette, not as your superior, but as your coworker and a gentleman, I would like to tell you how I personally feel about last night."

Nicollette noticed a distinct softening in his voice. He was calmer, friendlier, and there was even a hint of a smile.

"Your actions were certainly brazen, but also very brave. You took control of the situation with confidence and courage. You, Miss, drove that lorry competently under the most dire circumstances. You made the decision to stop for the wounded only after you positioned the lorry for maximum safety for not only you, but the trailing vehicle as well. Your actions may have saved the lives of those severely injured men. Finally, you took the initiative to leave your vehicle and approach the unknown. This was foolish and risky, but also took great courage.

You were willing to put your life in jeopardy to protect others."

He paused and walked behind Nicollette, placing his hand on her shoulder.

"Miss Nicollette Beverley, I have known you for just a short time and I am impressed with you. You handle yourself far beyond your years and I'm glad to work with you."

He stood in front of Nicollette and offered his hand. Nicollette felt unsteady as she stood and offered her hand in return, not feeling quite sure of what just happened.

"Just remember, there are consequences for not listening to directions and not all situations end favorably. Take what happened last night and learn from it," he concluded as he went towards the door.

"What about Mr. Johnson?" she asked. "Is he ok?"

"We are looking after him. He sustained a shoulder wound and a small wound on his leg. Now get some rest, Miss Beverley."

I didn't know he was hit in the leg as well. He was hit twice and I am responsible!

The escort guided Nicollette from the room and past a dozen soldiers in the lobby before climbing four flights of stairs to her room. A soldier was posted on each landing and two more on her floor as they walked down the faded green, concrete block hallway to her room, stopping in front of a simple wood door.

"If there is anything you need, Miss."

"Thank you."

There was no lock on the door as she entered the room and walked to the small window. She pulled back the well-worn curtains and looked at the street below. The military vehicles were still there, the clouds were thick, and it was raining softly. She turned away from the window and looked around the room. It was a simple room, like the dorm room she had at Brize during training. There was a small bed, a chest and mirror. There was a small bathroom off to one side. A wobbly ceiling fan spinning wildly offered some relief to the stifling heat. Nicollette turned the bath spigot on and, surprisingly, hot water started to flow. She found a robe and walked into the main room to undress.

She stood in front of the mirror and could hardly recognize herself. Her face was dirty and her hair was wet and matted down. Her shirt was hanging out of her shorts and torn open just below her bra. Her shorts were filthy and damp. Welts and scratches covered her legs. Large patches of blood were over her clothes and body, reminding her about Peter. Finally, underneath her untucked shirt, was the gun in the holster belt. *What a sight you are, Nicky, what a sight indeed!*

She slowly unbuckled her holster belt and checked the safety on the gun. She carefully laid it across the bed and undressed. The bath was waiting for her as she gingerly stepped into the hot water. The warm water enveloped her fatigued and sore body.

Twenty minutes later, wrapped in the robe, Nicollette walked past the heap of dirty clothes on the floor and grabbed the gun from the holster. She placed it under the pillow and fell onto the bed. Her mind drifted to her parents, her friends, and Brockwirth. She fell asleep still clutching the gun under her pillow.

Movement in the room quickly brought Nicollette out of her slumber. Her right hand instinctively gripped the gun under the pillow as she opened her reluctant eyes.

"What's going on?" she asked forcefully.

A small, Thai woman standing by the mirror turned and smiled. Nicollette repeated herself.

"What's going on and who are you?"

The woman picked up the dirty clothes from the floor and smiled at Nicollette as she started to leave the room.

"Wait! What are you doing?" she shouted while sitting up, covering herself with the blanket, hand tightly gripping the gun under her pillow.

"It's ok, Miss Beverley," the woman escort announced as she walked into the room. "We just wanted to bring you some clean clothes. I've brought you a make-up kit as well. It's nearly 1300 hours, we were going to wake you now anyway."

Nicollette looked at the top of the chest as the escort laid a small brown satchel next to a neatly stacked set of clothing. There was a fresh white shirt, tan shorts and white socks, and even some underwear. All this was a bit unnerving to her. *When did this happen? Did they do this for all of us? How did they get my size?* she wondered. Her boots were cleaned and dried. The brown satchel contained small cosmetics, combs and brushes, neatly arranged inside. There were even a couple of lipsticks. *Never,* she thought, a slight grin crossing her face.

At 1330 hours, Nicollette left her room carrying the small brown satchel. She felt refreshed and clean. The only physical reminders of last night's events were the sores on her legs and the weapon she was wearing around her waist.

The hallways and stairs were active with uniformed men and Thai women walking around with armloads of clothing and supplies. There was still a large military presence in the makeshift lobby as Nicollette entered the meeting room. She was the first in the group to arrive. Platters of food were being placed on the refreshment table. Nicollette's stomach rumbled at the sight. She hadn't eaten much of anything since yesterday and the sight of hot food had a hypnotic effect on her. She poured a bowl of good smelling soup into a bowl.

"Hello, Nicky!"

Nicollette turned to see Peter Johnson being pushed towards her in a wheelchair.

"Mr. Johnson!" She rushed to him. "How are you? Everything alright?"

"I'm fine, Nicky, feeling much better."

"But what about this?" Nicollette asked, pointing to his arm and the wheelchair. His face grimaced with each movement.

He's in pain! He was shot just hours ago and now he's up and about? Something is not right!

"Blast this bloody chair!" he responded. "They want to restrict my movements so my sutures won't open. Blast this chair."

Peter's leg bandaging was protruding below his shorts. His left arm was in a cotton sling and the two top buttons of his white shirt were unbuttoned, exposing his heavily wrapped shoulder. Small bits of blood were visible on top of the bandaging. *He is putting on a brave show, no doubt.*

The remainder of the group shuffled into the room. The NATO officer and three Thai counterparts walked to the front of the room. Two guards shut the door and stood at either side. The NATO officer asked for attention and was handed a small stack of papers by one of the Thais.

"Good afternoon. I trust you had some rest. This is our Chaing Rai exit briefing. As you know, our mission was to provide on the ground communications and intelligence to our respective agencies regarding the routes and components of the opioid trade here in northern Thailand." The Officer paused and opened the stack of papers. "I'd like to read you this update I received early this afternoon. I'll skip the formalities.

"At approximately 0800 hours, a force of five hundred was quickly deployed about twenty-five kilometers northwest of Chiang Rai. Using the information from the advance intelligence unit, the objective was to destroy the North Trail and auxiliary routes of drug trafficking. The lead group of troops found the abandoned outpost of the advance intelligence unit. It was totally ransacked, burned, and destroyed. The main force entered the areas around the North Trail at approximately 1000 hours. At 1100 hours, the main force entered the North Trail and engaged a caravan of transport vehicles. Twelve vehicles were destroyed and several bandits killed or wounded. Two bandits were taken prisoner. The force pursued the remaining bandits ten kilometers up the North Trail to an unmarked village, Kab Nein Khea, literally meaning against the hill. The village was secured. A road was discovered leading to a series of caves. This communication says the caves are not yet fully secured, but so far have yielded a treasure trove of everything from raw opium, manufacturing facilities, and distribution materials. Operations are ongoing. Updates to follow.'"

The NATO officer put the paper down and looked at the group.

"I believe this message confirms that our mission was a success. Thank you."

There was a buzz of conversation, pats on the back, and hand shaking amongst the group. Nicollette reached down and lightly hugged her wounded co-worker.

"We did good, Nicky," Peter said wearily, "we did good."

"Miss Beverley." Nicollette turned to see the NATO officer. "I want to thank you for a job well done."

He offered his hand to her and Peter. "You too, Mr. Johnson. I hope you are feeling better. Well done."

At exactly 1430 hours, the Officer asked the group to follow him into the lobby and commanded everyone to break into three groups. He explained there were five vehicles parked outside, the middle three reserved for the group.

"I would ask for you to get into the vehicles quickly. It is about thirty minutes to the airport."

A soldier came to push Peter to the transport. Nicollette waved him away. "I can do it," she announced.

The lobby door was opened, and a quick procession proceeded to the waiting vehicles.

The heavy humidity and afternoon heat felt hot on her face as she pushed Peter down the short temporary ramp. There were heavily armed soldiers on either side of the procession and even more in the street. Nicollette assisted Peter from his wheelchair as they entered the middle vehicle. They were joined by three others. Two soldiers pushed the rear gate shut and the lorry started moving.

Subconsciously, she reached for her holstered weapon and took a deep sigh. *The first step on the way home,* she thought.

The lorry came to a stop and two soldiers pulled back the canvas covering and opened the gate. They assisted Peter to a wheelchair and directed the group to a waiting aircraft behind them. The engine was running and the propellers were spinning as they boarded the plane. Peter was helped aboard by two soldiers. The NATO officer was last to board and the door was immediately closed behind him. Fifteen minutes later, they were in the air.

It's warm inside the plane but not too bad, Nicollette thought as she sat back in her chair. *The air conditioning must not be working very well.* She glanced over at Peter, trying to keep his eyes open. She closed her eyes, her mind drifting back to the events over the last twenty-four hours and then to Bangkok and home. *Bangkok and home, home...*

Brussels

The sun was setting when the plane landed at Don Muang Royal Thai AFB just outside Bangkok. The plane rolled to a stop and three military men came aboard.

"We are preparing your plane for the trip back to Brussels. We estimate take-off in about thirty minutes."

"At least we're comfortable," Nicollette whispered to a sleeping Peter Johnson. She closed her eyes, savoring the last few minutes of cool air as the emotional and physical toll of the mission was now coming fully to bear. It felt like her body was in a different time zone than her brain. The only sleep she had had were a few hours in Chiang Rai and a brief nap on the plane. The flight to Brussels would take about twelve hours. *Maybe that will get me in order,* she thought.

A military man announced it was time to deplane. Nicollette helped Peter to his feet and onto a waiting wheelchair. She could see he was still visibly in pain as they headed towards an exit ramp. At the ramp, a firm hand gripped Nicollette's shoulder.

"I'll have that, Miss," a military policeman stated firmly as he pointed to her holstered gun.

She looked at Peter and he nodded. Nicollette unbuckled the holster belt and handed it gently to the soldier. In and of itself, it was a simple act, handing her weapon over to the soldier, but to Nicollette, it meant much more. The weapon had become more than a security blanket, it had become part of her, a symbol of her growth, capabilities, and the trust others placed in her, even more so because she was young and a woman, surrounded by older and more experienced men. But most importantly to Nicollette, the holstered piece of metal was one part of the commitment she had made to herself: to be in control, capable, strong and confident. Mission being accomplished, she thought.

Nicollette gave a small smile to the soldier as she helped Peter Johnson up the stairs and onto the plane. Inside, her eyes opened wide to see the interior was the same as the plane she had taken to Brussels during her training. Quite different from the coach seat on the commercial flight she had taken from London to Bangkok just a couple of weeks ago. The seat rows had been replaced by sofas, chairs, and tables. It was more like the lobby in a luxury hotel than the interior of an airplane.

"Welcome to the Savoy in the air," Nicollette whispered to Peter as they found an unoccupied sofa.

"I wonder if they have room service," Peter replied.

That innocent remark reminded Nicollette of the drugging she had received on the flight to Brussels during her training. *A long time ago,* Nicollette thought as she smiled back at Peter. He leaned back on the leather sofa and closed his eyes, his injuries and physical stress overtaking him as he fell asleep. *His pain medicine is really knocking him out. Sleep well, my friend.*

Once flight altitude was reached, she stood and stretched, trying to knock the cobwebs from her body. A refreshment area was set up and Nicollette poured herself a cup of tea. *First decent cuppa in a fortnight.* She saw a group of soldiers and well-dressed men in the rear area of the room. Amongst them were the NATO officer and the German analyst. She did not recognize any of the others. Nicollette wandered to a seat near the rear of the room to try and listen in. None of her other colleagues seemed to notice the discussion taking place.

"We are flying to Brussels for a group debriefing and afterwards they want to talk with us individually," the NATO officer offered the group.

"This is standard operating procedure for those returning from a mission," one of the well-dressed civilians said.

"Everything is reviewed."

Nicollette understood the requirement for a general debriefing, but her heart skipped a beat at the thought of being interviewed individually. Thoughts were racing through her mind. *This seems awfully unusual! Who are "they?" What do they want with us? Me? What are they searching for?* A sudden shock shot up her spine as she thought about the actions she took during the escape from the jungle. *What if I'm asked about that?*

Reconciling her thoughts, Nicollette walked back towards the sofa, accidentally bumping into a small table. *Silly me.* On the table were yesterday's copies of The London Times. Nicollette picked up one of the folded newspapers and found her seat next to a still sleeping Peter. *Maybe this will help me get my mind off of Brussels.*

Nicollette opened the paper to the sport section, looking for cricket results. She had grown up a Worcestershire fan and always enjoyed a day at New Road, even getting to know a couple of the players. *Looks like they lost a couple of matches. Inconsistent batting, I'd say.* The paper featured articles about England's economic situation, turmoil in the Mideast, and commodity prices. *Nothing new, really.* However, an article in the International News section caught her eye. It was a small piece discussing the results of the government's investigations of the "South Atlantic flashes" that took place off the coast of South Africa about a year ago. Nicollette knew that her friends Val Davies and Sarah Green were sent to the British Embassy in Pretoria about that time, only a few months after the mission in the UAE. Sudden flashbacks crossed her mind about the UAE mission, the preparation, the firefight, and her friend Peg Wilson.

She remembered the worry and concern after they heard that Peg's Dhow had been blown up in the Gulf. Nicollette recalled the emotional high of receiving a medal from the Sheik earlier in the day and the angst of waiting hours for word about her friend and coworker later that same day. She remembered how time seemed to stand still and the world just seemed to stop while they waited for news. *Poor Peg, Poor Peg.* Finally, there was a communication from one of the rescue vessels. "Miss Wilson, Peg had been found alive." The sudden euphoria and relief at the news faded away with the memory of seeing Peg, motionless, lying on a gurney, a picture that still brought tears to Nicollette's eyes.

For the first time in a fortnight, there was no mosquito net covering a well-worn cot. Instead, Nicollette relaxed on a comfortable sofa, immersed in cool dry air on a luxury airplane. Importantly, she could now rest without feeling vulnerable, without having to sleep with one eye open and prepared to spring into action. She felt safe, allowing herself to completely let go of her subconscious alert sense. The worries of what might face her in Brussels seemed to drift away, replaced by pleasant thoughts of her friends, family, and home. She fell asleep.

It was midday and the sun's rays were beaming through the small windows as the plane approached Brussels International Airport. With Peter, Nicollette discussed her concerns about what she had overheard from the small group in the rear of the plane. She described the group that included the NATO officer, the German analyst, and other men she had never seen before.

Nicollette told Peter what she overheard. "We are going to be debriefed as a group and then individually. One of the well-dressed men quickly and abruptly added that 'this was standard procedure.' What do you think of all of this?"

"Let's take a walk and stretch your legs, Nicky, I could use a cuppa," Peter said.

She assisted Peter slowly onto the wheelchair, his eyes scanning the room as they made their way to the tea. Later, back at their seats, he asked Nicollette if she recognized anyone in the area who had participated in the rear room discussion.

"I didn't see our officer, the German analyst, nor anyone else in that little group. Not a single one. I don't know where they could have gone."

"Let's not be too hasty jumping to speculation or conclusions, Nicollette. Besides, what are we going to do in an airplane? I'm sure everything is in order."

Nicollette looked hard at Peter Johnson's face. Despite his casual comment and reassuring grin, his eyes were telling a different story. She could see the underlying concern going through his mind and forced a smile back at him. "I guess you're right, probably some simple explanation in order. I'm getting another cup and a snack, can I bring you something?"

"Thanks, Nicollette, another tea and some biscuits would be fine."

Nicollette's mind was flooded with thoughts. *Peter Johnson is one of the most experienced in our group. He has seen and witnessed almost everything! What's he hiding from me?*

She sighed as she poured the tea and selected a few biscuits. Her palms were moist, and she gripped the tray tightly. *Mustn't let Peter see that I'm concerned.*

Nicollette took a deep calming breath as she approached the sofa.

"Thanks, Nicollette."

Maybe he's right not to worry, but my insides say differently. Take a deep breath and try to relax, Nicky, try to relax.

The plane rolled to a stop at the embarkation point well away from the commercial terminal. Three military police, two men, and a woman walked into the cabin. The woman announced in an "all business" voice, "Welcome to Brussels. The local time is 1217 hours, the temperature is fifteen, and the sky is clear. We will de-plane in twenty minutes."

An announcement from a military policeman said that it was time to disembark and that transportation was ready.

"We have brought some light jackets for you. Please help yourself if you would like one."

Nicollette thought a jacket would be a good idea. Although it was warm by Brussels's standards, it was still very cool compared to the thirty degree temperatures in Thailand. She started to walk towards the box of jackets when she heard Peter. "Please grab me one as well, Nicollette," he asked weakly.

She grabbed two jackets from the box.

"Please help me to the chair, Nicky."

Something isn't right with him, she thought as she helped him up. Her suspicions became reality as Peter stood. She noticed a rather large red stain on his white shirt in the area of the wounded shoulder.

"You're bleeding, Peter," she exclaimed. "Why didn't you say something?"

"Help me with the jacket, quickly please."

Nicollette helped him put the jacket over his shoulder. She could see him wince in pain as the jacket went over the sling holding his arm in place.

"Zip me up halfway, please, Nicollette," he asked, ignoring her question. "Let's go."

Nicollette assisted him off the plane and onto a waiting coach. There was no doubt in her mind that he was putting on an extraordinary effort to hide his wound and pretend he was feeling better. *But why?*

At Peter's insistence, the two of them found a seat on the bench at the back of the coach. Again, Nicollette noticed that everyone on the Thai team was on the bus with the exception of the NATO officer and the German analyst. *This is very peculiar! I can see why the officer isn't on the bus with us, but the German analyst? He's part of the Thai team! Last I saw him was in that 'back of the room' meeting and not since! Now I don't see him on the coach. Very strange.*

Nicollette kept a worried eye on Peter during the trip. His

complexion had become very pale and he was having trouble keeping his eyes open. *He's really suffering.*

The coach went through several security checks and stopped in front of a large, ordinary office building. The group was escorted off the bus, into elevators, and then to a secluded, windowless conference room.

Nicollette helped Peter onto a chair. The NATO officer and the well-dressed men from the plane entered the room. They were followed by two other military men. The NATO officer asked the group for their attention as a screen descended from the ceiling. The lights were dimmed as he addressed the group.

"I know it's been a long journey, but I trust your flight was comfortable. We will make this final de-briefing short, I know we are all anxious to get home."

The NATO officer used a pointer to indicate positions on the map projected on the screen. "To review: our mission was to gather on-the-ground intelligence regarding the illegal drug activity in this area of Thailand. Previous air reconnaissance of the area had proven less reliable. Our operation started functioning four weeks ago with our initial reports to Bangkok and concluded two days ago with the evacuation of the operation. Our last intelligence communication to Bangkok detailed the location of illicit activity along the North Trail. This information was used to track the location of a large-scale clandestine processing and warehouse facility in the small village of 'Kab Nein Khea.' The facility was hidden inside a mountain and therefore undetectable by air reconnaissance. The latest intelligence report I have indicates the area is now under complete Thai and multinational military control and the facility and warehouse operation is neutralized. There is a multi-ton recovery of illegal material and a large number of arrests."

The NATO officer asked for the screen to be raised and the lights turned on. He cleared his throat and continued.

"The illegal activity in the region has been eliminated. We

have literally cut the head off the beast and driven a dagger through its heart. Mission accomplished. Thank you."

The officer paused, his sterile, informative, robot-like voice changing into a more heart-driven human communication. With inflection in his delivery, he continued. "However, with the success came a cost. During the evacuation and resulting firefight, there were casualties. Our group sustained two fatalities: Lieutenant Gustav Olufsen of Special Forces and Sergeant Charn Chai of the Royal Thai Guards. There were two of our group wounded as well. The rescue recovery force sustained four dead and six wounded."

The officer continued as he walked around the room.

"I want to take a moment to recognize the group for strength and bravery under dangerous and treacherous conditions. I realize you are civilians, but you acted like seasoned veterans and I commend you."

The NATO officer paused for a moment and continued, "When your name is called, you will be escorted to your individual debriefings. After your meeting, you will be directed to the release desk to complete your paperwork and obtain transportation to your home destinations."

Nicollette looked around the room as the NATO officer left. *Where is the German analyst? What's going on?* She turned to the barely awake Peter and whispered her concern.

"Probably first to interview, Nicky. No need to be concerned," he replied.

Nightmare

"Miss Beverley, Miss Nicollette Beverley."

Nicollette looked at Peter. "I'm being called. I guess this is it. Wish me luck."

"Everything will be alright, Nicky. Just relax, you don't need luck, you will be just fine."

She walked over to the escort, thoughts flowing through her mind. *I've been in the service for over three years and never had an exit interview. Briefings, yes, but an interview?*

Her palms were sweating as she was escorted down a long hallway to a wooden door. The sign on the side of the door identified the room as Conference Room PR-4. It was a small room, set up more like an office.

"Please come in, Miss Beverley. Take a seat," a well-dressed man called from behind the desk in the middle of the room.

It was easy for her to recognize his French accent.

"Good morning, Miss Beverley."

The NATO officer and three other men she recognized from the back of the room meeting on the airplane were in the room.

"Good morning," she responded with a nervous grin and hoarse voice as she sat down at the desk.

"Miss Beverley, my name is Henri Gistane and I'm a Senior Security Officer within the Overseas Operations Bureau. I, we," he pointed to the other men in the room, "would like to talk with you about your time in Thailand."

Mr. Gistane deliberately ruffled through a group of papers on his desk.

Nicollette tried to remain calm as her mind started to race with anticipation. *Review, what review? The NATO officer in charge knows all about my time! We didn't go anywhere or do anything! We were in the middle of nowhere! What's really going on here!*

Mr. Gistane looked up from the pile of papers. "Miss Nicollette Beverley, you are from British Intelligence Group 226/157 and you volunteered for this mission, is that right?"

Nicollette could tell by his manner of speech that Mr. Gistane was all business. His delivery was fast with no emotional inflection or hesitation. His French accent made him difficult to understand.

"Yes sir, that is correct," she responded, forcing the words through her dry throat.

"Please tell me about your normal day and please, Miss Beverley, all the details."

Nicollette looked him in the eyes, unflinching, and in as calm a voice as she could muster, she described her activities.

"Sir, my typical day would start at 0500. I would have a quick wash and breakfast, then be at my post by 0550. After a handover, I would be on the 'hotline.' That's what we called our live link to Bangkok. I would send a prescribed set of coded communications at specific intervals till my thirty-minute break at 1000 hours. If there was any new information, it would be inserted according to pre-established guidelines. My shift would conclude at 1430 and I would have eight hours till my next shift. Essentially, I was 'hot' for eight hours then off for eight every day."

Nicollette paused and Mr. Gistane quickly inserted a question.

"Miss Beverley, please describe your work and rest areas." *This is a bit off,* she thought, *surely the NATO officer would have given them that information. Why am I being asked this?*

Nicollette described the work hut, trying not to leave out even the smallest detail. She talked about the wooden desks and the uncomfortable chairs. The often muddy dirt floor, mosquito nets, and the small fire pit that was used to destroy notes as well as cover for the fumes of the gas generator. The locked cabinet of supplies and the muted buzzing of the equipment, even the steel trunk containing spare parts. She explained about the daily flow chart hanging, displaying the latest communication codes, and the large map with detailed information about current and past locations of the surveillance teams.

Before Nicollette could talk about the primitive living quarters, outdoor latrine, and tasteless food, Mr. Gistane, rather abruptly, interrupted her again. "So Miss Beverley, what you are saying is that everyone in the group had easy access to the communication codes and the whereabouts of the surveillance team. Is that right?"

"Yes sir."

"Including you?"

"Yes sir."

Mr. Gistane leaned back into his chair, his piercing eyes never leaving Nicollette's face.

"Tell me, Miss Beverley, how well did you know or get to know the people working with you?"

Nicollette started to wonder where this line of questioning, in fact what this whole interview, was leading to. Surely they knew the answers before they asked her.

"Well, sir, a few weeks ago, I didn't know any of them except for Mr. Peter Johnson. Mr. Johnson and I work together in British Intelligence, Group 226/157. We've worked together for several years now. I met the rest of our remote team the day I arrived."

Mr. Gistane rolled a pen between his thumb and forefinger.

"I see. Did you get to know anybody during your two week stay? I mean, more than professionally?"

Nicollette's mind started to go into overdrive with that question. *What is he talking about, more than professionally? What is he insinuating? Is this because I was one of only two women among all those men? I wonder if he asked the men the same question!*

Nicollette took a breath and looked directly at Mr. Gistane and gave a determined response. "No, Mr. Gistane, not really. I do my job and I do it well and with my schedule, there wasn't enough time for anything but simple conversation. Most of my free time was spent sleeping or reading."

"And Mr. Johnson?"

"We work together at home where he would be considered my boss. He is my friend."

"Did you have any contact with any of the locals, for example, the ones who would deliver supplies?"

"No, not really. I saw them only by chance the morning of the day we left. I was on a break, getting tea, when I saw two men bringing food supplies into our living area. Nothing seemed out of place. They brought in a couple of boxes and left. I finished my tea and went back to work."

Mr. Gistane reached into a drawer and pulled out a plastic bag and handed it to Nicollette.

"Miss Beverley, do you drink or smoke?"

Inside the bag was a crumpled cigarette package and bottle cap. Nicollette eyed the plastic bag carefully as she replied.

"No, I don't smoke and I certainly wouldn't drink on a mission."

"Miss Beverley, I want you to think carefully. Did you ever see anyone smoke or drink while you were stationed at the outpost? Think carefully, take your time."

Nicollette stared at the crumpled package and the red bottle cap. She didn't know of anyone in the group that smoked and alcohol was not permitted. Still, the more she stared at the bag, something triggered a thought in her mind. *All of our water jugs had blue or clear tops, but some medicines did have red tops, like a caution sign to the user. I know I've seen that top before, but where?*

Nicollette retraced her time in Thailand from her arrival to the flight from Bangkok, then it hit her.

"I remember seeing a red bottle cap when I first arrived in the jungle. I was given some 'mossie' pills by my guide bringing me to the base from Chiang Rai. The pill bottle had a red cap. And, I remember, he was a smoker!"

Mr. Gistane leaned in and focused his piercing eyes directly at Nicollette.

"Please, Miss Beverley, carefully open the bag and pull out the contents."

Nicollette did as instructed. She gingerly removed the bottle cap from the plastic bag and laid it in front of her. Next, she took the cigarette package and laid it next to the cap.

"Now, Miss Beverley, take a good look at the bottle cap and tell us what you see."

Nicollette brought the cap close to her eyes. It seemed like any other red bottle cap, a hard plastic, colored red. She looked at the underside of the cap and something caught her eye.

"Mr. Gistane, it appears the plastic liner under the cap has been tampered with. May I borrow a pen or tweezers please?"

Mr. Gistane handed Nicollette a pen. She very carefully used the pen point to remove the liner, revealing D4 written in very tiny letters on the inside.

Mr. Gistane immediately asked for her to unravel the crumpled cigarette package and examine it. Nicollette looked the package over. Having never smoked, she wasn't familiar with cigarettes and could not recognize any unusual characteristics of the pack. The outside of the pack only had hard printed information, no sign of added writing. The inside of the pack was clean and had a tobacco smell to it. She looked at the package again, this time with more intensity. Something on the label caught her attention and a thought crossed her mind. *As I remember, most cigarette packages contain twenty cigarettes, the label on the pack says this one only contains fifteen. Bottle cap D4, cigarettes fifteen?*

Nicollette looked up at the stoic eyes of Mr. Gistane.

"Yes, Miss Beverley, any thoughts?"

Nicollette thought hard about the bottle cap and the cigarette package. *What is the relationship? Think, Nicky, think.* She took a breath.

"Well, Mr. Gistane, just an idea. The D4 on the cap could refer to a specific area of our operations map. The map has a grid with letters on the top and numbers along the side. D4 could be one part of the coordinates of a specific area."

Mr. Gistane handed Nicollette a small copy of the map used in the outpost.

"Miss Beverley, could you identify area D4 on this map?"

Nicollette pointed to the spot.

"Here, sir."

Then it hit her.

"This is the area where our surveillance team was ambushed!"

"That's right, Miss Beverley," he responded smugly. "And the cigarette package? How does that figure in?"

"I arrived at the outpost exactly fifteen days before we had to escape, so this could be a message identifying where and when our surveillance team was going to be attacked?"

Mr. Gistane leaned back in his chair, his eyes on Nicollette, unyielding in intensity.

"We found these items less than five meters from the women's hut. Given the date you arrived coincides numerically with the attack on the surveillance team, is there anything else you want to tell us about, Miss Beverley?"

Nicollette took pause, her heart punching her chest full stop, as her mind raced to put all the pieces together. *This isn't an interview, it's an inquisition! They knew all the answers before they asked me! What's really going on here? Are they trying to pin the attack on me! Why? Are they looking for someone to blame? Is it because they think that because I'm a woman, I'm vulnerable? Is it because someone above me feels threatened by a strong young woman? I just put my life on the line, for heaven's sake! Nicollette took a breath. I do my job and I do it well! Damn them, damn them all!*

Thirty seconds went by, Mr. Gistane's intense stare still focusing on her.

"Well, Miss Beverly?"

Nicollette's heart was still vigorously pounding in her chest and a large amount of adrenaline was flowing through her body. Her inner anger metabolised into energy. *Must stay calm, Nicky, show them you are a professional and are bigger than this!*

Nicollette took another deep breath and looked directly into Mr. Gistane's eyes, responding to him in a deliberate and purposeful manner. She was fully aware that she had to be respectful, but also conscious that her career and the rest of her life may be at stake.

"Sir, my name is Nicollette Beverley, I am an Intelligence Officer in Her Majesty's service. I have been well trained and I believe I'm equal to any task. I volunteered for this mission and I recognize the importance of a successful conclusion. Although I am younger than most of my colleagues, I have been involved in operations at home and overseas. I conduct myself professionally at all times. Now I ask you, sir, do you think that from the time I left England to the time I arrived at the post in Thailand, I would have time to organize, facilitate, and activate a complete clandestine operation? For what or whom? Secondly, would I be as careless as to leave any obvious evidence pointing to *my* involvement? And how would I know the position of the surveillance team two weeks ahead of time on my first day? I'm not even involved with scheduling. Finally, would I have risked my life to pick up those wounded soldiers during our escape if I was a traitor? I ask you these questions while some of those soldiers are living when they could have easily died,"

Nicollette paused, but before Mr. Gistane could interrupt again, she continued, her eyes unflinching in their intensity.

"The Officer in charge of our post is sitting right behind you, why don't you ask him about my work and what he said to me the night of our escape?"

Then, still in control, but now in a calmer, softer voice, Nicollette concluded,

"Sir, Mr. Gistane, I don't want to be insubordinate, but I've said everything that I care to and I'm anxious to go home. Is there anything else?"

As she waited for his response, Nicollette felt a sense of urgency and discomfort replace the anger and energy she had drawn upon. Mr. Gistane's reaction in the next few seconds could be career and even life altering. She started to question herself as the seconds passed. *What did I just do? Was I insubordinate, brash, impolite or disrespectful? Was I justified? Did I overreact?*

The air in the room was thick. All the eyes in the room focused on her. *If I don't defend myself, then am I letting myself down and all I've learned gone to waste? Be strong, Nicky!*

A minute or two had passed when the silence was broken by a knock on the door. One of the men in the back of the room opened the door and a military policeman whispered something.

"Mr. Gistane is sitting at the desk," he responded.

Mr. Gistane withdrew his eyes from Nicollette and acknowledged the military policeman to come to the desk.

"Sir, you are needed in the hall right away, please."

"If you will excuse me, please," Mr. Gistane announced as he stood and left the room.

Nicollette's back was moist with perspiration and sticking to the chair as she tried to regain her composure. Her hands were numb from her tight grip on the chair handles. The NATO officer sitting just off to the side behind Mr. Gistane's desk was motionless, stiff, and sitting erect in his commanding posture. Her eyes momentarily met his; nothing needed to be said, it was all in the eyes. *He could have said something, surely. What about our chat after we escaped to Chiang Rai? Was that just for my benefit or was it for his?*

She turned away, her mind still trying to work out what just happened. The room was silent.

"Miss Beverley." Nicollette turned to see Mr. Gistane and the other men from the back of the room come through the door.

A sudden thought crossed her mind, *I was alone with the NATO officer all this time and nothing was said? Not a word?! Two weeks in the jungle under his command and all he can do is sit there? Something isn't right!*

Mr. Gistane stopped and whispered something to the NATO officer before resuming his place behind the desk. The NATO officer stood from his chair and gave a head nod to Mr. Gistane as he left the room. He never looked at Nicollette as she watched him leave.

"Now Miss Beverley, where were we?" Mr. Gistane asked while looking through the folder.

"Yes, we were talking about the red bottle cap and cigarette package."

Mr. Gistane leaned back in his chair, his demeanor changing to a less vigorous and more relaxed mood.

"Thank you for your cooperation and we will proceed no further at this point. Your flight leaves in two hours."

A military policeman entered the room and stood next to Nicollette.

"Sergeant Wouters will escort you to the staging area."

Mr. Gistane stood from the desk and offered his hand. "Thank you, Miss Beverley."

Nicollette rose from her chair and politely shook Mr. Gistane's hand as she left the room. The sergeant guided her to a staging area and offered her a coffee. Nicollette realized she was the only one in the room. She was numb, confused, and exhausted. *What just happened? What was the real intention?* She kept reliving the last hour in her mind. *Why did it end so abruptly? What made Mr. Gistane change his tone towards me? And what about the NATO officer? What's his story?*

The hot coffee felt good on the back of her throat, temporarily washing away her cottonmouth. She leaned back in the comfortable chair, closing her eyes to get just a few minutes of peace, while trying desperately to push aside the internal angst of the interview.

"Miss Beverley, Miss Beverley, we're ready to go."

Nicollette looked up to see Sergeant Wouters standing over her.

"Sorry, I must have dozed off. How long have I been here?"

The Sergeant looked at his watch. "About thirty minutes."

Nicollette stood up, had a brief stretch, and looked around the room. *Still the only one here.*

"This way, Miss," the Sergeant stated as he raised his arm and pointed to an exit.

"Sergeant, where is Mr. Peter Johnson? Shouldn't he be here with me? He and I are the only Brits here. We should be on the same flight. He was here when I went to my interview and now I don't see him. Can you find out about him for me please?"

With a disgusted look on his face, Sergeant Wouters looked at Nicollette. "My instructions, Miss, are to get you to the airport safely and watch you board your flight. Nothing else."

"Isn't there someone we could ask? I am not leaving till I find out. If you can't help me, then I will try to get answers myself!" she added defiantly, staring at his face.

Sergeant Wouters looked back at Nicollette, visibly agitated at being confronted by a young woman. He had his orders but realized that time would become a problem very soon. Nicollette watched the Sergeant's eyes soften as he reluctantly acquiesced to her demand.

"Wait here, please, Miss."

"No, Sergeant, I'm going with you."

The two of them left the staging area and headed down a long nondescript corridor, stopping in front of a large brown wooden door. Nicollette noticed there was no sign or number attached to the door.

"Wait here, Miss," the Sergeant commanded in a terse voice while opening the door. He strategically used his body to block any view Nicollette could have of the interior of the room.

Nicollette stood against the wall and looked up and down the hall as she waited. The halls were empty and very quiet. A disturbing thought crossed her mind. She was all alone here, with people she did not know, in a strange building, in a strange city. The only person she did know needed to be located for her and only at her insistence. She was not going to give up on finding Peter.

Nicollette looked at her watch, the same watch she'd been wearing since she was a teenager. *This watch has been with me for a long time, through my adventures and experiences. If it could talk, it might say that it didn't sign up for all of this when I first put it on my wrist, but like me, this is it and I am who I am. You are strong, Nicky!*

About three minutes passed when the brown door opened and Sergeant Wouters appeared with a dark suited man.

"This is Doctor Keller, he is in charge of the infirmary here."

Dr. Keller held out his hand and spoke to her in a heavily German accented voice. "Hello Miss Beverley. You want to know about your friend Peter Johnson, is that right?"

"Yes," she said as she shook the doctor's hand.

"Please enter my office. Sergeant, please wait outside, thank you."

Inside, Dr. Keller offered a chair and pulled one next to her. *No, please not bad news! Please!*

"Miss Beverley, Mr. Johnson has been transferred to hospital. He collapsed during his interview. His shoulder wound had reopened and was bleeding. We also noticed that his leg wound was not closed properly. Both procedures looked to be done in haste. Quite frankly, I don't know why the surgeon would even allow him to fly. Mr. Johnson is in surgery at this moment."

Dr. Keller squeezed her hand softly as he continued. "Miss Beverley, I can assure you, Mr. Johnson is in good hands."

There was silence. Nicollette let the doctor's words sink in. She looked back at him and, through her very dry throat, asked if she could see him. "I don't want him to be alone while he's recovering."

"We can arrange that, but you will miss your flight."

"There will be other flights," she replied. "I'm not going home without him."

The car was silent as Sergeant Wouters drove Nicollette to Queen Astrid Military Hospital. She found herself blankly staring out of the window, her mind overcrowded, thinking about the day's experiences.

At the hospital, Sergeant Wouters escorted Nicollette through a remote entrance, passing a large number of uniformed personnel as they approached a security desk. Sergeant Wouters spoke Dutch to the man behind the counter. The only words Nicollette understood were "Peter Johnson." The security officer picked up a phone, uttered a few words, and pointed to a group of chairs. Nicollette and the Sergeant waited about five minutes until they were greeted by a man in a military uniform. Sergeant Wouters and the man spoke a few words then turned to Nicollette.

"Mr. Johnson is in recovery, this man will escort us to a place where we can wait."

Nicollette heard the word 'we' and looked at the sergeant. "We? Are you going to stay with me?"

"My instructions are to stay with you until relieved. Miss,

I would like to point out that you are in Belgium, a foreign country to you. You have no identification, no connections, no money and you don't speak the language. Outside of headquarters, you are alone and vulnerable. I think you understand my instructions."

He's right. All I have are the clothes I'm wearing!

The escort took them to a small waiting area just outside the recovery area. A white-coated man approached Nicollette and Sergeant Wouters. He spoke Dutch to the sergeant then walked away.

"How is he? What's happening? Tell me please."

There was a pause.

"The doctor told me that Mr. Johnson is out of surgery and is in a recovery room. He said the procedures went well, but Mr. Johnson will not be able to see anyone till tomorrow morning. Miss, I must excuse myself to make a call."

Nicollette saw that her timing was lucky. There was nobody at the nurses' station in front of the recovery area. She watched the sergeant walk out of sight then ventured into recovery. There were twelve windowed rooms and she quickly walked past each one, trying desperately to find Peter. At room seven, Nicollette saw a chart hanging above the patient. Unfortunately, it was written in Dutch except for the name: Mr. Peter Johnson.

Nicollette peered through the glass. There was a breathing tube in Mr. Johnson's mouth and several tubes attached to his body. Suddenly, a strong hand landed on her shoulder, pulling her away from the window. A man in a blue coat spoke firmly to Nicollette in Dutch. She nodded, using her hands to show she didn't understand. The man took her arm and forcibly walked her past the nurses' station and back to the waiting area. He pointed to a seat and walked away.

Nicollette looked back at the recovery room area. *Heal fast, Peter! Please don't leave me!*

Mates

Sergeant Wouter gave a purposeful cough to get Nicollette's attention. "Miss, they want you back at HQ as soon as possible. Those are my instructions for you."

"What about Mr. Johnson?"

"I've spoken to the doctor. He says Mr. Johnson will be in the recovery room overnight as a precaution and transferred to a private room tomorrow. There's really no need for you to stay."

Nicollette felt helpless as she followed the sergeant down the hallway towards the exit. She now felt even more isolated in a strange place, Peter was the only connection to her normal reality, and all she could do was hope that everything would look better for him in the morning.

The sun was setting as the vehicle pulled up to a nondescript building.

"Out you get, Miss. I will meet you inside."

Nicollette exited the rear of the vehicle. The day had pushed her mind to the limit and now her body was following suit. Nicollette looked for a chair, but there was none to be found, just the well manned security desk in front of her.

"Can we help you, Miss?" one of the very serious looking guards asked.

Nicollette realized that she had no identification and probably looked in "a right state."

"Miss?" the guard asked again, more insistently, as he approached her from behind the desk. "Please state your business."

Remain calm, Nicky.

"I am waiting for Sergeant Wouters, he asked me to wait here for him."

The guard looked Nicollette up and down. *Probably a visual search.* The guard called back to another guard behind the desk.

"Maybe it's her. What is your name, Miss?"

"Nicollette Beverley," she responded in a very soft voice.

"It's her."

The desk guard picked up a blue phone on the desk.

"She's here."

Nicollette heard the words and her heart started to race. *They're expecting me! Is this from the interview or because I wouldn't leave Mr. Johnson?*

A minute or two went by, then out of nowhere, Nicollette heard her name.

"Miss Beverley, we've been expecting you."

It wasn't so much hearing her name called, but the voice, the accent. *That cockney accent! A Londoner! A fellow Brit!*

Nicollette turned to see a middle-aged woman approaching her from the side. "Hello Miss Beverley, my name is Elizabeth Brighall, but most people call me Betty, some even refer to me as Aunt Betty," she added with a smile. "I'm with the British Liaison Office here."

Betty Brighall offered her hand. Nicollette started to offer hers in return, but an overwhelming feeling inside her wanted to hug this stranger. Betty's voice, mannerisms, and welcoming smile appeared so friendly and inviting and after the events of the day, Nicollette could hardly contain herself. For just a moment, Nicollette let her guard down and hugged the receptive Betty.

"It's ok, Nicollette, you've had quite a day, my girl," she whispered as she patted Nicollette's back.

Nicollette pulled away. "I'm so sorry, Miss Brighall, it's just, it's just..."

"I know, Nicollette, I've been briefed. Now let's take a look at you, girl."

Betty Brighall took a step back and eyed her. "You are a sight.

First things first though. Come with me." Betty paused. "And it's Missus, by the way."

The sign on the door read British Liaison as Mrs. Brighall opened the door. "Come through, Miss Beverley."

Beautiful leather sofas surrounded a small table with a bowl of fruit. There was a tea cart off to the side and a basket of packaged sweets next to a large selection of teas. The walls were panelled and actual curtains covered the windows. A large portrait of the Queen was hanging behind the reception desk and the Union Jack stood proudly in the corner.

"This is a beautiful office, Mrs Brighall."

"Thank you, Miss Beverley, one must keep up appearances and be civilized." She smiled back at Nicollette, "Please have a seat and help yourself to refreshment."

Nicollette helped herself to tea and biscuits. *The tea bounced off her throat. Real tea! It's been over a fortnight! So good!*

"We're connected," the receptionist announced.

"Splendid. Give us a tick and put it through to room five, please. Nicollette, would you please come with me and bring your tea if you like."

Nicollette followed Mrs. Brighall to a small side room with a table and a couple of chairs. The phone on the table started to ring.

"That's for you, Miss Beverley."

"Me?"

"Go ahead and answer it, Nicollette."

Nicollette reached for the phone and put the receiver to her ear as Mrs Brighall quietly closed the door.

"Hello, Nicollette Beverley here."

"Hello Miss Beverley."

Upon hearing the voice on the line, Nicollette fell back into a chair. "Major Blasingame, ma'am, it's so good to hear your voice."

"How are you keeping?"

"Ma'am, I'm fine."

"Splendid. Now I want to talk with you for a moment. I have been fully briefed. Your mission was a success and you did us proud for your part. You showed initiative and resourcefulness, but Nicollette, these are dangerous people we put out of business. You must be careful, even in Brussels. So I want you to stay close to Mrs. Brighall, do as she says. I've known Betty a long time, she will look after you."

Nicollette felt reassured hearing the Major's voice.

"What about Mr. Johnson?"

There was a short silence on the line. "I know he is part of our team and your friend, but sometimes we have to draw the line with practicalities."

Nicollette heard the Major's words and tone but she was determined.

"Can we be practical next time, ma'am? I don't want Mr. Johnson to be alone here."

Another silent pause. "Nicollette, your mission was for up to twenty-five days. I think we can spare you for a few more days, but listen to me and listen to me good, my girl. You are to do everything Betty, I mean Mrs. Brighall, says. Full stop! You have two days and I want you back no matter what! Understand?"

"Yes ma'am and thank you."

"Now I need to speak to Mrs. Brighall. Good night, Miss Beverley."

Nicollette laid the phone down on the table and opened the door. Mrs. Brighall was waiting in the hall.

"Major Blasingame wishes to speak with you."

"Thank you, Miss Beverley, please wait in reception."

Several minutes passed till Mrs. Brighall walked back to reception, stopping at the reception desk and speaking to the receptionist. Despite her low voice, Nicollette could overhear the conversation. Mrs. Brighall was arranging secure transport to a place called "The House" but planning a stop along the way.

Nicollette felt better having spoken with Major Blasingame and she felt secure with Mrs Brighall, but she remembered the words of Captain McWilliams on her very first day of training: *Details, always remember the details. Never give anything away.*

Two military police walked into the room, a man and a woman. "Mrs. Brighall, transport is ready if you will follow us."

Nicollette sat in the back of a black sedan with the woman guard and Mrs. Brighall sat in front next to the driver. The car had dark tinted windows, obscuring the outside world. They drove for just over thirty minutes. The car suddenly stopped and Mrs. Brighall looked at Nicollette.

"First things first, Miss Beverley. We need to get you some supplies. We don't have Marks and Spencers here, but we do have Hemas."

Mrs. Brighall spoke to the driver as she and Nicollette exited the car. "We need forty minutes."

Nicollette entered the department store, her eyes having to adjust to the bright lights. Mrs. Brighall marched her quickly to the clothing area and pointed to a display of black and dark blue skirts. "We don't have a lot of time and no one is interested in fashion at this point. You know your size, Nicollette, pick one of each." Next it was white blouses then underwear and tights. A quick visit for comfortable shoes then off to the toiletries.

As she was filling her basket, Nicollette once again realized how vulnerable she was. She had nothing and was nobody, and yet she was being looked after well, even down to purchasing a toothbrush. Mrs. Brighall paid for the two bags of supplies and the two of them quickly entered the black sedan.

"Thank you, Betty."
She quickly realized her mistake,
"I mean, Mrs. Brighall."
Mrs. Brighall smiled at Nicollette. "This time Betty works just fine, Nicky."

The sedan stopped in front of a poorly lit area in front of an old warehouse.

As she and Mrs. Brighall approached the large steel double door entrance, two fully clad military policemen stopped them. With guns pointed, they asked for identification. After showing documentation and inspecting the bags, the large steel door was opened and they walked through a long foyer till they reached another checkpoint in front of a second steel door. Documents were exchanged and the security men opened the door to another security area. The light from inside was unexpectedly bright and caught Nicollette off guard as she raised her left hand to shield her eyes.

Nicollette looked around while Mrs. Brighall spoke with the guards behind the desk. As her eyes were scanning the lobby, Nicollette felt like she had been here before. Then she remembered! *This is the place we stayed at during our training!* Her mind revisited the events of that weekend. The organization and planning, the prisoner exchange, the grateful Colonel and his family and yes, the cold-blooded shooting by the East German guards. *The first time here, I was exposed to a shooting! It seems like a long time ago!*

Mrs Brighall and an escort brought Nicollette to her room. It was just as she remembered. The escort pointed to a binder next to a phone with three buttons sitting on top of the nightstand.

"Everything you need to know is in the binder, Miss," she announced as she walked away.

"Are you alright, Nicollette?" Mrs. Brighall asked.

"Yes, I'll be fine. I was here once before during my training."

"Would you like me to stay? We could have dinner together?"

"Thank you, Mrs. Brighall, I'll be fine. I just want to rest."

"If that's what you want, Nicollette. I will arrange transport for you in the morning at 10:00 a.m. Make sure you are in the lobby and ready to go and if you need anything, anything at all, you can reach me at this number."

The door shut behind Mrs. Brighall. The room was quiet, a calming silence giving Nicollette time to collect her thoughts. It had been a day! Starting out in Bangkok and finishing here in Brussels and everything in between. She organized the supplies and clothing, then a quick shower and a visit to the cafeteria. Nicollette checked her watch. It was nearly nine and she hadn't eaten much all day.

The warm water splashing against her felt soothing and relaxing to both her body and mind. She wrapped herself in a towel and sat on the bed, a numbness creeping over her. She fell back on the pillow. Quiet. Calm. Serene.

A natural awakening, no alarm, no sunlight and no gentle prodding. The body says it's had enough sleep, asking the senses to come back to reality and the mind to imagine all the possibilities of the day ahead. This was a rare occurrence for Nicollette, especially during the last fortnight, and she took advantage of it.

A quick look at her watch revealed it was half past seven. She had slept ten hours! Rare, very rare.

Her stomach insisting, Nicollette readied herself and headed to the cafeteria, returning later to the room and then on to the lobby.

At exactly ten, a security guard approached her. "Miss Beverley, transport is here."

Nicollette was escorted down a long hall, past a security desk and into a waiting sedan. Two solid jawed, stoic men sat next to her, never moving or taking their eyes away from the front or side windows. She remembered Major Blasingame telling her to be careful. There were still dangers for her even in Brussels. *Looks like I am well protected.*

Nicollette was taken to the security desk outside the recovery area. Her escort handed her a card, "contacten," and walked away. The security guard eyed her. "Missen?"

Nicollette understood that Missen was Dutch for Miss.

"English?" she responded.

"Engels? Nee, wacht hier."

It was just another reminder of where she was and how vulnerable she could be. *I have no identification! No papers! Why would the escort leave me? What if they detain me or worse?*

Another security guard approached her.

"Miss, your business here?"

English, thank goodness for that.

"I'm here to see Mr. Peter Johnson. He was in recovery last night and should be in a room this morning."

"Papers please, Miss," the guard insisted.

Nicollette's nightmare was happening. "I do not have any. All I have is this."

The guard looked at the card, both sides, then back at Nicollette. "One minute, Miss."

He made a quick call, returned Nicollette's card, and motioned for her to follow him. They stopped at the nurses' station where words were exchanged and names written down. The security guard raised three fingers and pointed to the left. Finally, she was at Peter Johnson's room. She took a deep breath as she entered the room, not knowing in what condition Peter would be in or how receptive he would be to her visit

"Hello Peter," Nicollette announced.

He was lying on the bed, struggling with a straw from a water cup. "Hello Nicky," he whispered back in a dry throaty rasp.

"Let me help you with that."

Nicollette adjusted the straw and Mr. Johnson took a healthy drink. She could see he was still feeling the effects of last evening's surgery. His right arm was wrapped and strapped to his chest and there was a large bandage covering his right thigh. There was a tube running a clear liquid through into his right arm and a cable from his right shoulder to some sort of monitoring machine on the wall. His complexion was pale and his face had three days' worth of growth on it.

"How are you feeling, Peter?"

"Much better since they brought me here," he whispered. "They say I fainted during the interview. To tell you the truth, Nicky, I don't remember much about last evening."

He paused for a breath and asked for another sip of water.

"I knew the treatment given to me in Thailand was just a patch job. I was just hoping to make it home in time to see it right. I just didn't want to be left behind in Chiang Rai, no matter what." He took another sip of water. "I could feel I wasn't well on the flight, but I really thought I could make it." He gave a slight smile. "Turns out I was wrong."

"Never mind, Peter, you will be back home soon."

A doctor and nurse walked into the room.

"Good morning, Mr. Johnson," the doctor announced in heavily Dutch accented English. "Let's see how you are this morning."

The doctor motioned for Nicollette to wait outside. After fifteen minutes, the nurse walked out of the room followed by the doctor. Nicollette reached out to gain the doctor's attention. His facial expression was all business as he turned to her. "Ja, Missen?"

"Please, sir, how is he? When might he be well enough to travel?"

"Mr. Johnson is doing well. We, how would you say, put right the mend. We even found a small piece of old metal in his shoulder. He needs rest, at least twenty-four to thirty-six hours. We will know better tomorrow."

Peter was sitting up in the bed, his torso supported by pillows. He was still pale but a small glint of color was returning to his cheeks. "I really am glad to see you, Nicky."

He used his finger to beckon her to come closer. She pulled the chair closer and offered him a drink. He motioned the cup away and reached for her hand.

"How did your briefing go?"

Nicollette paused before responding. She wanted to tell him everything but did not want to get him upset or agitated.

"I think we should find a better time for that conversation."

He squeezed her hand.

At noon, a nurse brought in a lunch tray. She was followed by Mrs. Brighall. "Hello, Peter! How's the patient?"

"This is a pleasant surprise, Betty! I'm a little tired but much better, thank you."

"I was hoping to steal Nicollette for lunch and give you a chance to rest."

"Go ahead, Nicky, I'll be fine."

Mrs. Brighall brought Nicollette to a waiting sedan. "I know a lovely little bistro nearby. I hope you like French food."

The sedan pulled in front of a stone building across the street from a park. The two sat down at an outdoor table and Mrs. Brighall ordered a bottle of wine. "We're off duty, Nicollette."

Nicollette felt comfortable for the first time since arriving in Brussells. She had made it through the exit briefing, *more like a cross-examination,* had a good sleep, and spent time with Peter. Mrs. Brighall had come to her rescue. It was a lovely afternoon. The sun was warm, the air fresh, and the scent of blooming flowers wafted in the air. It was hard to believe that less than three days ago, bandits were shooting at her.

The peaceful afternoon snapped back to reality as the driver approached Mrs. Brighall and reminded her of the time. Forty-five minutes later, Nicollette was back in Peter's room.

She found a football match on the tele and settled in while he slept. She closed her eyes.

The creak of a trolley awakened her. Nicollette checked her watch. *Nearly seven o'clock!*

Peter was awake and very alert as he chuckled. "You've been asleep all afternoon."

His voice was stronger and he was now sitting up in bed.

"You look much better," she offered.

"Thank you," he responded. "Must be the company."

The next morning, Nicollette was surprised to see Peter standing by the bed when she arrived. He had color in his cheeks and his facial stubble was gone.

"Well, you look so much better," she exclaimed.

"I had a good night. I still feel a little stiff, but certainly on the mend."

The day went by as the two laughed and talked about home. Despite her hints, Nicollette felt like Peter was avoiding talking about the briefing. The thought crossed her mind that he may have information and was hiding it from her. But she trusted him and felt assured that if it was important, he would tell her.

The dinner trays were just being carried away when a familiar voice permeated the room.

"Hello, you two layabouts! Time to come back to work," Val Davies proclaimed as she embraced Nicollette.

"Val, so good to see you! What are you doing here?"

"Thought you might want some company on your flight home, and," Val leaned in and in a soft voice, "a certain 'Bigwig' kinda asked me to come along."

"Hello, Miss Beverley."

Nicollette's knees buckled as she turned to see Major Blasingame enter the room with Betty Brighall.

"Somebody has to be in charge of the operation," Major Blasingame stated as she gave a smile and offered her hand to Nicollette. "Good to see you, Nicollette."

Nicollette shook hands with the Major. "It's good to see you as well, ma'am."

There was small talk and pleasantries in the room until the doctor arrived for the evening check. Nicollette and Val were asked to leave the room, leaving the Major and Betty Brighall inside.

Nicollette and Val made their way to the waiting area. Val explained how the Major had a meeting in Brussels and wanted a day or two to catch up with the Brits here. She also thought Peter might need help getting home.

"Why did you stay here, Nicky? You could have come home yesterday."

Nicollette thought about the question. Was it instinct, friendship, a sense of obligation or a fear that one day, she could be in a hospital room alone?

"Because we are mates, Val, teammates and mates."

Val nodded and leaned in to whisper to Nicollette. "It seemed like the Major was anxious to check on Peter Johnson but even more keen to talk with him. I'm not sure why, Nicky, but I bet it's about Thailand. I know she wants to get him home."

The two of them continued small talk while Nicollette's mind focused on Val's words. Thailand.

Bullocks!

A hand on her shoulder brought Nicollette out of her sleep.

"It's time to leave, Miss," the nurse's soft voice whispered.

A man in a doctor's coat was walking towards Peter, sound asleep on the hospital bed. The tele was still on as Nicollette regained full consciousness. *Must have dozed off.* A quick look at her watch gave the local time of just after 1:00 a.m. She nudged Val.

"Wakey, wakey, Sleeping Beauty," Nicollette whispered.

"Wha...what's going on?" Val asked drowsily.

"I think we're leaving."

Nicollette pointed to the doctor waking up Peter Johnson.

"This kind of reminds me of our training, me having to wake you up every day," Nicollette added with a smile.

"Cheeky devil," Val responded.

The doctor motioned for the two of them to leave the room as another doctor joined him. A nurse followed and asked the young ladies to leave the room so Mr. Johnson could be prepped.

The hall and waiting areas were eerily quiet, in fact, there seemed to be no one about. Nicollette spotted three men and a security guard at the desk at the end of the hallway. On the shoulders of the three men, she could just make out what looked to be Uzis. Nicollette recognized the Uzi from her training days. She remembered the weapon as firing a large number of bullets very fast. She had to fight to hold the Uzi down. *It has a tendency to rise, barrel towards the sky, so aim low,* the instructor taught them. *A very dangerous weapon!*

"Let's get a coffee." She gently tugged Val's arm.

They walked to the nurses' station, where there was a pot of old coffee sitting on the burner. Nicollette grabbed Val's arm as they quickly ducked into an empty room off to the side.

"This coffee tastes like lead!" Val exclaimed.

"Forget the damn coffee! Did you see the extra security at the end of the hallway?"

"No, not really. What's up, Nicky?"

"This area is very quiet. The only activity seems to be us! There is nobody in the halls and the nurses' station is empty. Where is everybody? Why all the security? Is it for us? It's bloody one in the morning!"

"You are imagining things, Nicky, you aren't on a mission," Val responded.

"Besides, this is a secure area."

"I'm not imagining the Uzis I saw on those men, Val! Why didn't the Major inform us about getting Peter ready to leave the hospital or send Mrs Brighall? I mean, a nurse we don't know tells us to leave so he can be prepped! Prepared for what? Something isn't right, Val, and Major Blasingame made it very clear to me to be extra careful in Brussels."

Val pulled slightly away from Nicollette. "Now you've got me thinking. Suppose you're right. What do you have in mind?"

Nicollette pulled out the small piece of paper that Betty Brighall had given her the night before.

"If we could just call Mrs. Brighall, she could sort this out and if I'm wrong, then there is nothing to worry about, but if I am right....We can't call from this floor because if this is a situation, the phone will be tapped or cut. You must go down a couple of floors and find a phone."

"Easy for you to say."

"Now listen, Val, when we were at the nurses' station, I noticed a stairway entrance across the hall. That door is hidden from the view of the security desk. We can crawl back and you can leave from there. I will wait behind the counter. We have to act fast, we probably don't have much time. Let's go."

Nicollette looked down the hall at the four men at the security desk. It was a long way down the corridor and they didn't seem to notice the two women crawling to the nurses' station. Val continued on to the stairway door, quietly opened it, and disappeared. Nicollette's heart was racing, her adrenaline flowing, her mind overflowing with information.

Her thoughts were suddenly cast aside as she heard a soft groan coming from the area around the staircase door. Nicollette crawled across the hallway towards the door. Another soft groan. The noise seemed to be coming from a green door next to the staircase entrance. Fortunately, the green door was hidden from the armed men at the other end of the hall. Nicollette carefully opened the green door and slowly entered the dark room. The soft groan was now more emphatic as she gently closed the door. Keeping one hand on the door handle, Nicollette used her other hand to feel for a light switch. Her hand was successful, her heart pounding as she took a breath, *one...two...three....*

Immediately the room became illuminated, revealing a closet that was used for medical storage. A small trail of blood led behind some large cardboard boxes. She slowly stepped towards the boxes as the soft groaning increased in intensity.

Very deliberately, Nicollette moved one of the boxes and looked behind. A set of eyes blinked uncontrollably back at her. Nicollette quickly removed another box and dropped to her knees. The groans were coming from a bound woman in a nurse's uniform. Her mouth was covered and there was wet blood on her face and hair. Nicollette removed the tape covering the nurse's mouth.

"Are you alright? What's your name? What happened here?"

"Klien engels," the injured nurse replied and pointed to her badge.

"You are Anneke Janssen, yes?" Nicollette asked.

Anneke nodded. Blood seeped from a large wound on the

side of her head.

"My name is Nicky," Nicollette whispered, using her nickname to keep it easy. "We need to get you a bandage." She used her hands to demonstrate.

"Verbandan," Anneke responded as she pointed to a shelf.

Nicollette found a pair of scissors and ripped open a box of medical gauze. While freeing the nurse and applying the gauze, Nicollette's mind started churning. *Here I am in a closet with a badly injured woman. There are four, maybe even more, strange men at the security desk and Peter is alone in his room with a nurse and two doctors who may not even be who they are. Isn't this supposed to be a secure hospital? And Val...*

Anneke held her hand out for Nicollette to assist her to stand. She stood gingerly but soon regained her balance. She looked at Nicollette and held up three fingers. She held one finger, "Slechte dokter," then another finger, "Slechte verpleegster," and her third finger, "Goede dokter."

Nicollette understood the words Goede Dokter meant Good Doctor, but not the word slechte or verpleegster. She repeated them for Anneke. "Slechte Verpleegster?" Anneke nodded her head again as she pointed to her badge, "Ja! Verpleegster!" She then pointed to her head wound with her pointer finger extended and her thumb upright. "Slechte!"

She's imitating a gun with her hand. Nicollette responded, "Slechte...bad!"

"Ja, bad."

Nearly twenty-five minutes had gone by since they had left Peter in the room. Nicollette had a sense they were running out of time. She motioned to Anneke to be quiet and watch for her signal as she slowly opened the closet door. *Must get back to the nurses' station first.* The hallway was still quiet as Nicollette crawled behind the counter. She pointed back at Anneke and gestured for her to crawl to the station. *So far, so good...*

Val appeared from the stairway door and made her way

behind the counter. "Any luck?"

"The two floors below us have been emptied," Val explained. "I had to go down three floors till I found somebody, and then they nearly blew my head off as I left the staircase. The floor is teeming with security people, soldiers and staff. There are patients everywhere. This floor and the two below it have been cordoned off. I asked about making a call, but security wouldn't let me, even after I explained who I was. They wouldn't even let me come back here though I tried to explain that you were still on this floor. I was able to sneak away, so now, the security people know there are at least three of us here, including Peter."

Val paused to catch her breath and then leaned in to Nicollette.

"Nicky, there must be a hundred well-armed people downstairs and I heard the word 'hostage.' The authorities downstairs told me there are at least ten attackers and maybe more. The attackers have weapons and it appears they are well organized. Security thinks there may even be explosives around, plus, hold onto your hat, my friend, I heard the words 'Tang,' Baader Meinhof, and Haviken."

Val paused to catch her composure.

"Nicky, these are serious people! They mean business! They aren't playing!"

Val was right to be concerned. The Tang Organization was the largest drug group in Southeast Asia and their scope of business was worldwide. Baader and Haviken were local connections, perhaps providing logistics or muscle or both.

Is this revenge for the operation in Thailand? How could this have been organized in seventy-two hours? Nicollette drew a breath. Too many questions! *Must deal with the situation at hand first.*

"Hostage situation, you mean Peter Johnson is a hostage?"

"It would appear that way, Nicky, and, my girl, there's you

and now me."

Nicollette drew back.

"You and I hostages?"

"Think about it, Nicky. Peter is the only patient left on this floor. You and I are just visitors. Someone has gone to a great deal of trouble to get Peter. They weren't expecting us, probably didn't even know we were here. After all, we fell asleep in the room last night and didn't head out."

Val paused.

"Say, what happened in Thailand and by the way, who's this?" She pointed to the bloodied nurse.

Nicollette explained about hearing the soft groaning and finding Anneke in the closet. She told Val about the two doctors, one good, one bad, and the bad nurse, all in the room with Peter.

"As for Thailand, we'll chat later. Right now we need a plan."

"Perhaps this will help." Val reached behind her back and produced two pistols.

"Crikey! Where did you get those?" Nicollette asked.

"There were two dead men on the stairway. I reckoned they wouldn't need them, so I picked up the pistols on my way back up."

Nicollette looked at Val and grabbed her shoulders. In a firm voice full of concern and with a piercing stare, she spoke to her friend.

"Remember our training? Those bodies could have been planted and baited with explosives! I hope you took all the precautions!"

"We, Nicky, were trained well."

Nicollette checked the first weapon. There was a full magazine. Same for the second gun.

"Val, what kind of clothes were they wearing?"

"Are you kidding me, Nicky? They were dead."

"Think, girl. I know it sounds silly, but it may be important."

"I don't know, Nicky, plain clothes, I guess."

"Look at the four men at the security desk. Was it like them?"

Val crawled to the edge of the counter and peered down the hall.

"Yes, Nicky, sort of like them, only now there are only three there."

Nicollette looked down the hallway. Val was right, there were only three men at the desk. *Where is number four?*

Nicollette tucked the gun into her waistband behind her back. She instructed Val to do the same.

"We don't want to engage Uzis with pistols if we don't have to."

Nicollette formulated an idea in her mind. There was only her and Val on this floor and maybe Anneke could help in some way. They would most certainly be outnumbered and definitely outgunned, but they must get to Peter, and soon.

"Val, what if the hostages took hostages?"

Val just looked at Nicollette. "What the devil are you thinking? Are you mad?"

"I just may be, but it's the best I can come up with. We are running out of time. We left Peter's room nearly thirty minutes ago, don't you think they might be getting suspicious?"

"What's your plan?"

"We know there are at least two plotters in the room with Peter. We also know that this is a hostage situation and the security people downstairs have to be working on something. If we can get back to the room and neutralize the two plotters, we may be able to signal the security people below."

Val's face was expressionless. "Nicky, you *are* mad!"

Nicollette's heart was now in full throttle, her body was damp with nervous sweat, but her voice was strong and decisive.

"Listen, Val," she said. "You said that there were two dead men in the staircase, right? And you didn't see anyone else in the staircase, right?"

Val nodded.

"Then I think those two men were plotters and their friends on this floor don't know they are dead, plus it was probably one of those two that bonked Anneke on the head! Those men were probably watching over the stairway and were neutralized. I also think that the stairway is the avenue that security is going to use to mount an assault. I would guess they purposely let you come back to this floor to see if the stairs were clear!"

"You mean I was used as a pawn?"

"Maybe. I'm hoping."

Anneke tugged on Nicollette's blouse and pointed to Peter Johnson's room. The missing man from the security desk was entering the room. He was carrying an Uzi.

"Val, when those security men find out we're not in the room, they'll come looking for us. We must act fast."

Nicollette grabbed Anneke's arm and pointed to a fire alarm next to the stairway. She used her fingers to pantomime herself and Val walking back to the room. She looked at Anneke, hoping she would understand, as she displayed her watch.

"In three minutes, pull the switch!"

Nicollette used her right hand in a pulling motion and raised three fingers with her left. Anneke nodded affirmatively, "Ja."

Val looked at Nicollette.

"Damn, I hope she gets it! Now what about us, Nicky?"

"We have an element of surprise and we are going to use it. First, the plotters don't know we understand what's going on. Secondly, they don't know the stairway is a secure route for the security forces downstairs to get to this floor. We have Anneka to signal an alarm, and most important..."

Nicollette grabbed Val's arm tightly and stared directly into her eyes.

"They think they're dealing with two weak, scared women, who'll probably just start crying and won't put up any trouble. Well, my friend, they're going to learn a hard lesson real fast!!"

"Damn right! What's the plan?"

"We are going to each get a cup of coffee, the same you said was like lead. Well, that leaded liquid is now a weapon. We are going to casually walk back to the room. Hopefully, the Uzi man will escort us. Be sure to loosen your blouse and unbutton the top two buttons. Hopefully, a little 'skin' will distract him to your chest and he won't pay too much attention to your backside. Plus, the loosened blouse will cover the gun sticking out of your skirt. We don't want him to know we are armed. Once in the room, on your third step, I want you to stop suddenly and turn back at Uzi man. I will push him hard and you throw the coffee in his face. I will disarm him and you take control of the room with your pistol. By that time, Anneka should have set off the alarm. If the Uzi man is not fully neutralized or if any of the others try to resist, don't hesitate, shoot them low in the legs. They are our hostages. If this works, we will have three hostages and a stairway full of reinforcements."

Nicollette paused.

"Val, you are my colleague and friend. This is very dangerous. I will switch places with you, it's up to you."

Without hesitation, Val responded: "Bullocks!"

Instincts

Nicollette peered down the hall. The Uzi man was out of Peter's room and heading towards the nurses' station, looking into rooms along the hallway.

"Ready, Val? Let's go!"

Nicollette stood and went to the coffee pot. She poured two large cups of the pitch-black liquid.

"Follow my lead," she whispered to Val.

The two women walked from behind the nurses' station and into the hallway, revealing themselves. Nicollette engaged Val in some light conversation. The Uzi man saw the two and quickly approached them. In broken English and in a heavy German accent, he asked where they had been. Nicollette responded that her friend had a dodgy stomach and had to use the loo.

"Loo?" he asked. "Vat's loo?"

"Toilet," Val responded.

Val followed along by pointing to her stomach. The Uzi man then lowered his weapon from his shoulder and pointed it at the two women.

"You are vanted back in za room."

Nicollette and Val, as if on que, immediately changed their expression to one of fear, each remembering their training to "appear vulnerable, letting the aggressor gain a false sense of control, use the psychology to their advantage, then strike back with vengeance!"

The three of them walked back towards Peter Johnson's room. There were now eight armed plotters at the security desk at the end of the hall. Two were talking into some kind of device. *They must have help on the outside and maybe even more help inside the hospital. Two in the stairwell plus those eight plus our 'escort' makes at least eleven. And then there are two imposters in with Peter as well. This is a major operation!*

The group was now just a few steps from the entrance to Peter Johnson's room. Although the Uzi was lowered in ready position, their escort appeared to have taken "the bait." He had subconsciously allowed her to walk about a half a step behind him on his right side while Val continued to walk directly in front. Nicollette's full being was in overdrive as they walked through the entrance to the room. There wasn't a dry spot on her body and it felt like all her blood was replaced with adrenaline. *This is it, Nicky!* She told herself. *One step into the room, followed by another, then a third...*

Val suddenly stopped and turned back to face the Uzi man. She pointed to her stomach and on que, Nicollette bumped his right shoulder as hard as she could. Val threw the hot coffee in his face. By instinct, he pulled the trigger of the Uzi, shooting blindly several rounds harmlessly into the chair that Nicollette was sleeping in less than an hour ago. Nicollette continued her advantage, pulling out her pistol and cracking it across his right arm. He immediately released his grip on the Uzi. Then she followed up with a pistol strike across the right side of his head. *That's for Anneke!*

The Uzi man fell to the floor, unconscious, his left hand still covering his face. Nicollette grabbed the Uzi.

She looked back to see Val holding her pistol at the three attending Peter. Val forcefully asked for their hands to be raised, quickly checked them for weapons, and guided them away from Peter's bed. He was lying on the bed, fully dressed, but unconscious. A drip tube was attached to his arm that wasn't there earlier. *He's not going to be much help.*

"Keep an eye on them, Val, I'm going to check the hallway."

"But what about the good doctor?"

"We'll sort that later. Just keep an eye on them, and Val, don't hesitate to shoot."

Nicollette crawled towards the doorway. Surely the others heard the gunfire. *Must act fast! Must use our advantage!*

She carefully peered down the corridor. Two men ran towards Peter's room. *Now Nicky, now!* She pointed the Uzi at the men racing towards the door and gently squeezed the trigger, remembering to aim low. Tat...tat...tat...tat....A dozen rounds off in seconds. Both men fell to the floor, yelling painfully in some foreign language.

Nicollette ducked in the doorway as return fire was hitting high all around the door. There was a moment's pause in the gunfire. She lowered her head and gingerly glanced down the hallway towards the security desk. A man was rushing towards his wounded comrades, his weapon now firing right at the doorway. *His aim is high! One shot, Nicky!*

Nicollette rolled flat on her belly to the doorway, bullets still flying high at the door's edge. *One...two...three...go!*

She pulled herself along the floor just outside of the doorway, quickly aimed and pulled the trigger. Tat...tat...tat... The bullets found their mark. The rushing man received the full impact as he fell backwards, spurting blood as he fell dead on the floor.

The hallway was silent except for the continued groans of pain coming from the two injured plotters. Nicollette couldn't see anyone at the security desk and there was no return fire. *Where the hell are they?*

The two wounded men were about ten meters away and their dead companion behind them. There was a large puddle of blood between them. She yelled back at Val, "You ok?"

"No problem here, Nicky. You?"

"Good here. All under control." *Where is Anneke?*

Twenty minutes had passed since they left the nurses' station. The alarm certainly would have sounded by now if Anneke had made it and understood the directions.

"Nicky," Val called, "Uzi man is coming around."

"Is he secure?"

"I found some bandage tape, so he's taped up."

Nicollette took another look down the hall again. Still no movement. *Something must be up.*

The hallway was quiet, the painful groaning from the wounded men had subsided. Nicollette fired a couple of rounds in the area of the security desk. No responding fire. She rolled back into the room and saw Val pointing her gun at the two doctors and the nurse. The Uzi man was groggily sitting against the wall, hands behind his back. He had blood on his head and blood stains on his shirt.

Nicollette handed the Uzi to Val and pulled the groggy Uzi man to his feet.

"If anyone acts up, shoot 'em, Val!"

Nicollette pulled her pistol from her skirt and placed it against the back of the Uzi man, using her free hand to force him to the door. At the doorway, she told him, "Halt." The light switch on the wall gave her an idea. *Must try to signal outside. It's dark outside so someone should see the lights.* She moved the gun to the back of Uzi man's head and used her other hand to start flickering the lights.

"What the bloody hell are you doing?" Val called.

"Morse code. We must try to communicate our position, Val."

Nicollette recalled the lesson from her training. *Morse code, a series of dots and dashes, primitive, but effective in the right situation.* She flickered the lights again, hoping she remembered the sequences correctly, waited a minute, and did it once more.

There was no immediate response from the outside world to Nicollette's signal. *Maybe later. For now, I must focus on the task at hand; hostages.*

She pushed her gun against the Uzi man's head, urging him to advance past the doorway and into the hallway.

"Hey, you out there, hold your fire, we've got three hostages here."

Nicollette waited for a response. None. She nudged the Uzi man a little further into the hallway, being very careful to keep him between her and the security desk.

"Perhaps you didn't hear me. We've got hostages! Show yourselves and lay down your weapons!"

Nicollette knew a surrender was unlikely, but she had to show a position of strength and there was always a possibility of a slip up by the enemy.

Standing in the hallway with her gun on the head of a groggy, but still much bigger male, Nicollette felt as if time had slowed to a crawl. Seconds seemed like minutes. *I know there are others. Where the bloody hell are they! Could they have left? Is this situation all over? Where is the security force?*

Two minutes went by, then a third and a fourth. A slight noise broke the silence. Nicollette could barely make it out, but she was sure it came from one of the empty patient rooms.

She watched down the hall from behind the Uzi man, first the left side, then the right. Nothing, but yet, she knew the noise she heard was real. *Listen, Nicky. Focus.*

Her heart was racing and she felt weighted by her wet blouse, but her instincts were on point. A whisper came from a room on the left, I'm sure I heard it!

Her eyes focused on the seven or so doorways on the left side. *Come on, show yourself you pieces of shite! Damn you!*

Nicollette announced herself again, still no response. Her ears and eyes strained to pick up even the slightest hint of sound or movement. Then it happened. She saw it. The short barrel of an Uzi in a doorway. *I must react now!* Guessing what was about to happen, Nicollette pushed the Uzi man forward towards the two rooms and dove back into a room just as a burst of gunfire filled the hallway. A trail of bullets followed her into the room, then an eerie quiet ascended. She leaned against the wall just inside the door. Her chest heaving up and down, encouraged by deep breathing. She rolled onto her stomach again and very slowly crawled to the doorway. Looking down the hallway revealed the Uzi man, just two meters away, lying in a pool of blood. Motionless.

In the room, Val was still pointing her Uzi at the hostages.

"What the hell is going on, Nicky?"

Nicollette looked back at her friend.

"They were waiting for me. They shot Uzi man!"

Val walked slowly towards the doorway, never taking her eyes off of the hostages.

"Let us have a look, Nicky."

"Stay low and be careful."

The two traded places, Nicollette swapping her Uzi for the pistol. Val was on her stomach at the door's edge and Nicollette was watching over the hostages. The whole area, from the security desk to the room, was ghostly quiet. Nicollette walked towards Peter's bed, never taking her eyes off the hostages.

At his bedside, she looked at her sleeping friend. He looked peaceful and comfortable. *If only he knew what was happening.* She looked at the drip tower. A clear liquid slowly continued to drip through the tube and into his arm. *Maybe it's water, perhaps he is dehydrated.* She looked up at the plastic bag holding the fluid. There was no label or identifier. As she turned to the small stand next to the bed, her left foot hit something under the bed. Nicollette pointed her gun at the hostages and bent down, reaching under the bed. Her hand felt a rather heavy object as she pulled it out from under the bed. It was a black, hardshell suitcase. *Peter doesn't have one of these.*

Nicollette pushed the suitcase between her and the hostages. Her left hand felt around the edges for potential booby traps and found the metal clasps. She squeezed the clasps and the case opened. Her eyes scanned the contents of the case while she pointed the pistol at the hostages. *Crikey!*

Inside the case were several bags of clear liquid, a bag of green pills, and most stunningly of all, a recording device complete with tapes and cables.

Nicollette grabbed one of the bags of clear liquid. A label was still taped to the outside. The writing appeared to be in German, but the ingredient was clear. *Sodium Pentothal! Truth Serum!* She rose to her feet and stared at the three hostages. Her heart pumped wildly as a sense of anger ran through her veins!

"I don't know which one of you is a real doctor or nurse and I don't bloody care, but you have ten seconds before I blow each of your brains out if you don't reveal yourself!"

She paused for a breath.

"Ten!"

"Nicky, what the hell is going on! What's happening?" Val yelled from the doorway.

"Nine!"

"Nicky?!"

"Eight! They have been drugging Peter Johnson! Seven!"

"What?!"

"Six! Sodium Pentothal."

"Five!"

Nicollette raised her pistol and fired a shot into the wall.

"I mean business! Four!"

"It's me, don't shoot! Please don't shoot! I'm a doctor!"

It was the woman hostage speaking out. The two male hostages quickly tried to subdue the doctor. Nicollette fired another shot into the wall and Val fired a short burst as well.

"Let her go now! We won't miss next time!"

Nicollette reached in with her left hand and grabbed the doctor and pulled her away from the small scuffle. She was still wearing her ID badge.

"Dokter Ilse Hoebeek, so you are the doctor. What about the other two?"

With a heavy accent, Doctor Ilse Hoebeek responded, "Bedriger, how you would say it, imposters!"

Nicollette looked at the two male hostages with their hands over their heads. She looked at the first badge, Pieter van der Berg, Dokter, then the second badge, Gerda Bakker, Verpleegster, nurse.

"You are no Gerda—and certainly, you are no nurse!" she exclaimed as she pushed the badge back into the chest of the imposter and motioned for the two men to sit with their hands on their heads against the wall.

"Do not move!" she commanded them. Then to the doctor, "Get that damn thing out of his arm."

"Ja," the doctor responded as she turned a clip that stopped the liquid flowing into Peter's arm.

Doctor Hoebeck found a roll of tape and some cotton wool as she pulled the needle from Peter Johnson's arm and covered the wound.

"Pass me the tape," Nicollette instructed. "Anything happening, Val?"

"Still quiet, Nicky."

"Cover me."

Val took another quick look into the hallway, then turned back to the room.

"All clear, Nicky."

"If they try anything, shoot!"

Nicollette used her gun to motion for the two hostages to separate themselves from each other and directed the first hostage to stand and come forward. She turned the hostage around and placed his hands together behind his back. Using her teeth, she pulled a length of tape from the roll and wrapped his hands, including his fingers, remembering a disabling technique she learned in training. *Without the fingers, the hands are useless.*

Satisfied with her work and while still holding her gun in

one hand, she quickly searched the hostage for any type of weapon that was obtained or hidden. She knew Val was trained on proper searches, but being overly careful could be the difference between survival or not. "This one is clear."

Nicollette then motioned for the second man to come forward and started the same procedure. Dr. Ilse stood next to the bed, not moving, frozen, just watching Nicollette go through her process.

There was something odd about Dr. Isle, Nicollette thought. *She knew enough to stop the flow of liquid into Peter's arm, but anyone who could see could do that. Removing a needle and bandaging was easy as well. Easy first aid! But standing by his bedside and doing nothing for him, just watching me, that does seem strange.* Then it hit her like an electric shock running through her body. *Anneke! She could have easily alerted me to who the real doctor was by saying it was a woman! How simple is that! Must keep an eye on her!*

Nicollette quickly finished wrapping the second hostage's hands, while switching eye contact between the doctor and the hostage. There was just enough tape left to secure the man tightly.

She started her search of the second hostage from his shoulders to his waist. *All clear so far.* Now from his legs upward. *So far so good, now his waist.*

He softly chuckled when she reached around to search his front. She whispered to him, "Don't get too excited, I'm really not interested." *Clear again.*

Checking his backside, she could feel something unusual around his waistband. She pushed her gun against his head as her left hand reached into his shorts, retrieving four micro cassettes. With no pockets in her skirt, Nicollette quickly put the cassettes down the front of her knickers. *Just try and get them.*

She turned the hostage around and pushed him to his spot against the wall. Movement out of the corner of her eye caught

Dr. Ilse, slowly and very deliberately, opening the top drawer of the bedside table. *She waited till my back was turned and was being very careful not to bring attention to herself. What's going on here?*

"Stop!" Nicollette commanded Dr. Ilse. "Now!" she added while pointing her gun directly at the doctor.

The sudden outburst caught Val's attention.

"What's going on, Nicky?"

"Not sure, Val, not sure."

Val shifted her position in the doorway, slightly exposing herself but making it easier to see down the hallway and give cover to Nicollette at the same time.

"Now, Doctor, slowly bring your hands above your head!" Nicollette commanded. "But I'm a doctor," Ilse protested.

"I don't care if you are the queen! Do as I say or I'll blow your brains out!"

Nicollette's voice was strong and clear, she was focused, her pistol hand was steady, aiming a pistol at the doctor. Dr. Ilse stared back at Nicollette and their eyes met in visual combat. *Don't break, Nicky! Your life may depend on it!*

The battle of wills continued, neither side yielding. Ten seconds, twenty seconds, a half a minute passed. Nicollette understood that Dr. Ilse had played her card when she refused to comply with the command. *She's one of them! That little tussle was just a charade! Who is she? What the hell is going on here!!*

Nicollette's strength was in full throttle, she was unyielding as the battle of wits between her and the doctor continued. Forty seconds, then a minute passed.

"I'm going to count to five, Madame Doctor, and you are going to put your hands on your head! One! Two!"

"You are bluffing! You're just a little girl playing with guns. Besides, we have you surrounded. It's Peter Johnson we want. So put the gun down and behave," the doctor proclaimed.

"Three!"

"You won't shoot, little girl. Now playtime is over, put down your gun!" Dr. Ilse calmly cajoled.

A million thoughts crossed Nicollette's mind. *This is the moment! Now is the time! Stay strong, Nicky! Focus, Nicky!* "Four!"

The doctor just smiled smugly back at Nicollette as she slowly began to pull one of her hands from the drawer.

"You won't shoot, little girl, you should let the adults be in charge."

"Five!"

At that moment the doctor pulled a black object from the drawer. Dr. Ilse's expression immediately changed from smug to serious. Everything seemed to be in slow motion as a microsecond seemed like a minute. *Now, Nicky!*

Nicollette's brain yelled to her right hand to act when she saw the black object was a gun. The right hand received the signal and passed it onto the trigger finger. Pow! Pow! Pow! Three shots! The doctor's gun falling to the floor, splashes of blood flying in the air. One shot in the arm and one grazing her hand.

"Nicky!" Val's scream breaking Nicollette's trance. "Nicky!" she continued to yell as she ran into the room.

"I'm ok, Val, I'm ok."

"Move, Doctor, or whatever the hell you are!" Nicollette commanded.

"But I'm bleeding."

"You'll bleed a whole lot more if you don't move; now!"

Dr. Ilse moved away from the bedside cabinet and walked gingerly to a spot against the wall next to her co-conspirators. There was a box of cotton wool on the bedside cabinet. Nicollette threw the box to her.

"Now you can play doctor for real!"

Endgame

Nicollette stood next to Peter's bed, her eyes firmly focused on the three hostages sitting against the wall. The two male hostages had their eyes closed and the woman pretending to be Dr. Ilse Hoebeek was holding her injured right arm and hand. A piece of a ripped sheet, used as a bandage covering her arm, was stained a pinkish red color. The imposter's eyes never left Nicollette.

The room and hallway were quiet, too quiet, a calm one experiences just before the arrival of a storm, knowing it's coming but still not sure when or how severe. Val had her Uzi at the ready, still diligently eyeing the hallway from the door entryway. At that moment, Val looked back at Nicollette. Their eyes met with an accompanying mutual nod of heads. Nothing needed to be said, both of them fully aware of how dangerous the situation was and what their responsibilities were: staying alive!

It was nearly 3:30 in the morning, two and a half hours since she was awakened from her comfortable chair and the nightmare began. *They must have wanted Val and me out of the room so they could interrogate Peter! And after that, were they going to drug us? Then who knows what would have happened!*

Nicollette looked at her watch again. *Two and a half hours. One hundred eighty minutes. There are at least two men dead and two injured in the hallway, perhaps more. We have three hostages, one is badly injured. What happened to Anneke? There has been no contact with the outside and it's been quiet here for over an hour. Did anyone see my signal? Val and I are outgunned and outmanned and Peter is still asleep. Did they get any information from him? The tapes? What is going to happen? Only a couple of hours till daybreak. How long do we have to wait? Can we hold out? Nicollette answered her own question, At least in this room, we are in control and most importantly, still alive!*

"Ummmmm. Oh, Oh. Ummm."

Nicollette heard Peter's groans and turned to see his eyes opening. His mouth moved. "Nicky, what's happening?"

"It's a long story, we'll talk about it later. How do you feel?"

"My throat is dry and I feel like I've been run over by a large lorry! Last thing I remember was the medical staff coming in to check me over. They said I was dehydrated and put a tube in my arm."

Nicollette reached behind Peter with her left arm while keeping her gun pointed at the three hostages sitting against the wall. She gently helped him to sit up. The color started to return to his face.

"Val, he's awake."

"Welcome back, Mr. Johnson, feeling better?"

"Better now, Miss Davies, thank you."

"Splendid," Val replied as she went back to her position at the doorway.

Peter grabbed Nicollette's left arm tightly. In a quiet but firm whisper, he asked, "Nicky, what the hell is going on here? Why are you pointing a weapon at the medical staff and what's Val doing with an Uzi?"

Despite his groggy tone, Nicollette could hear the concern in his voice. She knew she needed to give him some sort of answer.

"These 'medical staff' you see are actually part of a plot to get information from you and take you hostage. These imposters are part of a much bigger group and they control this entire floor. The hospital has emptied this floor and the two below us."

Nicollette paused for a moment to let her answer sink in, then continued, "Peter, there are two dead men in the hall and at least three wounded. We are two against who knows how many but we, the hostages, have our own prisoners and we could really use your help. Do you feel comfortable enough to watch our hostages?"

Peter looked at the three prisoners then back at Nicollette. "Still a bit groggy, just give me a tick. Some water would help."

Nicollette waited a minute then handed the second gun to Peter Johnson. She slowly rounded the bed and walked to the bathroom to get him a drink.

"He's with us," she said to Val while opening the bathroom door.

There was a pungent odor in the bathroom as Nicollette entered. She ignored it. *It's a hospital. There are going to be smells.* She found a stack of plastic cups and quickly filled one for Peter. The pungent odor was stronger and it was getting hard for her to breathe.

She accidentally knocked over a stack of plastic cups and some of the cups rolled off to one side towards the large bathing area. Nicollette knelt down to reach for the cups and nearly choked as she saw the fingertips of a human hand protruding from under the privacy curtain. Pulling the curtain back, she saw two bodies stacked on the floor of the shower. The victims were in hospital uniforms and had been shot dead. There was a large pool of blood around them and the stench was nauseating. One of the victim's eyes stared back at Nicollette, displaying the terror of impending death.

Nicollette dropped the cup of water and vomited in the toilet.

"What's going on there, Nicky? You alright? What's that smell? Nicky?" Val yelled from the doorway.

Grabbing a wet paper towel, Nicollette wiped and covered her mouth, quickly pulling the curtain closed. Closing the bathroom door, she placed a couple of towels around the bottom of the door to restrict the spread of the odor.

"There are two more dead in there, Val."

"What the hell, Nicky! Can we do this? Are we going to end up like them?"

Nicollette let Val's question rest before replying. Her heart was now pounding out of her chest and her palms were sweating. Her nose still carried the stench and her stomach, although empty, continued to feel sick. For the first time during this situation, she started to feel vulnerable and concerned. It was becoming more difficult to hide her growing anxiousness, but she knew that there was no alternative. Giving up was not an option and dying, well, that just wasn't going to happen. *Must remain strong! For Val, Peter, and myself! Mustn't give in. Stay sharp, Nicky, and stay alive!*

Whether it was false bravado or just trying to convince herself or both, Nicollette placed a hand on Val's shoulder and whispered back, "We're going to make it, Val. We'll be fine. And now, there are three of us! They don't have a chance!"

"What's your plan, Nicky?" Peter asked, sipping his water.

Nicollette ignored the question, unable to respond. Instead she looked at the hostages against the wall. Dr. Ilse was having a hard time keeping her eyes open and the other two hadn't moved. Val was still diligently watching the hallway. Looking out of the window, Nicollette could see a few flashing red lights and some light activity, which struck her as strange. *Shouldn't there be more going on? There doesn't seem to be any type of urgency! Are they coming or have they given up on us?* She checked her watch, it was just 4:35. The sun would be up in about forty minutes.

Peter repeated his question. "Any ideas, Nicky?"

"I really don't have an endgame plan, Peter. I was hoping Anneke, the injured nurse I found, would find help, but that hasn't worked. I thought these hostages could be used as negotiating pieces, but there has been no contact. At least we have a better chance of staying alive while we have them. But since we haven't received any communication from anywhere and have discovered those two in the bathroom, I'm not so sure. My guess is we just have to be patient and wait, no matter how hard or dangerous that might be. At least they know we mean business. I used the Uzi earlier and I know Val is capable as well."

"Gas! Gas!" Val yelled frantically.

Nicollette rushed to the edge of the door and crawled next to Val.

A steady stream of a dense, grayish white gas was permeating the hallway and moving quickly in their direction. There was screaming coming from all directions and in multiple languages. Nicollette yelled back into the room, "Peter, if anyone gives you trouble, shoot them!"

The situation in the hallway quickly descended into chaos, screams echoing heard in the blinding fog and red tracer bullets started flying from everywhere. The noise was deafening.

"They must be using the gas to blind us! The shooting is more intense and there's a lot more of it! This is too dangerous for us, Val! Our only chance may be to set up defensively back in the room."

The women both understood the reality. They were in a dangerous profession. An unspoken realization that this could be the end for the three of them. Nicollette remembered the "death" document she signed before her first mission. To her, death was opaque, a faraway fear, buried somewhere deep in her brain. *It didn't happen at Little Tunb Island and I'll be damned if it's going to happen now!*

Nicollette grabbed Val's arm.

"Val, we're not going down without a fight, but if something happens…"

"I know, I know."

The two of them retreated into the room and stood behind

the bed. Peter hoisted himself off the bed, whilst holding his gun at the fully alert prisoners. He took a quick glance at the two young women next to him and gave them a slight, albeit weak smile.

Nothing needed to be said, each knew what the other was thinking, they were together in mind and deed, focused on the challenge ahead.

Val aimed the Uzi at the doorway and Nicollette yelled at the prisoners to remain quiet, waving her pistol to back up her instructions. No one in the room moved. It was a deadly still-ness, almost surreal. Outside the room, the gunfire continued unabated. The once ornate wood doorway was reduced to splinters. The shouting seemed to get louder. The three of them knew their adversaries were getting closer. Nicollette could feel her hands sweating, her heart racing and legs becoming numb. The grayish white cloud was beginning to permeate the room.

Nicollette grabbed pillow cases off the bed and ripped off several strips to be used as masks for the gas.

"Better alive than dead," she whispered to Val and Peter.

The vapor became more intense but oddly, the shooting seemed to be tapering off. The loud screaming was drifting away from the door entrance and seemed to be heading fur-ther down the hall. The three held their weapons at the ready.

The vapor was now fully in the room. The prisoners, just a few feet away, were mere shadows, and the doorway was almost invisible. The shooting outside the room had all but stopped. The hallway was quiet.

A terrible feeling swept through Nicollette. *Have they won? Have the bad guys removed any resistance? Are they now com-ing for us?* Her sweaty hand tightened around the gun.

Through the soupy vapor, Nicollette saw a hint of a shadow at the door. She nudged Val and Peter and pointed with her gun to the entryway.

"Someone is coming."

All three of them focused on the slow moving shadow. Nicollette held her finger on the trigger, her arms holding the weapon steady. A second shadow now appeared at the doorway following the first one slowly into the room.

The shadows came closer, ten feet away, nine, eight.

"Stop!" Nicollette yelled with everything she had. "We've got hostages and we'll shoot!"

There was no response.

Nicollette repeated herself. "We've got hostages and we'll shoot!"

This time there was no delay. The first shadow replied in a British accent. "No, Miss, you do not have hostages, you have prisoners!"

Not to be fooled or deceived, Nicollette asked the shadows to raise their hands, slowly step forward, and reveal themselves.

"Yes, Miss."

Nicollette, Val and Peter stood behind the bed with their guns pointing at the human shadows stepping forward. *This is it, Nicky! Be a brave girl!* The shadows were now just a few feet away. Nicollette could almost hear their breathing.

"Is it secure?" a voice yelled into the room.

Nicollette, Val, and Peter immediately recognized the voice. It was Major Blasingame!

"Yes ma'am," the first shadow responded.

"Well, open up a damn window!" the Major ordered, "I can't see a bloody thing!"

It was over. The three of them had prevailed, and more importantly, stayed alive. The dense fog quickly dissipated through the open window. Soon the room was filled with soldiers and the Major took control of the situation. The three hostages were handcuffed, searched, and led from the room. Soldiers with stretchers carried the dead bodies out of the bathroom.

The Major looked at Nicollette, Val, and Peter, all still stand-ing, frozen behind the bed.

"Sit on the bed and breathe. This is not a request, it's an or-der!" she commanded with a grin on her face.

Nicollette sat softly on the bed, the tension in her body slowly going away. Val stared out of the window, watching the day break over Brussels.

Nicollette placed her arm around Val and looked out the window with her. "It's beautiful, isn't it," she whispered to her friend.

I Lived It!

The siege had ended. The hospital room was cleared, the prisoners taken away, the bodies removed from the bathroom and the blinding gray vapor long since evaporated out of the window. Now, it was just the four of them in the empty room. The Major had asked for the forensic team to give the group some time.

Major Blasingame walked about the room, searching for clues and gathering her thoughts together, trying to formulate a theory about what had taken place. She rubbed her hands along the bullet holes in the wall and stared at the blood along the floor.

In the bathroom, the Major stood over the shower stall. A bloody handprint on the privacy curtain revealed a last grip on life for one of the victims. The doorway was riddled with holes, the Major losing count after thirty. The ornate wooden trim was just splinters. She took a quick venture down the hallway, stopping to see three circles marked on the floor just a few meters from the room. Two circles had a W written inside and one circle had a K. *Two wounded, one killed,* the Major thought.

She continued towards the security desk, shell casings everywhere. There were two more circles near the desk, one more wounded and another dead.

Major Blasingame shook her head. She had seen enough and walked back to the room.

Nicollette stood up from the bed and stretched, trying to fend off the creeping fatigue as the Major re-entered the room. She had been so numb earlier, she hadn't noticed that Major Blasingame was dressed in full military fatigues, complete with a holstered pistol at her side. It was the first time she had seen the Major in a soldier's uniform. There was too much to talk about but not much to say.

"We will be leaving here as soon as we're cleared," the Major said, breaking the quiet.

"I can't wait to leave, I want to go home," Val replied, climbing off the bed.

"I think we all feel the same way, Val," Peter whispered, leaning against the bed.

A soldier walked into the room and announced that transport was ready to leave when they were. He was followed in the room by a white coated man.

"Before we can leave, Mr. Johnson, I want you checked over. Don't worry, he's one of us," the Major added.

"Have a seat on the bed, mate," the doctor directed Peter.

"I think we'll excuse ourselves," the Major announced as she motioned for Nicollette and Val to join her in the hallway.

There was a flurry of activity in the hallway, all sorts of people coming in and out of the rooms. Bursts of light from photo flashes and the soft sound of machinery permeated the hallway. The three circles on the hallway floor caught Nicollette's eye. Two w's and one k. A sudden chill ran up her spine. *That was me!*

The doctor emerged from the room, pushing Peter Johnson in a wheelchair.

"His wounds seem to be healing nicely but it's still very early since surgery. I'm reluctant to allow him to travel, but if he has to, he must be very careful. I recommend resting. He may also have some slight residual from the sodium pentothal, but he is not impaired. Have him checked out again when he gets to England."

"Thank you, Captain O'Brian," Major Blasingame said as the two saluted.

Captain O'Brian turned to Peter. "You take care, 'Old Man,' and remember: rest."

An orderly took over Peter's wheelchair.

"Blast this chair!"

"Glad you're feeling better, Mr. Johnson," Nicollette said.

"Cheeky, Nicky."

As the group started down the hallway, Nicollette stopped at the three circles on the floor and suddenly felt a strong need to see the room one last time.

"Ma'am, could I have a quick minute to go back into the room."

"Ok, but be quick about it."

Nicollette walked back into the room and straight to the chair she was sleeping in peacefully just eight or so hours ago. She ran her hand over the soft padding, stopping at the bullet holes. She noticed some blood stains and shell casings on the floor. Pow, pow! Her mind revisited the shots she fired at the woman posing as a doctor. *Little girl, she called me. Who does she think she is? What a cow! She's lucky I've got good aim!*

At the nightstand, Nicollette slowly opened the large top drawer. *This is where the imposter's gun was hidden. I wonder if there is anything else?* Her suspicions were spot on. Besides the usual medical supplies, there was a second weapon and a rather large manilla envelope. Nicollette checked the safety and removed the full cartridge from the weapon. *They brought a spare gun or was it for one of the other imposters? We were really outgunned for certain.*

She carefully emptied the envelope onto the bed. There were several more mini-cassette tapes and a larger box containing a Betamax tape as well as some documents paper-clipped together. The documents were written in German and French. She placed them aside while instinctively reaching down the front of her skirt to feel for the tapes she had hidden earlier. *Still there.*

She then pulled out a dozen or so photographs from the envelope and sat on the edge of the bed as she went through the stack. The first photos were of the communications huts and their surroundings in Thailand. The next several photos were even more concerning. There were photos of most of the analysts, the supporting soldiers, and the Thai guides. Each photo was marked with the identity and nationality of the person written on it. When she saw the photos of Peter Johnson and herself, a distinct chill ran up her spine. *When and where did they get that? And more importantly, what were they going to do with them?*

She glanced through the remaining pictures and quickly put everything back in the manilla envelope. The case with the equipment was still under the bed. Nicollette pulled it out and placed it on the bed. She opened it, carefully placing the tapes, the loaded gun cartridge, and the manilla envelope inside.

On her way out, Nicollette walked into the bathroom. She could smell some residual stench as she looked in the mirror. Her face and hair needed a good washing. Not much on vanity, she let that go, but it was her eyes that stood out. Nicollette could see in the reflection that her eyes could tell a story. They were clear and bright, yet troubled and concerned, like they had lived a lifetime in the last eight hours.

She turned to the shower bath privacy curtain and noticed the bloody hand markings in the lower corner. Staring at the shower floor, her mind envisioned the open eyes of one of the victims looking back at her. She sat down on top of the toilet, still staring at the bloody print and shower floor. Her mind would not let that picture go, those eyes looking out as the victim entered the journey of death. Nicollette was numb, powerless to move, her entire being caught up in that memory; those eyes. She knew that image would stay with her for a long time.

"Nicky, Nicky!" Val's voice broke the silence.

It felt like an alarm clock bringing her out of deep sleep as Nicollette responded sheepishly, "In here, Val."

"We've been waiting for you. Major Blasingame was worried. You alright?"

"Yes, I'm ok. Let's go."

Nicollette grabbed the gun and the case from the floor as the two of them left the bathroom.

"What the hell is that?" Val exclaimed, pointing at the case and gun.

"I found some interesting things in the night stand, Val, including this gun and an envelope I think the Major would like to see." She whispered, "We were very lucky, Val, very very lucky indeed."

In the hallway, Nicollette handed the Major the case and the gun.

"This was in the room under the bed and I thought you should have it. There's lots of interesting things inside the envelope and I also have these, Ma'am."

Nicollette reached into her skirt and handed Major Blasingame the additional tapes. "These are the tapes that were in the case with the recording device. The blue one was in the recording device when I first found it."

The Major took the case and the gun from Nicollette. She placed the gun into her belt. Nicollette's mind allowed her a very brief bit of levity. Major Blasingame looked like an American cowboy with a gun on either side of her waist.

Two large black sedans were waiting for them as they exited from a rear door of the hospital. The sun was very bright and Nicollette had to shield her eyes. Even so, she could still make out a large number of military personnel and security vehicles around, some with their lights still flashing. The orderly assisted Peter Johnson from his wheelchair into one of the vehicles.

"You can keep the bloody chair," he said to the soldier. "I won't be needing it. Thank you very much."

The drivers wasted no time in leaving, but as the car drove

to the front of the hospital, it became apparent to Nicollette just how extensive the rescue operation was. There were far more vehicles and personnel around than what she could see from the hospital room. There were even a handful of trucks labelled "Bomb Defusing Unit." Crikey.

It was a quiet ride to the airport. The city was alive with activity, people coming in and out of shops and buildings, sitting in outdoor cafes, and waiting on corners to cross the streets. *Normal, everything seems normal. They are oblivious to what happened just blocks away. People are just going about their business. Life goes on. Normal for some, dangerous for me. I must live in a different reality.*

Nicollette sighed, her thoughts turned towards home.

The small village of Brockwirth would be filled with activity this time of year. People coming up from London and down from Birmingham, seeking a quiet respite. The shops and cafes would be busy and there would be different dialects in the pubs.

Nicollette thought about her parents with unease as she wondered just how they would react if they knew what her job with the government really was. *Would they be surprised to learn about the extensive training she went through, the coding and signaling, courses of intensive self-defense, and special driving skills? What would their response be to the weapons training she received and the dangers she faced, like the gun battle in Brussels? How shocked would they be if they found out that their daughter shot her weapon at another human with the intent to kill!*

Maybe out of a sense of guilt or maybe the need for some sort of calm, Nicollette suddenly felt a deep desire to see her parents, to hear their voices, and revisit what "normal" felt like.

The two vehicles drove to a small airport and directly up to a waiting plane. It was a small aircraft, not like the large luxury one they had flown to Brussels from Bangkok.

"They brought us a Lear jet," Peter exclaimed sarcastically. "They must want us home in a hurry."

The door to the plane was about to close when Betty Brighall rushed aboard and sat down next to the Major. Val quietly asked who she was. Nicollette explained that Betty was a Liaison Officer for the British who were working in Brussels. She told Val how kind she was, taking her to lunch and even buying her new clothes. As she was talking to Val about the new clothes, Nicollette realized that all she had in her possession were those same clothes, the ones she'd been wearing for the last three days. And most importantly, the tapes she took from the hospital were still in her pants.

It was a cloudy, misty day when the plane landed at the Brize-Norton RAF base. Nicollette and Val assisted Peter off the plane and into a waiting car. They arrived a few minutes later in front of a three-story white building.

Major Blasingame walked to the security desk and returned with three keys.

"You lot have had quite a morning and I think you should try and rest a while. Here are your room keys. If you're hungry, the dining area is over there. Otherwise, I want you down here at 1600 hours."

Betty Brighall put her arm around Nicollette. "You did good, Nicky, and I am proud of you. We'll talk later."

Betty and Major Blasingame left Nicollette, Val, and Peter alone in the lobby. The three of them stood there, not quite knowing what to do. Nicollette and Peter were back in England after being away for a long three weeks. For Val, it had only been a couple of days, but for each of them, the last twenty-four hours seemed like a lifetime.

Nicollette opened the door to her room and gasped. This was no dorm room, more like the fancy hotel in London, even down to the luxury toiletries and soft robe. She put the hot water tap on and readied for a bath. The soothing water accelerated her fatigue. Her body had used a great deal of energy and now was begging for a recharge.

Laying on the bed, Nicollette's body was winning the battle, but her mind was still active, reliving Brussels, from the interview to the hospital, to her lunch with Betty, to the action at Peter's room. She could still smell the stench from the bodies in Peter's hospital room bathroom. The visions of the bloody handprint and the victim's opened eyes staring back at her seemed to be permanently etched in her brain. Nicollette tried to think of more pleasant thoughts: Brockwirth and home.

She closed her eyes.

The phone at the side of the bed rang, relentlessly. Nicollette fumbled with the receiver.

"Hello," she answered, half asleep.

It was a reminder call that it was 1515 hours and that she needed to be in the lobby at 1600 hours. Almost simultaneously, there was a knock on the door. Nicollette wrapped herself in the extra-large bath towel. She looked through the small peep hole in the door while asking who it was.

"Corporal Tanjun with a package for Miss Nicollette Beverley. I will leave the package by the door."

Nicollette watched her leave down the hallway. She quickly retrieved the package and placed it on the bed. She unwrapped the brown paper to reveal a white blouse and dark blue mid-length skirt. There was a pair of stockings and a blue belt as well. *This is Air Force women's officer clothing,* she thought. *I'll look like I'm in the RAF! Well, at least it's clean and fresh.*

Val and Nicollette walked and Peter hobbled into the lobby where Majors' Blasingame and Hartwell and Betty Brighall were waiting for them.

"I hope you had a good rest," the Major greeted the three of them.

The Major directed them to a room down a corridor. Before she opened the door, Major Blasingame looked at Val.

"Miss Davies, we are going to discuss the mission. You will be exposed to information you are unaware of. You are a professional and I don't need to remind you of your responsibilities. Understood?"

Major Hartwell, Mr. Henri Gistane, and the NATO Officer in charge of the Thai operation were sitting at an oval table inside. Nicollette nearly jumped out of her shoes when Mr. Charles Thompson walked into the room. Major Blasingame offered seats on either side of her to Nicollette and Peter. Val was motioned to a seat next to Betty Brighall.

Nicollette's hands were wet. *Is this a repeat of the interview in Brussels? Do I have to do that again? Haven't they got enough out of me? And what are Major Hartwell and Charles Thompson doing here?*

Major Hartwell opened the discussion with a brief agenda. They were going to review the operation in Thailand first, then spend time talking about Brussels.

She asked the NATO Officer to begin.

The NATO Officer shared his notes and mission forms with the group. He gave a brief, albeit detailed, description of the mission. He talked about the location, support, and personnel, all of which had been carefully chosen for the operation. He detailed the day-to-day activities of the group. The NATO officer then talked in depth about the last day and the escape into the jungle. How he used the last few minutes of operation to send out the secret distress code and identify which emergency plan the group was going to follow. He stressed the speed at which the huts had to be abandoned and the need not to leave anything of significance behind.

"We left with everything important, literally carrying all our work on our backs."

Nicollette listened to the NATO Officer's account, knowing full well what he was going to talk about next: the escape from the jungle. She could feel a numbness creep through her body, only interrupted by the drumming of her heart against her chest. *Here it comes, Val,* she thought, taking a quick peek at her friend across the table. *What happened in Thailand.*

The NATO officer described the group's escape journey on the small trail through the jungle, the insistent pounding rain, the noise from the thunder and lightning, the mud, and the heated pursuit of the bandits. The terrible conditions were only made worse by the weighted packs that were being carried and the insatiable appetite of the mossies. He described the river crossing and arriving at the dirt road. Hiding from the approaching lorries and the uncertainty whether the group of armed men searching the road were friend or foe.

The room was silent as the NATO Officer continued his briefing.

"We felt fortunate to be rescued on the dirt road and on our way to Chiang Rai until we were ambushed a few minutes later. There was a heavy firefight and we took on several casualties. Two of our four lorries were destroyed. The armed men escorting us laid down rounds of covering fire as we reloaded the remaining lorries and started down the dirt road. Miss Beverley drove the lead vehicle and I drove the trailing lorry. Despite my instructions not to, Miss Beverley's truck stopped to pick up four severely wounded men. I want to add at this point that Miss Beverley's actions saved the lives of those men and her driving skills were superb under extreme conditions. She had strategically placed her vehicle in the optimum position to offer maximum protection for both lorries. At this point, I drove my lorry to the lead and reached a rescue party further down the road. Unfortunately, one of the Senior Analysts, Mr. Peter Johnson, was wounded en route. He is here with us today. We arrived in Chiang Rai at 0650 hours."

Nicollette had prepared herself to hear the NATO officer's account of her disobedience during the briefing, but not the recognition of heroism. *Everyone on that mission was a hero!*

Anyone would have done what I did! And what about the dead and wounded? Surely they are heroes!

Major Hartwell asked if there were any questions. A few were offered regarding preparedness of the outpost and communication issues, but none about the escape. *Odd,* Nicollette thought, *odd.*

The NATO officer concluded his briefing with information about the stay in Chiang Rai and the flights to Bangkok and Brussels. Again, only a couple of queries about logistics and communications.

Just like that, it was over. The briefing on Thailand was completed and put away. *Nearly two weeks in some back of nowhere place and twelve hours of terror in the jungle, now just entries in some folder, in some file, in some building,* Nicollette thought. Admittedly, she knew she didn't pay as much attention as maybe she should have during the long briefing. Her mind had been racing through a fog of memories, her thinking may have been distorted. *Maybe there was and information brief that I missed, but after all, I lived it!*

Revelation

Henri Gistane started to brief about the activity in Brussels. Nicollette had already experienced a storm of emotions reliving the details about Thailand. Now it was going to be Brussels and Henri Gistane. *That man put me through hell! Now I have to sit here and listen to him! Why is he even here? What's going on?*

Major Blasingame put her hand on Nicollette's shoulder. "Deep breaths, Miss Beverley, deep breaths. I'm sure everything is going to be alright."

The Major's calming voice offered a brief respite.

"My name is Henri Gistane and I am the Chief Security Officer for the Special Operations Unit in Brussels. Our intelligence division in Bangkok first made us aware of a potential breach in security at our remote Thai operation about three weeks ago. We made the officer in charge aware of the situation and asked him to exercise caution in his daily functions. Codes and procedures were changed, but the breaches continued. The gathering of intelligence by the remote group was becoming increasingly harder to obtain. On a few occasions, our spotters in the field would only find a small bit of information, but not enough to substantiate any action. It seemed our adversary was one step ahead of us. At this point, we knew our position in the jungle was becoming more tenuous. There was a sense of urgency to stop the breach and secure the lines of communications. The success of our mission and, more importantly, the safety of our team, became our top concern. A week ago, we thought we had a break. One of our team discovered evidence of subversion in, of all things, a cigarette. There were only a few smokers on our team and one of the smokers innocently asked another for a cigarette. A simple act among co-workers."

Henri Gistane stopped and took a sip of water from his glass. Nicollette's attention was squarely on the man who mentally tortured her just a few days ago. Now, that same man was going to provide answers to some of the many questions she still had.

"A simple cigarette was the break we needed. The agent who received the cigarette noticed the label on the pack did not match the cigarette brand they were smoking. The coloring of the label indicated 'menthol' but the cigarette was not. The agent didn't think much of it at the time. He thought there probably was a simple explanation. Also of interest was when another agent spotted two unidentified Thai men in a tent they were not allowed to be in. When confronted, the two just responded 'supplies.' Our supplies were normally delivered by Thai personnel, so not too out of the ordinary. However, as required, this event was still reported to the officer in charge. Upon investigation of the 'supplies,' the officer found several packs of cigarettes with the seals broken. A more thorough investigation of the tent and surrounding area turned up more interesting items, a red bottle cap and an empty, crumpled cigarette package. The officer received permission from Bangkok to alert the second in command, the senior agent at the post, of this discovery. We were unable to continue our search for the source of the breach because the next evening, Friday last week, is when the post was abandoned and the group headed back to Chiang Rai."

Nicollette was on high alert, both mentally and physically. The information she was hearing sounded like the basis for the series of questions she was bombarded with in Brussels. The cigarettes and the bottle cap seemed to be central to the investigation. *But why me? Everyone used the mossie pills from the red capped bottle and I do not smoke!*

Another drink of water for Mr. Gistane. Nicollette was using every last ounce of energy she had to focus on every word Mr. Gistane was speaking, hopefully revealing the answers to her many questions.

"With the Major's permission, I'm going to advance my briefing directly to Brussels. The reasons will become clearer as we proceed. Ma'am?"

"Proceed, Mr. Gistane."

"Thank you. By the time the group landed in Brussels, we had narrowed our suspects for the breach down to three. Under the guise of an 'exit interview,' we interrogated our three suspects. Just when we thought we were about to get a confession from one of the suspects, a new witness came forward. We used the new information to obtain a thorough, detailed admission of guilt from an agent who wasn't even one of our original three suspects."

Mr. Gistane paused and gathered his notes. *What three? A new witness? Who? What the devil is happening here?*

"Now I would like to continue with information that will lead us into the situation at the hospital. The tent where the two Thai men were found was our women's quarters. There were only two women in our group, Maria Alderete and Nicollette Beverley. Neither were smokers that we knew of, but both women were recent additions to our group. The timing of their arrivals coincided with an uptick of compromised information. We applied a great deal of pressure on our original three suspects. At the last minute, Mr. Peter Johnson, the second in command and senior member of the post, brought forth information that directly pointed to the traitor. Mr. Johnson was wounded on the road to Chiang Rai. He said he would have come to us earlier, but he was incapacitated in Chiang Rai for a short time. In Brussels, despite his wounds, he refused medical attention until he was able to speak to one of the operational security personnel. Mr. Johnson had confronted the two Thai men in the women's quarters and later witnessed some peculiar behaviour by another agent. Mr. Johnson had seen the perpetrator drop the cigarette package and bottle cap less than five meters from the women's quarters. Only later were we able to tie the two events together."

Nicollette nearly jumped out of her seat. Her angst was quickly turning to anger. *They thought it was me, I was one of the suspects! They were going to blame me! I was being set up! Damn them! Damn all of them!*

A firm hand on her leg was all that kept Nicollette from standing from her chair and voicing her thoughts to the group. Major Blasingame knew an outburst here would put a big damper on Nicollette's career and bring into question the ability of a woman to handle the severe pressures of the job. Nicollette was too valuable to group 226/157. In addition to losing a great analyst, all the time, training and money spent on the MOD's Women's Initiative would be called into question.

Major Blasingame pushed her hand down on Nicollette's leg even harder to gain her attention. In a soft yet firm tone, she whispered, " I know it is hard but you must compose yourself. There is too much to lose for you and group 226/157. Nicollette, you are a great example to the women in training now and the future. Think of them. Think of the barriers you have broken and will continue to break. You are a valuable asset to the team. Look around you and you see people who are here because, as a team, we have your back."

Slowly, Nicollette rolled her left hand on top of the Major's and took a deep breath.

"You have my back?" she whispered to the Major.

"Damn right."

Henri Gistane then revealed that the German analyst was the "mole" and he had carefully devised a scheme to implicate the two women of the surveillance team.

"The German analyst thought the women would be easy

targets and buy him time until he could get away in Brussels, and it almost worked. He has been arrested and is in our custody."

The bastard! I wish they shot him on the road to Chiang Rai!

"After a brief investigation, we found the German analyst was leaking information to the Tang Organization in exchange for a nice full bank account in Switzerland. Tuesday evening, we received communications that a local drug gang, Haviken, working with the Tangs, wanted to make a hostage exchange for the German. The information about the hostage they were holding was rather vague and we had very limited time to gain any clarity. We are currently investigating how the arrest of the German analyst was disclosed. Nonetheless, we proceeded. The instructions directed us to a hotel room by the airport. Inside the room, we found the Spanish analyst, Maria Fuentes, one of the two women on the Thailand surveillance team, dead in the bathtub from an apparent drowning. She had been stripped naked and the words, 'We know everything' and 'we mean business' were written across her chest. We immediately called off the exchange."

Nicollette's stomach started to turn violently when she heard Mr. Gistane talk about the Spanish analyst. They had been bunkmates just a few days ago and shared a common bond of being young women in a dangerous profession, surrounded by dangerous people, in a dangerous land. *Now, Maria is dead because she was doing her job! Her humanity has been reduced to just a name and number. Death! Just another pawn in this nasty business!*

"Late Monday evening, we received communication from the Haviken group, setting new terms for an exchange: we give them the German prisoner and they give us a portfolio of sensitive information. We were now in full response mode. Our forensics team was feverishly searching every potential clue and the tactical team was activated. Our agents in Southeast Asia were placed on alert. All lines of communications were being closely monitored and security forces were dispersed across the city. We were ready."

Henri Gistane took his seat and a well-dressed man in a three piece blue striped suit stood to speak.

"I'm Hans Ten Haken and I am the Director of Security for Special Operations in Brussels. As Mr. Gistane explained, we activated all security procedures and we were on full alert. We decided not to respond to the set of demands left for us, rather we wanted to be patient and be fully prepared. By 6:00 p.m. Tuesday, we received another set of demands. The exchange became more expensive, the German prisoner and a large bit of cash, ten million US dollars, in exchange for the portfolio and one of our Senior Operatives. No identity was given for our 'senior operative.' We were given a deadline of 10:00 p.m. To search and contact all of our agents was an impossible task, so we focused our search on Brussels and nearby regions. The 10:00 p.m. deadline passed. At 10:30 p.m, we received another communication stating there were now two agents being held and they would both be dead if we did not respond by 2:00 a.m. Wednesday. This time the agent was named, Mr. Peter Johnson. Mr. Johnson was recovering at a military hospital. We contacted security at the hospital and were advised that there was unusual activity on the sixth floor. Without waiting for details, we immediately put our full resources in place at the hospital and assessed the situation."

Nicollette was in shock. She forced herself to stand and numbly walked towards the wall, wanting a private moment to digest the information. *The bastards already had Peter as a hostage! Val and I were there visiting. The 'outside' knew we were there!*

The hospital situation was becoming clearer to her. Major Blasingame was in Brussels not for a meeting like she said, but to be involved with the crisis. Two of her analysts were, at the time of her arrival, potential targets of a kidnapping. Val said she "tagged" along, but maybe the reality was she was asked to join the Major and be with Nicollette and Peter. *Reinforcements. Another set of eyes and ears in the room; maybe.*

Mr. Ten Haken continued his briefing.

"We soon discovered this was a well-planned and coordinated effort. Our intelligence put the number of gunmen at fifteen and total plotters at twenty-five. At approximately 11:10 p.m., our team encountered two gunmen in a third story stairwell. They were installing some type of device. A quick firefight ensued and they were eliminated. Silencers were used so as not to alarm anyone. The device turned out to be an eavesdropping instrument, so now we had 'their ear' at our disposal. Our team left the dead gunmen propped up in the stairway to set up a false impression. We continued to have our forces in place as the situation solidified. At approximately 1:20 a.m. Wednesday morning, Miss Valerie Davis, a British Agent who was visiting Mr. Johnson, came through the stairway door on the third floor. She was able to give us an update of the situation on the sixth floor. Miss Davies explained that heavily armed gunmen were at the security desk and that she and Miss Beverley were asked to leave Mr. Peter Johnson's room by a nurse. There were two doctors in the room as well, she added. Despite our efforts to stop her, she went back up the staircase. At approximately 1:40 a.m., a severely wounded woman fell through the stairway door. She was a nurse on the sixth floor who had been beaten and left for dead by the gunmen. She was able to give us vital intelligence, through a translator, about the situation on the sixth floor. She said she was found by a British woman named Nicky and that a second British woman joined them later. The nurse told us she gave information to Nicky about a doctor and a nurse in Mr. Johnson's room who were imposters. She seemed to think that Nicky had a plan and had asked her, using hand motions, to pull the fire alarm and go down the stairway. As a precaution, we had disabled the alarm for security reasons, but Miss Beverley and Miss Davies did not know that. She also said that Miss Davies gave Miss Beverley a gun."

Nicollette was envisioning the moment in her mind. *Annike had pulled the alarm, but it didn't work. That explains that. But she did get to the security operators, at least that's something.*

Mr. Ten Haken took a sip of water, cleared his throat, and continued.

"At this moment, this is what we knew. There were heavily armed gunmen on the sixth floor. Mr. Peter Johnson was alone in his room with at least two kidnappers posing as doctor and nurse. We had two British Agents, armed, and seemingly able to act independently on the sixth floor. At 2:00 a.m., we received a final set of demands and a warning from Haviken. The communication also announced that explosives had been placed in and around the hospital and if demands were not met by 6:00 a.m. Wednesday morning, they would be detonated. The communication stated that this was their final warning. Failure to act would have dire consequences. Needless to say, especially after finding evidence of a bomb device among the two perpetrators in the stairwell, we were scrambling to get results. To complicate matters, we heard gunshots coming from the sixth floor. Our initial reaction was that our three agents were in perilous danger."

Nicollette heard Mr. Haken say the words "perilous danger." *They thought we were in perilous danger? What they really meant was dead! Dead! Does he think that because we were outgunned or does he believe two young women can't handle themselves? He doesn't give us any credit at all! Were they even going to try and get us or were they just going through the motions?*

"Just a few minutes later, we heard more shooting from the sixth floor. At the same time, one of our observers stationed outside the building told us of some unusual flashing of lights from a room on the sixth floor. It was determined that this was some sort of signal coming from Mr. Peter Johnson's room. The observer said that a crude morse code asking for help was being sent. He added the signal also included something about 'horses or hopscotch' or something. It was put before us that perhaps the sender meant the word 'hostages.' We now knew there possibly were hostages in the room, but we couldn't determine if our agents were prisoners of the gunmen or the women had prisoners of their own. A quick, yet thorough search of the outside areas of the hospital where the room signal would be visible came back clean. We now continued under the assumption that our two agents had prisoners of their own. This assumption, if true, would give us a useful asset on the sixth floor. Our forces went into overdrive. We had less than three hours till dawn."

Mr. Haken resumed his seat at the table. A soldier in a NATO uniform stood and introduced himself as Major Alberto Ruffini of Special Tactical Operations. He had a very hard Italian accent, but his English was perfect.

"At 0300 hours, the security team held a planning session and we discussed several options. We knew we had to deal with the situation with great care and precision accuracy. We did not want to alert our adversaries or make an unstable situation worse.

"Our three objectives were to isolate the enemy in the hospital by eliminating any outside assistance on the grounds and in the immediate vicinity of the building. Secondly, we needed to put in maximum effort to find any explosives and neutralize them. And, finally, we needed to retake the sixth floor safely. We put the time to accomplish our objectives at 0500 hours, an hour earlier than the deadline the enemy had given us to meet their demands.

"Our tactical bomb team went to work right away using specially trained dogs to detect explosives. Our communications were secured and monitored with electronic interference to block any foreign devices. By 0430 hours, we had disarmed four explosive devices, two in the building and two on the grounds. Although the devices were crude, they would have caused major damage had they detonated. The perimeter team located and arrested an additional ten enemy accomplices and captured four vehicles. I might add this was done without a single shot.

"Now the final objective, to clear the sixth floor. We decided on a plan of surprise. Firstly, we took advantage of the stairwell we knew was clear and sent our main tactical force to the sixth floor. We would also send a small squad up the second staircase on the opposite side of the hallway. At the prescribed time, we cut power to the floor, shutting down the lights and elevators. The main force would then shoot 'steam bombs' into the hallway to further blind the enemy. These 'steam bombs' act like a smoke bomb but instead of smoke, they create a dense fog and raise temperatures by as much as fifteen degrees. The steam leaves only a water vapor residue, very useful in situations such as these. The smaller force and the main force would then rush to clear out the blinded enemy. We were very confident with our plan."

Major Ruffini was handed a piece of paper by a soldier sitting behind him and continued.

"At 0435 hours, we were confident that our first two objectives were completed and moved on to phase three. Our tactical units fired the 'steam bombs' into the hallway and moved in. A firefight ensued and we were quickly able to contain the situation. At 0500 hours, the floor was deemed secure and our agents rescued. The terrorists suffered thirteen casualties with eight dead, five wounded, and fifteen taken prisoner. We suffered one wounded soldier during the operation. There were an additional six civilian casualties, including three dead and three wounded. We are currently pursuing additional terrorists outside of this operation."

Mr. Gistane stood and announced that a forensic team was busy at work on a satchel that was recovered in the hospital room containing tapes and photographs. He continued stating that initial findings from the forensic team led him to believe the tapes and photographs may have been the information the kidnappers were attempting to bargain with.

"A written report will be available in forty-eight hours and any updates and further information will be forwarded to the respective parties. Any questions should come through my office."

Mr. Gistane thanked everyone involved for their professionalism and courage and ended the briefing.

There was muted mumbling as the room cleared out. Nicollette could not move. Her body felt like it was glued to the chair. Thailand, the escape, Brussels, the interview, Peter, Val, the horror of the hospital and this highly clinical briefing. *Six days! I lived it! For most, just fiction, something on tele, for a very small few, a rare partial reality. But for me, I lived a lifetime in those six days, and I'm alive!*

The room was now cleared. Only Val, Peter Johnson, Charles Thompson, Betty Brighall, Majors Blasingame and Hartwell, and Nicollette remained. There was a deafening silence in the room, like life had turned off the volume and left the room. Charles Thompson shut the conference room doors and stood next to Nicollette.

Major Hartwell's normally firm voice changed into a soft, gentle tone, as she asked Nicollette how she was feeling.

Nicollette was torn between feelings of anger, abuse, resentment and hurt. A small part of her wanted to jump out of the chair and resign, but her better sense prevailed. Now, as she was trying to form an answer to the Major's question, all she could come up with was a simple response.

"They didn't trust us, Major. They didn't believe we could

do the job. We were pawns in the game just like the Spanish analyst and...I don't want to end up like her."

Before Nicollette could continue, Val, her friend, the young woman whom she had known since training, as a roommate, friend, and later as a co-agent, stood from her chair and announced in a firm voice, "But I trusted you, Nicky. With my life, I did! And I'm damn glad I did!"

Peter stood gingerly from his chair using Major Blasingame's arm for support. "Nicollette, you were nothing less than amazing last night. If you hadn't acted, who knows what information they would have attained from me and it's anyone's guess what they would have done with me, Val, and you. The outcome at the hospital might have—No, *would* have been—totally different. Nicollette, you were brave and resourceful and handled yourself with professionalism well beyond your years and if the people in Brussels don't see it, well then, shame on them! You and Val saved my life and maybe a great many more." Peter turned to Val. "Thank you, Val, for your courage and professionalism and for being a good friend. You both are a credit to our group and our country."

Nicollette was digesting the kind words from Val and Peter. A bit of energy was returning to her body and the color was returning to her face. The positive reinforcing comments from her two colleagues was helping to take some of the sting out of the clinical briefing from Mr. Gistane. She was even able to share a small smile and say thank you to her friends.

"I would like to add something, Major, with your permission," Charles said.

"Certainly," Major Hartwell responded.

"Thank you. Miss Beverley, Miss Davies, and my friend Peter Johnson, you lot may be wondering why I'm here. I arrived in Bangkok a few days after you arrived. I was sent on an assignment to investigate the security breach within the operation in the jungle. Only Majors Hartwell and Blasingame knew of this mission. For some time now, we had suspected a possible leak in our communications regarding the mission in Thailand. Last month's bombing raids seemed to be too precise to fail, but they failed. We felt it had to be someone on the inside passing secure information to the drug lords. We alerted the NATO Captain and he discreetly kept watch. The investigation narrowed it to three members of the surveillance group and a couple of the Thai support team. The three analysts were the only ones whose time in the jungle overlapped with the failed bombing raids. We certainly knew that Nicollette and Peter were above any suspicion, leaving us one suspect. We then focused our investigation down to the last suspect, the German analyst. We were convinced of the German analyst's involvement but we still needed solid proof. I was on the same flight back to Brussels as you, keeping an eye on our 'friend' but also staying away from anyone who would recognize me. In Brussels, we kept a very close watch on the German. Your interview, Nicollette, gave us just what we needed. We subsequently arrested him and he confessed."

Charles Thompson bent over and spoke to Nicollette.

"Nicky, I was outside the door when we gave Mr. Gistane the news of the confession, but I couldn't say anything till now. Sorry. I heard your 'interview.' You were magnificent in a very stressful situation and acted well beyond what others expected. Bravo."

Nicollette smiled back and forced a whispered thank you. She looked around the room, remembering what had just been said about her. Despite all the emotional and physical angst she had been through the last day, a feeling deep down rose to the surface; she really loved her job. Sure, it was challenging, even dangerous, but she was well trained and confident in her position. The pressures of being a young woman in a male-dominated field seemed to give her additional motivation to complete her tasks. Nicollette picked up little reminders all the time, evidence that even five years after being formed, people were still watching Group 226/157. She also understood that she was a part of something bigger than just herself, she was part of a movement, trailblazing new roles for women for positions within British Intelligence that were normally just reserved for men.

Nicollette remembered being told during training, *Self-doubt is common, but it can be very disruptive and menacing to your abilities to do the task. As hard as it is, you must push it aside and be confident in yourself and those around you. Trust yourself, your life may be dependent on that.*

A thought was crystalizing in Nicollette's mind. *Perhaps this experience was a test for me, helping me prove to myself that this career is right for me and that these people in the room and the rest of Group 226/157 have become my family, my new family. The "normal" I was raised with and hoping to find again in Brockwirth is actually here in front of me! This is my normal! Of course, I will always love my real family and Brockwirth, but this is what I want to do and these are the people I want to be a part of. I am right now committing to being the best I can be, for me personally and my new family!*

After nearly five years, the ever-present question of whether to completely commit to this new life had been percolating inside her. Now there was clarity. This was her choice, her career, and her life. A deep burden was lifted from her. She recognized the challenges and the dangers of her decision. *I am ready!*

In a tired, but clear voice, Nicollette addressed her two superiors, "Majors Hartwell and Blasingame, I would very much like to go home please."

Maria Fuentes

The government car turned down a dark street in Prestbury, a small village just outside Cheltenham, a single light pole offering the only illumination as the vehicle stopped in front of Peter's semi-detached house. It was the first time either Nicollette or Val had seen where he lived. He was to be dropped off first, despite being adamant that Nicollette and Val should be.

The driver was asked to wait as the two women escorted Peter into his home. A key was hidden in a flower box attached to the stone face of the house. When Nicollette asked about security, Peter replied, "For the neighbor."

It was a simple house inside with comfortable yet basic furniture around a gas fireplace in the sitting room. The dining area consisted of a small wooden table and a couple of chairs and the kitchen was simple with a cooker and small refrigerator. There were bedrooms and a bathroom upstairs. There was the luxury of a second small bathroom on the first floor.

Nicollette and Val settled Peter on the couch at his insistence, saying he would be more comfortable there. As she looked around the room, Nicollette realized she knew very little about his life outside work. *His life is a real mystery and he is very private. Until tonight, I didn't even know where he lived!*

The few details she did know about him were that he was about her father's age and had been working in the Intelligence service for a long time. Nicollette knew he lived alone and had never mentioned ever having been married before. Still, it all seemed quite peculiar to her. *He's a Senior Level Agent living in this very modest home. He doesn't even own a car! He has to be doing well financially, but it looks like he doesn't spend any money. I wonder what his story is. Very private indeed!*

Val found the teapot and brought Peter a cup. He insisted the two women join him but it was late and Nicollette and Val were anxious to get back to their respective flats. They could see he was struggling to stay awake and knew it was time for them to leave. He sleepily assured the two that he was fine as they started to leave.

Nicollette found a piece of paper by the phone and made a note of his number. She would ring him tomorrow. As they were driven away, the two women could see the light in the front room turn off.

The driver stopped in front of Nicollette and Val's building and insisted on escorting them to their flats. "Orders, Misses."

Nicollette was home! It had been three tumultuous weeks since she had left for Thailand. *Three bloody weeks!*

She was too tired for tea and had thoughts about a bath, but the soft pillows and the comfortable bed won that argument. She unconsciously reached for the mossie net, rolled over, and fell into a deep sleep, still dressed in her RAF outfit.

The incessant ringing of the telephone brought Nicollette back to reality. *That's one thing I haven't missed over the last three weeks!*

"Good morning, sleepyhead. My turn to pay you back from those early morning days at training!"

"Good morning, Val," Nicollette replied. "What's up?"

"I've organized a taxi to take us to Peter Johnson's house. I thought we'd pick up some lunch for him on the way. The taxi will be outside in an hour."

"Ok, have you called him? We should let him know the plan."

"He said fine, in fact, he asked us to bring fish and chips, so he must be feeling better. Also, Nicky, did you get a call from Captain Blankin?"

"No, why?"

"It seems they want us at work today at three."

"Did the Captain say why?"

"No, nothing other than to come to work. Ok then, see you in an hour."

Nicollette's inquisitive mind started to run as she stepped into the hot shower. *I thought we were off for a couple of days? Multiple scenarios were crossing her mind, Another mission? No, too soon. Probably just paperwork.*

She was enjoying the endless stream of hot water when she heard the phone ring again. A quick towel and a rush to answer. It was Captain Blankin calling to check in on her and invite her to the 3:00 p.m. meeting. It was an all business call, no small talk.

Peter was sitting at a small table in his front garden as the cab dropped off Val and Nicollette. The three of them enjoyed the fish and chips under the blue skies of an English summer. Unlike the night before, there was small talk amongst the three, sharing stories of past assignments. Val was all ears when the conversation turned towards Thailand. There was a chuckle around the table as they talked about some comical moments at the remote outpost.

It was getting close to the time the cab was returning to take the three of them to the afternoon meeting. Nicollette asked if she could go inside for a minute. "The beer is catching up to me."

"You are out of practice, Nicky," Val responded.

On her way out of the house, the photos Nicollette had spotted last night in the sitting room caught her eye.

There were a couple of color photos of what looked like Peter posing with a family in a country setting and one of him kneeling with a dog. Behind these photos were some rather old black and white pictures of what looked like a young Peter dressed in a military uniform. In one photo, he was posing with other soldiers in front of a tent and in another photo, he was sitting in a GP vehicle. In a third photo, he was posing with a mounted machine gun on the back of a GP vehicle.

Nicollette could see by Peter's uniform he was a Lieutenant and, given her guess as to his age, these photos were probably taken in WWII. There was another stack of photos, but Val announced through the door that the cab had arrived.

Nicollette, Val and Peter walked into the conference room at three. The two Majors, Captain Blankin and Mr. Charles Thompson, were already seated at the conference table. There were four other civilians seated at the table that Nicollette didn't recognize. In the center of the table was a large piece of equipment.

Major Hartwell thanked everyone for coming on such short notice. She explained the reason for the meeting was that the forensic team had reviewed the tapes and prepared an analysis of their content.

Major Hartwell introduced Mr. Wilf Simonson, Deputy Director of the Forensic Department, to the group.

Mr. Simonson explained that the team was faced with two issues in the task. First, there was the translation. The tapes were recorded in Dutch, German, French and even some Thai. Next was the task of creating some sort of timeline. The Beta tape was easy to analyze.

"Because of the length of the tapes, Major Hartwell has asked me not to play all of them, but merely the relevant ones to this group."

Mr. Simonson added that some of the recordings about to be played might be disturbing. He placed the first tape in the machine and Nicollette could recognize right away the voice of the Spanish analyst.

"This is a recording of the questioning of Maria Fuentes, the Spanish analyst, in her hotel room."

As the tape was playing, Mr. Simonson translated the conversation taking place between the intruders and Miss Fuentes. He noted the German accents of the intruders as they asked for detailed information. Nicollette's Spanish was a little rough, but she could understand that Maria was repeating "I don't know" and heard the elevated anxiety in Maria's voice. The intruders sounded more and more frustrated with Maria. The tapes played what sounded like physical punishment being applied to the young lady. Multiple slaps, punches, and even a belt whip were accompanied by Maria's painful grunting responses. The intruders were now screaming their questions. Maria continued to respond, "No sé."

It was increasingly apparent that Maria's voice was starting to fail. *She is weakening, her body is being beaten, but she is staying firm.* Then an ear-piercing shriek permeated the room.

Mr. Simonson explained they believe that this was when Miss Fuentes was stripped and placed in the bathtub. There was the distinct sound of water splashing and human coughing while questions continued to bombard Maria as she was gasping for every breath. "No sé! No sé!"

The intruders were giving no ground. The screaming questions, splashing water, coughing and gasping for air were becoming almost unbearable to listen to. At once, the noise stopped and Nicollette could faintly hear the words, "Necesito ir al hospital."

There was one final loud splash, then silence. Maria Fuentes was gone. She had resisted to the end of her strength.

Mr. Simonson removed the tape and placed another in the machine. Nicollette's stomach was turning. *What an awful death! All that's left is a tape, a bloody tape!*

"Maria Fuentes," Nicollete spoke aloud, "her name was Maria Fuentes."

The voice on the second tape was even more familiar. A very groggy Peter Johnson was being questioned by a woman. *It's the imposter doctor! The one I shot!*

Mr. Simonson stopped the tape and explained that this is one of two tapes recovered from the recording machine in the room. *The tapes I found, sir!* Nicollette thought.

Mr. Simonson added that Mr. Peter Johnson was under the influence of Sodium Pentethal, "the truth serum." He continued by identifying the woman doing the interrogation, "A Miss Greta Franke."

The name didn't mean anything to Nicollette, but a numbness crept over her when Mr. Simonson explained that Miss Franke was a notorious criminal with direct connections to several terrorist and drug groups, including The Tang Organization and Baader, two of the three groups involved in the hospital siege.

"She is wanted internationally for multiple crimes from illegal drug and weapons charges to outright murder. Miss Franke and her small group of mercenaries are merciless killers and very bad actors on the world stage. Interpol has been after her for years, but she is extremely detail oriented and always has an escape planned. She is multilingual and a master of disguises. We have no doubt that she was the mastermind behind the hospital siege."

Mr. Simonson concluded that the two dead victims in the hospital room bathroom were probably killed by her.

"Our agents in the hospital room were very lucky. Truly very lucky."

Major Hartwell quickly added, "And we've got her! Miss Franke is now in custody and being held in a secure location."

Mr. Simonson placed a new tape in the machine. Nicollette's mind wandered back to the confrontation she had with Miss Franke, remembering her condescending attitude and her belittling comments. *She called me a little girl. Little girl, my arse! I should have wasted her! That bitch! May she rot in hell!*

As the recording played, the group could hear Peter shakily responding to questions about Thailand. He revealed the identities and nationalities of the analysts and the NATO Captain. When asked about the German, he said, "That traitor!

Glad we got 'em!" Miss Greta Franke then asked for detailed information as to how information was gathered and relayed back to Bangkok. Peter talked about the coding schedule, rotation, and electronic equipment. Many of the questions were repeated for clarity. As the questioning continued, a shiver went up Nicollette's spine when Peter was asked about the women analysts he was working with in Thailand. When asked how weak they were, Mr Johnson replied the team were all very good.

"Maria Fuentes and Nicollette Beverley, the two women, are excellent."

The tape was about forty minutes long. Nicollette looked at Peter, his head bent over between his two hands. He had given Miss Franke a wealth of secret information on the activities of the clandestine operation in the jungle and how secret communications worked, and, most frightening, the identities of the agents. The sodium pentothal had worked.

Nicollette reached over to him and spoke softly, "It isn't your fault, and we have the tapes."

Major Hartwell announced that this was enough for today and thanked Mr. Simonson for his report. A satchel was given to one of the civilians and he and the rest of the civilians were excused from the room.

"Peter," Major Hartwell said, "you were incapacitated and unaware of what was happening. Please don't be hard on yourself, it's not your fault. You know full well the dangers of what we do. You are a damn good agent and an invaluable member of this group. And Peter, you are alive!"

"Here, here!" added Major Blasingame. "And we have the tapes! As sensitive as the information is, it is highly unlikely that there was enough time to duplicate the tapes, and Miss Franke and her accomplices aren't going anywhere! Well done, Miss Beverley, for your quick thinking."

Nicollette was moved at being recognized by her superiors.

In the entirety of the formal briefing led by Mr. Gistane, her name was never mentioned once. *That man just couldn't do it,* Nicollette thought. *He couldn't recognize a woman by name for bravery and a job well done. Old sod!*

Nicollette was surprised at the way Major Hartwell addressed Mr. Johnson by his first name. She had never heard either major address any of the team by their first name in a professional setting before and then talk so candidly in front of everyone. Peter raised his head and thanked the two majors for voicing their confidence in him.

Major Hartwell stood from her chair and glared at each of her personnel around the table, each in turn. In a clear and impassioned voice, she exclaimed, "You lot listen and listen good! I know I speak for Major Blasingame as well when I say to you that we have your back! No one, but no one, is going to take anything away from the fine work that you and the rest of Group 226/157 has done or will do in the future. We have worked too damn hard to get to this point. I don't care if it's a senior analyst or a new recruit, we have your back!"

The Major paused for a moment and pulled out a folded piece of paper from her chest pocket. She carefully unfolded it and proceeded to talk about the contents of a letter she received earlier that day. All eyes were upon Major Hartwell as she described how the Ministry of Defence was proud of the work and accomplishments that Group 226/157 had achieved in the last five years and that funding for another year of new recruitment and training was being discussed.

"So there you have it. We are being recognized. Think about it. A section of British Intelligence made up of mostly women is now being recognized as capable and important to the MOD! I know there is still a long way to go, many still don't believe we can do the job, as we've experienced the last few days, but ladies, we've accomplished so much. The ball is rolling! This is happening!"

The Major paused to calm her excitement, then continued, "Peter and Charles, you are and continue to be a great help in the success of this group and you should take pride in what has been achieved and I, we all, thank you. So there you have it. I'm very proud of you lot. Very proud!"

The Two Mes

Nicollette's hand was shaking and wet from perspiration as she held the receiver. *Why am I so anxious? I'm just calling home, it's very simple and I've done it hundreds of times! What is bothering me? Is it the experiences of this last mission or the little fibs I tell my parents about my job? Or maybe both?*

She took a deep breath hoping it would help calm her down. A second round of rings and then an answer.

"760652."

"Hello Mum, it's me, Nicollette, I'm back early from my trip and I was hoping to see you and Dad tonight."

"Hello Nicky, so happy to hear your voice. When did you get in?"

"Very late last night, so I had a 'lie in' to help with the jet lag. I'm off today so I was hoping to come and see you and Dad for tea."

"Smashing Nicky, see you then. Bye."

"Bye, Mum, and...I love you."

Nicollette's hand shook as she put down the receiver. *Where did that come from? On the phone no less?* She talked to her parents frequently over the phone, but almost never ended the conversation with "I love you." Love was assumed, seldom vocalised, and certainly not over the phone. Sure, she loved her parents deeply and would do nothing to let them believe otherwise, but to express it when not in person, *that's just cold, empty, and meaningless.* However, today was different.

"What is your story going to be when you see your parents?" Val asked as she took a bite of the still warm donuts they were enjoying together at the local coffee shop.

"Our original cover story, and the one I've told them, was that we were being sent out to make arrangements for our rugby and football teams tour of Australia, New Zealand, and India, and we were also to start work on several future cricket test matches. All in all, we were to tell people we were going to be away for as much as a month."

"But you were away for just three weeks?"

"I know. I'll say that our work didn't take that long and I was anxious to get home. There shouldn't be too many questions."

It was easy to make up their cover story, almost too easy, seemingly belittling the extreme danger they experienced during their missions. Secrecy was part of their job and their reality. Now it has become a permanent fixture in their brains. Storytelling and fibbing had become weapons in their arsenal of deceit.

"It's open, come through, Nicky," Peter called from inside his house.

Nicollette walked into the sitting room to find Peter relaxing on the couch. His feet were propped on the coffee table and a football match was on the tele.

The kettle boiled and Nicollette sat in the overstuffed chair next to the sofa. She poured the tea and offered a fresh donut to Peter.

"Are you sure you will be alright, Peter?" she asked.

He was adamant he would be alright. He told her that he had a cleaner come to the house twice a week to do the washing and tidy up.

"And if I am a 'good lad,' she will even do some cooking for me as well. Remember the key outside, Nicky?"

It was getting late in the afternoon and Nicollette used the phone to call for a cab. Peter asked about her plans for the evening. She told him that she was off to Brockwirth to have tea with her parents but she was a bit uneasy about the visit.

"Since Al Sha'am and now, Thailand and Brussels, whenever there was danger, my mind thinks of my parents. They have no idea what I really do or how dangerous it can be. It's been nearly five years and it's getting harder to keep the story going. They didn't train us for this. Have you ever felt that way?"

Nicollette caught herself immediately after asking Peter that last question. He was very private about his life and as far as she knew, he was a bachelor, not having to answer to anyone. *He could just say he works for the government or something and no one would know the difference.*

He leaned back on the sofa. Nicollette could tell by his tone that the conversation was about to get serious.

"That is a very interesting question, Nicky, and there really isn't one right answer. Five years isn't enough time to get comfortable with telling stories to your family, no amount of time is. In fact, you will never be ok with telling fibs to the ones you love. I know this sounds callous, Nicky, and this is important, you have to grow comfortable with the idea of never, and I repeat never, telling anyone what you really are and what you do." Peter leaned forward. "Some people say 'ignorance is bliss' and maybe there is some truth to that. Regular people don't have to worry about all the malignancies and bad actors out there, we do that for them. For the rest of your life, there are going to be two yous. One you is Nicollette Beverley who works for British Intelligence, living a clandestine life of secrets, missions, and danger. A life she has been highly trained for and has become very good at. Her second life is in the outside world. A life of being seemingly normal, just a young woman with a normal government job and doing normal activities. Your challenge, and I know this is hard, especially now, is to separate the two yous. A line has to be drawn right down the middle, black and white, there can be no gray area. None."

Peter grinned as he continued, "If you can handle the challenges you just went through in Brussels, I am confident you can handle this."

Nicollette *felt* every word he said. It was as if he had looked into her mind and knew exactly what to say. *It sounds so simple! There must be two mes. After all, it's not what I am or what I do, it's who I am: Nicollette Beverley! That's all it can be.*

The Secret

"Yoohoo, hello, I'm here, anybody home?" Nicollette announced as she walked through the unlocked door of her parents' home.

"I'm in the kitchen," her mum called.

Nicollette was excited and yet still a bit anxious as she walked into the kitchen. The words her friend Peter had told her forty minutes ago still played in her mind. But all that seemed to fade away as she saw her Mum standing over the sink wearing the same old pink apron she always wore and drying her hands on the same old blue dish cloth. *Same old, same old. I'm home!*

Nicollette reached for her mum as she turned from the sink and they gave each other a tight hug. Nicollette felt tears well up in her eyes.

"What's all this?" Alice asked as she spotted the wetness on Nicollette's cheek as she pulled away.

"I'm just happy to see you, Mum. It was a long, hard trip."

"Well, you'll just have to tell me and your father all about it over tea. He'll be home shortly."

"I've brought a sweet, Mum."

Nicollette opened the cardboard box to reveal a chocolate cake.

"Your father's favorite and...mine," she responded cheekily.

Alice was baking the sausage rolls and frying the chips as Nicollette prepared the salad. They could hear the car door shut beside the house and the front door open.

"Where's my Nicky?" her father asked.

Nicollette walked into the sitting room and greeted her father with another tight hug. *No tears this time, just inner joy!*

"Let's take a look at you, Nicky!"

Nicollette twirled in front of her father.

"I believe you've lost some weight. Your clothes look too big on you. Don't they feed you on your trips? What do you think, Alice?"

"Too skinny for my liking, but we'll soon sort that out. Tea's ready!"

The three had a laugh as they walked into the kitchen. *If only they knew,* Nicollette thought, *and they will never know.*

"What's this, Mum?" Nicollette asked as she spotted a note taped to the refrigerator.

"Oh. Carol called while you were away. She said she tried to reach you at your flat several times and you didn't reply, so she called here. I told her you were called away on business."

Nicollette unfolded the note. Carol wanted to get together to catch-up and talk about her wedding plans. *Is the wedding that soon? Time has flown!*

Nicollette and Carol had been friends since primary school and were inseparable for a time. But over the last few years, their lives took different paths. Still, she and Carol remained good friends. Carol had asked Nicollette to be a bridesmaid. *Fingers crossed I won't be away,* she thought at the time.

It was a casual evening with her parents in the warm, safe environment of the sitting room. An empty bottle of red was standing next to the half-eaten chocolate cake on top of the sideboard. The conversation was light, mostly about the family and past trips. When asked about her recent work trip, Nicollette gave vague answers with just enough detail as to not raise questions. *I'm glad I know my geography,* she thought as she talked about New Zealand and Australia.

Nicollette looked at her watch. It was getting late. Her father had volunteered to drive her home, but he could barely keep his eyes open. At her mum's insistence, Nicollette would spend the night with them in Brockwirth. "We are going into

Cheltenham tomorrow morning anyway, so easy enough to drop you off."

It was a strange, yet comfortable feeling walking into her old bedroom. Even after four and a half years, there was still clothing of hers in the dresser and wardrobe. Nicollette saw her old pair of Nike running shoes, battered but clean, on the floor. *I should go for a run tomorrow morning. It might help clear my head,* she thought.

In the dresser, she found the clothes she wore for her training at Brize, neatly folded in the bottom drawer along with her old Field Hockey jersey. She gingerly laid her jersey across the bed and then carefully placed her training gear next to it. A numbness crept over her as she sat next to the bed, never taking her eyes off the garments. *Four and a half years ago, this was me. It seems so long ago, but it really wasn't. It was a different Nicky back then, fresh and innocent, ready to conquer the world. I never would have dreamed I would have this life. My world is very different now and...I love it.*

The milkman's van was driving past the house as Nicollette sat on the porch and put on her running shoes. It was a clear, cool morning. She ran the same route she always had but this time it seemed to take longer to reach Brockwirth Tower. Sitting on the bench at the Tower, Nicollette thought, *Have I gotten slower? Am I out of shape? Or maybe, just maybe, I slowed down to enjoy the run.*

The bench on the Tower grounds had always offered a respite for Nicollette, from the time when she first started running and even in those days she just walked. It was peaceful and pastoral and the view of the village below was magnificent. The air always seemed to be fresher and clearer on the grounds. It was her place to think, solving many of the world's problems in her head and her homework on paper.

But today, the bench was her place to meditate and review her life, what she had experienced and what she had become.

She took a deep breath and closed her eyes as she recalled Peter talking to her about who she was.

Nicollette had sat on the same bench, meditating over her involvement in the elimination of the Bulgarian General and his family. *They called it collateral damage!* Then it was the mission on the Lesser Tunb Island. *Shoot the damn gun, Miss Beverley!* Now it was running for their lives in Thailand, the accusations against her during the after-action interview and, finally, the deadly hostage situation in Brussels. *I shot a man in front of me! I pulled the trigger and could see his face as life left him.* The image of Mr. Gistane grilling her at the interview and accusing her of being a traitor! *Thinking I'm weak because I'm a young woman! To hell with that! To hell with them!*

"Miss, you alright? Miss?"

Nicollette opened her eyes and turned to see one of the local "Bobbies" standing behind her.

"Yes, I'm alright, just resting my eyes after my run."

"Well, it's such a lovely morning and the view is beautiful here, I don't blame you. Good morning to you, Miss."

As he walked away, Nicollette looked at the view of the village. *Bulgaria was a restless night, Lesser Tunb was a bad dream, Thailand and Brussels were absolute nightmares, but I'm still here, alive and strong!*

She took a deep breath of the fresh air and headed down the hill to her parents' home. *And despite all the changes in my life, all the experiences both good and bad, the traveling and the secrets, deep down, I will always be a Brockwirth girl.*

It was mid-afternoon when her parents dropped her off at the flat. Nicollette invited her parents in for a cuppa, but they declined, knowing she had things to do for herself.

"You are coming for Sunday lunch tomorrow, right?" her mum asked in a directive tone.

"Sure Mum, I'll be there."

Nicollette was relaxing in front of the tele when the phone announced its presence. *That's one thing I didn't miss in Thailand, the damn phone!*

Nicollette recognized Peter's voice instantly.

"How are you feeling, Peter?

"Much better thank you. I was hoping you would join me for dinner later, there is a great Chinese take-away on the next street. And I have some movies on Beta we could watch."

Nicollette thought for a moment, *I reckon he's lonely.*

"Sure."

The door was open as Nicollette walked into Peter's home. He was sitting back in his chair, remnants of breakfast or lunch or both still sitting on the small table in front of the sofa. Peter apologized for the mess, saying his "lady" didn't come today. Nicollette cleared the table and pulled two Cokes from the refrigerator.

"They know you well at the Chinese, Peter," she said as she sat down on the sofa, "and whatever you ordered smells delicious."

As they were eating and having light conversation, Nicollette thought about Peter's situation. *The takeaway knew him when I mentioned his name for pick up, probably because he eats from there all the time. I'll bet he hasn't had a proper Sunday lunch in a long time.*

As she was getting ready to leave, she asked him if he would like to join her at her parents' house in Brockwirth for Sunday lunch. Peter Johnson didn't hesitate to reply.

"Yes, that would be lovely."

It was just before 10:00 p.m. when Nicollette called home. Her parents would still be up on a Saturday night, probably watching a special on tele. Nicollette asked her mum if she could bring a guest for Sunday lunch. She could hear her Mum get a little excited on the phone when she asked about the friend.

"Yes, Mum, it is a man, but no, Mum, he is a supervisor, co-worker, and much older. He's just a friend."

Nicollette explained that Mr. Johnson had an accident on the work trip and he needed a home cooked meal. Nicollette knew her Mum was a little hard of hearing so when she asked his name again, it was no surprise.

"Mr. Peter Johnson, Mum. His name is Mr. Peter Johnson."

Riding to Brockwirth, Nicollette reviewed their cover story with Peter, noting that her parents weren't too inquisitive, but they should be on the same page to be safe.

"So this is where you grew up, Nicky," Peter commented as Nicollette helped him navigate the three steps into the house.

"Hello, we're here!" Nicollette announced as they walked into the small sitting room. Alice and James walked in from the kitchen and gave Nicollette a parental hug. James held out his hand to shake hands with Peter as Nicollette introduced him to her parents.

"Thank you for inviting me, lunch smells delicious."

"Lunch will be ready shortly. Make yourselves comfortable," Alice announced as she went back into the kitchen.

James asked Nicollette to take Peter's coat as the two men sat in the room. Nicollette helped him take off his coat and went to hang it in the small foyer. As she was placing the coat on a peg, she noticed two envelopes inside the jacket inner pocket. *None of my business really.*

The conversation was light as James asked Peter about his injuries. As rehearsed, he explained how he mis-stepped and fell down a few steps onto a hard floor in Canberra.

"It was just before a meeting in, of all places, the Department of Home Affairs Building in Sydney. Quite silly really. It's much better now."

There was some more chatter about the planning, tedium, and bureaucracy that the group had to deal with. "But that's why we have to send our athletes overseas."

"We are lucky to have Nicollette, James. She is meticulous and precise. She makes my job much easier."

Nicollette felt uneasy telling tales to her father, but she remembered what Peter had said to her about "never, never."

James responded by talking about Nicky's Field Hockey days and the County Championship.

As the small talk continued, Nicollette could tell there was something going on between her father and Peter. There was a forced politeness and pleasantness in the conversation, but that was natural given they just met. *No, there is something underneath making them a little uncomfortable. I can just tell by my father's expression and tone and Peter's body language. I know my father knows that we just are friends and cowork-ers, but why does he seem so overprotective of me? And Peter, he sometimes looks like he's treading water trying to make con-versation. Like he's talking to a ghost! At least they are friendly. Maybe a bit nervous or something.*

Alice announced lunch was served, her father poured a red wine, and everyone raised a glass to the hostess. Nicollette was impressed by how Mr. Johnson was able to use his utensils even with one arm in a sling. *Knowing him, he probably prac-ticed before we came.*

Alice laid out the eclairs and offered tea and coffee. "Where are you from, Peter?"

Peter took a sip of tea and explained that his family moved to Prestbury from London after the war, that his father had a job with the government and later was able to secure a job for him locally.

"Were you in the forces?"

Nicollette could see Peter struggling for an answer in his mind as he sipped some more tea. She noticed her father's ex-pression changing quickly to one of concern. He politely inter-rupted, "That's not a nice question, Alice. The war was a long time ago. Let's talk about these splendid eclairs."

This was highly unusual for her father, Nicollette thought. *He never interrupts Mum or abruptly changes the conversation. Something must be going on.*

However, Peter replied politely, "Yes, Alice, for a short time. And the owner of a little bakery in Prestbury is one of my neighbors. You should stop there sometime. It's just off Mill Street. A local secret."

After dinner, there was more light conversation in the sitting room and another glass of wine. It was getting late in the afternoon and Peter asked to call a cab.

"Don't be silly," Alice replied. "James will take you."

"No problem, I'll get my coat," James added.

"Splendid, thank you and thank you for a wonderful lunch," Peter replied as Nicollette brought in his jacket from the foyer, the two white envelopes still in the jacket pocket.

Pleasantries were said and thank yous repeated as the three of them left the house. Nicollette noticed her father placing a small wooden box in the boot of the car.

"What's that, Dad?" she asked as he shut the boot.

"Oh nothing, Nicky, just something I've been meaning to bring to work."

Nicollette shrugged it off. Her father had always been a little forgetful, so his answer was not out of the ordinary.

The ride was eerily quiet. As they reached the outskirts of Winchcombe, James broke the silence by asking if anyone wanted a nightcap.

"There is a good local nearby and they are open."

The three of them walked into the pub and found a table off to one side. Nicollette brought three pints from the bar. Her father and Peter were just looking at each other, like two players in a chess match, waiting for the other to blink.

Peter broke the stare and raised his glass. "To a wonderful lunch."

"And to good company," James added.

"Speaking of company," Nicollette asked, "what's up with you two? The two of you have been stressed since you first met. Now, what's really going on?"

Nicollette turned her head from her father to Peter and back again. "Well?"

Peter broke the silent tension. "I think you should tell her, James, I think it's time."

James took a deep breath. "You're right, Pete, it's time."

Nicollette almost fell out of her chair. Her mind worked feverishly to digest what she just heard. *What! Time for what? Tell me what! And did I just hear Peter call my Dad James? And Dad called Peter Pete? What the hell is going on here!*

Her father excused himself momentarily, then returned and laid the small wooden box on the table. At the same time, Peter pulled the two white envelopes out of his jacket pocket.

James took a sip of his beer. "Nicollette, you know how much I love you and what I'm going to tell you, I've been holding for a long time."

All Nicollette could do was acknowledge her father with a head nod. Her body was paralyzed. All of her senses were focused on her father. All the familiar background noises of the pub seemed to vanish. All the patrons in the pub seemed to disappear.

"I have talked about my war experience with you and Edward before. My rank was sergeant and yes, I was a boxer. This is true."

"They called him 'Beast Beverley,'" Peter injected.

Nicollette's father gave a slight grin at the comment, then returned to his story.

"We would travel around France and Belgium, entertaining the troops by putting on boxing matches. Sometimes there might even be a singer or comedian joining us as well. We were often near the frontlines so the events were always in front of smaller gatherings. We didn't want to give the Germans any easy targets of large concentrations of unprepared troops. Peter, here, was our sergeant in charge of the events. His nickname was 'Packer Pete' because he always wore two pistols around his waist, like you see in those American Western movies. There were ten total in our group, including 'Packer' and myself. Pete, do you want to add anything?"

"Your father was a hell of a boxer! He even had thoughts of turning pro after the war! But also during our time together, your father was a good soldier and one hell of an intelligence agent."

Nicollette abruptly stood from her chair, her body acting on its own as a reaction to what she just heard. *What the hell did I just hear! My dad worked in intelligence!*

For her whole life, she believed her father to be a boxer who traveled around Europe entertaining the troops, barely seeing any action other than the boxing ring. Now she was hearing a whole new story, a totally different side to the man she knew ten minutes ago and had lived with all her life. Her body was still standing and her arms felt like they were nailed to the table.

James asked Nicky to sit down, took a sip of his beer, and continued.

"In the late summer of '44, we were giving Gerry a proper thrashing across Northern France and Belgium. Monty, I mean General Montgomery, appeared to be in competition with the American General Patton as to who could advance faster to end the war, so he pushed to make sure that nothing would get in his way. He relied heavily on Intelligence to make his plans and even recruited locals to gain information. In early September, General Montgomery wanted to make a dramatic move. Intelligence informed him of a gap between two large German forces. This gap opened a pathway directly into the center of Holland and into a city called Arnhem. There was a strategically located bridge over the Rhine in the city. If Monty could pull this off, he would have a direct shot into Germany.

He named the mission 'Operation Market Garden.' Nicky, you remember the movie *A Bridge Too Far*?"

Nicollette, by now, was so captured by her father's story, that all she could do was nod.

"Before getting shipped off to France, I was with the lads at Bletchley Park," Peter said. "I was involved primarily with the electronics, building, fixing, and maintaining what would now be considered antique radio and signaling devices. They taught me some coding along the way so I could be more useful. Before Bletchley, I was a Maths and Engineering student at University. When I was called up, I initially was trained in explosives, munitions, and small arms. The Army found out about my technical background and sent me to Intelligence. Quite a contrast really, between shooting and signaling. One day you are destroying and the next you are building! Now your father has a different story. Right, James?"

"Nicky, when I first joined the Army, we were given hand-to-hand training. I was bigger than most of the other lads, so I found it easy to win fights. Of course growing up in a tough part of London helped. When they found out I had some boxing training in school, I was placed with the traveling show. Just a few weeks before we went to Europe, the officer in charge sent me to an intense course in interrogation. They figured my size and tough demeanour would be useful in extracting information from prisoners. Next thing I know, I'm working for the Security Services and being trained at a secret Special Operations Executive camp outside Paris. You may have heard of the S.O.E., Nicky. This is where I'm joined up with Peter. And that's how it started."

Peter picked up the story. "Our little boxing group was quite successful. The lads loved the matches and we obtained some valuable information along the way, including exposing a German ring of infiltrators dressed as American soldiers. Now let's get back to 'Market Garden,' shall we? I'm sure you'll want to hear about that, Nicky."

Again, Nicollette nodded as Peter continued.

"As your father stated earlier, General Montgomery was determined to make a bold move into Holland. He wanted every aspect of the mission to be on course to give the highest possibility of success. Monty knew that failure would be devastating to his plans and embarrassing for him in front of the Allies and Patton. Our little 'boxing group' was brought from Paris to a meeting in Belgium where we were briefed on the operation by members of Montgomery's staff. Our objective was to gain as much local information as possible and, most importantly, expose any German infiltration into our ranks. Our group consisted of your father, me, and eight others. We were instructed to put on a match at a base camp near the frontlines, outside a town called Arandock. We arrived a day before our 'show' to set up and reconnoitre the area. One of our men found some unauthorized radio equipment in a nearby wood. He reported to me later that evening that the equipment was rather old and not working and was probably discarded from the German invasion of 1940. Not wanting to leave anything to chance, your father and I went to check it out. The equipment by then had been moved and despite our best efforts, we could not locate the radio anywhere. We became very suspicious and reported what we found to the Commanding Officer, who had been briefed about our mission. We also heard some interesting conversation among the troops. A group of reservists had arrived at the camp and there was talk about seeing large amounts of armor and equipment on the roads leading to the front. This loose talk and the disappearance of the radio gave us reason to be concerned. We had to be vigilant."

Peter finished his beer.

"Now is when it gets interesting, Nicky. Your turn, James."

"Nicky, we pulled all stops out to locate the missing equipment and find the people involved. We were not successful, but the show had to go on. I fought with a couple of volunteers."

"And made short work of them," Peter added.

"Yes, they were easy matches. In the meantime, two of our crew were getting something from the back of our lorry when they discovered the missing equipment hidden under a tarp in the back. Probably the last place we would look. Anyways, as our men started to unload, they were jumped, taken hostage, and forced at gunpoint to drive the lorry away from the camp. A third member of our team, a corporal, saw what was happening and fired a few rounds as the lorry was driving away. Peter and I were heading back to our quarters when he found us. He told us what happened and we immediately got our group together and took off after the lorry. We left the corporal behind to get to the commanding officer. Jeeps are faster than lorries and we caught up about four kilometers down the road. We tailed her for about five kilometers when the lorry disappeared, vanishing into thin air. We continued slowly. It was very dark in the woods and we certainly did not know where we were. We approached a bend in the road and proceeded carefully. About fifty meters down the trail, we were showered with small arms fire. It was an ambush. The tailing jeep pulled alongside and we set up a perimeter. It was bad. We were pinned down and two of our men were already killed. There were two Bren guns and a couple of rifles in the Jeeps, as well as a few grenades. We returned fire as best we could and lobbed grenades at a German machine gun. Through the gunfight, we could see our lorry off to one side. Peter decided to make a dash for it to free the hostages and destroy the lorry, but he didn't get far. He caught one in the shoulder."

This is when Peter got his wound.

"Your father saved my life, Nicky, right there and then!" Peter interjected. "He crawled out to get me all whilst being shot at and then managed to get me back to the Jeep. He dressed my wound and handed me one of the Brens. 'My turn,' he said, grabbing a couple of grenades and a long rifle and crawling to the lorry. For a big man, your father moves very well, Nicky. He crept up on the two Germans by the lorry and knocked both of them out with his fists! Our two lads jumped out of the lorry in quick form and James handed one of the lads the long rifle. James then pulled the grenades from his pocket, tossed one into the lorry, and quickly crawled away. The explosion got Gerry's attention and your father threw the second grenade at the machine gun. Boom! The machine gun was finished. Your father then crawled back to the Jeep. There was smoke everywhere but Gerry's fire was almost gone. About thirty minutes later, we could see headlights behind us on the trail. We turned to make a stand, but they were our lads.

"We were rescued, the lads cleaned up what was left of the Germans, and took two prisoners, both of them in our uniforms! While the medic looked at me and some of the others, he noticed your father had a distinct limp and had difficulties walking. Turns out, he had several deep shrapnel wounds in his thigh. We were sent to a field hospital in France and soon back to London."

Peter continued, "An officer, a Major Hartwell from the Secret Service, visited us in London. He explained that our 'little mission' helped bring down a syndicate of German agents posing as our lads. When the Secret Service briefed General Montgomery, he believed that Operation Market Garden was not compromised and proceeded. 'Too late in the game,' he said. The Major and his adjunct presented your father and me with 'Distinguished Service Accommodations.' Major Hartwell then handed your father a sealed brown envelope. 'From General Montgomery's staff, Mr. Beverley,' he said. Your father opened the envelope and his expression changed from curious to amazement. He was to receive the MCS, Military Conduct Award! He tried to stand to salute the Major, but his dodgy leg wouldn't work. The Major received the salute and returned the honor. It was a very proud moment for us."

Nicollette's brain was working in overdrive. Her father, the man she loved and had trusted for her entire life, had just revealed a buried but important secret about himself. Not a deep, dark secret, but one of courage, purpose, and duty. *My father is a hero, like those names on the War Memorial in Brockwirth! And I never knew, no one knew! Why didn't he talk about it? Why carry this secret all these years? In addition, he and Peter already knew each other. Surely Peter would have made the connection with my last name. Why didn't he say something? What is going on?*

She took a deep breath, sighed, and placed her hand on her father's arm. Nothing needed to be said, it was all understood.

Not a Word

"Sit down and take a look at some of these old pictures of me and your co-worker, Nicky," her father said as she slid her seat nearer to him.

"Here is Peter standing with me and a few of the crew and another snap of me in my boxing kit with Peter holding my spit bucket."

Nicollette looked at the old grainy pictures. Her father was almost unrecognizable in his boxing gear. He was thinner and fitter and even had a head of hair. Peter, on the other hand, was easy to spot. Except for a bit of gray on his head and a few wrinkles, he looked virtually the same.

There was still a good stack of pictures to see between Peter's envelope and her father's box, but Nicollette noticed it was after seven. It was getting late and she and Peter were going into work tomorrow for the first time in a month.

"Even though this has been very interesting, to say the least, I want to remind you two that we all have to work tomorrow," Nicollette suggested after looking at her watch.

"Crikey, is it really past seven already?" Peter responded. "You're right, Nicky. I guess we'll have to do this again, eh James?"

James held out his hand to Peter and the two men shook hands. "It's a date then. But before we go, there is one last thing I want to show you, Nicollette, and I know Peter will remember this."

James then reached into the box and pulled out a brown envelope. He wiped the table in front of him using a paper napkin. Her father then carefully pulled a folded-up document from the envelope and gingerly laid it on top of a handkerchief, then very delicately unfolded it.

"Nicollette," he started.

Nicollette knew that what her father was about to say and what she was about to see were very important. Ever since she was a little girl, he would only refer to her as Nicollette when he was angry with her or when there was something serious to talk about.

"Nicollette, this is what Major Hartwell brought to me in the hospital thirty-seven years ago. I want you to read it."

Nicollette looked at the yellowed paper. The ink had faded, but the message was clear, her father had been awarded the Military Cross. The letter continued, "for gallantry during active operations against the enemy." In addition, her father was awarded the honor of having the initials MC at the end of his name. There would be a ceremony at a later date. The letter was signed by Major General Francis Wilfred deGuingand, Chief of Staff to Field Marshall Bernard Montgomery.

James handed the opened wooden box to his daughter. She could see the medal, a silver cross with a blue and white ribbon comfortably laying on a dark red velvet bed.

"I don't really know what to say, Dad, except it's beautiful and...I'm so very proud of you."

"Before we go, I'd like to share something with you as well, Nicky," Peter added, handing her another brown envelope.

Nicollette slowly opened it and pulled out an old typed letter with a weathered, yellowing newspaper clipping attached. She read the letter quietly.

"You were awarded an 'MiD', 'Mentioned in Despatches', for the same mission, Peter! Crikey!"

Nicollette meticulously unfolded the newspaper clipping to reveal both her father's and Peter's names listed in The London Gazette for being awarded their medals.

"Crikey you two!"

Peter looked at Nicollette and then back at James. "I'm glad we were able to get reacquainted. It's been a long time, in fact, too long. Almost forgotten in time. But then I saw Nicollette Beverley's name on the group's roster, it all started coming back. I thought it might just be a coincidence, but to be sure, I did a little snooping and my suspicions were right. You are James and Alice's daughter. So, I brought the photos and letters today, looking for the right opportunity. I hope I didn't spoil the day?"

"Nonsense," James replied. "We were good friends then and we are good friends now."

The two shook hands and Nicollette placed her hands on top. Nothing more needed to be said.

Nicollette and James assisted Peter to the car. As her father turned the car out of the car park and headed towards Cheltenham, Nicollette could not contain herself. "I went into the Pub with my father and my friend and walked out with two War Heroes! Blimey!"

"And a million questions, I bet," Peter added.

"And a million questions," she responded.

Outside her flat, talking to her father, she said, "This evening was very revealing, there is so much I want to find out. I have many questions. How about a quick cuppa, Dad?"

"Sure, but a quick one."

Nicollette put the pot to boil, poured the tea, and sat on the sofa next to her father. "Dad, why? Why after all these years, you didn't tell Mum about the medal or anyone else for that matter? That medal was earned and awarded to you for heroism. You could've put letters at the end of your name like a doctor. Weren't you proud of it? You're a hero, Dad."

"At first, I was humbled and honored to have been awarded the MC. I was just a young man from the tough side of London. There weren't many medal winners in my neighborhood. It's true that growing up, I learned to use my fists to take care of myself. I was a little guy among bigger mates, always being picked on. Then, when I was in secondary school, I grew bigger. There were some 'debts' I wanted to repay and after a few of my 'repayments,' I was suspended from school for a short while. Your grandfather was furious with me and my backside was very sore. One evening, the phone rang and a boxing coach called to invite me and your grandfather to a boxing club. The coach had heard about me from one of his students who attended my school and he wanted to see what I could do. At the club, I was given a used, smelly kit and some boxing gloves. The coach asked me into the ring. I had no training in formal fighting and quickly took a few punches from my opponent. When I gathered myself, I put my opponent on the mat with my right hand. The same for my next two opponents. The coach told me to get dressed while he and your grandfather had a chat. Next thing you know, I'm back at school and working out in the club. I became very good, Nicky, winning most of my fights. After one particularly tough bout, my opponent said fighting me was like fighting 'a beast' and that's how I got my nickname."

Her father paused and took a sip of tea.

"When I came out of school, I went into the army like most chaps. We saw what Gerry was doing to our city and country and all we could think about was getting a chance to get at him and give him what's what. We were excited to serve, but naive as to what lay ahead of us. During training, I did very well in hand-to-hand combat, shooting, and surprisingly Maths. I made many friends in camp, and found it quite easy.

"When I came out of the basic training, the Sergeant referred me to a 'New Section' for specialized work. In the new unit, I was taught about interrogation and hush hush work. The army created this new unit in response to Gerry's infiltration of our front lines. The enemy would put on our uniforms and become one of us. They would typically use an excuse about being lost or their unit being wiped out or something. Once Gerry was in the group, he would gather information and send it back to his superiors and we would be compromised.

"An idea to build a counter force to seek out the infiltrators was put forward and approved. We would go into an area and perform, and at the same time, mingle with the lads and locals to seek out any traitors. And this is how I ended up in a camp outside Paris.

"Now for the medal. Nicollette, I did what I did on that night because it was my job. I couldn't let one or any of our chaps just lay there wounded and die. And if we didn't get to that radio and stop the Germans, how many more of our lads would have met their fate. I didn't have time to think, only to act and those few minutes of my life, I had luck with me.

"The next morning, I was called into the commanding officer's tent. A major reviewed my details about the last evening's event while a corporal took notes. When I finished, the major told me that the operation was quite successful. He added they found what was left of the radio, including a second radio that was hidden and a case of British uniforms. He then very casually mentioned that the rescue group found eight dead Germans.

"After being dismissed, and while I was on my way to the field hospital to see Peter, a strange feeling came over me, one like I've never felt before. A numbness was quickly creeping over me. I had to sit down, it seemed my whole body was paralyzed. However, my brain was running amok with thoughts. I kept thinking about how easy it was for the major to talk about the number of dead Germans, almost like he was keeping score. The thought wouldn't clear my mind. These were *men* who died, not numbers. Maybe they had families as well. They were people, human beings, and the Major simply said we killed eight.

"And that is when it hit me, like a right hook squarely on my jaw. *I* killed them. I realized that all the training, all the motivation, everything we learned prepared us for this moment. Then the moment happens and your instincts take over, you don't think, you don't question, you do what needs to be done to live and survive. What they don't train you for is the moment after *that*, when you realize it was you who took the life of another human being. I did it, I killed. The thought wouldn't leave me. Nicollette, it's one thing to fight a man in the boxing ring, that is sport, but truly another to kill one."

James reached for Nicollette's hand.

"The medal was and still is a very humbling experience for me and I am truly honored by it, but it also is a reminder of what I did to earn it and how I felt on that bench thirty-seven years ago. I knew that if I wore it or talked about the medal or used the 'MC' initials after my name, people would ask questions. I would always be reminded of that moment, not so much the rescue of Peter or the smashing of the radios, but when I took another's life. War is a terrible companion, one that I chose to live without."

Nicollette squeezed her father's hand lovingly. He had open-ed up to her despite his British instinctual reserve. Position and regard are never easily obtained, but Nicollette knew her father had just given her both with the understanding that she was his daughter and he loved her dearly.

At the door, as he was saying goodbye, James said, "One last thing I want to tell you, Nicky. Peter Johnson was the fellow student that spoke to the boxing coach about me and.... I know if you are working with him, you are doing something serious and maybe dangerous. We'll talk about him later, I promise, but for now, please, please be careful."

Nicollette sat on her sofa, having a quiet moment before bed. She knew she could never talk about her position in the group, nor what she had done in the past. But, she also realized that her dad had a good idea there was something secretive, myste-rious, and perhaps dangerous in her job. There was also an un-derstanding of how similar she was to her father. Visions of the action, years ago, on the Lesser Tunb Island danced across her head. *Shoot the damn gun, Miss Beverley! Shoot the damn gun!*

She walked into her bedroom and opened the small drawer in her chest of drawers. Nicollette pulled out an old, wooden jewelery box her father had made for her when she was a little girl. She removed the small purse from inside and opened the top. There it was, wrapped in tan silk, the beautiful medal she was awarded by the Sheik in Oman. *For bravery in action. Bravery, what is bravery in this nasty business?*

Nicollette placed the medal under her pillow as she crawled into bed. Her hand reached for it as her head hit the pillow. *So much like my father. Like him, I also can't share my award with anyone. Maybe living with the secret, the memory, that's the bravest bit of all.*

The alarm sounded, giving no mercy to the quiet of the early morning.

The hot water brought her back to reality. *Such luxury, a hot shower.* The events of the last evening were rapidly being replaced by the idea of going in to work for the first time in over a month. She felt apprehension and excitement as she met up with Val and Peg for the walk to work.

"Where's Sarah?" Nicollette asked, not sure if she had been informed.

"Sarah's been posted to Argentina," Peg replied. "She's going to the embassy there for a year's assignment to work in communications. You just missed her, Nicky, she left last week."

It was a bright sunny morning. *Quite a difference between walking into work here and rolling out of bed onto a muddy floor and the stifling heat in Thailand.*

The three of them had a few laughs and even a few questions when Peg started talking about her date on Saturday night. Nicollette listened to Peg describing the details of the date, but her eyes drifted down to Peg's legs. It was a couple of years ago when Peg was rescued from the Persian Gulf. Nicollette thought about those anxious hours, waiting in the camp for any news about her missing friend. She remembered rushing to the pier to see Peg lying on a stretcher, barely conscious, her lower body covered with a blood-soaked towel. Then the helicopter arriving in the camp to take Peg to the HMS Sheffield for emergency treatment and Major Hartwell briefing the group later that day saying that Margaret was alive, in the recovery bay, in stable condition and would recover...but that she had lost her right leg above the knee and all of her left foot.

Peg was off work for nearly a year, but provisions were made for her to stay with the group. Her role changed. She could no longer be in the field, but instead, she would work as Major Hartwell and Major Blasingame's Administrative Assistant and Liaison. Peg took on the new position fervently and her physical abilities expanded as she became more comfortable with her artificial limbs. Now, as they walked to work, Peg was only using a walking stick. *And now she is dating! I'm so proud of her!*

Nicollette looked at the assignments board on the wall as she walked towards her desk. Her assignments were to monitor relatively quiet areas in South America. It felt a little strange to be back at her desk in the communications room. The quiet humming of the computers and the comfortable surroundings were in stark contrast to her experience in Thailand. She subconsciously touched her right thigh, searching for her weapon. *Silly me,* she thought, *no need for that here!*

Nicollette looked over her specific communications log and schedule. A small smile crossed her face when she saw Buenos Aires as a contact point. *Sarah is there!*

Nicollette knew full well neither of them could use their names across the communications lines, but she also knew that Sarah was very good at her job, concise, confident, and sure.

A slight tug on her shoulder brought Nicollette's attention from her screen.

"Nicky, may I sit with you for a tick?" Peg asked.

"Sure, it's good to see you, Peg. How are you?"

"Doing well, Nicky, but I had to see you. I just finished reading the transcripts of your briefing last week and...holy shite, girl!"

Peg paused for a moment. It was highly unusual for Peg to use such language and Nicollette could see the concern on her face and could feel her hand on hers as she continued. "Nicky, we've known each other since training and you are my friend for life. We've both been in some very serious situations, even life and death. Please, Nicky, please, please, please be careful and take care of yourself."

Nicollette touched Peg's artificial leg with her free hand. "You are a good friend Peg and I'm very happy we work together. And yes, I'll be careful. I promise."

"Am I interrupting something?" Peter's voice broke into the moment between Nicollette and Peg. "I was wondering if you two want to join me in the cafeteria for lunch."

"The Major wants the report finished today, so I'm pretty much here, but thank you anyways, Mr. Johnson," Peg replied as she gingerly stood from the chair and headed out of the room.

"I'll join you, Peter, I could use a bite."

The two of them found a table and Peter placed his crutches on the side. As they settled in, Nicollette asked if they could talk about last night.

"It was truly enlightening, Peter. There are so many questions I would like to ask you."

"I'll do my best," he answered as he took a bite from his sandwich, "but any questions about your father and me should be answered by him. All I can tell you is that your father is a good man and we were best mates for a while."

That reply took some of the wind out of "Nicollette's sail." She knew it was a polite, yet deflecting answer. *Maybe he doesn't want to talk about it or maybe he is hiding something.*

"Well, Peter, something you said last night is still with me. You mentioned that Major Hartwell brought you and my father the awards, any relation to our Major Hartwell?"

Nicollette wondered if she had surprised him with the question and he wasn't sure how to reply. She knew how private he kept his life, but maybe, just maybe, that door was about to be opened.

Peter's facial expression turned from pleasant to anxious, his face reddened and his eyebrows curled above his squinted eyes. Nicollette realized she may have hit a sore spot with that question and, seeing his physical response, quickly injected, "I'm sorry, Peter, maybe it's none of my business."

There was a pause. "I married his daughter. She's my wife. She's my wife, Nicky, and you must never tell anyone!"

What? When? How long? And why the secret?

She realized that not only had the door to Peter's private life opened, she was one of the only people to be allowed inside. Through a dry throat, Nicollette whispered back, "I won't say a thing, Peter, I promise. But why all the secrecy?"

"I'll keep it short. I thought you might put two and two together, I mean with me knowing your father and all, so when I mentioned Major Hartwell last night, I was hoping you wouldn't put the pieces right. I guess you are just too good at puzzle solving.

"It's a bit of a long story, Nicky, but simply put, Liz, I mean Elizabeth and I met by chance at an officer's club. She was a lieutenant. We fell in love and were married. In fact, James, your father, was my best man! Elizabeth had just finished her officer's course and was going to train for an Intelligence job. Her father arranged our move to Brize and later to Cheltenham. Liz and I, because of the nature of our work, decided to be very secretive about our lives, keeping our family surnames and living separate lives at work. We didn't want to be compromised in any way. You remember I mentioned a woman who comes into my home a couple of times a week?"

Peter took the last sip of his now cold tea.

"Well, she actually lives with me! Liz was upstairs when you came over last Saturday. I was going to tell you then, but I had to be sure that you were James's daughter first. So here we are, Nicky, not a word. Please, not a word!"

Back to Work

Carol's wedding was in the local church, followed by a reception at the posh Evesham Tennis Club. Nicollette still bore bitterness when it came to the members of the club, except for Carol, her family, and a very few other members. To her, the rich walked around with their noses up in the air when it came to working class families like Nicollette's. She felt uncomfortable whenever Carol would invite her to the club. Even more important, although it was almost five years ago, was the memory of the New Year's Eve assault on her by a rich club member and Peter's Ansley's friend, Garrett. Nicollette could feel a shiver across her body when she remembered the feeling of helplessness and what might have happened if her brother hadn't rescued her. That moment became a driving force in her life. *Never again! That feeling won't ever happen to me again!*

Nicollette bit her lip while finishing the last bit of makeup on her face. She never liked using cosmetics, preferring to be natural. *Makeup is what clowns use, but this is a wedding and one must make an effort,* she thought.

The dress flowed over her head and fell into place as she closed the snaps in the back and shifted the garment just slightly. She took a step back from the mirror to take in the whole picture and realized this was the first time she would be dressed up and in a large social gathering since she had joined British Intelligence. There hadn't been many opportunities the last few years to "go fancy" other than the rare "company do."

At the church, Nicollette was greeted by Carol's older brother and their mutual friend Ashley Tran. The three of them went to a room off to the side and Nicollette immediately spotted Garrett, standing in the corner talking to Carol's sister. As their eyes briefly met, a slow anger started to rise within her, making her want to pay him back.

She forcefully restrained that feeling. The gratification of giving Garrett a bloody nose or worse just wasn't worth it. *He has to face me as well,* she thought. *Maybe the guilt and shame, if he has any, will be enough payback.*

Nicollette was quite relieved when she learned that she was to be paired with Carol's brother to walk down the aisle. Their friend Ashley would have the "honor" of being with Garrett.

As the wedding party stood on the altar, Carol and her father slowly made their way towards them. *She's so beautiful in her wedding gown, so grown up,* Nicollette thought as visions of the two becoming friends at the Primary School playground danced across her mind.

Throughout the ceremony, Nicollette started to think about herself. Other than the rare flirtation at work or the Pub, she hadn't had a date in a long time, let alone have many single male friends. Her work had become her life and she was unsure about balancing much of anything else with that. *How could she honestly explain the sudden travel or any other details of her job? Who would want to date me? I can never be truthful about the "other me" and any type of commitment...well...*

A smile crossed Nicollette's face when Carol and Peter shared their first kiss as Mr. and Mrs. Ansley. Two of Nicollette's best mates from her "normal side" were married, leaving her only three close friends who were still single. Carol's brother reached for Nicollette's hand to escort her to the back of the church. As they were walking hand in hand, Nicollette's mind had a pleasant reset. It had been a long time since someone held her hand. *Is this something I want? Am I ready? Maybe, just maybe, there's someone for me. Patience, Nicky, enjoy the day, patience.*

After several requests, Nicollette found herself on the dance floor. A slight, accidental bump caused Nicollette to turn and see Garrett. This was the moment she had dreaded all day, standing face to face with the man who had attempted to rape her five years ago.

"Pardon me," Garrett stated in a condescending tone.

Nicollette had prepared for this moment, knowing full well her capabilities to enact revenge. She took a deep, calming breath and nodded her head in acknowledgement of the accidental bump.

As Garrett turned away, Nicollette grabbed his arm, gently forcing him to turn back and face her. In a calm and confident voice, she softly spoke, "I will never forget what you did and neither should you."

Garrett's face turned white as Nicollette squeezed his arm very tightly. *I could snap it with a simple move.* Only the voice of his dancing partner broke Nicollette's vice-like grip.

Nicollette turned towards her dancing partner.

"What was that all about?" he asked.

"Just a little history, " she responded, "a long time ago."

The phone woke her the next morning. Val was calling to invite her for a walk up Cleeve's Hill, just outside Cheltenham.

"It's a beautiful day and I bet you could use the air," she added.

Nicollette crawled out of bed despite her body's resistance. She looked in the mirror. Her hair was a mess and the cosmetics on her face looked more like a two-year-old had applied them. The dull drumming in her head reminded her she had too many glasses of champagne from the night before. She immediately got a hold of her senses when she spotted the Bridal Bouquet on her dresser and felt the garter just above her left knee. *It felt good to feel normal again. I really needed it!*

Val brought a lunch basket as she and Nicollette started their hike up Cleeve's Hill. The steep trail led to a beautiful view at the top. They found a clearing amongst the gorse, the long-stranded grass that flourished on the hillside, and had their lunch.

A panoramic view of Cheltenham stretched out before them, only blemished by the grouping of satellite towers off to the side. She remembered when she was a child, during one of the many family walks around Cleeve Hill, asking her father about such odd-looking structures and what they were for. He would respond with a smile, "So we can talk to space."

"Like Martians, Dad?"

"I guess, Nicky, maybe one day you will find out."

Now, years later, Nicollette understood what those towers were for. She smiled as she thought, *In a way, I guess I am talking to space.*

There were handout binders waiting on the conference table when Nicollette, Val, and Peg arrived for work Monday morning.

It was not uncommon to have a sheet or two at the morning briefing, but a prepared binder was a bit unusual. *Something important must be happening.*

Just before Major Hartwell opened the briefing, several additional people walked into the room. Nicollette was a little surprised to see Charles Thompson. *I thought he was away in South America.*

"Good morning. I trust everyone had a good weekend. There's a lot to get through this morning so please, everyone take a binder and we will get started."

Nicollette reached for two binders and handed one to Peg. The major introduced Mr. Paul Richards to the group, announcing he was an expert on Polish internal affairs. Mr. Richards asked for the binders to be opened and started to review some recent Polish history. On the first page, there was a standard issue map of Poland, but with several dozen different colored points identified throughout the country.

"You are all aware of the Polish group, Solidarity, and its leader, Lech Walesa."

There were several affirmative responses from the group.

"Solidarity has been gaining momentum in the last few months and the Communist regime is starting to get nervous. Prime Minister Wojciech Jaruzelski wants to crack down very hard on Solidarity and its leader, Lech Walesa. Jaruzelski, his government, and their Soviet benefactors believed the 'Solidarity movement' could become a large internal threat to the 'iron fisted' rule of the Polish communist government. If not stopped, and soon, it could spread throughout the Eastern Bloc."

Mr. Richards retrieved some papers from a stack in front of him.

"Now I know we've stated the obvious. We all know the Russians and their satellite countries, headed by their puppet governments, including Poland, would never allow any type of public dissent or unrest. It is also clear that dramatic actions to stop such activities are clearly on the table; witness 1956 Hungary and 1968 Czechoslovakia. The Polish, Soviet, and other communist regimes are watching this very closely because, as Solidarity gains in Poland, there have been sympathetic rumblings in Czechoslovakia, Hungary, and East Germany. Additionally, keep in mind that Poland shares a border with two of those countries and with the Soviet Union as well. Any questions so far?" The room was silent, but Nicollette knew everyone was thinking the same question in their minds. *How does this affect the UK and British Intelligence?*

It was nearly five years ago when, just out of training, she had her first mission. She was asked to participate in the communications, planning, and execution of an operation to eliminate a Bulgarian General. Bulgaria. *It seems like a long time ago. Bulgaria was and still is a satellite communist country. Not much has changed.*

The briefing continued with Mr. Richards talking about the importance of the Polish events to the UK.

"We have several areas of concern with the developments in Poland. I will talk about them briefly. First off, we have a small but very active Polish population in the UK of about 80,000, many of whom still have family ties in Poland. This is a vocal group and they have already voiced their support of Solidarity and against the Communists. Secondly, we do have some economic ties to Poland, albeit small, but nonetheless active. Thirdly, we have a history of support with the Poles. We were their allies in the second world war and today, we have significant assets inside Poland providing us and NATO valuable information. As I've said earlier, Poland is geographically central to the East European Bloc, a perfect spot for intelligence gathering. So you may ask, why all the interest now?"

Mr. Richards paused to put on a pair of glasses as he shared one of the papers with the group.

"I have here the latest intelligence from Warsaw. Our sources, very high up in the government I might add, have indicated that a severe and harsh crackdown by the Jaruzelski regime is imminent and that all suspected foreign agents will be arrested or worse. The regime believes that Solidarity would not survive without foreign help. Their intent is to eliminate all internal foreign influence and crush Solidarity. Our sources also have information about several very high-level meetings with the KGB and London is very worried about the safety of our assets. We would not like to lose our sources and be publicly humiliated to the world about our intelligence capabilities. That said, the prospects of a successful overthrow of the Polish Communist regime by Solidarity is very intriguing. London wants to walk a tightrope—support Solidarity and maintain ours and other Western assets, safe and secure. Here is a directive from the Ministry of Defence. The M.O.D. wants us to establish multiple lines of secure communications with our Polish assets and I quote, 'For every second of every minute, of every hour, of every day.' That is where you come in."

Mr. Richards sat back in his seat and Major Harwell resumed the briefing.

"Our group is going to merge with other communication and mission groups on this assignment. Each of those multi-colored dots on the Polish map represents an asset. Their importance and security levels are indicated by the color of the dot. Mr. Peter Johnson will spearhead the communications portion and review with you the new procedures and protocols as well as your schedule. Major Blasingame will be assisting the work on mission planning. Are there any questions? None? Good. Please follow Mr. Johnson into the communications room for further instructions. Thank you."

"This is very serious, ladies," Nicollette whispered to Val and Peg. "Looks like some long days ahead."

Lieutenant Blankin softly tapped Nicollette's and Val's shoulder. "The Major needs you two to stay."

Nicollette watched as the room emptied. Sergeant Durbin made sure the doors to the room were secure as Major Hartwell asked for the women to take a seat.

"We have another task," Major Hartwell started, "and this one smaller, but still very serious and important. Mr. Thompson will brief you."

Charles Thompson stayed seated as he started to speak; he preferred to be more casual with the smaller group. Charles was Nicollette's sponsor into the program five years ago and he frequently appeared to be behind the scenes of several of the group's missions. He had many responsibilities within the organization and always seemed to be traveling to some "hot spot" or performing other important work. As words started to flow from his mouth, Nicollette noticed that perhaps the position was starting to take a toll on him. His hair was thinning and threads of gray were interwoven amongst their darker brown partners. His face was starting to show weathering around his cheeks and eyes. *Perhaps it's just age, or maybe it's all the traveling and the dangerous situations he's had to endure,* Nicollette thought. *I wonder what I will look like twenty years from now...*

"In brief, as you are all well aware, we receive daily reports from our Embassy in Buenos Aires, Argentina. Recently, these reports have caused us increased concern. We know that over the last seven years, the civilian-military government has been waging a severe crackdown on so-called left-wing dissidents and government protesters. Our estimates are that as many as twenty-five thousand people have been killed or simply disappeared. In reality, this is no civilian government, but a military Junta headed by General Jorge Rafael Videla. They are ruthless and committed to eliminating any form of dissent or protest. The Junta have labelled this dirty war 'Operation Condor.' Over the last year, and despite fears of severe repercussions, there has been an uptick in civil strife and protests. These demonstrations have become not only more frequent, but much larger in scale and increasingly more violent. The protesters are motivated by many factors, but primarily by a failing economy and a very unpopular government. Fortunately, as of now, foreign companies, expats, and embassies have not been targeted by either side, but our staff in Buenos Aires are becoming very concerned with their safety. Our embassy is taking additional steps to ensure security. I will be leaving for Argentina tomorrow."

Major Hartwell continued. "Thank you, Mr. Thompson. I want to talk about where we are today. Like Mr. Thompson has said, Intelligence has reported several findings we are looking into. First, there have been multiple sightings of unflagged shipping vessels in the harbor of Buenos Aires. We are working on tracking the source or sources of these ships and their cargoes. Secondly, there has been stepped up activity at several Argentinian military installations, both Air Force and

Army. We are working to see if this is a reaction to the unrest or something more devious. Thirdly, we have received unconfirmable reports of increased Argentine Naval activity in the South Atlantic, off the east coast of Argentina and around the South Georgia and Sandwich Islands. Note that the Falklands are between South Georgia and the Argentine mainland. And finally, well-placed sources have heard whispers of the Junta planning some sort of action as a way to unite the country, to take the focus away from the conditions inside Argentina and ultimately strengthening the military Junta. Perhaps these events are coincidental, but we are continuing to monitor the situation. Our Embassies in Chile, Brazil, Paraguay, and Uruguay have all been placed on alert."

Major Hartwell looked at a stack of papers in front of her and continued.

"I have just returned from a sensitive meeting in London where the current state of affairs in Argentina was discussed at the highest levels. It is believed there are three outcomes to this situation. One, the dynamic doesn't change inside Argentina and all the peripheral activities are purely coincidental. Two, the Junta is going to amp up repression of the protestors and work on crushing any dissent by using extraordinary force. We think it's possible the unidentified ships in Buenos Aires could be secretly bringing in supplies and equipment in preparation for any worldwide condemnation, including embargoes or sanctions, in response to the severe Junta crackdown. Third, and highly speculative, the possibility of an Argentine military foray into a neighboring country. London has looked at these possibilities and concluded, at least for now, that military action is less likely. Chile is protected by the Andes mountains and Brazil is far too strong. This leaves the weaker countries of Uruguay and Paraguay. Of the two, Paraguay is the most likely. It is landlocked and very weak. It is the headwaters of the Parana River, a vital transportation avenue in this area of South America, making it potentially a reward for an invasion. However, Intelligence believes Argentine military action against any land neighbor would be very expensive for Argentina, both domestically and internationally. Finally, there is the Falklands. Here is where it gets a bit tricky. Historically, Argentina has claimed the Falkland Islands as their own, referring to them as the Malvinas. The Islands are only about three hundred miles away from the Argentine mainland and are well within reach of Argentine air power. The Falklands are defended by about thirty Royal Marines on the east Island, all based around Port Stanley. The west island is undefended. In the event of an invasion, it is estimated it would take a week to assemble and reinforce our forces into enough strength for any clash with the Argentines. There are about seventeen hundred people living on the east island and about three hundred on the west island. There are about two hundred times more sheep than people in the Falklands."

Major Hartwell paused for a breath. "Here is where it gets interesting. London thinks an invasion of the Falklands is less likely, but still possible. It would be a risky military action for Argentina and politically, this situation could be very tricky. Argentina could receive support internationally by claiming to just be recapturing its own territory from a former colonial power—England. We also need to be aware that Argentina has a strong relationship with the United States and we all know about our special relationship with America. The unanswered question is how the Americans would react to an invasion of one ally's territory from another ally.

"On the surface, London feels an invasion of the Falklands would be too great of a risk for the Junta. The results could lead to political and international suicide. Communications between Washington and London are already taking place and the Ministry of Defence believes the Americans will be very persuasive in halting the Argentines from military action anywhere. The final opinion from the meetings in London is that despite the Falklands' military vulnerability, there is just not enough strategic and economic value for the risk of an invasion. Notwithstanding the potential consequences of international condemnation. Therefore, they believe an invasion is not likely. However, all is not as it seems either.

"The Ministry still wants very quiet preparations to proceed just in case. These preparations must be very secretive. We don't want to incite and justify an Argentine reaction. We are proceeding with naval and air plannings domestically, however, we cannot be seen as 'poking the bees' nest,' so any visible changes in our security forces stationed on the Islands is off the table. This is where our group comes into action. Miss Davies and Miss Beverley, you are going to have a warm winter."

"Star Gazer"

The room was silent. Nicollette's mind was in full gear. *What does the Major mean by a warm winter? Where am I going and for how long? The Major's briefing was all about Argentina. Am I going to Argentina?*

A well-dressed man in a three-piece pinstripe suit walked to the front of the table and found a seat next to Major Hartwell. Val asked if Peg or Nicollette knew who the man was. Nicollette shook her head.

"He must have snuck in," Peg said. "I didn't notice him before."

"Let me introduce Vice Admiral Sir Harold Stanley, ACNS, Special Operations for Naval Intelligence," Major Hartwell announced.

"He has traveled from London to personally review the plans of a special mission for group 226/157, code named 'Operation Star Gazer.'"

Peg whispered, "I've heard of him! He's the Assistant Chief of the Naval Staff. He's damn important!"

A leather-bound binder was passed over Nicollette's shoulder and laid in front of her. Same for Val, Peg, and everyone sitting at the table. It was a jet-black leather binder with the Royal Navy seal embossed in the front, quite a contrast to the basic one used for the briefing on Poland.

The Vice Admiral nodded towards his adjutant to proceed.

Bloody hell, this must be a serious mission. The bigwigs are here to personally brief us. Surely there are other assets. Why us?

"As Major Hartwell mentioned, we are in the process of making preparations for any and all possibilities regarding the Falklands. We've already started to prepare militarily, albeit very slowly, so as not to raise any suspicions. Also, we cannot reinforce our small garrison of Royal Marines at Port Stanley on the eastern Falkland island either. We don't know who is watching and we don't want to provoke any retaliation from the Argentines."

The Adjutant paused and asked for everyone to open their binders. Inside, Nicollette unfolded a highly detailed, double page map of both the eastern and western Falkland Islands. Her eyes immediately were drawn to the large red circle around Port Stanley, "Davies" in green lettering just above the circle. She turned her attention to the Western Falklands and a cold shiver rolled across her body. There it was, in the southwest corner of the island, a small gold dot with the name "Beverley" next to it. *Val and I are going to the Falklands!*

"This is our current situation around the Falklands," the adjutant continued. "Looking at your maps, the two dark blue dots in the South Atlantic represent current submarine deployments and the gray dot is the HMS Endurance, an Ice Patrol Ship, making the rounds near St. George Island. As thin as we are in the area and to make matters worse, we don't have 'eyes or ears' on the West Falkland Island. Our only source of intelligence from the Falklands is in Port Stanley. Thirty Royal Marines cannot keep a close eye on the hundreds of miles of coastline. We need a way to gather intelligence from that area without raising any eyebrows. Recently, the very limited surveillance we do have in the area has shown some unusual activity near Weddell Island, on the west coast of the western Island. Several large ships have been spotted traveling very close to the island, leaving the standard shipping lanes by as much as four hundred kilometers. Plus, there has been a noticeable uptick of smaller vessels in the area. Typically these are fishing and whaling boats, but we need to know for certain about this increase in activity. Is this normal or is there some alternative reason? Should we be concerned?"

The adjutant gathered his papers and walked to where he had been standing against the back wall. Sir Harold Stanley looked directly at Nicollette, Val, and Peg. Nicollette could feel his hard stare. She knew by his title and position that he was a man of no nonsense, everything was yes or no and black and white. There was no room for maybes or gray areas and least of all failure. She could tell by his demeanor that he was tough and strict. His jutting jaw and erect posture revealed the Vice Admiral was strong and confident. And now this Senior Naval Intelligence Officer, a man who worked directly with the Minister of Defence and even the Prime Minister, was looking at her for a special mission.

Nicollette would be challenged, no matter how serious or dangerous the mission, but she also realized, if she were to fail, the consequences to her career, the group, assets on the Island, and potentially her life could be devastating.

In a deep voice and with perfect inflection, Vice Admiral Sir Harold Stanley asked the group to turn to page four of the binder. The heading was Falklands Reconnaissance, Operation Stargazer.

Sir Harold elaborated the details of the mission. The room was quiet, absolutely still, every ear acutely tuned to the Vice Admiral's voice.

"As you've heard, we have a need for 'on the ground' intelligence on the West Falklands Island. Understanding the sensitivity and politics of the region, this has to be an 'under the radar' operation. My group has come up with a plan of operation that is simple, discreet, and, by all accounts, has a good chance of success. Please turn to page eight."

Nicollette heard the words, "a good chance." *What does he mean, "a good chance"? How can he even hint at the possibility of failure! Am I just fodder to something even bigger? It's me who's life could be on the line! Me!*

On page eight, there was a large picture of an older couple

and a ranch style home. There were smaller pictures of sheep in a field and of a small village store.

"I want to present some background of our mission by introducing you to Mr. Geoffrey Clarke and his wife, Joanne. Mr. Clarke was a frontline decoder with the 6th Airborne Division in Northern Europe during the War. His small group would be parachuted into enemy territory ahead of an advance. In March of 1945, we were ready to march into Northern Germany and expedite the end of the war. Our air surveillance picked up a large German force south of Hamburg. This area was still under German control and the City of Hamburg, what was left of it, was well defended on the ground. On 9 April 1945, Captain Clarke and his group were dropped approximately twenty-five kilometers outside of Hamburg to report on German strength and reconnoiter a clearer route of advance. Captain Clarke's team landed safely and headed south. He reported there was a large amount of activity at a railhead around the small town of Bergen. His group sent back vital information and a secure route of advance was established. Captain Clarke's group was instructed to stay in the area and continue to report. On 14 April, Captain Clarke's group was reunited with the 11th Armoured Division as they advanced. On 15 April, the 11th discovered and liberated the Bergen-Belson concentration camp. Captain Clarke would be permanently affected by what he witnessed that day. He was so moved by the experience that he volunteered to stay on at the camp to assist the liberation and relief process.

"After the war, he stayed on in Army Intelligence, but became very quiet and withdrawn. He became unreliable at work and wanted to resign his commission. The Army stepped in and granted him disability retirement. His wife would say that Geoffrey, the man who loved being with people, the life of the party, always telling a joke or two, suddenly wanted nothing to do with anyone. He could never get past the experience of what he witnessed at the Bergen-Belsen Concentration Camp. Joanne recalled the nightmares, the restlessness, and screams of his sleepless nights. He would tell her he just couldn't get past the question of how any human being could do something so horrible as he witnessed at Bergen-Belson. 'It became unbearable,' she stated, 'so I convinced him to get help.'

"An Army doctor noted that Captain Clarke's situation was worse than 'Army Fatigue' and prescribed a 'quiet change in scenery.' In 1948, he and Joanne left England and moved to the Falklands. They bought a small abandoned farm near Port Stevens on the West Island. Geoffrey and Joanne raised sheep and ran a small general store. The quiet life seemed to help him regain a bit of normalcy in his life. The couple had no children and used local labor to help with the farm. Sadly, Geoffrey Clarke died about five years ago. Joanne is currently in England receiving treatment for cancer. Now here's our connection, path, and mission."

"Whilst serving in post-war Intelligence, Geoffrey Clarke worked with a junior analyst, Mr. Peter Johnson. Given Mr. Clarke's condition, Mr. Johnson was the nearest thing to being a friend to both him and his wife. In fact, it was Mr. Johnson who found the army doctor for Geoffrey Clarke. They remained connected all these years, with letters and holiday cards and the like. Now here is our path. Joanne had an estranged married sister living in London when the Clarkes left England in 1948. That sister had a daughter, an only child, Linda, born in 1955. Both of Linda's parents died three years ago in a car accident. Linda is our key, she is the niece of Geoffrey and Joanne. Please turn to page ten."

Nicollette turned the page as instructed and nearly jumped in reaction to what she saw. On the page were two black and white photographs, mounted side by side, of two young women. The two women looked to be about the same build and height and looked similar enough as to 'tick by' any passing scrutiny. Only the difference in hair styles was the most easily recognizable distinction. *Oh my God! The picture on the right is me! That other woman could be my sister or even my double! Oh my God! What is going on here?!*

The Vice Admiral placed his left hand on his binder, raised his right hand, and pointed at her.

"You, Miss Beverley, will become Linda Crowther, the niece of Joanne Clarke, and most importantly, the 'Star Gazer.'"

There was a deafening silence in the room. All the eyes around the conference table watched Nicollette, carefully. She went to swallow, but her mouth felt like it was full of cotton wool. The silence was finally broken when Sir Harold asked if Nicollette and Val understood what he just talked about. All Nicollette could do was nod affirmatively.

"Splendid, Miss Beverley and Miss Davies," the Vice Admiral announced. "Major Hartwell will review the particulars with you. I must return to London but my office will remain in contact."

Everyone rose as Vice Admiral Sir Harold Stanley stood. He thanked the group for their attention. As he was leaving, he first offered his hand to Nicollette and then to Val while whispering, "I'm confident in the two of you. We're depending on you. Best of luck." And then he was gone, exiting the room as surreptitiously as he had entered.

Cease to Exist

Major Hartwell called for a break. A hand on Nicollette's shoulder brought her partially back to reality.

"You look like you could use a cup of tea, Nicky."

Nicollette turned to Charles as a cart with tea and food was wheeled into the room.

"Major Hartwell's orders, we're all to eat together. A working lunch, she called it."

She took her seat at the table as Charles brought her a lunch plate and a hot cup of tea. The hot liquid made short work of the dry wool in her mouth. Although she wasn't hungry, a couple of bites from the roast beef sandwich seemed to energize her. *Perhaps it's the hot mustard.* She glanced at Val hungrily enjoying her lunch. *She'll be coming to the Falklands with me. I wonder what her role is going to be?*

The door to the conference room was opened to allow Peter Johnson and a few other civilians into the room. Nicollette was glad to see her friend and understood his importance to the assignment. His friendship with the Clarkes would play a vital role in convincing Joanne to participate in the ruse.

Lieutenant Blankin asked everyone to find a seat. Nicollette realized she and Val hadn't spoken since the beginning of the briefing. The two of them had worked together on nearly every mission and had built a special friendship. They could trust and depend on one another. It was very reassuring to each of them to have such a co-worker and friend, especially in this line of work.

"The Vice Admiral has asked me to present a more detailed overview of 'Operation Stargazer'," Major Hartwell announced. "Please turn to page twelve of your binder. There are lots of gears to this machine and for this mission to work, all of them have to be in sync. There are five spokes to the communications wheel. The center of this wheel is Miss Valerie Davies. Miss Davies will be stationed at Port Stanley and will be joining Sir Rex Hunt, the British Governor of the Falklands, as a member of his staff. Sir Rex has been briefed and is the only one in the Falklands, other than the participants, who knows about the mission. Miss Davies' cover title is Administrator of External Communications. Miss Davies' mission will be to act as the relay operator in the Falklands, sending and receiving coded information. She will be supplied with a specific coding manual based on the recipient of her information. Mr. Charles Thompson will be heading to Buenos Aires to work with our analyst already in place there, Miss Sarah Green. He will be available to handle any immediate need regarding security and safety of our mission. Peter Johnson will head up the communications group here in Cheltenham. We will conduct daily briefings to review any and all information pertaining to our mission. There could be Naval, Royal Marine, and others represented at our meetings. Link number four is the Vice Admiral's office. Sir Harold wants to be informed and briefed every day. He is ultimately in command and responsible for this mission. The final and the most important spoke of this wheel is Miss Nicollette Beverley, aka Linda Crowther, aka the 'Star Gazer.'"

Despite the pressure being levied on her, Nicollette started to feel more confident. *They chose me for this mission. Me! Of all the other agents, male or female, they chose me, Nicollette Beverley. They must have a great deal of confidence in me. I will not let them or myself down! No matter what, I, here and now, promise this to myself.*

The Major asked Lieutenant Blankin to proceed with details pertaining to Nicollette.

"Miss Beverley will be positioned at the Clarkes' ranch, located in the southwest corner of the West Falkland Island, about five kilometers from Port Stephens. Miss Beverley will be posing as Linda Crowther, Joanne Clarke's niece. Miss Crowther is a doctoral candidate working on her dissertation about climate change and its effect on the environment. She is currently enrolled at the Imperial College of London. Miss Beverley's cover role as Miss Crowther has three advantages. First, Joanne Clarke is suffering from cancer and the small community on the West Island could easily believe her niece from the UK would be coming to assist on the ranch. Secondly, by posing as a science academic, it would be entirely understandable for Linda to have specialized instruments for her research. This makes it less suspicious for the amount of equipment Miss Beverley, I mean Miss Crowther, brings to the ranch. Her field of study should also defer any questions from anyone who sees her in unusual places or times around the island. Finally and by pure chance, Miss Beverley and Miss Crowther look similar and could 'quick glance' pass for each other in the very, very rare chance of any recognition. These factors combined with the small local population should allow our 'Star Gazer' unbridled freedom and easy access to move about the island. Two additional points, first, Mr. Johnson has visited Mrs. Joanne Clarke. She was given a very general briefing by him and has agreed to this arrangement. She understands Miss Beverley is posing as her niece for 'something about the government and academic studies.' But ultimately, according to Mr. Johnson, Mrs. Clarke wasn't very concerned about Miss Beverley's job or the use of a false identity. She realizes whatever the reason is, it must be very important. Ultimately, according to Mr. Johnson, Mrs. Clarke just relished the idea of having some company; fancy that."

With that last comment, there were grins and a few muted smirks. Nicollette started to imagine herself on some 'spit of land' in the middle of nowhere, providing company to someone she didn't even know, all whilst being alert and focused on a very critical assignment. She hoped Peter made it clear to Mrs Clarke that this was not going to be a rest holiday, sharing tea and playing cards with some senior. She was the center of an operation that could have international ramifications. *An interesting dichotomy!*

"Point two. The Clarkes have had very little contact with their niece over the years. To our knowledge, they have never met or spoken, just the odd letter and holiday card by all accounts. These factors, combined together, should give Miss Beverley and the mission a very high likelihood of success."

Major Hartwell concluded the briefing by announcing that each section of the mission would be individually briefed during the coming days and that Sir Harold wanted Star Gazer fully operational by 7 January 1982. "And in his words, 'no excuses'!"

Major Hartwell stood from her chair.

"A schedule of operational preparations and briefings will be distributed later today." The Major paused and looked around the table. "I don't need to remind you of the seriousness of this assignment. Despite the low probabilities of any hostilities, our group needs to be ready and prepared for any and all eventualities."

Major Hartwell leaned forward and continued looking at the group around her. She slapped her hand on the table while confidently expressing, "And we damn well shall be!"

The briefing was adjourned and a reminder was given that there was still other work that needed attention. Nicollette glanced at the clock. It was past three. She needed a stretch and a break before heading back to the communications room and finishing the day.

Lieutenant Blankin stopped her as she was leaving the room. "The Major wants you in her office when you return. Please be quick about it, Nicollette."

Nicollette knocked quietly on Major Hartwell's office. Inside were Peg, Val, and Lieutenant Blankin. Nicollette was surprised to see Charles Thompson, Peter Johnson, and Sir Harold's adjunct. Major Hartwell introduced the adjunct as Captain Cyril Morley and explained his presence.

"Captain Morley will be rotating between here and London for the duration of the operation. He will be attending all pertinent activities regarding the mission and function as the direct liaison between Group 226/157 and the Vice Admiral. And now for you, Linda."

"Yes ma'am," Nicollette responded quietly.

"Well done, Miss Beverley, you're going to have to get used to living as Linda Crowther, because the second your feet hit the ground in Port Stanley, Nicollette Beverley ceases to exist."

That last comment from the Major brought a chill up Nicollette's spine as the reality firmly set in. *Cease to exist.*

"Let's review your plan," the Major continued. "You will have five weeks of training. When you are finished, you will know the terrain of the West Falklands and you will understand how to operate and maintain sophisticated communication devices. The training will include how to send and receive photo images, the use of infra-red cameras as well as telescoping equipment. Linda Crowther is an academic working on climate change, so you will be given enough background information to pass as such. Remember, there is no need for any complicated answers to any questions about what you are doing. No need to risk exposure. Most people wouldn't even know what climate change is anyways. We will review the pertinent information about Linda Crowther's life and the relationship you have with your Aunt Joanne."

Lieutenant Blankin handed out a double-sided single sheet of paper containing the biography of Linda Crowther. The information was rather routine: birthday, parental information, addresses and education. She noticed that Linda had only a few friends and was strictly single. At the bottom of the second page, Nicollette saw that Linda was working for a research organization studying climate change and was currently based in Thule, Greenland. She would be traveling around the North Pole doing research for the next twelve months.

"As you can see, Miss Beverley," Major Hartwell continued, "you are about as far apart from the real Linda Crowther as you can get. She is at the North Pole, probably feeling very cold, whilst you will be enjoying a warm winter in the South Atlantic."

A slight grin crossed the Major's face with that last remark. Major Hartwell very rarely showed any outward emotion when talking about an assignment or a mission. Typically, she was all business, but somehow, this slight grin from the Major, this simple sign of emotion, caused a warm, calming feeling to rise within Nicollette, giving her a sense of reassurance and confidence with the task at hand.

"Nicollette," the Major resumed, "as Captain Morely will attest, Sir Harold's office has gone through a great deal of time in creating, planning, and organizing 'Star Gazer.' The mission is critical. When Sir Harold's office contacted Group 226/157 and described the operation to Major Blasingame, Lieutenant Blankin, Charles Thompson and myself, we knew you were the one to handle the assignment. Your name was offered to Sir Harold and he personally approved our choice. Rest assured, Miss Beverley, you will have a great team with you. The 'wheel spokes' in the operation are people you know and can depend on. We have the utmost confidence in you and the team to achieve success. Does anyone else have anything to add?"

Peter Johnson reminded the Major about the meeting tomorrow.

"Thank you, please continue, Mr. Johnson."

"Tomorrow, Nicollette, you, Major Hartwell, and I have a lunch date with Mrs. Clarke. We thought it might be wise for you two to meet and get to know each other a bit before you move in. I will contact Joanne, I mean Mrs. Clarke, tomorrow to make sure she is feeling well enough to go out. I might also add that even though this is work related, I want you to dress casual, jeans preferably. We want Mrs Clarke not to feel intimidated or uncomfortable by any formalities. After all, you might be her houseguest for up to a year, so she should see you tomorrow as she would see you in the Falklands, don't you think?"

All Nicollette could do was nod, her mind too busy latching on to the words "up to a year." It was the first mention of the duration of the mission that was brought up in the briefings. *A year! I could be away for a year! What about my family? My friends! Me!*

Even the Wellies

This must be what it feels like when waiting for a blind date to arrive, Nicollette thought. *Here I am waiting to meet the woman whose house I will be staying in for up to a whole year and I know very little about her. What if she doesn't like me or asks too many questions?*

She took a deep breath, trying to shake off the nervousness as they waited for Peter and Joanne Clarke to arrive at the restaurant. Major Hartwell had asked Val to join them at this lunch meeting for two reasons. First, in the off chance that Val would visit Nicollette at Joanne Clark's ranch and secondly, to offer Nicollette a bit of stability and reassurance in meeting her future "house mum."

Val also knew that this was a big step and unlike any assignment the two had been on before. The Major had sensed the collective tension of the two young women when Nicollette and Val first sat in the car. She tried to offer small talk during the ride to London by passing along some stories and even a few dated jokes. It was natural for them to be nervous.

Peter arrived with Mrs. Clarke. Nicollette, Val, and the Major all stood to greet her as they introduced themselves and exchanged pleasantries. She was a stout, firmly built woman, a little shorter than Nicollette. She was very pale and her facial features and skin were visibly weathered. *Probably from the years living in the Falklands and her treatments here.* She guessed Mrs. Clarke's age was late fifties to early sixties, a bit older than her father and Peter. It was easy to see the cancer treatments were also having an effect on her mobility as Peter gingerly helped her to the seat next to Nicollette.

Mrs. Clarke started the table conversation after drinks were ordered. "So you are Nicollette Beverley or should I say Linda Crowther, my niece? Please tell me a little bit about yourself."

"Well, I'm working on my doctorate at London's Imperial College. I am researching the effects of climate change on local weather and environments for my dissertation and I can't wait to get started in the Falklands. Between the Island's proximity to Antarctica and the local biosphere, the Falklands provides brilliant conditions to do my research. And I want to say thank you, Auntie, for the opportunity and inviting me into your home. I hope I won't be any bother."

Nicollette was pleased she had forced herself to review some of the information the Major provided her in preparation for today's lunch. "It might come in handy tomorrow," the Major stated as she handed Nicollette a folder when they both left the conference room yesterday.

"No bother at all, but all that study stuff is all well and good for Linda, but I want to know about who you are, my dear," Mrs. Clarke replied.

A slight uneasy feeling crossed through her body as she wondered if Mrs. Clarke was genuinely interested in her or merely testing for a response. She realized she had to be very careful with the conversation. She had to appear genuine but not too forthcoming with unnecessary personal or professional information. *Just enough to answer, but not enough to create more questions.*

"Well, Mrs. Clarke," Nicollette smiled. "You know my name is Nicollette Beverley and I'm from a small village called Brockwirth. I attended the local schools and played club field hockey. My team won the Midlands championship. My parents still live there and I have an older brother who works overseas. Pretty dull stuff, I'm afraid."

Joanne Clarke smiled back at Nicollette. "Come, come, my girl. Do you have any hobbies? Special interests? Boyfriends?"

Nicollette hadn't prepared in advance to answer this type of inquiry; she'd just have to wing it.

"I'm sorry Mrs. Clarke, no hobbies that stand out although I like to travel and as it is, I haven't a boyfriend at the moment."

"Well, I do hope you like animals because I have four dogs and lots of sheep on the ranch. And, Linda, you can call me Jo."

"Thank you, Jo, and I do like dogs."

It was the moment, the click, that connection was made. Nicollette had passed the test and was in with Mrs. Clarke. First name basis after twenty minutes. *She called me Linda and I can call her Jo!* Nicollette could sense a collective sigh of relief from Major Hartwell, Val, and Peter Johnson. The last hurdle, Mrs. Clarke's final acceptance, was out of the way. The operation was a go.

During the ride back to Cheltenham, some doubting thoughts in the back of her mind made Nicollette feel a little uneasy about the lunch with Jo. *Did our connection fall into place too easily? This woman is allowing a complete stranger into her home to do some kind of private work for the government after just a few questions about boyfriends and dogs? Am I just overthinking this? Relax, Nicky!*

Nicollette's training started just after the next morning's briefing. In Major Hartwell's office, Nicollette was given a schedule and timeline for the next six weeks. She was going to be very busy training. As she was getting up to leave, the Major casually announced that Nicollette's cover was still being processed and that everything should be in place in the next few days.

A little hammer in Nicollette's head started to pound out the words: cover, a year, twelve months, and three hundred sixty-five days. Visions of her friends, Brockwirth, her family, and her outside life flashed across her eyes in a relentless parade. She found herself in the women's room, splashing cold water on her face. *A time frame of a year is easier to talk about in words, but much harder to do in practice!*

The first weekend in December was circled in Nicollette's diary. This was the time when Nicollette would join her parents in Brockwirth to start the family Christmas preparations, a tradition that began when she first moved into her own flat. There would be the usual activities like cleaning and decorating the house. Her mum would start the baking and her father would make a large batch of his Brockwirth Brew. Saturday night was the holiday party at the Cricket Club and Sunday was a walk down the village followed by a traditional Sunday lunch with the extended family. It was a weekend she looked forward to every year and although it was for only a couple of days, she would be able to leave work behind and completely relax in the safety, security, and love of her parents' home.

This time might be different, Nicollette thought as she entered the cab for the ride to Brockwirth. *I've got to tell my parents that I may be gone for as much as a year!*

"Yo hoo, I'm home!" Nicollette announced as she walked in the front door.

The smell of something in the oven greeted her, a giveaway that her mum had already started the baking.

"In the kitchen, Nicky," her mum responded. "I'll put the kettle on."

Nicollette's mum was still wearing that same old holiday apron she wore every year. A sudden feeling of guilt crossed her mind as Nicollette watched her mum baking. She is such a loving person. *I feel so bad that I keep her oblivious and totally unaware of what I do and what I've done.*

"I love you, Mum," Nicollette announced as she poured the tea.

"I love you too, Nicky." Her mum smiled back.

Over fish and chips later, her father asked about work.

"Well, work is as busy. End of the year stuff and organizing for next year. Speaking of planning, I do have some news and it's rather important." Nicollette put her fork down and looked at her parents. "My boss has me going to America! The Embassy in Washington D.C.!"

A big smile crossed her mum's face. "That's wonderful, Nicky!"

Her father's response wasn't as excited, but seemingly happy just the same. "Good news, Nicky! Tell us all about it."

Major Hartwell had thoroughly reviewed Nicollette's cover with her. Her pretence was she would be heading to the Embassy in Washington, D.C. at the beginning of the year. She would be filling in for an administrator in the local affairs office who would be away on maternity leave. Nicollette explained to her parents that the Embassy reached out to her group to provide someone with experience with visas, certificates, and the like.

"They also wanted someone single," Nicollette added. "Who knows, maybe I'll meet an American. Chance be a fine thing!"

Later that night, after her mum had gone off to bed, her father poured a brandy for Nicollette and himself.

"Nicky, I'm excited for you to go to the States, but I'm concerned because of who you work for. If I may, and you might not be able to answer me, I would like to ask you some questions to set my mind at ease."

Despite his calm demeanor, there was concern in his expression.

"I'll try to answer as best I can. What's on your mind?"

"Is Peter going with you?"

At first, Nicollette thought this to be a peculiar question, then she realized her father knew of Peter's background. *I guess he thinks that if Peter isn't with me, the assignment isn't dangerous.*

"No Dad, he is not coming with me."

"Is your friend Valerie going with you?"

"No, she isn't coming with me either. I'm the only one going to Washington." *I hate stretching the truth to my father. She isn't going to America with me, but she is going to the Falklands with me. Maybe he feels that if Val is along with me, there would be two of us to face any challenges.*

James grinned as he asked another question. "How do you really feel about your assignment, Nicky?"

"Actually, I'm pretty excited to go to the Embassy in Washington. I know I will be busy and challenged, but it could be fun."

"Just be safe and keep your head…and do a good job."

The afternoon before Christmas Eve, there was a planned gathering of Group 226/157 in a large conference room. There was a sign at the entrance to the room; Please Leave Work Outside.

Majors Hartwell and Blasingame greeted each member as they entered the festive room. There was a small bar and plenty of food. Holiday music was playing in the background.

"This is perfect," Nicollette said to Val as they tapped their beer bottles together. "We sure deserve this after all the work we've put in."

Major Hartwell walked over to the two women.

"Enjoying yourselves?"

"Yes ma'am."

"I know what the sign says at the door, but I need to tell you two that I want you back here the day after Boxing Day."

Nicollette and Val's expressions gave away their disappointment with the Major's announcement.

The Major quickly added, "Don't be so glum, we are only going shopping! You two are going away for a while and we want to make sure you are properly supplied." The Major offered up her glass to Nicollette and Val. "Cheers and happy holidays!"

It was dark when Nicollette arrived in Brockwirth later that evening. After getting settled in, Nicollette was able to sneak away for a late walk up to Brockwirth Tower. Sitting on her favorite bench and looking down on the village, she could see that Brockwirth was lit up and shining. *A beacon to the Cotswolds of the beauty of Christmas,* she thought.

Nicollette could sense that this was no ordinary 'shopping trip' when Major Hartwell escorted her and Val to a waiting car two days later. Inside the vehicle, the Major announced they were headed to London and handed each of them a list.

"And before you ask why London, let me answer by saying we wouldn't want to run into anyone we know, now would we?"

First stop was a high-end outdoorsy type store. Nicollette and Val tried on workman hiking boots. The three of them had a laugh when Nicollette put on a pair of over the calf boots.

"I look a right Wally in these Wellies!" she exclaimed.

"You'll be glad of them with all those sheep about," Major Hartwell responded.

It was late when the driver stopped in front of their building. The Major and the driver helped Val and Nicollette with their abundant packages. First into Val's then Nicollette's. Major Hartwell gave instructions. "All of the clothing purchased today must be washed before being packed and even the shoes must be worn as well."

"Even the Wellies, ma'am?"

"Yes, even the Wellies, Miss Beverley."

New Year's Eve was bittersweet for Nicollette. There was the joy of spending the time with her parents and friends conflicting with the realization that this might be the last time she would be in Brockwirth for some time. The party at the Cricket Club was the same as it always was and Nicollette enjoyed every minute of it. The reminder about what happened to her six years ago just outside the club had become blurred and foggy, partly because of the alcohol and partly because she understood that she was different now. Her life had changed dramatically from innocent village girl to confident, strong, and experienced agent in British Intelligence.

The clock struck midnight. Nicollette looked around to see couples embracing with a New Year's kiss. A feeling of being alone suddenly flashed across her as she hugged her parents. She started to think, albeit briefly, about that portion of her life that was missing. *My work has been and still is my priority, but it would be nice to have somebody. Maybe, just maybe.*

For Nicollette, Monday the fourth of January started before dawn. A last-minute look around her flat and check of her papers, then an early drive to Heathrow and the flight to Miami, Florida. There she would board a flight to Buenos Aires and connect to Port Stanley in the Falklands, arriving there late afternoon on Tuesday. Val, Peter, and Charles Thompson had left earlier on the second. They would be traveling on a Naval vessel and transported by helicopter to Moody Brook Barracks, the Royal Marine Base outside Port Stanley. Seeing a helicopter land at the base would not raise any suspicions as supplies were sometimes brought in that way. Val would stay on base while Nicollette would be greeted by Peter and Charles at Port Stanley Airport. The two men would disguise themselves as transport company personnel. The three of them would drive to the ferry connecting to the West Island, then on to Joanne Clark's ranch. If all went well, the group would arrive at the ranch in the late afternoon of the sixth.

"Have a safe trip, Miss Crowder," the ticket collector said as Nicollette boarded the airplane.

"Thank you," she responded as the collector handed back her papers.

I am now Linda Crowder, Nicollette Beverley has ceased to exist, she thought as she settled into a Business Class seat for the first step of her long journey.

The smaller DC 9 landed at Port Stanley airport an hour early.

Nicollette had spent the last day and a half traveling from London to get here. Despite the upgraded accommodations, she hadn't had much sleep and her body was paying the toll. Half of her was numb and the other half was too tired to feel anything. She remembered Major Hartwell telling her "to be prepared for a rough trip, but this way is necessary to avoid any external suspicion." *Easy for her to say*, Nicollette thought.

A sudden rush of adrenaline flowed across her weary body when Nicollette saw Peter holding a small sign for Linda Crowder when she entered the baggage claim area of the airport. He was dressed in working man's clothing and was unshaven.

"Miss Crowder, I'm here to take you to your hotel," he announced after giving a quick wink.

"Thank you," she replied whilst trying very hard to contain her amusement at the way Peter was dressed.

It was a short ride to the Malvina House Hotel. All arrangements had been made in advance for Linda Crowder. Peter walked her into the lobby and slipped her a small piece of paper when Nicollette tipped him, as was part of the plan.

Nicollette opened her room and placed the luggage on a rack. She had a quick look around and the room was clean, not only physically, but from any unwanted surveillance devices. *So far, so good,* she thought when she turned on the shower. As she was getting undressed, Nicollette opened the little piece of paper Peter had given her: Pick-up at ten. Sleep well. Oh, and thanks for the tip.

The next morning, Nicollette was in the lobby when Charles entered. He was barely recognizable and it was all she could do to contain herself when she saw him. He hadn't shaved in a couple of days and was sporting a dark brown moustache. Charles Thompson, the man who was always very well dressed, was now carrying her luggage dressed in ill-fitting, stained clothing, complete with a distinctive odor. He shook his head as he mumbled quietly, 'No me conoces,' in crudely accented Spanish as he opened the door to a green van.

"Good morning, Linda!"

Nicollette nearly stumbled when she heard the greeting coming from inside the van.

"Good morning to you, Jo," she responded. "I didn't expect to see you here."

"I decided to come here a day early to get some supplies organized and I wanted to spend some time with my new housemate."

It was a six-or-so hour drive to the ranch on the West Island. The view from the van reminded Nicollette of Scotland. Hardscrabble landscape, with valleys nestled in between rolling hills and flatlands closer to the water. Nicollette noticed there weren't any trees around but she did see that sheep seemed to be everywhere. They took the ferry to the West Island and soon after, the roads became mostly unpaved dirt tracks. They drove through Port Stevens, where Joanne pointed out the large sheep station and the port area. *Not much of a port, just some buildings and a couple of large docks,* Nicollette thought. *We really are in the middle of nowhere!*

They arrived at Joanne Clarke's ranch just after four in the afternoon and were promptly greeted by her four dogs. "They run the place for me," Joanne exclaimed as the dogs investigated the three newcomers. "They're Falkland Shepherds, very useful in these parts. They're friendly, really."

Joanne introduced the dogs by name to Linda as Peter and Charles started unloading the van. Besides her personal luggage and Joanne's supplies, Nicollette could see three large trunks in the back of the van. One of the trunks was the one Major Hartwell gave her to pack the new clothing, the other two she did not recognize.

"Let's get you organized, Linda." Joanne put her arm around Nicollette and led her into the house.

It was a good-sized home with a large kitchen and sitting room. The view from the sitting room overlooked a stretch of water about a mile away. "That's Queen Charlotte Bay," Jo pointed out, "and you have the same view from your room. Let me show you."

Joanne led Nicollette down a hallway, past a bathroom to a closed door. "Here's your room, Linda," she announced as she opened the door. It was a large room with two windows facing the bay. There was a big closet, chest of drawers, and a double bed. "I hope you will be comfortable here."

"I'm sure I will. Thanks, Jo."

Charles left the room after carrying in the last trunk and Peter closed the bedroom door behind him.

"Let's get started and we need to be quick, Nicky. I'll leave you your personal unpacking for later."

Peter opened the first trunk and pulled out a large suitcase with a hard cover. He opened it to reveal a complete portable radio system. Nicollette found an electrical outlet by the bed and plugged the unit in. She remembered from training to keep the battery charged just in case. She ran a long black wire along the base of the wall to the window nearest her bed. She opened the window as Peter handed her a two-foot metal rod for the antenna. The rod could extend up to ten feet high, easily clearing the roof. Nicollette quickly mounted the rod on the side of the window using specially designed hooks and tape. Peter switched the unit on and there was a static noise. "We're on, Nicky."

Nicollette unplugged the wire and brought the antenna back into the room. She recoiled the wire and repacked everything into the case and slid it under her bed. Peter reviewed the rest of the equipment with her. There were binoculars, a portable telescope, and a small metal detector. The second trunk contained a small two-way radio that had been preset to reach Val in the event of an emergency. At the bottom of the second trunk was a black leather case. Inside the case was her service weapon, the Browning Hi Power FN-635 Pistol, along with three magazines and four boxes of ammunition.

"Hopefully you won't need it, Nicky."

Nicollette had noticed two shotguns hanging on the wall near the kitchen. She would ask Jo about them later.

The equipment was checked and organized back into the trunks.

"You are open for business." Peter opened the third trunk out of curiosity and to be helpful to Nicollette. With a big smile, he pulled out the Wellington Boots. "Wellies, Nicky?"

Nicollette smiled back. "Yes, Wellies. After all, I'm on a sheep ranch in the Falklands!"

Nicollette and Peter joined Mrs. Clarke in the dining area for tea and sandwiches. She asked if the other delivery man outside would care to join them. "I'll take something out to him."

Charles was walking around the front of the ranch with two of the dogs.

"This is a pretty large place, Nicky, and you're in luck, there's an old Range Rover parked behind one of the barns." He then firmly put his hands on her shoulders and whispered, "Be careful and use your head, Nicollette. This operation could mean nothing or everything. You are the right person for the job!"

Peter stayed inside with Joanne Clarke for nearly forty-five minutes, finally excusing himself, explaining they had to make their way back to Port Howard before dark. They would take the ferry back to East Island in the morning.

Nicollette watched as the van traveled down the dirt road towards Port Stephens. As she turned to walk back into the house, it became very real to her that she might not see Peter or Charles for some time. She was now alone, in the back of beyond on the West Falkland Island, with Joanne Clarke, four dogs, thousands of sheep, and her Wellies!

Early Days

Joanne Clarke was sitting at the table and poured another cup of tea for Nicollette. "How about we make an early start tomorrow and I'll give you a tour of the ranch, Linda?"

Nicollette could see that the drive from Stanley had taken a toll on Jo. She watched her take a glass of water and swallow a fistful of multi-colored pills. Jo said good night and walked down the hallway to her room, a couple of dogs in tow. The shadows against the wall said that the sun was setting. Nicollette checked her watch, nearly 9:00 p.m.

Walking down the hall to her room, she passed a closed door across from hers. Curiosity getting the better of her, she looked to see if the crack at the bottom of Jo's door was dark. She's asleep. Nicollette opened the closed door and turned on a light, softly closing the door behind her. A quick glance revealed the room to be a study or office. There were photographs on the wall and a line of bookshelves behind an old wooden desk. The top of the desk was a flurry of papers. It appeared that the room wasn't used much.

A sudden scratch against the door ended Nicollette's curiosity for the evening. She opened the door to find one of the dogs waiting for her. She remembered his name, Monty, and invited him into her room as she finished unpacking.

Just before she rolled into bed, Nicollette took a look out of her bedroom window. It was now dark over the bay, not much to see. She thought she saw some lights in the distance, but after blinking her eyes, the lights were gone. *Probably my imagination. It's been a long day. I'm just tired.* She pulled back the sheets on the bed and noticed a green envelope protruding just slightly from under her pillow. I wonder what this is all about?

She opened the envelope and unfolded a handwritten note. It was from Peter;

Nicky,

Just a reminder that Sir Harold wants the operation fully functional by tomorrow. Keep in mind that there's a five hour time difference between you and London. Send a signal out before you go to sleep. Talk about anything, sheep, teas, cricket scores, dogs or whatever. We just want to get all phases synced. You will get a received signal back within one hour. Use code 'green' and pattern A-7285463. Nicky, this could be a serious situation, so please look after yourself. You can trust Jo, but be careful with everyone else. Take a day or two to become acclimated. Follow your instincts and hopefully, we can finish our mission safely and soon.

Peter

PS Looking forward to seeing James at the pub next week.

Nicollette folded the letter and looked at Monty. "Looks like we have some work to do before we get some sleep."

She carefully opened the case containing the radio and opened the window to install the antenna. *Brilliant,* she thought as the antenna quickly went into place. Nicollette placed the headphones over her ears and turned the radio on. She set the controls to the proper pattern and wavelengths prescribed in the code book. "What shall we talk about, Monty? How about dogs?"

Nicollette entered a paragraph describing her new friend, Monty, and pressed the send coordinates. She looked at Monty, petting his head. "Now we wait, my friend. You're going to be famous."

The yellow light on the receiver started to blink in a pattern, two blinks then a pause, a single blink, then another pause, and another two blinks. This was repeated three times. Nicollette looked at her watch. *One hour, right on schedule.* The yellow light was a sign of connection and the pattern of the blinks confirmed the five spokes of the communications wheel.

"We are up and running, Monty. Now let's get some rest, old boy, tomorrow's going to be a busy day."

A stream of daylight pierced through the window, chasing the night darkness away. It was after seven when she felt an insistent wet nose against her cheek. Nicollette dressed and followed Monty out of her room. He walked to the doggie door and outside.

"Good morning, Linda," Jo called from the kitchen.

"Good morning to you, Jo," she responded.

"I hope you slept well."

"Yes, I did. It's so quiet and peaceful here, I was tired and I had Monty for company as well."

"Monty is an old softy."

Jo swallowed a handful of multi-colored pills and reached for the keys to the Land Rover. The sun was bright and there was a warm breeze as they headed out the front door. There was the sound of sheep in the distance as Nicollette got her first look at the ranch. Jo pointed out her vegetable garden next to three large barns and two fenced in pens.

"Let's see if she starts," Jo said as the two of them sat in the Land Rover.

She turned the key and the engine gave an enthusiastic roar. The dogs must have heard the noise and jumped into the rear.

"I guess we have company."

"It's a bit bumpy, Linda, so hold on tight."

They drove along a path about a mile to the top of a hill. "This is the highest point on my ranch, Linda."

From her seat in the truck, Nicollette could see what seemed to be an endless mass of white sheep. "That is my flock." Jo pointed. "Almost three thousand head."

Nicollette had seen sheep before around Brockwirth, but never in such numbers in one place. The dogs jumped from the back of the vehicle and ran towards the sheep. "They just want a bit of fun," Jo added. Nicollette asked if she could walk around a bit. *Sure glad about the wellies,* she thought as she stepped out onto the grassy ground.

The small set of binoculars came in handy as Nicollette walked away from the truck and looked over the ranch to the bay and scanned northward. She saw what appeared to be some buildings, standing alone, in the distance to the north-west. Nicollette turned her head eastward and could see a small plume of gray smoke in the distance to her right. She would remember this hill. It would serve as a good vantage point to see a large part of the southern area of the West Island.

Nicollette sat back in the truck and looked at Jo.

"I hope you don't mind me asking, but how do you do it, Jo? There are so many sheep and so much to do."

"We, I mean Geoffrey and I, stopped working the ranch nearly six years ago. What with our age and our health, it was just too much, but it was hard to get help. You see that bit of smoke over there?"

Nicollette had seen the smoke earlier through the binoculars.

"That is the Van Ghent place. They have been here since the turn of the century, five generations now. They have one of the largest farms on the Island and are my closest neighbors. They are my partners. I provide the sheep and land and they run it for me. It's mutually beneficial. We'll drive over and say hello, their place is quite impressive. The dogs know the way home."

They drove over a rutted road several miles to the Van Ghent Ranch. Driving through the large iron front gate, it was easy to see this place dwarfed the Clarkes' many times over. There were several huge barns and outbuildings either side of a wide avenue leading to a castle-like two-story home. Nicollette counted a number of utility trucks and tractors. There were four Land Rovers parked near the house. *This place is massive, almost too big for this small island,* she thought. Jo tapped the horn as the two of them left the truck.

"Hello, Jo!" a man called out. "Great to see you!" he continued as he walked towards Joanne and Nicollette. "How was London? How are you feeling? Is everything alright?"

"Everything is fine, Mark. I'm showing my niece around and I wanted to introduce her to my partners. This is Linda Crowley. She is a doctoral scholar in London. She will be staying with me for a while. Linda, this is Mark Van Ghent, my neighbor and friend."

"Pleasure to meet you, Linda."

"Nice to meet you too, Mr. Van Ghent," Nicollette responded as she held out her hand to shake his. She suspected Mark Van Ghent was in his late fifties. He was slightly balding with a weathered face and with a slight continental accent.

"You must come inside for tea," Mark insisted. "Ellen would love to see you."

They walked into a big foyer with a large staircase on one side leading up to a second-floor landing. Straight ahead was an arched entryway to a sitting room. Multiple floor-to-ceiling windows made up the entire rear of the sitting room. Art hung on all the walls with small statues on pedestals in every corner. *This place is like a museum!* She continued to look around, trying not to be too nosy or obvious.

Ellen Van Ghent entered the room and greeted Jo with the traditional European two cheek kiss. Jo introduced Linda and Mrs. Van Ghent summoned a uniformed house helper to bring tea and biscuits.

Tea was served and there was light talk at the table. Ellen asked Linda about her studies in London and mentioned that her son was studying Agricultural Studies and Agribusiness at the University of Maryland in the states. She said her oldest daughter Maria and her husband Miguel were already helping out working and managing the farm. She brought over a picture and proudly presented her grandson John. "My, he is getting so big," Jo commented.

"He's grown so much since you've been away, Jo. Nearly two now."

Jo seemed to be getting a bit tired and Nicollette excused the two of them for her. Mark offered an invitation for dinner on Saturday. "I would love it," Jo responded.

Jo handed Nicollette the keys to the Land Rover and they drove off towards the Clarkes' ranch. It was easy to tell that the Van Ghents were very friendly people, but in the back of her mind, a couple of questions still remained. *Why such a palatial home in this backwater of an Island? It's like a movie! Is there that much money here? In sheep? I can see they like Jo and they're very friendly, but is that covering something? Then there's the accent, could it be normal? But the family has been here over eighty years. And what about Miguel? A Hispanic name for sure. Where is he from? What's the story there?*

Nicollette glanced over at Jo, who was struggling to close her eyes due to the bumpy ride. *Am I being too nosy about the Van Ghents? I don't want to stir up anything, especially for Jo's sake, but something just doesn't feel right...something.*

When they arrived back at the house, Joe announced she was going for a nap. "We'll have supper at six, Linda. Why don't you take the truck and go exploring a bit on your own? You can't get too lost. Take Monty with you."

Nicollette drove past the entry gate and headed across the field down towards Queen Charlotte Bay. She wanted to get a better look around the shoreline, about a mile away. The land flattened out the closer they came to the water. The coarse grassland gave way to a small marshy shore. Nicollette stopped the truck and Monty jumped out. The two of them walked along the water as she grabbed her binoculars and looked out over the bay. The water was calm and she couldn't see any traffic on the water. *A postcard moment.*

The two of them continued to walk along the shore in a northern direction until a small estuary blocked their path. She could see the northern shoreline of a large inlet coming off the bay, about three kilometers across from her. *I wonder if Jo has a map? I'm merely guessing at this point.*

Looking northeast across the inlet, something caught her eye a couple of kilometers or so up the inlet. She could just make out what looked like the ruins of some buildings. *I wonder if that is what I saw earlier from the hill outside Jo's ranch?*

Nicollette sat down on a protruding rock and drew a rough map of what she saw along with accompanying notes. Multiple questions crossed her mind. She realized there was so much more to learn about the island's people and topography than she had learned during her brief training. She called Monty and the two of them headed back to the truck.

The tea kettle was hot when Nicollette arrived back at the ranch. Jo was sitting at the table and the smell of something in the oven permeated the room.

"Have a good look around, Linda?"

"I did, Jo. Took Monty down by the Bay and had a long walk. Would you have a local map, Jo? I'm trying to find a good place for my studies."

"There might be one in the cupboard by the window. Top middle drawer. Take a look."

Nicollette started to sort through the cluttered drawer. Deep in the back, under the odd, unusual, and insubstantial jumble of papers, a light brown envelope caught her eye. She pulled it from the tangle. On the outside of the envelope, the Clarkes' names were handwritten and oddly, there wasn't any postage, either stamp or seal. She glanced over at Jo, now in the kitchen. Nicollette turned her back towards Jo and tried very gently to open the envelope. The seal was so old, it had resealed itself.

"Any luck, Linda?" Jo asked while removing whatever was baking in the oven.

"No, I'm afraid not."

"No worries, after supper I'll check the office. There's bound to be one in there."

"Jo, that's the first time I've had lamb casserole and it was delicious. I'll wash up and put the tea on."

"I'll go look for that map while you do that."

Jo rose gingerly from the table and slowly walked down the hallway towards the room across from Nicollette's bedroom. She watched as Jo walked into the office and shut the door behind her. *She must really be private about that office, she didn't even ask me to help look. I'll have a sneak sometime later. Let's see about getting this letter opened.*

Nicollette quickly put the kettle on and returned to the table for the dishes. The kettle whistled and a steady stream of steam flowed through the spout. *Perfect!*

Very delicately and deliberately, she pulled the envelope open. Nicollette quickly folded back the envelope's flap and stuffed the letter into her front pocket as the sound of a door shutting came from the hallway. Jo sat down in her seat as Nicollette brought the tea tray in.

"I found one," Jo announced, "although it's a couple of years old. Not much changes around here, Linda."

The two of them finished their second cup of tea. It was nearly half past eight and Jo said she was off to bed. Nicollette helped her from the chair and watched as she went into the kitchen and downed another fistful of pills from the cabinet.

"Goodnight, Linda, see you in the morning," Jo announced as she walked down the hallway to her bedroom, one dog trailing her.

Nicollette poured another cup of tea and unfolded the map. It was dated 1975 and was part of an advert for the ferry company that operated between the east and west islands. The map contained the locations of the various ranches on the West Falklands, the majority of which were in the north part of the Island. The map also showed a finger of the Queen Charlotte Bay nearly splitting the west island in two. *That must be the inlet I was at today!*

The crack on the bottom of Jo's bedroom door was dark. She's fast asleep. Nicollette grabbed the envelope from her pocket and laid it next to Jo's map, carefully opening it and removing the three yellowing pages inside. The letter was typed except for the Clarkes' names, which were handwritten. The letter's only reference of origin was Port Stanley. The date was 10 November 1965. The letter looked to be an official notification from some government official in Port Stanley announcing a work project on the northwestern shore of Queen Charlotte Bay. The letter described the work as "erosion mitigation and shore stabilization," with a completion time of about six months. The letter continued that "due to the nature of the project, Queen Charlotte Bay would be closed to unauthorized vessels for the duration of the project." The letter concluded with an apology for any inconvenience and was signed by a Mr. William Fields, Project Manager, Port Stanley.

The last page was a map of Queen Charlotte Bay, with the areas affected by the work clearly identified. The waters of the bay were almost all off limits as well as the surrounding land area about two kilometers inland from the shore. The Clarke and Van Ghent ranches were within the work area as well as a third farm, labeled Smythe, located on the northwestern shore of the inlet, about five miles inland from the main body of water.

Multiple questions flowed through Nicollette's head, starting with the authenticity of the letter. *I know they are casual here in the Falklands, but this is a bit too informal for such a big project. No real detail or budget information. Not even the name or contact information of the construction company! The letter was designed to look official, but there is no government seal or signature. And then there's the map identifying a farm just about where I saw the remains of old buildings today. Was that the Smythe place? I wonder what happened to them and their farm? It couldn't have just disappeared over eighteen years, could it? What's the story there?"*

It was half past nine as Nicollette scribbled some notes on the small pad she carried with her. This was just her first full day on the ranch and already there seemed to be a hundred questions that needed to be addressed. She placed the letter back into the envelope and purposely left Jo's map on the table. Monty dutifully followed her into the bedroom as Nicolette commented, "We've got lots to talk about, Monty, let's get cracking."

Nicollette installed the equipment and waited for the return signal from Val in Port Stanley. The radio signal changed from yellow to green. "We're on, Monty."

Nicollette formulated in her mind what she wanted to say as she placed the proper code cover over the keyboard. Her hands deftly crossed the keyboard as she described the visit to the Van Ghents and the resulting invitation to dinner on Saturday night. Nicollette then described her trip along the Queen Charlotte Bay coastline; the project letter from Port Stanley with an eighteen-year-old map and the discrepancies that map had with a newer map; then the Smythe Farm. She asked Val for some deeper research into the Smythes.

The signal was sent and the yellow light confirming receipt started to flash. Forty-five minutes later, Nicollette received a response from Val. She looked at Monty. "They want me to be patient for now, Monty, but continue to get the flavor of this part of the Island. 'Early days,' they said, 'early days.'"

Questions

The sky was overcast and there was a slight drizzle as Nicollette drove herself and Jo Clarke to the Van Ghents for Saturday night dinner. The truck seemed to automatically know the route there and the slippery path was no match for the Land Rover.

Despite being at the Clarkes' ranch for less than a week, it was becoming increasingly apparent to Nicollette that Jo was far more ill than she was letting on. She was good in the morning and after her lunchtime nap, but she faded quickly after tea time and slept soundly through the night. *And all those pills she takes!*

Still, Nicollette was looking forward to dinner with the Van Ghents. The past few days had been quiet at the ranch, but had given her a little more time to explore the island, including an interesting trip with Monty to Port Stephens for supplies, mail, and petrol.

Port Stephens wasn't much of a port, but it was the largest sheep station on the Island. Nicollette had exchanged pleasantries with the clerk at the petrol station who introduced himself, Cyril Robinson. Nicollette introduced herself as Linda Crowther, niece of Joanne Clarke, and said that she was here to study and help her Aunt Jo at the ranch. Cyril asked how Joanne was doing, mentioning that he hadn't seen her since she went to England and she was doing poorly then. He added that Joanne and her late husband Geoffrey were partners with him in the petrol station and small market. Cyril walked with "Linda" to the truck. Monty was quick to greet him, enjoying Cyril's affectionate petting. "Tell Jo I said hello and I'll ring her soon," Cyril said as he closed the door for "Linda."

Nicollette drove past the iron gates of the Van Ghent Ranch and straight through the array of work buildings to the front of the large home. She helped Jo from the truck and they walked arm in arm to the front door where Ellen and Mark Van Ghent were waiting for them. They introduced their daughter Maria and her husband Miguel.

Nicollette saw a much older gentleman speaking with Joanne by the drinks table. Jo caught "Linda's" attention and motioned for her to come and be introduced. "This is Luuk Claassen, Ellen's Uncle."

"Pleased to meet you, Miss Crowther."

"Pleased to meet you as well, Mr. Claassen," "Linda" responded.

"Please, we're family on this island, call me Luuk."

"And you can call me Linda." Nicollette smiled back.

Mark Van Ghent invited everyone to have a seat as dinner was about to be served. Mr. Claassen held Joanne's arm and escorted her to her seat. Thoughts were swirling in her head about Mr. Claassen. *His accent is more pronounced than the Van Ghents and his voice inflection indicates to me that he was well brought up and educated. Even his posture is perfect and correct, which is unusual for his age and anyone on this Island.*

The dinner conversation was light and cheerful. Nicollette took the opportunity to compliment Ellen Van Ghent on the lovely artwork in the home and Ellen asked if she would like a tour after dinner.

"Have you an interest in art, Linda?" she asked.

"A little. I've visited the National Gallery in London a few times. I found it a wonderful place to step away from my studies, to relax and clear my mind."

Joanne seemed comfortable among the Van Ghents and was enjoying herself. There were several light questions directed at "Linda" regarding her visit and studies. Linda answered them easily with a smile and the conversation turned to the weather, prices, and sheep.

All throughout dinner, Nicollette felt Miguel's eyes upon her. He hadn't said much, nor changed his expression throughout the evening. *Is he suspicious of me or doesn't like newcomers?* This was in sharp contrast to his wife, Maria, who was much more engaging with the group.

Mark brought around a bottle of brandy after dessert. Nicollette glanced at her watch, noticing Jo was starting to fade. "Linda" declined the offer of a brandy and followed Ellen back into the house for her tour. Ellen enthusiastically described each painting and piece of art as if she had created it. Nicollette felt like she was a student in an advanced art appreciation class as the two of them traveled through the first floor of the house. They must've seen a dozen pieces, including works by Picasso, Van Gogh, and Chagall. Arriving back in the dining room, she thanked Ellen for the tour. "It was like I was in a small art museum."

Ellen smiled and acknowledged "Linda's" appreciation. However, Ellen's demeanor changed when "Linda" commented about the amount of effort it must have taken to organize and accumulate such a wonderful group of art.

"That's for another time, Linda," she commented rather tersely as the two of them rejoined the party.

The rain had stopped and it was a clear night for the drive back to the ranch. Nicollette looked over at Jo. Her eyes were closed and she was resting soundly.

About halfway home, at the top of a hill, Nicollette slowed the truck down and looked out over the bay. Maybe it was her imagination playing with her again, but she was sure she saw a faint blinking light in the distance. Another quick look at Jo, still asleep, and Nicollette stopped the truck. She grabbed her binoculars from under the seat and stood on the steprail, looking towards the direction of the blinking light. A minute or two went by and there it was again, an orange light followed by two quick flashes of white.

Nicollette marked the time on her watch and waited to see what might follow. Two minutes passed and then another series of flashes. She scribbled notes on her pad about the flashes and the visit with the Van Ghents. *Val and I sure have a lot to talk about,* she thought as the truck pulled into the ranch.

Nicollette helped Jo to her room and gingerly closed the door behind her. She knew Jo would be asleep very shortly. In the meantime, she put the kettle on and continued with her notes. As she was writing, questions were flowing freely through her head. *What is the real story behind the Van Ghents? What about Ellen's uncle and Maria's husband Miguel? And the artwork? Ellen showed me some museum-quality works. I mean here, in the Falklands? How and why? Then there are the flashes I saw from the Bay. Normal signals or something else?* Nicollette also noted that she did not see any return flashes from land, or at least, none that she could see.

The crack under Jo's door was dark and the house was quiet except for a soft snore coming from Monty. Nicollette closed her bedroom door and set up her equipment. It was nearly midnight when the confirming connecting signal flashed on her radio. *They're not going to like this in England. It's five o'clock Sunday morning there!*

She pulled out her pad and transmitted her questions about the Van Ghents, the artwork, Miguel, and Mr. Claassen. As soon as the received signal started to flash, Nicollette sent her information about the lights she had seen on Queen Charlotte Bay, carefully noting the sequence, color, and timing. She pressed the final send button and twenty-five minutes later, she received a good night from Val.

The smell of pancakes permeated the house the next morning. Nicollette walked into the dining area to see Joanne at the table, drinking a cup of tea.

"There's pancakes and bacon in the kitchen, Linda," she announced.

The clock on the wall said half nine. "I must've overslept," Nicollette commented and followed by asking Jo how she slept.

This is perfect, Nicollette thought, *a natural opening to ask questions without being too nosy. Maybe I can get some answers from Jo.*

"I had a nice time last night, the food was great and I enjoyed meeting everyone. How long have you known the Van Ghents?"

"They were here when Gerald and I first arrived and we've been friends ever since. They are wonderful neighbors. Did you know they have the largest operation on the West Island?"

"I bet they do," Nicollette responded and continued, "Was Ellen's Uncle, Mr. Claassen, here when you first arrived?"

"Yes, Luuk was here with Irina, his wife, Ellen's aunt, but she died about thirty years ago. We just barely knew her, and she didn't socialize much, that one."

Jo took a sip of her tea as "Linda" took a bite of her pancakes.

Nicollette thought that now was the time to ask a nosier question.

"Have you seen all the artwork they have?"

"Yes. Mark and Ellen travel a bit and I guess they pick up pieces while away. They are always adding a piece or two and probably have two or three dozen paintings, quite a few statues, and other bits and pieces."

"Well, their collection is very impressive and I enjoyed the tour and the whole evening a great deal."

Without knowing it, Jo had very casually revealed a great deal of information about the Van Ghent family.

Despite the picturesque Sunday afternoon, Nicollette was having a hard time relaxing. She was dealing with a load of information and questions and just couldn't sit still. Even though she had been there for a week, Nicollette had yet to have a good look around the farm buildings off to the side of the ranch.

"Mind if I take a walk around the buildings, Jo?"

"Suit yourself, Linda, but be careful. It's been some time since I've been in them."

The first building Nicollette visited was a very large barn. The side door was unlocked and she strolled in. The inside seemed massive with a large floor area and a high-pitched roof. It looked to Nicollette that it had recently been used. There were the odd bits of straw and hay on the floor and portable fencing was organized on one side. She could see remains of imprinted sheep hooves and work boots all around the dirt floor. Nicollette placed her boot over one of the imprints and estimated a size twelve. *Big man,* she thought.

The silos outside the barn contained a mixture of hay and straw. Nothing unusual there. She saw a well-worn dirt track leading from between the silos to the barns and then off towards the front of the ranch. *Nothing unusual here either.*

Before she entered the second large barn, she noticed a much smaller, grayish building, slightly hidden from view, just down a small hill from the second barn.

Nicollette had seen the two larger buildings and the silos from the front of the ranch, but this third building was a surprise to her. Curiosity taking over, she walked towards the building. There was no identified pathway, just a few bare spots and some small eroded soil gullies. *This building hasn't seen too many visitors,* she thought as she walked the fifty meters or so to the building.

She walked around the building, passing a shuttered window, to find the entrance. On the bay-facing side, she found a double wood door. There was an old brown padlock that was rusted open hanging on the latch.

It took a lot of effort to open one of the doors. The hinges were rusty and soil had accumulated around the base of the doors. *This building hasn't had any visitors for a long time,* she thought as she very carefully entered the dark insides.

The sun's rays only illuminated a small portion of the interior and there was no electric light, but from what she could see, the building seemed to be used as some sort of oversized shed or workshop. *I need to get a torch or lantern.*

Sudden insistent barking from Monty gained her attention and Nicollette spotted him up by the silos. She called for him, but oddly, he did not come for her. She called again, and again, but Monty just waited for her to climb the small hill back to the silos. Nicollette reached out to Monty and gave him a good petting. "You follow me everywhere, old boy, but you wouldn't come to me down the hill to the building. What's the matter, Monty? Are you afraid of something?"

Monty, tail wagging in excitement, just looked up at her and urged her to follow him back to the ranch house.

Jo was sleeping peacefully in her outdoor chair when they arrived back at the ranch house. Nicollette looked at her watch and realized she had been gone for over two hours. She picked up Jo's empty lemonade glass and walked into the ranch house to get her equipment. Nicollette gathered her torch and camera. Something inside her was telling her to be careful, after seeing the way Monty had acted towards her at the building. She reached for the case containing her gun and strapped on the holster. The safety was on and there was a full magazine in the weapon when Nicollette placed it in the holster. She untucked her dark green shirt from her pants to cover the holstered weapon, not wanting to upset Jo.

When she and Monty approached the hill above the gray building, Nicollette urged Monty to come with her. "There's nothing to be afraid of. I'm here with you, Monty." But as hard as she tried, Monty would not budge. "Just wait for me here, I won't be long." Nicollette started down the hill, taking a quick glance back at Monty, sitting patiently, waiting for her to return.

Nicollette came to the door, unstrapped her weapon, and turned on her torch. The inside of the building was damp and there was a very pronounced musty odor. Cobwebs covered everything and the floor was deep in dust, making it harder to breathe. She placed a kerchief over her mouth and carefully walked back to the window, avoiding the clutter on the floor. The window was stuck firm. *In for a penny, in for a pound!* Using a piece of lumber, she broke through the glass pane and freed the outside shutter.

The sunlight illuminated a messy room. Bits and pieces of junk were scattered all over the place, but of particular interest to Nicollette were two rather large workbenches on the opposite wall. She laid the flashlight on top of an old cardboard box to maximise her light. The first bench was covered with small machinery parts and oily tools. *Mr. Clarke must have used this bench to do his repairs.* Using a screwdriver, Nicollette filtered through the jumble. Nothing too interesting here. Underneath the bench, there were several tool boxes filled with a variety of hand tools, reminding her of the small work area her father used in the garage. The second bench, just off to the left, was dramatically different. The work area was clear, there were no tools or spare parts; in fact, there was nothing on top of the bench. *This is rather odd.*

Nicollette took a step back to survey the bench. As she stepped, she felt a small crunch and a crackling sound under her boot. She brought the torch over to fully illuminate the area. A sparkle of light revealed the source, a small shard of thin glass, maybe a couple of centimeters big. Nicollette carefully picked up the shard and held it close to the light. There was a small gray marking on the fragment, which looked to her like a number 7. She got on her knees and used the torch to scan the area more closely, discovering a few smaller shards of the thin glass. But under the lower shelf of the workbench, a small round black object caught her attention. It was a peculiar looking thing, with bits of silk-like metal on one side and three wider prongs on the other side. She placed the round object next to the shard of glass and focused hard on the two, trying to come up with an answer. Then it hit her. She remembered her father fixing their old black and white tele by replacing a cylindrical glass tube. *This is the remains of an old tube!*

Her heart was beating fast as Nicollette continued her search around the second workbench. She found several more pieces of broken tubes scattered under the dust, but her heart nearly stopped when she moved a large wooden box next to the workbench and found a tube chassis behind. She placed the chassis on the workbench and looked for some sort of identification of the equipment, model number, serial number, or manufacturer, but there was nothing. She walked towards the rear of the room where two metal cabinets stood. The cabinets were locked. Nicollette used a screwdriver and forced the door open to one of the cabinets. She brought the torch around and nearly stumbled when she removed a stack of small boxes from inside the cabinet. There, behind the boxes, she saw a small spool of coaxial cable and some old tube boxes with the tubes still inside. She recognized the coaxial cable from the mission at Little Tunb Island. *This cable was hanging all over the place in our hut,* she remembered.

A picture was starting to form in Nicollette's mind. There were just a few more pieces to find before she could solve this puzzle. She pointed her torch towards the top of the walls, slowly guiding the light across the room. And then she saw it! Neatly tucked in the corner against the wall, she saw a black coaxial cable going into the ceiling. Using her torch to shine on the trail of the cable, Nicollette could see where it ended. It was actually severed, cut clean by a wire cutter or very sharp knife. *Someone wanted this to be cut. Now let's see where the remaining cable leads us to.*

Nicollette remembered there was a slight pitch to the roof,

maybe just a meter or so from the sides to the peak. She slowly brought the torch's light across the ceiling. *There must be an access point to the attic area here somewhere.*

At first glance, the ceiling appeared solid, with longboards spanning the entire width. There was no easy visible access to the attic. The only break in the ceiling were two chains hanging from a pair of pulleys that were mounted to metal plates screwed into the wood longboards. Nicollette found an old step ladder in the corner and placed it under the metal plates. The pulleys were attached to iron rings that were welded to the plates. She pulled the first chain. The iron ring would not budge. When she tried the second chain, Nicollette thought she felt the ring turn counter-clockwise. She found an old metal bar and inserted it through the ring. It took almost everything she had to get the ring to turn. The ring unscrewed about half a turn from the steel plate, then stopped. Maybe out of anger or from frustration, Nicollette took the steel rod and took a hard swing with a hammer at the obstinate ring. The entire plate, ring, chain and all, fell crashing to the floor, just missing her on the ladder.

The downed plate revealed quite a clever design. The ring controlled four flat metal strips that held the plate on the ceiling. When the ring turned, the strips retracted into the plate, freeing the plate to fall and exposing the opening above. *Ingenious! But why the secrecy? What's going on here?*

Flashlight in hand, Nicollette climbed the ladder and poked her head through the opening. She flashed the torch in the direction of where the coaxial cable came through the ceiling and into the attic, ending at a steel rod hanging through the rafters. *An antenna!* She guided the torch across the attic. There were some small boxes and various pieces of lumber scattered throughout the small space. A pile of material in the opposite corner caught her eye. She laid the torch on the attic floor and very carefully hoisted herself into the tight attic space.

Unsure of the stability of the joists, she crawled on her stomach very slowly towards the pile of material. Using a piece of lumber, she pushed the top layers of the pile off to one side. *Curtains and towels.* The next layer offered much more resistance. It was a rolled-up piece of carpet. Nicollette crawled closer, the boards below her starting to groan from the additional weight. Gingerly, she used her hands to pull the rolled-up rug away from the side wall, exposing the end of the roll. She shined her torch into the opening. A piece of white material was bundled inside the rolled-up rug. Despite the noise of the boards below her, she positioned herself to reach in and grab the white material. Gently, she pulled the material towards the opening. It was much heavier than just a piece of cloth and required using both hands. Finally, with a final tug, Nicollette pulled the white material free. *It's a pillow case! A damn pillow case!* She reached inside the case and pulled out one of several notebooks. The book was old and the writing inside was hard to see in the limited light.

The faint sound of a dog barking quickly caught Nicollette's attention. Monty! She dragged the pillow case with its contents across the attic floor to the opening and quickly descended the ladder. She hurriedly reattached the metal plate to the ceiling and moved the ladder as Monty's bark became more insistent. A quick clear of the workbench top and a final look to see if there were any obvious traces of her presence.

Nicollette reached for the wooden door and her heart stopped. On the inside edge of the door frame, barely visible in the limited light, looked to be a bloody handprint. Despite Monty's urging, Nicollette pulled her torch out and found two other large red marks on the inside of the door. She took a brief look around the door frame and saw a small wooden box. It was the same type of box her father would keep chisels or drill bits in, except when she opened this box, it had two slots embedded on a black velvety lining.

Nicollette placed the box into the pillow case and pulled the wooden door shut. She reapplied the rusty lock. Monty on the top of the hill, his tail was erect and his body was moving up and down while continuing the loud barking. *Something must really be bothering the old boy!* Nicollette threw the pillowcase over her shoulder, pulled out her gun and slowly climbed the small hill towards Monty.

"What's the matter, Monty?" she asked, noticing there didn't seem to be anyone around. Nicollette guessed as to what was bothering Monty, as the other dogs were joining them in their walk back. "Jo must've sent them to look for us." Nicollette placed the gun back into the holster and covered it with her shirttail.

When they arrived at the ranch house, Jo was not outside anymore. Nicollette checked her watch. It was nearly half-past four, and she realized she had been away most of the afternoon. She carried the pillowcase around the back of the house and placed it under her bedroom window. *No need to have to explain any of this to Jo. I'll get it later.*

"You're a right sight, Missy!" Jo shouted from the kitchen table. "Did you have a good look around?"

Nicollette understood she must look like a mess and could use a good bath.

"It was a good afternoon, Jo. I guess I should have a quick bath before tea."

"I think you should, Linda, and remember, you're making tea tonight."

Nicollette smiled back at Jo and walked down the hallway to her bedroom. She quickly opened the window and pulled the pillowcase inside, placing it under her bed behind her luggage. She put her gun away and grabbed her robe.

"So where did you wander off to this afternoon, Linda?" Jo asked as the two were eating.

Nicollette slowly chewed her food, buying some time to

give a reply. *Better to be honest, but be vague.*

"I had a walk around the barns with Monty. They sure are big, Jo. Biggest I've ever seen."

Joanne smiled back at "Linda." "At one time, they were used a lot, but now, since Geoffrey died, everything is taken care of by the Van Ghents. Nothing much gets done here anymore. Shame really, they are nice buildings."

Nicollette thought she would test the water with Jo and inquire about the small building. "I saw a small building down the hill from the barns. I thought I would take a look. Oddly though, Monty would not follow me."

Jo's expression flipped one hundred eighty degrees. Her smile turned upside down and her lower lip started to quiver. Nicollette knew at once she had hit a nerve. She immediately followed up. "I'm sorry, Jo, was I out of bounds?"

Joanne reached for a napkin and wiped the tears from her eyes. She took a deep breath and forced a reply. "No, you were not violating anything. But that building has a sad history with me and Monty."

Jo took a sip of water and another deep breath. Looking directly at "Linda," she continued. "I've never actually talked about this before, Linda, but you are so friendly and nice. Well, now is a good time to start. Please bear with me."

Nicollette nodded.

"That building was Geoffrey's place. He built it when we first arrived. He would go there to build and fix things. He would be there at all hours maintaining something or trying to get something to work. 'Tinkering,' he would call it. Geoffrey would get so involved that I would have to send Monty down to fetch him for a meal or even to come to bed. I rarely went down there, it was his area, and given his past experiences, I felt like he needed a space. I wasn't going to disturb him."

She reached again for the napkin to dab her cheeks.

"One evening, Geoffrey was in his building and I had a nice

tea on the table. I sent Monty down to fetch him. A couple of minutes later, Monty, normally a quiet dog, was barking up a storm. He was very loud and his bark was nothing like I had ever heard before. I rushed past the barns and down to the building. That's where I found Geoffrey, lying there at the side. Monty was using his paw to touch him, but Geoffrey wasn't moving. I checked his breathing, but it had stopped and he had no pulse. I tried everything to revive him, but he was gone. I asked Monty to stay with him, while I ran back here to call the authorities at Fox Bay. The constable and the doctor arrived in a small helicopter and landed right in front of the house. The doctor looked at Geoffrey's body and determined that he died a few hours earlier of a massive heart attack. He said there wasn't anything anyone could do. The constable asked the doctor about some blood that was on Geoffrey's right hand and his right arm. The doctor replied that Geoffrey must have scratched himself when he fell and it was not related to his death."

It took Nicollette a lot of strength to hold her emotions in check. She was well trained and had experienced other tragic situations before, but this one really tugged at her heart. She had only known Joanne Clarke for a week, but she had become like the auntie that Nicollette never had. She left her seat and reached for Jo, a comforting hug as both women shed tears.

Jo asked "Linda" to get a torch and follow her outside. It was now dark as Joanne grabbed Nicollette's arm for support as they walked to a secluded area just outside the house. Jo motioned for "Linda" to point the light in one direction and there it was; amongst several small stones was the larger stone marker of Geoffrey Clarke. "He always loved this farm and his dogs, so I thought it only appropriate to bury him here. This is where he belongs."

The two women just stood there. The stillness and quiet seemed to have a comforting, calming effect. The sky was clear, allowing the full moon and stars to shine brightly. To Nicollette, it seemed like a magical moment, like Geoffrey Clarke was looking down on Joanne and herself. A sudden, slight breeze coming from the bay felt like Geoffrey was whispering to his wife that all would be alright and to Nicollette to keep looking for answers.

Jo indicated that she was ready to go back inside and get ready for bed. She thanked "Linda" for listening and for being here with her. As Jo walked to her room, Monty followed. He took a look back at Nicollette, as if to say goodnight, then followed Joanne into her room.

The light under her bedroom door was soon off and Nicollette knew that Jo was probably fast asleep. She boiled a cup of tea and headed into her room, quietly shutting the door and placing the pillowcase from the outbuilding on her bed. There were about two hours before the daily communications to Val in Port Stanley was due. *Just enough time to get started on the hidden notebooks and perhaps get some idea as to what was really going on in that building. What was Geoffrey Clarke doing? How does a fit man suddenly die of a heart attack? Is there some sort of big secret? What is it and how does it relate to why I'm here!*

Call Me Nicky

Nicollette spread the contents of the pillow case across her bed. The small velvet-lined box caught her attention first. She held it under the bedside light and started to examine it with a magnifying glass. At first glance, it appeared like some kind of jewelery box for a necklace and bracelet combination, but the two slots in the velvet lining weren't the right size. Nicollette grabbed a small screwdriver from her kit and used it to probe around the inside edge to see if the velvet lining would release from the box. The top corner gave way as she cautiously worked around the edge to free the lining.

What Nicollette found next nearly caused her heart to skip a beat. On the exposed area underneath the velvet lining, embossed in the wood, was the Nazi symbol of a circled swastika. There was also a small piece of white paper stuck to the bunched-up lining. Her hands were sweaty as she carefully removed the paper and unfolded it under the light. She did not speak German, but what she saw did not need any translation:

Achtung

Das Gift

Zyanid

The box contained a tool of death, cyanide, and the means to administer it, a syringe. A million questions were flowing through her head as she carefully put the box back together and into the pillow case.

Nicollette stared out of her window, trying to organize her thoughts. *Where did the cyanide come from? Who had it? Nazis? In the Falklands? This is 1982! Was Geoffrey Clarke murdered? Was the blood on his hand from a fall or from a sloppy injection? The attending doctor said it was a heart attack, plain and simple, but cyanide can cause just that and since there was no autopsy, no one would know! But why? What is going on here?*

A chill ran up Nicollette's spine with the possibility that something very devious could be in play. Her mission was to "eyeball" the coast to enhance the limited warning systems on the west island and communicate her findings, but now she felt like she was sinking into a quicksand of a much more serious nature.

She sat on her bed and opened the first notebook while unconsciously reaching for a biscuit on the night table. Nicollette heard scratching on her bedroom door as she took a couple of bites from the sweet. *Monty wants to come in.* She opened the door and Monty walked straight to the night table, eyeing the plate of biscuits.

Nicollette obliged her furry friend with a piece of biscuit and sat back on the bed. Then it hit her like a brick. *Monty!! Now it makes sense. Dogs have keen senses of hearing and smell. Monty must've smelled the minute remnants of cyanide around Geoffrey's body. Now I understand his fear of that building. That strange smell killed his master and friend. Geoffrey Clarke was murdered!*

Nicollette gave Monty the remaining piece of biscuit while stroking his head. "We're going to work hard to solve this, old boy, that's a promise. Perhaps there are some clues in these notebooks."

A sudden surge of adrenaline ran through her body as she turned the pages of Geoffrey Clarke's books. It became immediately apparent that Geoffrey Clarke was a ham radio enthusiast. *Those bits and pieces I found today were from his ham radios.*

The first notebook contained pages that looked like a phone book, only in reverse. There was a column of letters and numbers followed by a corresponding column of initials. A third column contained single digit numbers and the last column showed a single letter, either an A, B or C.

Nicollette had some experience, albeit a very small one, with ham radios. A friend of her father's was an operator and he would talk about the conversations he had with people all around the world. She once asked him about all of his world-wide friends and how he could remember all their names. He answered that each friend had a call sign. A number was their name.

The first column was Geoffrey's contacts directory. The second column, made up of initials, appeared to indicate locations. There were quite a few UK, US, and HO as well as a few GY, FR, and PO. *Holland, Germany, France, and Poland.* It was becoming obvious that Geoffrey Clarke had quite a few connections around the globe.

The largest binder appeared to be the record of who he talked to and where they were from. The first entry was 17 April 1950 to someone in GY. Over thirty years ago. There was the number 5 and a B following the GY. Glancing over the log sheets Geoffrey Clarke created, it appeared his first few months of contacts were other operators from the UK, Germany, Poland, France, Holland and the US. A second binder contained the same type of log with the first entry being 17 April 1960 and the third binder started with the same date as the first two: 17 April 1970.

He kept one binder for each decade. I wonder why he used the date 17 April as his starting point for each of his logs? And why does each log book start at the beginning of a new decade? Does that date have some significance? A clue perhaps?

Nicollette noticed the last entry Geoffrey Clarke made in his logbook was 23 November 1978, just over four years ago. She pulled her pad out and scribbled down the call sign and related information. The country was HO, Holland, the number was 5 and the letter was B. She noticed over the last few pages of Geoffrey's log that there had been many contacts with that call sign over the previous months. Nicollette noticed four other call signs that were prominent during that same time period. From France, UK, US, and Germany. *Just a piece of the puzzle,* she thought. *What I need to find is what the letters and numbers mean in the logbook.*

Monty was asleep on the floor and it was nearly two in the morning when fatigue caught up to Nicollette. She had spent the last several hours going through Geoffrey Clarke's logbooks, trying desperately to find any significance between his ham radio activities and his very suspicious death. She knew there was still work to be done, however, she could not talk of her findings to Jo, at least not yet.

The rain was pounding the roof of the ranch house and a sudden boom of thunder brought Nicollette out of her sleep. She saw it was half ten and wandered into the dining area to find Jo and the four dogs. The wind had picked up and now was driving the rain against the windows.

"Good morning, Linda. Terrible storm we're having. You're probably not going too far today."

Nicollette remembered days like this when she was growing up in Brockwirth. Her mum, during those long rainy days, would get everyone together to do a cleaning and sort out of the house.

"Jo, how about I start earning my keep and do some housework around here? You could supervise and we could chat. I always find company and a good 'chin wag' makes the task go faster."

The front end of the house cleaned up quickly as Jo normally kept the kitchen and dining area very tidy. The sitting room just needed a hoover and a freshen up. Nicollette started to hoover the hallway leading to the bedrooms. She stopped at the door to the room she had secretly entered a few nights ago.

"Should I clean in here, Jo?" she asked.

Jo was in the sitting room, legs up, sipping tea. "Let's do that room last and just leave my room alone, Linda," she shouted back. "Just finish your room and have some tea with me."

The rain was still bucketing down as "Linda" finished her cup of tea with Jo. "Now, Linda, grab the hoover and duster and follow me."

Jo stopped at the closed door and turned to "Linda."

"You are the first person since Geoffrey died that I've allowed in this room, in fact, I've only been in this room just a few times myself over the last four years."

It was easy to hear a stumble in Joanne's voice as she spoke. *The room must bring back special memories, probably still a bit painful for her.*

"This was our office and study. Geoffrey and I would conduct the business of the farm here and we also used this room as our library."

Joanne turned on the light and walked across the room and opened the large curtain. A plume of dust flowed in the air.

Nicollette had to be careful not to let on that she already had been inside the room, albeit very briefly. She started to hoover while Jo sorted through the papers on top of the desk. Whilst cleaning, Nicollette looked at the framed old black and white photos hanging on the wall. There were several of Geoffrey Clarke working on the farm with the sheep, near a tractor, or in front of the barn buildings. But one in particular caught Nicollette's eyes. It was a photo of Geoffrey and Joanne with another couple in front of a house. There were some sheep standing around the group so she believed the photo was taken here, on the West Falkland Island. *Who are these people? They don't look like the Van Ghents.* Joanne saw "Linda" looking at the photo, "Something interesting? Bring it here and let's take a look."

Nicollette carefully removed the framed picture, exposing a marked difference between the color of the wall behind the frame and the surrounding wall. She handed the picture to Jo.

"Yes, I remember this picture."

Jo asked "Linda" to pull up a chair and sit down next to her.

"This is Geoffrey and me," pointing to the photo, "and these are the Smythes, Maureen and Michael. We used to call them 'M and M' like the American candy. They had a farm across the bay about the size of ours. We were good friends and spent lots of time together. Turns out, Michael, Geoffrey, and your friend Peter all worked together during and just after the war. In the end, we all came here around the same time, except for your Peter Johnson, of course."

Jo took a deep breath and sighed, looking at "Linda."

"Very sad story about Michael and Maureen, Linda. Michael loved to fish and had all the gear, even a small boat. He and Maureen would go out very early in the morning and we would have fish and chips later that night. Loads of fun, great memories. One day they went out on the Bay and never came back. They just disappeared! It's been fifteen years and they never found any trace of them or the boat. It's like they just vanished into thin air! It's all so strange because he was a good boatsman. Very sad, very sad indeed!"

Nicollette pulled a tissue out of her pocket and handed it to Jo. It was obvious that Jo was struggling with the memories, but felt comfortable enough to talk with her.

"I want to show you something, Linda, something I haven't shared with anyone."

Nicollette's leg started to twitch. *Whatever is she going to share with me? Whatever it is, it must be deeply personal and very private.*

Joanne reached down to a lower drawer on the desk. She emptied the few contents of the drawer and then pulled the drawer completely out from the desk. She laid the drawer upside down on the desktop, revealing an old large brown envelope taped to the bottom. There was a red government stamp on the left-hand corner of the envelope. Jo carefully undid the clasp and pulled out a stack of larger photos.

"I want you to see these. I've kept these hidden for a long time, even Geoffrey didn't know I had saved them. I didn't want to upset him or his recovery."

Jo handed the photos one by one to "Linda." The first few photos were of Geoffrey Clarke in his Army uniform. "He was an officer and I was so proud of him."

Then Jo showed "Linda" a photo that sent a bolt of lightning through her body. Nicollette's hand started to shake. She was holding a picture of several army men in and around a jeep. She immediately recognized the photo. *It's just like the one my father has in his wooden box! What? How? When?*

"That's Geoffrey and Peter here. Do you know who this is?" Joanne asked.

Nicollette tried to calm her shaking hand and clear her throat. "That's my father," she whispered back.

"Look at this one," Jo said, handing her another picture.

It was a photo of Geoffrey Clarke and Peter Johnson with James and Alice Beverley.

"This is Mum and Dad's wedding!"

There were several minutes of a deafening quiet between the two women. Only the rain pounding on the roof and the occasional boom of thunder interrupted the silence.

Nicollette couldn't stop staring at her parents' wedding photo while a million ideas flowed across her brain. *How did Joanne find out? Is there a history I need to know about? How come Mum didn't recognize him at our house? Or did she? How does this affect me? My mission? Who else knows? What am I going to do?*

Joanne Clarke reached for Nicollette's arm.

"I know who you are, Nicollette. You are James and Alice's daughter. The six of us, your parents, Peter and Elizabeth and me and Geoffrey, were all good friends, even during Geoffrey's tough times just after the war. When I was in London and Peter contacted me about hosting someone on my ranch for some government work, of course I had a lot of questions, who wouldn't? But then he told me who that someone was, James and Alice's daughter, Nicollette. You could have knocked me over with a feather! I knew about your brother, Edward, but never knew that James and Alice had a daughter. Peter and I talked for some time and I was convinced of two things. First, if Peter was involved in some government project, then it must be important and second, if Nicollette Beverley is the daughter of James and Alice, then she must be alright too. And here you are."

The two of them just let the moment evolve, each looking into the other's eyes. Nicollette was at a loss for words. She knew she needed to say something, but what to say? There was still a job to do, a mission to complete, and potential danger to both her and Joanne. She understood that everything she did or said from now on must be thought through thoroughly.

"Now here's something I've never seen before," Jo exclaimed as she gathered a small stack of letters that had fallen from inside an accounts book. A small piece of red ribbon bound the papers together. "Shall we take a look?"

Nicollette nodded her head affirmatively as Joanne carefully untied the red ribbon. The postage mark on the envelope showed that the letter originated in the Allied portion of Berlin on 25 February 1949.

"That's not long after we arrived here. We'd only been here a month or so," Jo exclaimed as she opened the envelope and retrieved the letter. She read the single, handwritten page, and then handed it to Nicollette.

"This makes no sense to me and I don't know any Paddy, nor do I remember Gerald mentioning that name."

Nicollette read the letter.

23 Feb 1949
British Zone

Occupied Berlin
Gerald,

We have followed up the inquiry you gave us, but to no avail.

However, some new information has come to our attention and we are working hard on it now. We have a contact we must see in Kiel and we are working to get transport out of the Berlin zone so we can get there.

Paddy

"What does it mean, Nicky?" Jo asked.

"I'm not sure, but it reads like Gerald had contacts in the occupational Army. It sounds like they were looking for an answer or something, Jo. See if there is another envelope with a later postdate."

Joanne picked up the next envelope, postdated 17 March 1949.

15 March 1949
British Zone
Occupied Germany
Gerald,

We finally made it to Kiel. The contact here has given us some useful information. Your picture was helpful. We are working on it now. Your thoughts may have some reality in them!

Paddy

"This is the last letter. It's postdated 10 April 1949." Nicollette opened the letter and her eyes went wide as she read the text.

Gerald,

Your suspicions may be right. It's possible it's the same man. We are going through the records of the whereabouts,

arrests, and other missing officers.It is a slow process however, there's a lot of interest in these men, from the military
courts, the police, fellow underground Nazis, co-conspirators and even vigilante private citizens. We must be careful,
the pitch is getting rather crowded. Are you operational?

    Paddy (XYM3ZAB7HQ41749)

Nicollette laid the letter down slowly, her heart pounding
through her chest as she realized that she was getting knee
deep in some serious muck, far beyond her mission. She saw
the angst in Jo's face as she digested the words of the three
letters.

"Geoffrey must have made some inquiries to some old war
friends working in the occupation zones regarding something
he heard or saw or stumbled across, Jo."

"But we're in the Falklands! Europe is thousands of miles
away and at that time, Geoffrey was still dealing with those
painful memories! How could this be?"

Nicollette wanted to say something, but she still didn't have
all the pieces of the puzzle and certainly didn't want to frighten
Jo with speculation. All that came to mind in response to Jo's
question was, "Maybe it's all related, Jo. Maybe Geoffrey was
working on something before you moved here and just wanted
to tie up loose ends."

"Maybe," Jo replied, "maybe."

Nicollette prepared the tea and Jo asked her to bring over
the pill box. In all the excitement of the afternoon, she had
forgotten to take her handful of pills.

"This reminds me, Nicollette, that Dr. Khan will be here
Tuesday to look me over. He comes a couple of times a year
to the West Island to check us out. Don't worry, Linda, I'll
remember."

Joanne finished her sweet and walked off to bed with three
dogs in tow. It was just past eight. *Today must've really worn*

her out, Nicollette thought as she waited for the light under Jo's door to go off.

In her room, she set up the radio and signaled to Val. While she was waiting for the connection reply, Nicollette pulled out her notepad and gathered her thoughts. The normal mission nightly communication would be brief, there was not much to report. Queen Charlotte Bay had been quiet. However, she was thinking that she may have stumbled across something that was too big for her to handle on her own. There was too much information to communicate over the radio. She needed to see Val in person, ending the evening's message with:

> Just been fishing and caught a big one! I needed help to reel it in.
> Can't wait to fry it up with chips!

After ten minutes, Val responded;

> I would love to join you! I'll bring the malt vinegar!

Time Warp

Dr. Azir Khan arrived promptly at 10:00 a.m. Tuesday. Joanne introduced her niece "Linda" to him and they talked briefly about London. "Linda" excused herself and went to her bedroom, carefully leaving the door cracked open so she might be able to hear some of the conversation. She noticed Jo was carrying a large envelope when she accompanied the doctor into the sitting room. More out of concern than curiosity, Nicollette laid on the floor with her ears by the door.

Nicollette could just make out the normal sounds of Dr. Khan checking out Joanne. She heard Jo say, "Here is the information from the hospital," as she handed him the envelope. There were several minutes of quiet.

"Well, what does it say, Doctor?" Jo asked impatiently. "And please be honest with me."

Again, there was a moment of silence until Dr. Khan responded. His voice was soft and hard to hear, so Nicollette carefully opened her door and crawled down the hallway.

"Joanne, I've known you for some time now and I will be very straightforward. Your condition is not so good. The hospital report says that you may be on limited time, there wasn't much they could do. They prescribed some strong medication for you, but you might want to start to make arrangements."

Another minute or two of silence.

"How much time?" Joanne asked in a quivering voice.

"Hard to tell, maybe two to six months. Are you feeling any symptoms? Pain?"

"No pain but I get tired easily. Too easily."

"That is to be expected. Do you need any more medicine?"

"I think so, let me check."

Nicollette rushed back into her room as she heard Joanne walk into the kitchen. She laid across her bed, wiping the tears from her eyes. She had suspected that Jo was in poor health, but now those suspicions had been confirmed.

The front door closed and Nicollette could hear the doctor's truck leave the ranch. She walked out of her room and saw Jo coming up the hallway.

"How did it go, Jo?"

"Everything as expected, Nicky, and I was just coming to get you. Fancy a trip to Port Stanley, maybe Thursday into Friday? I have to pick up some medications and Dr. Khan wants to see me in his office."

"Ok, but I'm driving, Jo."

"So who else?" Jo replied with a smile. "I'll make the arrangements at the hotel."

That night, Nicollette communicated to Val that she would be in Port Stanley Thursday and Friday. She coded in the message that she would be bringing some fish and asked how it should be packed. Val responded, "How big are the fish?" Nicollette indicated, "More than enough for four." Val coded back that she should use the small case and wrap the fish real good. Nicollette remembered the two of them had the same sets of luggage, so they could meet, exchange cases and no one would know. Val planned a rendezvous for the two of them at the Government House on Ross Rd. Nicollette would ring twice and hang up, signaling Val to send a cab to the Malvinas Hotel to collect her for the meeting. The evening's signal ended with, "Remember to keep the fish iced."

There was one very important task Nicollette wanted to complete before meeting Val in Port Stanley. *I must make a trip to the old Smythe Farm.* Early Wednesday morning, she retrieved the old envelope containing the government letter with the dated map and the more recent map Jo had given her. *These two maps will give me a good idea as to where I'm going.* Jo reminded her about the early start for Port Stanley the next morning and to make sure there was enough petrol in the Rover.

"Take Monty with you if you want," she added.

Nicollette loaded the truck with some scientific equipment and related gear and the two of them headed off. As they left the ranch, Nicollette felt her right thigh one last time for her holstered gun. *I hope I don't need it!*

They picked up the main road about five kilometers to the east and then drove north another thirty or so to where they headed west towards the old Smythe place.

The main road was one of the few that were paved or at least hardened on the West Island. It served as the main route for the small amount of traffic and led to the ferry to the East Island at Fox Bay. Nicollette was very aware that they would drive within a few kilometers of the Van Ghent ranch and even though it was not likely, it was possible to be spotted.

As they headed north, Nicollette saw a small tanker truck in her rearview mirror. She slowed down to allow the truck to pass her, then tailed the truck until they approached the area near the Van Ghents place. She would use the truck as a shield. *Thank goodness for the left-hand roads and limited traffic here!*

Nicollette accelerated into the oncoming traffic lane and kept pace with the tanker. She glanced up at the driver and could see him shouting at her. She just smiled and waved back, making the driver act even more animated towards her. She drove on the wrong side of the road for over three kilometers with the tanker as a cover until she saw a vehicle coming straight at her. She accelerated in front of the tanker and was serenaded with a rather lengthy blast from his horn.

She was able to put some distance between herself and the tanker truck when she came to the rutted dirt road leading to the Smythes' place. As they turned down the track, she could just make out the silhouettes of buildings in the distance. They were well below the grade of the main road, so it was highly unlikely the driver of the tanker could see her.

Nicollette carefully drove the very rutted trail until she came upon a locked gate blocking the way. She left the truck to inspect the gate. A sign warned, "Danger! No Trespassing! Private Government Property!"

The lock and chain on the gate were rusted but no match for the five-pound sledge and jimmy bar in the back of the truck. Three whacks on the hinges and the chain fell free. Nicollette drove the truck through the gate, stopped, and carefully reattached the hinges to the post. "We don't want any uninvited guests now, do we, Monty?" She could now see the ruins of the farmhouse more clearly, less than a kilometer up the trail.

The area around the farmhouse and outbuildings was visibly unkempt and overgrown. Nicollette parked and let Monty out and took a quick look around the outside of the house. The house looked to be in quite a state. The windows were boarded up and the front and rear doors were blocked with wood planks. There was another "No Trespassing" and "Government Warning" sign attached to the front door. A large section of the roof had collapsed and there were visible loose shingles all around the ground. The back of the house faced straight to the Queen Charlotte Bay inlet about half a kilometer away. The house itself was only about three or four meters above the bay, with a very soft slope to the water. Shame. It's a magnificent view!

After gathering her camera, torch, and jimmy bar from the truck, she headed towards the barns, passing two large aboveground tanks. *Probably propane and fuel for the equipment.*

There were two barns, much like the Clarkes' place. The first barn was easily accessible through the unlocked door. Once inside, the stench nearly knocked Nicollette over and caused Monty to stay outside. There was the smell of rotted hay, decomposed waste, mildew, and building rot. A couple of holes in the roof provided some light, but also allowed the rain to turn the dirt floor into mud. Rusted farm implements were against an exterior wall, but no mechanical equipment inside. There was abundant evidence on the floor, of birds living in the rafters and eaves. Nicollette used her shirt tail to cover her nose and mouth as she quickly investigated the building. It appeared to her that the barn hadn't been used since the last day the Smythes were alive, almost fifteen years ago.

The second barn proved to be much different from the start. The side door and the large barn doors were bolted by padlocks. Nicollette saw what appeared to be a wide trail leading from the barn to the back area of the house. The large rainstorm the day before had matted down the vegetation covering the rutted track. *Looks big enough for a truck or large tractor,* she thought.

It took some effort and a large stone, but the jimmy bar soon did its work and the side door was opened.

There was quite a contrast between the two buildings. The inside of this barn was clean and in much better shape. The roof was solid and even the electricity was working. There was no evidence of agricultural use at all. No hay or farm equipment of any type, in fact. Despite the well-worn look of the outside, the inside of this barn looked to Nicollette like a new building. Very odd. There was also something very different to any barn or farm building Nicollette had ever been in before. *There was a cement floor! It's more like a warehouse than a farm building.*

Monty was all too happy to scamper inside as Nicollette followed. The building was practically empty, only occupied by large stacks of pallets and crates along one of the exterior walls. The opposite wall was made up of three rather large block wall rooms, none of which had windows. The doors to the rooms were made of some very heavy metal and were bolted in three places. *It would take an explosive to open these doors. They're like large bank vaults!*

A fourth room in the rear of the barn had an interior window next to the door. The door was locked and the jimmy bar wasn't enough to budge it. However, it worked well on the glass window. Through the broken glass, Nicollette carefully climbed into the room.

Inside the room, Nicollette found the light switch and unlocked the door from the inside as a precaution. The sound of crunching glass greeted each step as she walked towards some filing cabinets behind three desks. The cabinets were completely empty. She investigated under and behind each drawer. Nothing. The first and second desk had the same results as the filing cabinets. Nothing. Nicollette did, however, find two folded papers under the bottom drawer of the third desk. *They must have slipped down between the top drawers.*

She unfolded the papers on the desk. It looked like a shipping ticket, similar to the ones she used at her old job at Russells. The numbers were fine but she didn't recognize the lettering, in fact, the whole paper was written in some language she hadn't seen before. The date on the paper was 1979, followed by some foreign characters: a two followed by some foreign characters, a twenty-six followed by some foreign characters. Nicollette deduced that the date on the paper was 2/26/1979. *That's just a couple of months after the Smythes died.*

The second paper was columned and all in foreign print, except for the same date and what looked to her like a quantity column. *An inventory sheet perhaps?* She folded up the papers and placed them in her front pocket. *Must show these to Val!*

Turning to leave the room, a quick flash of a shiny object sticking out from behind the file cabinet caught her eye. Nicollette saw it was the head of an electric cord like the kind that would be plugged into a tele or radio. She pulled the cabinet from the wall to reveal a service outlet and an unfamiliar set of prongs in the wall. She made a quick sketch and took a picture. *Val is going to be busy!*

The pallets and crates against the wall appeared to be empty, but then Nicollette noticed some faded black markings on the concrete floor. *Just like the kind that were on the floor of the storage buildings at Russells! They're made by forklift tires shuffling around. This isn't a barn, it's a warehouse!*

Two silos were at the back of the barn building. Again, they looked very weather- worn, like the outsides of the barn buildings, and both access doors were locked.

Nicollette looked around the closest silo and saw a pair of cables coming from the inside of the barn building and climbing up to the top of the silo. The jimmy bar did short work of the silo's locked door. She reached for her torch and walked onto a concrete floor inside the tall cylindrical building, guessing the silo was about five meters across and about twenty-five meters high. There was a clear view to the top of the silo. The small access door near the roof was open, allowing a small amount of light to illuminate the ceiling area. She could see two large hooks at the ends of a chain about a meter or so above her. The chains extended all the way to the roof. She was looking up at the top of the silo and walking further into it when her left foot tripped over something. She pointed her torch downwards. There was a large round metal plate embedded in the floor. The plate was over a meter across and firmly buried into the concrete. *Like a manhole cover!* There was a large padlock anchoring the cover to the floor.

Nicollette shook the lock, surprised to find that the lock arm was not engaged, simply pushed together and easily removed. A notch on either side of the cover allowed the jemmy bar to fit inside perfectly. Nicollette sat on the floor and used her leg to budge the cover off its metal ring and onto the concrete floor. *That cover must weigh at least five stone!* She aimed the torch down the hole and could see the bottom. There was a thin steel ladder attached to the underside of the floor. Nicollette looked at Monty. "Shall I, old boy?"

Before she ascended, she remembered one of the rules her instructors had talked about: "Check your areas. Be sure of your surroundings before compromising your safety. Always give yourself an avenue of escape and proceed with caution."

Nicollette walked out of the barn and took a quick look around the grounds. All clear. She gathered a rope from the truck and went back to the silo. After securing the rope to the door frame, she tied the rope around her waist. While using her left hand to hold the torch, she used her right hand to slowly descend the ladder.

The ladder ended about half a meter from the floor, about six or seven meters down. She stepped onto a concrete floor and used her torch to illuminate the space. She spotted a wire running from the ceiling to a switch. She flipped the switch on and several lights illuminated the room.

Nicollette was in a room about eight meters square. *Someone has gone to a lot of trouble to build this!* Each wall was filled from floor to ceiling with small wooden and metal boxes. *There must be a couple hundred or more here!* She walked over to the nearest stack of boxes and her senses went into overdrive as she saw a small Nazi swastika emblem on the outside of each box. Beneath the emblem were the words "der Zunder." She walked around the room and saw the same Nazi markings on every box and name labels like Schalten, Sicherungen, Kabelbaum, and Elektronische Schaltung. She did not understand German but the labels on the last large stack of boxes gave her pause. Der Timers and Ballistiks. *That's timers and ballistics in my language! Explosives? Bombs?*

Nicollette held her hands steady as she took pictures of the boxes and made notes on her small pad. A sudden chill ran up her spine. Had she stumbled upon a very complex and serious situation? *A secret storage of World War II armaments!*

She knew full well that this discovery could have very dangerous and potentially dire consequences for her and for many people. A million questions were flowing through her brain. *Someone is storing a hoard of Nazi war equipment. The war has been over for almost forty years. Who put it here? How did it get here? What are they going to do with it? Does this have anything to do with the Falklands? Val needs to get this information back to London fast!*

Nicollette wiped her wet hands on her shorts and climbed up the ladder, her heart still racing. She carefully pushed the manhole cover over the opening, fastened the padlock as she found it, and did her best to reattach the door to the silo. *No need to leave any trace of us from the outside, Monty!*

She and Monty walked past the second silo and back towards the ranch house. They had passed the two aboveground tanks before and hadn't paid any attention to them, but before Nicollette left the farm, she wanted to take a closer look. *Those two tanks seem a bit large for this size ranch, she thought, and why are they here years after this farm stopped working? Normally, a working farm would have one tank of propane for heating and cooking and a larger farm might have a tank for fuel, but this farm is much too small for that size tank. I wonder if these tanks have something to do with what I found?*

She approached the tanks and looked for some identification. The paint on both tanks was weather faded and unlabeled. Nicollette looked closer at the filling point and air valves on the first tank. There was a slight rusting around the caps and no detectable smell. She used her jemmy bar to hit the tank and could hear a hollow sound. When she hit the second tank, she heard a distinctly different sound. *This tank is full! Why? What could possibly be inside? Propane wouldn't make a full sound!*

Monty suddenly ran off down the trail to the water. Nicollette suspected he must have seen a rabbit or something. She called him, but he did not respond. She followed the trail about ten meters past the house, walking towards the water, when she stepped on something very hard. Covered by overgrowth and mud, she had walked onto a concrete path leading to the water.

Nicollette followed the path all the way to the bay, where it connected to a concrete apron that extended further into the water. The water in the bay was a bit murky, so it was not easy to tell the full distance the apron extended, but she guessed at least another five meters at least. Off to her right were the remnants of a wooden pier and four pylons sticking out of the water. *The Smythes were boating people and they probably used the wood pier. Would they have gone to the trouble of building a concrete launch? What would be the reason? I bet not! Maybe Jo can help?*

She called for Monty as she started up the path. Monty caught up with her about halfway. *Got away, did he, old boy,* she said whilst patting his head, even as her mind was digesting all the information she discovered.

The two of them loaded up, entered the main road, and headed south. Nicollette remembered to do one last look around before she left, making sure to eliminate any evidence of her visit. She was vigilant in reattaching the gate lock, her mind still trying to calibrate the discoveries and come up with theories as to what she saw; however, one simple thought continually interrupted her thoughts. *There is something very serious going on here. It's vast, and I'm in the middle of it! Must be very careful, Nicky! Very careful!* Subconsciously, she reached for the gun on her right thigh as they drove to get petrol in Port Stephens.

It was evening when Nicollette and Monty arrived back at the Clarke ranch. Jo had set out a meal for Monty and a cold plate for Nicollette along with a note.

> Remember our early start tomorrow. See you at 5:30. The ferry leaves promptly at 8.
> Jo.

Not Finished Yet

The sun was rising over the eastern horizon, illuminating the hardscrabble landscape. Nicollette and Joanne had finished loading the truck and were on the way to the ferry at Fox Bay. Jo reminded Nicollette about being "first on, first off" the ferry.

Just a few hours earlier, Nicollette had finished her packing and sent the evening signal. There was nothing to report on the bay this night. Nicollette noted there had been no activity for the last week. *Quiet, very quiet. Maybe too quiet.*

In preparing for the trip, Nicollette remembered Jo never locked her house and although they weren't expecting any guests, she followed the rule to expect the unexpected.

Nicollette was careful to organize her room to look as if an environmental research student was living there, careful to leave exposed only some meteorological gear and soil sample machines. She wrapped her sensitive equipment in a special bag and positioned it inside the mattress. The outside rain spout suited well for hiding the antenna and the radio equipment fit easily in the gap in the closet ceiling.

Trying to get a few hours kip before the trip, Nicollette laid down trying to relax, but her eyes just stared at the moonlit shadows dancing across the ceiling. Her heart pounded as her mind continued to try and work out the discoveries at the Smythe farm. Finally, out of exhaustion, Nicollette fell into a restless sleep, but not before deciding to bring her weapon with her on the trip to Port Stanley.

It was nearly 1:00 p.m. when they arrived at the Malvinas Hotel in Port Stanley. Joanne had booked two rooms. They were quickly checked in and agreed to have dinner together at six. As a precaution against pre-hidden surveillance devices, Nicollette asked Joanne to switch rooms when they were in the elevator, using a lame excuse about the sunlight and the view. "Of course, Linda, I understand," Jo replied with a smile as they exchanged keys.

The room was as expected and Nicollette did a quick search for any surveillance devices. *This room is clean. Can never be too sure though.* At 1:35, she followed Val's instructions for the cab and waited for its arrival in the lobby. The cab arrived at 1:45 and the driver asked for "a Miss Linda Crowther" at the desk.

Already in the lobby, Nicollette noticed the driver was a younger man with cropped short hair. *A soldier perhaps?* A preset coded verbal exchange was made between them and he escorted her to the cab for the short drive to Government House.

The cab drove through a side gate to a secluded entry of Government House and the "driver" escorted Nicollette to a basement door. As they were walking inside, a combination of anticipation and anxiety burst inside Nicollette. She was going to see her friend for the first time in weeks, then she would be giving a briefing about her discoveries. Just inside the door, at the security desk, an armed RAF Sergeant asked for identification while another soldier stood with a rifle.

Nicollette handed him her "Linda Crowther" information as Val had instructed. "Follow me, Miss," the RAF Sergeant instructed.

Nicollette was led to a small white door where the sergeant used a patterned knock on the door. Nicollette heard Val reply, "Enter." The sergeant opened the door and shut it immediately behind her. Nicollette and Val stared at each other for all of two seconds before rushing to hug each other. "What about me?" a man's voice inquired.

Nicollette nearly jumped out of her shoes when she saw

Charles Thompson in the corner. The two of them shook hands then hugged. "Now let's get down to work," he said. "You've brought a 'big fish,' Nicky, so we've got a lot to cover."

The three of them sat at a large table. Nicollette opened her case and handed Mr. Thompson the camera and rolls of undeveloped film. He went to the door, whispered something to the guard, and returned to the table. Val rolled out a large map of the West Falkland Island on the table. "Nicollette, let's start with Joanne Clarke."

Nicollette went into great detail about how Joanne lived and who she knew. She described how her farm land was leased to the Van Ghents and about Jo's interest in a small store in Port Stephens. "She's been really nice to me and hasn't asked any questions."

She discussed the visit to the Van Ghents' large house. Nicollette discussed the large amount of artwork the Van Ghents owned and how palatial the home was, "like a museum or even a castle." She recounted meeting the family and the suspicious looks she felt from the son-in-law Miguel. "I've found, though, the most interesting person of all is Ellen Van Ghent's Uncle, Luuk Claassen." Nicollette added, "He seems to me to look very much out of place in the Falklands. He's very 'old world,' continental, pert and proper, not very giving of information. He has a heavy accent and his posture is too erect for his older age. Like an athlete or career military man would have."

Charles turned to Val. "Make a note to look into the Van Ghents and especially this Luke Claassen fellow."

Val acknowledged him and Nicollette started talking about Geoffrey Clarke's workshop building. She went into great detail about finding the old broken radio components and the antenna in the attic. "But the two most interesting things I found were a hidden pillowcase in the attic. It had all his notes and this." Nicollette reached into her case and handed Charles the small wooden box. "I believe Geoffrey Clarke was murdered and this box contained the weapon."

Charles examined the box closely while Nicollette asked him to open the box and carefully pull back the velvet lining. She pointed out the Nazi inscription engraved in the wood and the small paper attached to the underside of the velvet.

"I remember reading about some German officers having a cyanide capsule implanted inside a tooth and other German officers being given different means of killing themselves. Perhaps this box is one of them," Val said.

"I want London to look at this, Nicky," Charles announced as he slid the box off to one side. "And let's keep Joanne in the dark. Even if what you speculate is true, I don't want to introduce new information about Geoffrey's death. No need for her to relive that sad time. Now let's look at the contents of the old pillow case, shall we."

Nicollette carefully emptied the contents of the dirty pillowcase onto the table. She pointed out that Geoffrey Clarke had organized the binders in chronological order, by decades, but had left no index or guide sheet. Val and Charles started thumbing through the binders. Nicollette then handed Charles and Val the small stack of letters that were in the bottom of the desk drawer.

"These are letters Jo and I found at the bottom of a drawer. Jo says she didn't recognize or know anything about them."

"Read them aloud please, Val."

When she finished reading the last letter, Val commented, "What do you make of it?"

A sudden knock on the door broke the conversation. Charles cracked open the door and was handed a manilla envelope. "Your photos Nicky," he exclaimed as he handed the envelope to Nicollette. "Let's take a look at them."

"These are the pictures I took at Maureen and Michael Smythes' farm yesterday." Nicollette described the reasoning behind her rising curiosity and subsequent visit. She talked about her sightings, the ruins of the buildings and the two maps.

"One map showed the farm and on the second map, albeit eight years later, the farm had disappeared. Literally, it had ceased to exist."

She handed Charles the letter the Clarkes received from the administration about a works project on Queen Charlotte Bay that also contained a map showing the Smythe farm. Nicollette also gave him the more current map showing the farm's disappearance.

"It does seem strange but maybe there is a logical explanation," Val implied. "Perhaps after their deaths, the farm was transferred to another owner who wanted privacy."

"And that's another thing," Nicollette said. "The circumstances around the Smythes deaths are suspicious as well. Jo tells me they died in a boating accident and neither the boat or their bodies were ever found. Jo also explained that the day Smythes went missing there was a calm sea, no storm or bad weather around. In addition, both Maureen and Michael were very experienced boaters. It all sounds a bit suspect to me."

"Let's look at those pictures, Nicky," Charles instructed.

The first group of pictures were the security gate and sign, the farm buildings, and the general landscape of the area. The next set of pictures drew Val's and Charles's immediate attention.

"This is the interior of the second farm building." Nicollette pointed out the office area, the cement flooring, and the tire tracks. "Highly unusual, I'd say."

The next set of photos were of the safe-like structures along the side wall of the barn.

"Whatever are these for?" Val blurted.

Charles stared silently at the photographs.

Nicollette pulled the last group of photographs from the

envelope. "This is the interior of the silo. Notice the chains hanging from the top. And here is the ultra large steel cover embedded in the floor."

Nicollette recalled how difficult it was to move the cover but how, once it was removed, it revealed the entrance to an underground warehouse. Her narration continued. "I climbed down several meters on a narrow ladder to a rather large room. I found a light switch and the electricity worked!"

Nicollette used the pictures to describe in detail the organized stacks of boxes with Nazi insignias and labels written in German. "When I saw the word Ballistik, I must admit, I had a shiver down my spine. There was a small armory down there!"

There was silence in the room. Charles investigated each photograph, then passed them on to Val. Each photo was marked and matched to her notes. Every so often, she would look at Nicky, her friend and co-worker in this dangerous game, but unlike earlier when they were passing smiles, Val's expression was blank, almost as if it was painted on. Nicollette had only seen this look once before, when the two of them were in Brussels. *Different time, different situation.*

Finally, after he finished the stack of photographs, Charles broke the silence. "Anything else, Nicollette?"

Nicollette handed him the photos she took from the rear of the Smythes' home and down to the edge of Queen Charlotte Bay. "I found this area very unusual for a small farm on the West Island. Oh, and then there were the two large tanks."

"Two tanks?"

"Yes. They are normally filled with gas or propane for the farm, but these tanks were more than twice the size of the ones at Jo's place."

She pointed out the tanks and the concrete road leading to the ramp that extended well into the water. Then the photo of the remains of the old wooden pier off to one side.

When Charles was finished analyzing the last of the photographs, he handed them off to Val and took a deep breath.

"What do you think, Nicollette?"

"I'm not too sure, Charles, but I have a suspicion that everything is related. From the circumstances around Geoffrey Clarke's death to the discoveries at the Smythes' farm. And I can't help but feel that the Van Ghents are involved somehow, some way. I mean, a palace in a sheep field? Add in Mr. Luuk Claassen, who appears way out of place here, and then there is Miguel."

Nicollette paused.

"Maybe I'm on the wrong train or have been around sheep too much, but I believe there is something, something."

"Maybe there's substance to your suspicions, or maybe not. Either way, I think it's best to keep on mission and stay alert until instructed otherwise. I'm going to take this information back to London, and Nicollette..." He reached for her hand. "You are on your own here. I want you to be careful, very careful."

Val gathered all the information and handed the pile of papers to Charles Thompson. As he stood to leave, he shook Val's hand and gave a brief hug.

"Thank you, Miss Davies. You should be careful too, Valerie." He turned to Nicollette, shook her hand and gave her a brief hug. "Thank you, Miss Beverley."

The door shut behind him and Charles was gone, leaving Nicollette and Val alone in the room. The two friends looked at each other as they sat down at the conference table. Val reached for Nicollette's hands and squeezed them.

"Nicky, you brought us a really big fish and I'm a little nervous for you. If what you're speculating is true, you could be in real trouble and I think Charles feels the same way. Think about how he said goodbye, using our formal names. He's right, you know, it's not like other missions, you are all alone in the middle of nowhere here."

She's right. I am on my own. If I'm right, whoever is behind all this means business. They murdered Geoffrey Clarke.

Nicollette realized this was no time for false bravado, it was alright to be human and be a little bit frightened. Perhaps a little fear would make her senses more acute and reactive. She knew she was well trained and had survived dangerous situations before. She recalled those words from training that were engraved in her brain: "All it takes is one slip up, one poor assumption, one mis-calculation, and it could be over."

"You and Charles are right. I need to be alert and stay on mission." She squeezed Val's hand tightly. "I'm not finished yet, Val, I'm not finished yet!"

It was nearly 5:30. Val had a dinner date with Jo at 6:00 The two young women walked to the exit door where the driver was waiting to take Nicollette back to the Malvina Hotel.

"Take care, Nicky," Val said. "Stay safe and on mission. Hopefully, this will all be over soon and we can go home."

"You too, Val. Be safe and watch out for those handsome soldiers!"

The bit of levity in Nicollette's remark brought a smile to Val. "By the way, I'm not completely alone, Val, I have my partner Monty."

"Monty?" Val questioned.

"Yes, Monty, the dog in the pictures. He's taken a liking to me."

As she looked back at Val from the window of the cab, she thought about Val's words. *"We can go home."* Home!

Chasing Rabbits

The soft sound of waves hitting the beach had an almost hypnotic, relaxing effect. Earlier at breakfast, Joanne explained that she had some morning business to attend to and that they would leave for the ferry to the west island around noon. She suggested that Nicollette visit the seaside.

An hour later, Nicollette found herself at Surf Beach, sitting on a towel, sand between her toes, listening to the songs of the birds overhead. The peace and serenity were quite a contrast to the meeting with Val and Charles yesterday. Just reporting her findings, describing the photographs, and reliving the experience caused anxiety to flow throughout her being. Now that was over and sitting on the beach watching the open stretch of sea in front of her gave pause to Nicollette's being and a chance to breathe. Her system decompressing. She closed her eyes and her thoughts turned to home. *Home!*

A sense of movement near her caused Nicollette to stir from the peace of her serenity. She opened her eyes to see two men walking just a couple of meters in front of her. Nicollette thought it was a bit strange that they would be walking so close to her with the water nearly twenty meters away. *There is no one on this beach!*

As they passed her, one of the men dropped what looked like a candy wrapper. Rather than yell at them and cause a scene, she stood from the blanket and picked up the bit of trash while giving an angry stare to the backs of the two men walking away. Sitting back down on the blanket, she subconsciously unravelled the red wrapper to see what kind of candy it was. *Kit Kat, I bet!* It was a Kit Kat wrapper, but there was a small white paper attached to the inside. Nicollette looked down at the beach. The two men were gone. She carefully opened the paper to find it was a note from Val.

Nicky,

    C left for London last night. He had a very concerned look on his face and was very quiet and subdued.

    Sarah sent a message to him before he left and I decoded it. She reported some new Argentine movement of troops and armor towards the coast as well as 2 squadrons of SkyhawkFighter Jets. Something big may be under way. London is talking to Washington this week. I thought you should know.

    The cab driver told us your whereabouts.

    Take care, V

Nicollette quickly stuffed the wrapper and note into her pocket. She glanced at her watch. It was past 11:00. There was just enough time to pick up a few things at the market before she met up with Jo for the ride home. *Something big? An invasion? Maybe just posturing, or maybe not.*

Jo slept for most of the six-hour drive back to the ranch. She told Nicky that the doctor did some tests and gave her new prescriptions. "Dr. Khan says the new medicine could make me a bit tired, so I hope I'm not too much of a burden, Nicky."

Jo was fighting to stay awake, her eyelids closing. Soon she was asleep. Nicollette didn't let on that she knew how sick Joanne was. "Never a burden, Jo. You get some rest."

Monty was excited to see the Range Rover drive through the gate. He scrambled to the truck and jumped on Nicollette. The other dogs accompanied Jo into the house. Nicollette prepared some soup and crispy bread for tea and started to unpack while it was cooking. Monty joined her in the room as Nicollette laid her cases on the bed. As she unzipped the cases, Monty jumped on the bed as if looking for a treat. "I didn't forget you, boy," she said as she handed him a dried ram's bone.

Nicollette noticed something sticking to his paw. "Let me see that paw, Monty." She softly grabbed his right front paw and saw a piece of double stick tape stuck to it. Nicollette gingerly pulled it off. "Now where did you get this, Monty?" She called out to Jo to see if she had any double stick tape around. Jo replied that she didn't have any.

Nicollette rushed back into her room and shut the door. *Double stick tape can be used to hide a device. Someone was sloppy. My room and maybe this house is bugged!* Frantically, she pushed all the furniture to the center of the room, pulling every drawer from the chest and laying them on the bed. She lay all the clothing on the floor and took the curtains down. She searched each inch of the closet, including the cracks in the floor and ceiling. *Nothing.* She then crawled along the floor around the perimeter of the room. *Still nothing!* The window and curtain hardware were also clean. *It's got to be here!*

Jo knocked and opened the door. "Whatever is going on here?"

Nicollette put her finger to her lips and made a quiet "shush" sound. She escorted Jo into the hallway and outside. "I think we've been bugged, Jo."

"I'll get the spray," Jo replied.

Nicollette was too anxious to smile at Jo's response.

"No, Jo. A secret listening device may have been placed here while we were in Port Stanley," she whispered back.

"You mean someone has been in my house while we were gone? What do we do?"

"It looks so. We need to find the device and disconnect it and you need to call me Linda all the time now."

"What does the device look like?"

"They're small with a piece of wire attached, and usually disguised to blend into the background. Look for something unusual."

The sun was setting and Nicollette turned on the light by her bedside. She turned the switch, but nothing happened. She tried again, no luck. She pulled the shade off and saw the bulb was loose and the socket was a different color metal than the shade brace. Nicollette whispered to Jo for a screwdriver and unplugged the lamp.

She used the screwdriver to unseat the socket, detach the wires, and pull the device from the lamp. Nicollette grabbed the socket and pointed to Jo to follow her outside.

"Here it is."

"What does this mean, Linda?"

Nicollette took a deep breath and explained to Jo that someone wanted to listen in to their conversations and that they would need to be more careful.

"We need to be extra cautious about what we talk about. There may be more of them, and whoever put them here could come back."

The tea was reheated and there was quiet among the two women, neither knowing what to say. While they were eating, a slight flicker of a light bulb in the overhead fixture gave away the location of a second bug. Jo stood from the table and excused herself, making her way towards the hall and stopping at the gun rack in the foyer. She grabbed a shotgun and a box of shells. "I'm off to bed. Let 'em try to come back!" she announced as she walked towards her bedroom, dogs in tow.

Nicollette set up her equipment outside the house for the evening's communications. She ran an extension cord through the bedroom window to power the transmitter. The air was still and the bright full moon illuminated a clear view of Queen Charlotte Bay. As she scanned the bay with her telescope, an odd colored flash crossed the bay. It was a pinkish flash of light that spread across the calm waters of the bay.

She scanned back and forth along the shoreline looking for

a response signal. After ten minutes of searching, she caught a double flash of white light coming from the northwest. *That's near the Smythes' farm!*

She glanced at her watch so she could time the response. Exactly five minutes passed and a triple flash followed by a longer burst of pink light crossed the bay towards the shore. This sequence of signals between ship and shore continued for nearly an hour. The combination of long and short flashes changed at each exchange. *Some sort of code. I just can't dissect it!*

It was late when the activity seemed to stop. Nicollette gave out a yawn. She would be late with her nightly report to Val.

It was after 1:00 a.m. when she started packing up her equipment. One final scan of the bay before going inside. Starting from the north shore and scanning towards the bay, all appeared to be quiet. Nicollette quickly sent a signal to Val. She was careful to open her report by saying her favorite candy was Kit Kat. Must let her know I got the message. Continuing her report, Nicollette coded in "the back garden lights had arrived. Not too sure about the colors, though."

"Just make sure they work alright," Val responded, "and they are plugged in properly."

Nicollette took a final unaided glance over the bay before heading inside. She thought she saw a small white and green flashing dot in the distance. *Maybe my eyes are tired or it's my imagination.*

She rubbed her eyes and looked again in the direction of the lights. It only took a few seconds for her to find the rotating green-white light. It seemed to her as though the dot was getting bigger. She quickly unpacked the telescope and focused on the light. A rush of adrenaline flowed through her veins as she saw the light moving along the bay. With the assistance of the light from the full moon, Nicollette could just make out the silhouette of a small boat through the telescope. She changed the lens and refocused. Her heart pounded as she counted five large rowboats and three platforms moving towards the north shore. The row boats looked to be filled by people, Nicollette guessed to be around ten on each boat. She was unable to see what was on the floating platforms. There seemed to be some kind of covering protecting the contents.

She decided to take a closer look. Monty was sound asleep on the floor as Nicollette quietly put her equipment away in her room. She changed into a dark sweatshirt and placed a nightcap over her head. *Hope I don't need this,* she thought, placing her gun into the back of her pants. Grabbing her binoculars, portable scope, camera, and boots, she headed towards the bay.

The moon provided light as Nicollette ascended carefully towards the water's edge. The ground was rough and uneven, making the footing a bit tricky. It was a slow process. *No need for a turned ankle.* To be evasive to any unseen eyes, she would occasionally hide behind the abundant gorse.

The flotilla of boats and barges were stealthily making their way to the north shore.

She reached a good vantage point about fifty meters from the water. A grouping of rocks and the surrounding vegetation provided cover for her observation nest.

It was nearly 2:30 a.m. when the first boat, about a kilometer away from her, passed her position. A white searchlight scanned the water and the shore just in front of her. When the light went by her, she used her night vision binoculars to get a closer look. She counted twelve people on the boat with two at the head carrying automatic weapons.

The rest of the five boats quietly passed her. She ducked back into the gorse as the searchlight from the fifth boat surveyed the shore. The platform barges followed, lumbering along at a slower pace. Each barge was carrying four people, one stationed at each corner. They were armed with automatic weapons. Nicollette could not make out too much about the cargo. The covers were securely attached to the barges. She could tell that whatever they were carrying, it was large.

It took nearly thirty minutes for the last barge to pass her position. At the end of the flotilla, a sixth boat appeared that Nicollette hadn't seen before. Unlike the earlier vessels, this boat looked to be a private fishing craft, with the cabin positioned higher than the deck and a series of antennas extending a couple of meters upward. The searchlight scanned all around the water and shore as it continued towards the north shore.

It was almost four when the last vessel reached the north shore. Nicollette maneuvered closer to the North Shore. She could see through the portable scope that the flotilla's docking area was Smythes' farm.

She watched as the people quickly disembarked their vessels and the boats headed back across the bay. The coverings were removed from each barge. Nicollette counted six forklifts exiting the first barge and they were immediately put to work, removing large crates. She could see the jitneys carrying their loads up the hill to the Smythes' place and returning to unload the second barge. *More crates.*

The first two barges were quickly unloaded and started back across the bay. When the third barge was unloaded, Nicollette gasped when the covering was removed. Three small artillery pieces and what looked to be crates of shells were revealed. Each artillery piece was chained to a jitney and pulled up the hill. By 5:30, the entire process was completed and all the vessels, including the fishing boat, were on their way back to open waters. A pink light on the horizon flash seemed to signal directions to the mother boat.

The sun would be rising shortly and Nicollette made her way carefully back to Jo's ranch house. She knew that Jo would sleep until at least 7:30, so there was enough time to send this information back to Val in Port Stanley.

Nicollette's hands were sweaty and shaking slightly as she assembled her equipment and started her communications.

Hung nine strands of lights and nearly 100 bulbs are not working. There appeared to be three shorts causing a popping sound when plugged in. Maybe too dangerous to use. I do like the pink, green, and white lights.

Please contact the Jones Company in Forkhill for assistance.

Nicollette pressed the send button and put her equipment away. She fell back onto her bed, exhausted. *Just a few hours' kip.*

"Linda. Linda. You alright? It's gone past ten!"

"I'm alright, Jo. Be out in a minute," she answered in a groggy voice.

Nicollette quickly changed out of her dark clothes and put on her normal attire. Monty was waiting outside her bedroom door and Jo was at the dining table. As Jo started to address her, Nicollette placed a finger to her mouth and pointed to the light fixture. She grabbed a tablet and wrote, "Let's not talk too much, we may still have bugs." Jo winked back. Nicollette wrote on the pad asking if she could take the truck and Monty for a drive to walk along the shoreline of the bay. Jo acknowledged and gave a thumbs up.

Nicollette put together a backpack with some scientific gear and some provisions. She tucked her gun into her jeans and grabbed the keys to the truck. With Monty alongside her, they drove north along Jo's property and turned west to the shoreline. She parked the truck and the two of them started to walk. "We need to get a little closer, old boy."

They walked along the shore to a point where Nicollette could get a good view of the Smythes' place from across the water. She gave Monty a drink and set up her equipment.

Nicollette dug a few small holes and filled her sample bottles with the soil and water from the bay. "We need to make this look good, Monty, just in case."

The high-powered binoculars were perfect for her to see across the water to the concrete docking area at the Smythes' place. *Everything looks quiet, like nothing happened! Even the bay is quiet.*

She wanted to get a closer look at the Smythes' place. Grabbing the backpack, she and Monty headed inland about a kilometer from the shore. They came upon an old wire fence that was in a terrible state of disrepair. Nicollette found a gap in the fence and climbed through it. *This must be a boundary of properties. Maybe the Smythes?*

They reached an area of higher ground that afforded a view of the Smythes' ranch. Nicollette set up her equipment. She scanned the ruins of the ranch house and the farm buildings. She noticed that the door of the big barn building was open and men were moving boxes in and out. There was also movement around the second building and the silo area, however, her view of the second silo was partially obstructed by the first barn building.

"Just want to get a little closer, Monty," she whispered to the obedient dog. They walked further up a hill to get a better view. Nicollette heard motorised vehicles at the ranch. She crouched down and looked through her binoculars. Her adrenaline flow increased when she saw the long barrels of three artillery pieces along the backside of the second building. *Artillery? Are they expecting an attack? What are they protecting?*

The Jitneys were busy moving stacks of boxes from the silo to the first barn building. She noticed two sandbagged positions in front of the ranch house on either side of the road leading in from the main highway. *Machine guns! They are making this place into a fortress! What is going on? Is this about all that German hardware in the silo? An invasion? Bloody hell, they're already here!*

A slight panic rushed through Nicollette's body when she heard the sound of vehicles in the distance. The sound from the motors were becoming louder. *Someone is coming!*

She realized the gravity of her situation and quickly understood the danger she could be in, knowing the odds that were heavily stacked against her. "We need to leave now, Monty."

Nicollette grabbed her equipment and the two of them headed towards the gap in the fence. She saw three large tricycle motorbikes riding along the fence and heading straight for them. Not wanting to show panic or concern, she and Monty continued to walk casually towards the gap in the fence.

The three vehicles caught up with them just as they were about to go through the fence. One of the drivers dismounted his motorbike and approached Nicollette. She could see a holstered pistol on his side. In accented English, he asked for her name and what she was doing here. Nicollette could see the other two men were also Hispanic and one had a rifle by his side. She purposely stood with her back against the fence, in case the outline of her pistol would become visible through her cotton blouse.

"My name is Linda Crowther and I'm Joanne Clarke's niece. I was doing some soil and weather experiments over there," Nicollette pointed to an area beyond the fence, "when my dog chased a rabbit through this fence. We didn't mean any harm. My Auntie Joanne's place is just over there."

The interrogator walked over to his vehicle and picked up the handset of a two-way radio. He spoke in Spanish. Nicollette could just make out what he was saying, her language training coming in very handy. Her ears perked up when he spoke her name and gave the story. He lowered the handset and held his hand in the air towards her and said, "Una moment, please."

A cold shiver ran down her spine when the interrogator turned to the other drivers and said in Spanish, "The boss wants to check her out." The man with the rifle slowly brought it to his lap, finger on the trigger.

Monty was getting anxious and Nicollette knelt to calm him down, keeping her back towards the fence. The last thing she needed was for him to run off and the men to discover she was armed.

Finally, a response came. The interrogator said, "Sí," and looked at Nicollette and smiled. "You can go. We fix the fence."

Nicollette walked through the gap in the fence, pulling Monty as an excuse to walk backwards. The three men drove away, leaving a wisp of dust behind them.

It was early evening when they arrived back at the ranch. Jo was sitting outside enjoying the peace of the early evening.

"Successful trip, Linda?"

"I think so. How was your day, Jo?"

Jo motioned for Nicollette to follow her to the back of the house.

"We can talk freely here, Linda. Ellen Van Ghent called me this afternoon. We had some small talk and she asked about you. I said you were busy doing research and that you had taken Monty and were headed towards the bay. She then told me she had some good news, that she and Mark had bought the old Smythe place and were going to fix it up for their son to live in when he comes back from university."

Jo looked hard at Nicollette, her stare piercing the air like a laser.

"Linda, I don't know what's going on here. Smythe's place has been abandoned for some time now. We were told the property was in the government's hands, but the land was being leased to the Van Ghents in the interim. They said London was going to build a weather station and lighthouse on the property and it was not for sale."

Jo paused and took a breath.

"I don't know what you are doing here, Linda, and I frankly

don't care, but what I do care about is you, young lady." A tear crossed Jo's face as she continued, "I have grown very fond of you these past weeks and I'm concerned for you. You know I'm not well, but you have brought a sense of joy and belonging to this house. I wish you really were my niece."

Nicollette did not know how to react, but instinct directed her to reach out and hug Jo.

"I care about you very much as well, Jo. You make a wonderful auntie. Don't worry, I will be safe."

Nicollette's nightly report to Val was lengthy. She described finding the bugs in the house, the traffic on Queen Charlotte Bay, and the activities around the Smythe ranch. "Someone is turning that place into a small fortress, Val!"

While typing, several questions crossed her mind. *Why bug this house? Am I compromised? Who knows? What is really going on at the Smythe place? How are the Van Ghents involved? What is Port Stanley going to do about it? What can they do?*

Later, as she laid in bed, the pieces of the puzzle started to form a theory in her head.

Geoffrey's radio, the Van Ghents, the artwork, the cyanide, the iron vaults, the underground warehouse of Nazi supplies, the secret boats, and now all those men and equipment, including artillery. What? What? What!

She theorized that the Van Ghents and the uncle, Luuk Claassen, were involved in some sort of conspiracy. *He is out of place here on the west island, but this might be a good place to hide. The back of nowhere. Perhaps all that artwork and those old military supplies are somehow integrated into some larger scheme. The main part could be the armaments. And what about those tanks and vaults? What was or is still in them? Did the murders of Geoffrey Clarke and the Smythes happen because they discovered something?*

The next morning, with her theories still fresh on her mind and having been given permission by Jo, Nicollette walked into the office room and started to scan the several hundred books on the shelves. *Maybe the answer is here somewhere.* Most of the first bookcase consisted of old classics including a large collection of works by Dickens, Wordsworth, and Shakespeare. A surge of energy flowed through her when she discovered a large group of rather obscure books about World War II on the second bookshelf. The books were primarily picture books about weapons, battles, and eyewitness accounts, but a stack of pamphlet type paperbacks caught her attention.

She carried the stack to the desk and searched the titles. Nicollette opened the first pamphlet and saw the paperbacks were published by the Allied military to be used as references for the occupying forces. Towards the bottom of the stack, she saw a pamphlet called "The Treasures of Merkers."

She read that the salt mines around the town of Merkers were used during the war to store stolen Nazi artwork and that inmates would be transferred from the Belsen Concentration camp to work in the mines. *Peter and Geoffrey and perhaps Michael Smythe helped liberate Belsen!*

She found an old atlas among the pamphlets and opened it to a map of Germany. She spotted Merkers just south of Belsen and saw that a main road connected the two towns. Nicollette noticed the same road continued north to the port city of Bremerhaven. *I vaguely remember learning in school that a U Boat facility was located there.* Her brain went into overload when she saw that the Dutch border was only a couple of hours away from Bremerhaven. *The Van Ghents!*

There was a knock on the door, bringing Nicollette out of her intense state of thought.

"Find anything useful, Linda?" Jo asked. She sounded like she was struggling.

Not wanting to raise any angst or difficulties for Jo, she responded there were some interesting books she had found.

"I would like to ask you a question, Jo. Are you up to it?"

Joanne held her hand out and Nicollette guided her slowly to the chair behind the desk. With complete disregard for the potential of bugs, Nicollette asked Jo if Geoffrey ever talked about Belsen.

"I know it was difficult for him and he carried it for the rest of his life, but did he ever talk or say anything that you can remember?"

"He held it in and it nearly destroyed him."

She took a pause and related to Nicollette the therapies and treatments. How Geoffrey withdrew from people and the world. And having to deal with the nightmares and screaming in the middle of the night.

"Jo, this is difficult, I know, but do you remember anything that Geoffrey screamed in his fits?"

Joanne looked at her hands as tears fell down her cheeks.

"One terrible night when we were still in London, Geoffrey was more restless in bed than usual. He kept tossing and kicking and then all at once, he sat up in bed and yelled very loudly, 'It's him! It's him! Stop those trains! Stop those trains!'"

Nicollette could see that Jo had given her everything she could. She walked her back to her bedroom and promised to bring a cup of tea. The pieces of the puzzle were taking shape.

My Turn

Nicollette checked in on Jo as the rain continued to pound against the house. The storm had been relentless for almost three days and the days were wet with very few breaks. These last few days, it was becoming increasingly apparent that Joanne Clarke's health was failing. She hadn't left her room or eaten anything other than some broth and toast. Nicollette would spend time with her, reading a book, telling a story, or just having conversation. Even the dogs, especially Monty, could tell something was wrong. Nicollette rang Dr. Khan in Port Stanley and he promised to come as soon as he could.

Ten days had passed since Nicollette communicated to Val about the large amount of activity around the bay and her subsequent visit to the Smythe place, concluding by adding her own theories to Val. But Val's responses were always the same. "Keep on mission."

Surely, London has spoken to Washington by now! Are they just going to let whatever this is just happen? It could be in advance of an invasion or some underlying plot for something even bigger. I can't believe that London is sitting on their hands!

That evening's communication to Val was the same as the night before and the night before that.

Queen Charlotte Bay was quiet. Too much rain. No unusual activity. Nicollette felt anxious and restless. Between the weather and Jo, she was limited leaving the house. She couldn't leave Jo alone for very long and now they needed supplies. The walls seemed like they were closing in on her, but deep down, there was a feeling that something, something big, very big, was about to happen.

The sun finally made a guest appearance and the ranch

seemed to bounce back to life. Dr. Khan would be there to see Jo tomorrow and Cyril was delivering supplies later that morning. Nicollette let the dogs outside for a run. They enjoyed romping in the mud and even old Monty got dirty. *I'll hose 'em down later!*

Jo appeared to regain some energy, joining Nicky for breakfast and later sharing a cup of tea outside together. The air was fresh, the sun was warm—it was late summer in the Falklands.

Cyril arrived with the supplies and sat with Jo. It had been a while since he'd visited the ranch and the two had much to discuss. "Linda" excused herself to bring out a pot of tea and the accounting books Jo had requested. Nicollette brought a chair to the back of the house and watched over the smooth waters of the Bay while sipping tea. All was calm, *maybe too calm.*

A sudden dull thump in the distance broke the peace and quickly gained Nicollette's attention. It wasn't very loud, more like a distant firework. She scanned Queen Charlotte Bay, subconsciously looking in the direction of the Smythe place. Then there was a second muffled thump and a cloud of yellow smoke followed. The smoke confirmed the sound was coming from the Smythe ranch. *Are they shooting artillery shells? Practice? Calibrating the weapons?*

Nicollette turned away from the north shore and looked towards the westward sky while gathering her thoughts. She stood from her chair and her heart began to race as her eyes could barely make out three vapor trails crossing the dark blue sky in the western horizon. *There are no flight patterns on this side of the Falklands! Who is flying those jets? Are they military jets? Is it related to the yellow smoke? Are they marking the Smythe place? Something is happening!*

Nicollette was anxious to get her information to Val in Port Stanley that night. *If those were fighter jets, then someone in the Queen's services must have seen them! They do have radar in Stanley.*

Nicollette had to breathe as she was typing the message, not wanting to get ahead of herself or let her emotions get in the way of her assignment.

At tea earlier that evening, Jo was able to sit with "Linda" in the dining room. It was obvious that the day's activities had taken a toll on her. Still, it was nice for her to have company as she ate. Nicollette talked about Jo's visit with Cyril, asking if he had any gossip to share. "Not too much, Linda," Jo replied, "but he did mention that the additional help for the lambing season had arrived at the Van Ghents."

Jo explained that each year, the Van Ghents would bring in workers from the mainland, usually Uruguay, Brazil, and Argentina, to help with the lambing. "But that isn't until mid-April. This is very, very early for that. Cyril also mentioned about some construction work taking place at the Smythe place. He explained that three men he had never seen before came into the store for some beer. Cyril said he wanted to make conversation and one of the men volunteered that they were working on an old ranch in the north. He said he was working for 'Mr. Miguel.'"

Nicollette included the news from Cyril about the early arrival of the lambing helpers and the construction workers from the mainland in the nightly communication.

We're supposed to have a party in the near future, and I don't have a clue what to do or where to start! There are too many people involved! It's hard to construct an event like this. I hope it just doesn't end in ruins! Sometimes I just want to forget about the whole thing.

Val's response was,

"Have a good time and stay on point."

Dr. Khan arrived late morning the next day. Jo was able to meet him in the front room where "Linda" had prepared tea for the two of them. "Linda" excused herself and walked to the back of the house with Monty in tow. She looked out over the bay. Her eyes glanced upon some small shapes on the western horizon. She rubbed her eyes and used her hand to shield the glare. *Something is there.*

Nicollette climbed through her bedroom window to get the binoculars, not wanting to disturb Jo and Dr. Khan. The binoculars confirmed what she had seen; a dozen or so fishing boats were heading inland.

Now she faced a big dilemma. *Do I break protocol and contact Val or wait until tonight's communications?* Breaking the rules was only to be used in an emergency. *Is this an emergency?*

She placed the binoculars on the window sill and walked to the front of the house. Dr. Khan met her at the front door and asked "Linda" to follow him to his car. At the car, he turned to her.

"Linda, Joanne and I had a nice chat and she is doing as well as expected."

He put his right hand on her shoulder. "You may have gathered that your Auntie is sick. Since you are her only family and after talking it over with her, we think it is best to let you know what is going on."

Nicollette stared back at Dr. Khan, unable to stop the tears welling up in her eyes.

"Joanne Clarke has terminal cancer. She will have some good days, but I'm afraid they will be fewer. All we can do is make her comfortable. She has medicines to help her with pain and keep her comfortable." Dr. Khan squeezed Nicollette's shoulder firmly. "The truth, Linda, is she may only have a month or two left, if that." He paused for a moment. "I'm very sorry."

The tears were now streaming down her face. Nicollette, an agent with Her Majesty's Intelligence Services, strong and confident, who had faced many dangerous and serious challenges in the past, was now incapacitated by the news about a woman she had just barely come to know.

Dr. Khan gave her a tissue. "I must leave, Linda, they are closing the airport later this afternoon. If there is anything you need, just ring me. Stay strong, young lady, your auntie really loves you."

And then he was gone. Nicollette wiped her face, forced a smile, and walked into the house.

Jo was sitting at the table and Nicollette had a strong desire to hug her.

"Why don't you put the kettle on, Linda, and we can chat."

While preparing the tea, something Dr. Khan said about the airport closure was staying with her. The airport was nothing more than a dirt track with a couple of small hangers. Everything was controlled at Port Stanley. *Why are they closing it? Maintenance? Repairs? Why weren't we notified? Is all of this related? Damn London! All this right under their eyes! Damn London!*

Nicollette poured the tea and added the right amount of milk and sugar to Jo's cup.

"Sit down, Linda, I want to talk with you."

"Linda" sat down next to Jo as instructed.

"Did Dr. Khan talk with you?"

"Linda" nodded.

"I'm glad he did, although I guessed you probably already knew that I wasn't well. You are a smart and bright young lady and I have grown very fond of you." Joanne Clarke paused and gathered a wheezy breath. "I want you to know that having you here with me these past weeks has brought a happiness that I haven't felt for some time. Linda, you have made my last days so much more than I can say and I wanted to say thank you and that I love you, my niece."

Tears were flowing down both their cheeks.

"I love you too, Auntie."

Jo left the table and walked slowly towards her bedroom. She turned to "Linda". "If there is anything you need, please let me know. If you need to find something, you know you are welcome to use the office. Good night, my niece. Sweet dreams."

"Good night, Auntie."

The sun had set and the dishes were put away. Nicollette gathered her equipment and her gun and headed to the back of the house and down towards the bay. She needed to clear her head of the emotional evening and refocus on the mission.

The moon wasn't so helpful tonight, and the ground was still wet, making her hike more challenging. She reached the same spot she used ten days ago and set up the telescope, camouflaging it with vegetation. Scanning the bay, Nicollette could see a pink and white light rotating off in the western horizon. There seemed to be no discernible pattern to the light, just a basic rotation. Looking northward, she spotted several white lights moving across the water. As she suspected, the lights were traveling towards the north shore. *The Smythe place! More troops? Equipment?*

Nicollette jumped to attention when she heard a slight noise off to her side. She moved her gun from the back elastic of her jeans.

The noise was coming closer. She thought it strange that there was no attempt for whoever was coming towards her not to be quieter or to hide themselves. They may not know I'm here. Nicollette knew that to hide and be discovered would be riskier than giving herself away. She put her right hand on her weapon, stood from behind the rocks, and aimed her torch along the water's edge. *Better to know what you are facing then to be surprised!*

Seeing the shoreline was clear, Nicollette flashed her light inland. Her heart nearly jumped out of her skin when she saw three silhouettes about twenty-five meters away. A return light shined on her from the approaching shadows. She could see the silhouettes moving towards the shoreline, using an easier path to reach her.

"Hello there," a voice in Spanish-accented English called out.

Nicollette waited for them to come closer before responding.

"Hello," she called out when she could see three men just ten meters or so away.

The adrenaline in her body was pumping furiously when she saw shouldered weapons on the men. Nicollette took a little pause when she saw two of the men carrying fishing poles and the third carrying a large tackle box.

"Good evening," the man with the heavily accented English announced. "We are looking for a fishing place. Can you help us?"

Nicollette formed a quick response. *A local would certainly know the best spots to fish.*

"There's an excellent spot about a kilometer this way," she stated while pointing southward. "Just look for where a stream flows into the bay."

Satisfied with her response, the man said, "Gracias, I mean, thank you."

Nicollette wished them good luck and the three men started walking away. They had walked only a couple of steps when the leader stopped and turned back towards her.

"Excuse me, but what are you doing here?"

Nicollette could feel his eyes looking over her body. She was alone and anything could happen. If he attacked her, she knew she could take him out and maybe one of the other men with her gun, but the third man would probably have enough time to get her with his rifle. *No odds here. I don't want to reveal myself either. Play it cool, Nicky.*

The man started to reach for her. Nicollette cleared her throat rather loudly, startling the man, and stated she was a scientist and Joanne Clarke's niece, pointing up the hill to the ranch house as she spoke. She told the man that she was doing some studies on the environment and it required nightwork. His hand dropped and he offered to shake hers.

"Good luck to you and your studies."

He turned and walked back to his friends. Nicollette could hear the men laugh as the leader said, "Ella es una científica! Probablemente virgen!"

She gathered her equipment and headed back to the ranch house as soon as they left her sight. She quickly set up her telescope and looked for the men along the shoreline. *Can't see them, too much clutter and a bad angle.*

She turned the telescope to the white lights in the bay. Now she could see eight vessels just off the north shore. *More men arriving at the Smythe place. There must be close to two hundred men there now!* A sudden thought crossed her mind about her earlier encounter. *Were those men really going fishing or patrolling the shore? Did I give anything away? Did they believe me? Am I compromised?*

She set up her radio equipment and started typing her evening report:

> Now there are more people coming to the party. Tested some fireworks earlier. It will be great fun! Hope you can make it! You can bring a dish. Also, the kite you gave me doesn't fly. I will try again soon.

Nicollete waited for the normal response to "stay on mission" or "have a good time," but no response came. She waited the standard fifteen-minute allowed response time and still no reply from Val. She checked her equipment and sent a cleansing signal to Val. Another fifteen minutes passed and still nothing. *What is going on? This is highly irregular! Val??*

Forty-five minutes passed when the green light finally

flashed on her radio. The message that Val sent raised panic in Nicollette;

> Sorry, my friend, but received bad news today. Family member is ill and must leave at once. Unable to come to the party. I will miss you!
> Sounds like a great time! Also...Ben saw Cywa & Eric!...

Her palms started to sweat and her hands shook as she decoded Val's communication. The three dots and ampersand indicated a more serious message and specific decoding instructions. Using the first letter of each word, the message read:

> "Being evacuated now. Stay alert. Will contact you when able. Eliminate routine intelligence communication."

Nicollette stood, clutching the scribbled decoded message in her left hand. Her thoughts were racing a million miles an hour, faster than she could ever begin to make sense of any of them. But one reality exploded in her brain: *I'm on my own now! Really on my own!*

Nicollette took a last look out of the window. *Very quiet now.* She tried taking relaxing breaths in the cooler evening air. *Not much help.*

Not wanting to disturb Jo, she softly walked down the hall to lock the normally unlocked front door. She stopped at the gun rack in the foyer. One was missing. *I suspect Jo still has that one.* Returning to her room, she placed her pistol under her pillow and tried to get some rest.

The first beams of light streamed through the window and drew Nicollette out of her restless slumber. Quickly out of bed and dressed, she bypassed breakfast, grabbed the Land Rover keys, and headed out the door. She wanted to get another look at the activity at Smythe Ranch.

Nicollette parked the truck where Jo's and the Smythe property met at the shore of Queen Charlotte Bay. She grabbed her backpack, put the gun in the holster on her right thigh, and hiked up the hill along Jo's side of the fence. It was better than a two hour's walk, even at a good pace, to reach the spot where she and Monty breached the fence the last time. It was easy to see the fence was recently repaired, but a split board fence wouldn't prevent anyone from merely passing through the boards or climbing over it.

Nicollette knew it was a simple act to go beyond the wooden barrier, but she also realized that this "simple act" could have serious repercussions. She thought through the possibilities while sipping from her canteen.

My mission was only to observe the activity on the bay. This will be unauthorized, so I'm on my own. I will be trespassing and I don't have Monty as an excuse. If I'm caught, it could have significant ramifications for me and many others, including Jo. And whatever I find, who can I tell? Val is shut down! But—but— I need to do this! I need to do this!

Nicollette pulled the binoculars from her backpack and canvased the fence each way. There was no sign of anybody around, however, she noticed the grass was matted down in two lines parallel to the fence. Tracks. *They must be patrolling the whole length of the fence!*

She decided to crawl under the lowest wood plank, carefully avoiding the matted grass. Once past the tracks, Nicollette crouch walked to a spot where she could conceal herself in the thick gorse and have a view overlooking the Smythe ranch. She could feel the prickly needles of the gorse pierce her body as she crawled into the plants.

There was nothing "abandoned" anymore about the Smythe ranch. *It's as busy as an ant colony!* From her vantage point, Nicollette watched as men, most of them bare chested and wearing camouflage military pants, were moving in and out of the farm buildings. The silo covering the underground warehouse had been removed and replaced by a large tent. Jitneys were moving boxes from under the tent to the backside of the ranch house. The three artillery pieces were now positioned openly in the front yard, two facing inland and one towards the bay. There were four sandbagged machine gun posts across the front of the property. They have really fortified the property. *What are they protecting? What are they expecting?*

The rumble sound of an off-road vehicle caused Nicollette to turn around, the gorse scratching her left arm and leg in the process. She looked through the bushes as two all-terrains rumbled past along the path by the fence. A sudden chill raced up her spine when she realized that if they continued down the path to the shore, they would find her truck in less than twenty minutes. She had to leave now, cross the fence, and get as far inland as possible so as not to be easily seen. Nicollette poked her head out from the gorse, all clear, and crouch walked to the fence.

So far, so good, Nicollette thought as she climbed through the fence and took a quick look up and down the path. *Still clear.*

Knowing she needed to get at least a kilometer inland from the fence, she tightened her backpack and started to run. Blisters were forming on her feet from the uneven ground and the heavy work boots. She ran for about ten minutes when she tripped on the uneven ground and landed face first, wincing in pain as her ankle swelled. She sat up, removed her boot, and rubbed the angry ankle. *Damn! Just what I need!*

Nicollette loosened the laces and gingerly put the boot back on the angry ankle. The pain from her ankle numbed only by the necessity to get back to her vehicle hastily. The noise from her ankle would just have to wait. She wanted to avoid any suspicions about her whereabouts should she encounter anyone, so it was imperative that she approach the truck from the south, from well within Jo's land.

It had been almost three hours since she left the observation point on Smythe Ranch. As she limped to the parked Range Rover, Nicollette could see the area was clear. Her heart sank though when she saw that one of the tires was flat. A closer examination showed that the tire had been slashed by a knife. *Sabotage!*

With a painful ankle and blood-stained arms, she released the spare from the truck and swapped out the bad tire. She stepped into the Range Rover and thought she heard laughter coming from beyond the fence. She looked in the rearview mirror and saw four men leaning on the border fence. One man pointed at her. "¡Mira, Carlos, el científico puede cambiar llantas!"

Nicollette knew exactly what was said. The scientist can change tires.

Anger rose within her and her right hand started to reach for the gun. *I bet they don't know that this scientist can shoot a gun! Damn them! Damn the whole lot of 'em!*

After a couple of deep breaths, sensibility quickly returned and she placed the weapon under her blouse. *Stay calm, Nicky, calm!*

Sitting in the cab, she looked back at the men laughing at the fence. "¡Yo también soy un buen científico!" (I'm a good scientist too!) she shouted.

Monty was waiting for her outside the front door. It was very quiet inside the house. Nicollette called for Jo, but there was no response. She locked the front door and hobbled to Joanne's room. Jo was asleep.

Nicollette limped into her bedroom and removed her boots, exposing the swollen ankle. Her reflection in the mirror showed she needed a bath. *But that will wait. I must try to reach someone!*

Setting up the radio antenna, she looked out of her window and noticed a lot of activity on Queen Charlotte Bay. *There's still some daylight. They're not even trying to hide whatever they are doing!*

Despite knowing she was breaking specific instructions, she started to send a message. *Maybe someone will pick it up*, she thought. *Fingers crossed!*

Her hands were shaking as she coded out the serious information. Her instinctual bell was ringing a warning that something serious was about to happen. *Too much is going on!* She closed the signal with:

> The plans for the party are set. We have even planned a few surprises for the guests! It's getting very exciting around here! Can't wait to tell you all about it! Hope your family is doing well...

Nicollette pressed the send button. There would be no return confirmation signal tonight.

In spite of all the thought traffic in her brain, fatigue and the sore ankle won out over the rest of her body. Thinking she would just lie down to get a few minutes' kip, Nicollette, still wet from her bath and wrapped only in a towel, was soon sound asleep.

A loud pounding on the front door brought Nicollette out of her deep slumber. Her watch said 3:00 a.m.

She quickly threw on some clothes as the pounding became more insistent. She grabbed her gun and limped down the hallway towards the front door. Then she heard something that sent her entire body into a nervous shake. A male voice screamed in a heavy Spanish accent, "Miss Beverley! We know you are in there! Open up now or we'll come in and get you!" And then he repeated the same instructions in Spanish.

Nicollette turned off the light in the entryway that was

normally left on in case the dogs needed to go out during the night. She drew her gun and positioned herself behind an upholstered chair, aiming her weapon at the front door.

"Miss Beverley, we know you are in there! Unless you come out now, we are coming in!" And again in Spanish.

Her heart was pounding fast and furious. Her mind was sending quick snapshots of her family across her eyes. *Is this the end?*

Nicollette was not a religious person, but in the moment, she asked for God's mercy and asked for her parents' forgiveness. *Amen!*

Maybe it was bravery or false bravado, but a surge of adrenaline started to flow inside her and she shouted back, "The door is open, you'll have to come and get me!"

In a matter of seconds, the front door slammed open, bright lights from the men's torches temporarily blinding her. She shielded her eyes with her left hand while pointing her gun towards the source of the lights. She could just make out six or seven attackers, fully dressed in black, aiming their machine guns straight forward.

"Miss Beverley, show yourself now! You are coming with us!"

Nicollette realized her situation was hopeless. She slowly stood from behind the chair, her gun now pointing at the figure with the commanding voice. At almost the exact moment she fully exposed herself to the attackers, the overhead light in the room flashed on.

"Oh no she's not!"

Nicollette turned to see Joanne Clarke in her night clothes, leaning against the hallway wall with a growling group of dogs by her side. She was pointing her old shotgun at the attackers.

Jo shouted again, "My niece is staying with me and you lot better leave now!"

There was now almost a deafening silence. Here was an

elderly woman in her mid-sixties, dressed only in her night dress aiming an old shotgun, and Nicollette with her service weapon, holding off a group of intruders with machine guns. For what seemed like an eternity, but was only about a minute or so, nobody moved or said anything. Finally, from behind the intruders and walking into the room, a woman's voice broke the silence.

"Oh yes you are Miss Beverly or should I say Nicky!" The woman pulled the black covering off her face. "Oh yes you are!"

Nicollette's knees almost collapsed from under her when she heard the voice and the hidden face was revealed.

"Lieutenant Amin? Is that you?"

"Yes, Nicky, although now it is Captain Amin of 'E' Squadron 173, but you're a civilian, so I guess you can call me Nazrine!"

"Why are you here? What's going on?"

Without saying a word, Nazrine grabbed Nicollette's arm and brought her outside. She pointed to what looked like distant fireworks exploding in the northern horizon, accompanied by sounds of muted booms. Nazarene brought her to the back of the ranch house and pointed across Queen Charlotte Bay. The bay was lit up with lights and white flashes and there was the distinct sound of helicopters in the distant sky.

Nazrine looked squarely at Nicollette.

"There's a battle taking place on the water to the west and at some ranch to the north. My mission is to get your backside out of here and soon! You'll get your briefing later. The way I figure, we've got about twenty minutes before a group of very angry Argentine Rangers get here. And I don't think it's for tea and small talk! How about it, Nicky?"

Nicollette limped back into the house, past the now group of unmasked soldiers and into her room. She threw everything willy nilly into her cases. Two soldiers helped remove the larger radio equipment and antenna.

Nicollette took one last look at her room, turned off the light, and walked into the front room. Jo was now sitting on a chair one of the soldiers had brought from the dining room. A large lump formed in her throat as she bent down in front of Joanne Clark. Their eyes met in an intense glare of love and respect.

Nicollette had tears in her eyes when she turned to Captain Amin. "What about Joanne? Surely we could bring her along or do something! We can't just leave her here!"

"You are welcome to come with us, Mrs. Clarke, if you wish," Captain Amin said. "We have room."

Nicollette turned to Joanne. "How about it, Jo? It may only be temporary."

Jo put both of her shaking hands on Nicollette's shoulder. "I can't leave the ranch, Nicky. I don't have much time left on this earth and I promised Geoffrey that I would be buried here with him, and that's what's going to happen!"

Sparks of simple humanity passed between the two women.

Jo squeezed Nicollette's shoulder. "Nicky, you've been the best thing to happen to us here at the ranch in a long time and I have grown very fond of you, but you must go. I'll be alright. I do have one favor to ask before you go. One last time, can you call me Auntie Jo?"

Nicollette hugged Joanne Clark tightly. As tears flowed freely down her cheek she whispered, "I love you, Auntie Jo!"

"I love you too, my niece, Nicollette!"

A soldier came running into the room. "Ma'am. The enemy has been spotted about ten minutes away, we better get cracking!"

Nicollette reached over and hugged Monty. She turned to Jo and asked if she could take him.

"Monty is an old dog, this is the only home he knows. If he follows you out of the door, then in his own way, he is saying yes. If he stays by me, then he wants to stay."

Nicollette said a quick goodbye to the other dogs and walked to the front door. She motioned for Monty to follow, but he just sat down next to Jo. Nicollette swallowed hard and blew him a kiss. She waved goodbye to Joanne Clark, turned and limped briskly with Captain Amin to a waiting vehicle.

As the truck headed south, Nicollette peppered the captain with questions. "Where are we headed, Nazrine? What do you think will happen at Joanne's place? And why did you come for me?"

"To answer your first question, Nicky, we're headed to a rendezvous point with your transportation off this island. Someone way above my grade thinks you're pretty important! To your second question, those angry Argentines will be surprised to find about two dozen of our lads waiting for them at the ranch. You, my girl, were probably too caught up in the moment to notice them. I'll bet Mrs. Clarke will be just fine. Now as for your third question."

Captain Nazrine Amin, normally quietly reserved and with an appearance that made her look tough as nails, started to choke up as she said to Nicollette, "I asked for this mission, Nicky. I figured I owed you one. You saved me on that stinking Persian Gulf island. You risked it all for me! And now it is my turn to return the favor, my turn to save you!"

A helicopter was waiting for Nicollette in a field just north of Port Stephens. Captain Amin escorted her to the helicopter's open side door as a soldier offered a hand to get aboard.

The noise from the rotors forced Nicollette to scream. "Are you coming with me, Nazrine?"

"No, I've got those men at the ranch to keep an eye on! Oh, I almost forgot, Mrs. Clarke gave this to one of my men to give to you and she said you are not to open it till you get back home. And that's an order! Good luck, Nicky."

Nicollette accepted the large, thick envelope and waved back as the helicopter quickly flew off the ground.

The attending airman buckled her into a seat. "All comfy, Miss?"

Nicollette looked up from the package she was holding from Jo. "Where are we going?"

"We are headed towards Saint George, Miss."

Everything is Fine

Nicollette slid into the soapy hot water. She would never have believed she would be soaking in a tub at the Savoy Hotel in London when, just a few days ago, she was extracted from Joanne Clarke's ranch and flown by helicopter to HMS Invincible. Despite her angry ankle, the three-day voyage to London on the carrier wasn't that bad. A doctor on board wrapped the ankle and offered crutches. "No thank you."

Nicollette had a private attendant and was the personal guest, throughout the journey, of one of the ship's superior officers. They assigned her private quarters and issued an officer's kit. Even a military style name plate was ready for her to wear on the white blouse. She was invited to the bridge each day, attended part of the daily briefing, and dined in the officer's mess. However, most of the time, she found herself in the communications center, hoping to find out anything about the West Falkland Island and, by default, Joanne Clarke. Now, with the steam rising from the oversized bathtub, she closed her eyes, thinking about tomorrow's special meeting at the Ministry of Defence and what she did to deserve all this special treatment.

A call from the front desk at 11:00 a.m. informed her that transportation to the meeting at the Ministry of Defence had arrived. Earlier that morning, while getting dressed, she realized that all she had to wear was the officer's kit from the Invincible and the clothing from her stay in the Falklands. She had to leave the hotel just after breakfast to find a shoe store. No way was she going to show up at the meeting wearing her work boots, dirty trainers, or wellies!

The driver stopped the vehicle just off to the side of a nondescript building in downtown London. He opened the door and accompanied her through the front door. At the reception desk, Nicollette was asked to wait for a moment. There was a quick call and within a minute, two full suited men arrived to escort her to a private elevator around the corner. One of the men inserted a card into a slot and the elevator door opened. Nicollette noticed there were no floor numbers inside the elevator and instead of going up, they were descending. About a minute later, the elevator opened into a spacious conference room with a large table in the center. The table was surrounded by fourteen leather chairs, one at each end and six at either side. It was a very posh office with wood paneling and two chandeliers hanging from the ceiling. A Union Jack stood in the corner and a large portrait of the Queen hung on the wall.

Nicollette was directed to a chair next to the head of the table and left there by the two men. The room was silent. She was all alone.

A sudden noise off to the side caused Nicollette to turn in her chair. She nearly jumped out of her seat when she saw Peg enter the room through a hidden side door. Nicollette's legs started to wobble and her heart raced when she saw Sarah, Val, Peter Johnson, Charles Thompson, Major Blasingame and Colonel Hartwell behind Peg. *Formalities be damned!* She rushed to greet her team with hugs and smiles.

"I hate to break up this reunion, but we need to be seated," Captain Morely, the liaison between group 226/157 and Sir Harold's office, announced as he walked to the table and pointed out the seating arrangements.

Once everyone was seated, Captain Morely acknowledged an unidentified suited man standing by the hidden door. Colonel Hartwell and Major Blasingame stood as Vice Admiral Sir Harold Stanley walked into the room, followed by the Home Secretary and Deputy Prime Minister, the Honorable Willie Whitelaw.

The Deputy Prime Minister! Nicollette thought. *Crikey! This must be some damn important meeting!*

Sir Harold asked all to be seated and welcomed everyone.

"With your permission, Sir Harold, we are here to brief and conclude the successful mission of 'Operation Stargazer,'" Captain Morely stood and announced.

The suited man by the door began handing out portfolios to the group while Captain Morely continued.

"To review, the stated objective of the mission was to place an agent on the west Falkland Island to serve as a set of eyes and ears on the ground with the specific purpose of observing the area around Queen Charlotte Bay. We believed that this area of the West Falklands was being set up to be used for future subversive activities. We were able to place our agent on the west island, at the ranch of Joanne Clarke. Her husband, Geoffrey, was with the British Intelligence services during the later stages of WWII. But as I said, that was the 'stated' objective. In reality, there were two priorities for 'Operation Stargazer.' We believed that a large amount of hidden military hardware and equipment had been moved from Argentina and was stored somewhere on the West Falkland Island. We estimated there were enough armaments to fully equip a force of maybe two to three hundred men. More importantly, we believed that among the cache of weapons was enough material and hardware for the production of between four and six atomic bombs. We just needed to find it and secure it."

The silence was deafening in the room, only the quiet hum of a film screen lowering from the ceiling could be heard. Nicollette could not believe what Captain Morely had just said. *A hidden armoury? Is that what I found at Smythe's Farm? Atomic bombs! Those big vaults! Did they contain bomb parts? Uranium? Seriously! I was never briefed on any of this! Was I just cannon fodder?*

She looked across the table at Colonel Hartwell, the Colonel's complexion almost pale white and her eyes unblinking in their returning stare. *Did they keep this information from her as well?*

Nicollette's mouth felt like it was full of cotton balls as she reached to pour a glass of water from the center of the table.

"Allow me, Miss Beverley," Sir Harold said, noticing her shaking hands.

Nicollette did not know whether to thank him or yell at him for keeping this serious and dangerous information from her. She nodded instead.

The lights were dimmed and Captain Morley continued as pictures appeared on the screen.

"This mission actually began in early 1945 when Joanne's husband, Goeffrey Clarke, was gathering intelligence in Western Germany. As his group was reconnoitring the assigned area one night, they came across a set of railroad tracks. Lieutenant Clarke checked and couldn't find this particular line on any of his maps. Shortly after the discovery, a darkened train ran past their position, in fact, it was two trains, one following the other. A total of two hundred and sixteen cars passed them heading north. Lieutenant Clarke radioed the information back to London and the response was to stay on mission and that 'perhaps he was using an outdated map'. Lieutenant Clarke was in disbelief. By this time of the war, just about anything that moved in Germany was bombed by the allies, so two large trains would surely have been targeted, he thought. Nevertheless, he carried out his orders, until a few days later, after the liberation of the Bergen-Belsen concentration camp, a squad of German soldiers entered the camp to surrender.

"Lieutenant Clarke was the only Intelligence Officer about, so he was put in charge of interrogating the prisoners. At first, Lieutenant Clarke kept the prisoners isolated, not wanting to risk their safety from revenging soldiers and former inmates of the concentration camp. The German prisoners, after three days of being paraded through the camp and fearing for their lives, agreed to talk with Lieutenant Clarke. With an interpreter, a scribe, and several bottles of Schnapps, Clarke started to interrogate the prisoners. The information he heard was quickly forwarded to London and to S.H.A.P.E., the Supreme Headquarters Allied Powers Europe.

"The German prisoners told of a secret laboratory and factory buried in the ground about fifteen kilometers away. They talked about the production of bombs so powerful, 'it would wipe a city clean off a map!' Several of the prisoners described the use of expendable slave labor from the camps. 'It was very dangerous to work in the factory, there was much sickness and death among the workers, so a steady supply of labor was needed.'"

Several grainy, black-and-white pictures of a German officer appeared on the screen.

"This is General Luke Klaus. General Klaus was in the inner circle of the EER, the Einsatzstab Reichsleiter Rosenberg, the group responsible for the looting and storage of stolen artwork for the Nazis. This group was under the direct control of Hitler."

Nicollette took a hard look at the old black and white photos on the screen. There was something about the pictures that was causing her unease, something familiar, but she just couldn't grasp it.

"By this time, most of the high-level German Command, except Hitler, knew the war was lost and would end soon. They realized preparations were needed for the future. To that end, General Klaus was ordered to remove as much of the stolen treasure as possible from the mines and caves where it was being held. Special arrangements were made to transport the treasure by train to Kiel. From there it would be loaded onto a Swedish freighter and escorted by several U Boats to Argentina. The plan was to take the treasure to Buenos Aires. This would give escaping Nazi leadership resources to live on. Two large trains were packed and headed towards Kiel when an Allied

Bombing mission came perilously close to the rail tracks. The trains were delayed at the bomb factory the squad of German prisoners talked about. General Klaus toured the facility and made a decision to include the laboratory and material to build these bombs of mass destruction to be placed on his trains. He thought the value of such a weapon was much greater than some 'paint on canvas.'

"Workers removed nearly all of the artwork from one of the trains and replaced it with the bomb-making material and equipment. It took several days to complete this task. General Klaus ordered the workers to work fourteen or fifteen hours a day and any stragglers were to be shot where they stood."

Captain Morely took a sip of water and continued.

"Once the task was completed, General Klaus ordered his troops to force all of the workers and anyone involved with the bomb project into one of the large caves. 'With a promise of additional food, no less.' Explosives were placed at the entrance to the cave and as the last train was leaving, the explosives were detonated, entombing those inside. General Klaus wanted 'no informants and no witnesses.' Lieutenant Clarke asked the prisoners how they escaped. They said they were lucky, they were out foraging for food and taking der piss."

The next pictures on the screen showed an old picture of the large port area in Buenos Aires. Captain Morely used a pointer to identify what was believed to be the Swedish tanker. He described how elaborately organized General Klaus's plan was, creating false paperwork to identify the ship as being used for the transport of refugees and displaced persons to the Netherland Antilles islands for resettlement. He even organized having yellow "Jude" stars sewn onto the garments worn by his troops, their families, and the other escaping Nazi officials.

"Lieutenant Clarke was shaken very badly by what he experienced at Bergen-Belsen and when he returned to London, he expressed to us the need to do something about the people responsible for Bergen-Belsen and insisted on being allowed to find the train, its contents, and General Klaus.

"He established a network of contacts throughout occupied Europe and when he moved to the Falklands, he used his amateur radio to continue his search. Although several Nazi hunting organizations were looking for him, Klaus seemed to just vanish. There were claims of sightings in Paraguay, Bolivia, and even in South Africa, but nothing definitive. Clarke continued to believe he was in South America, most probably in Argentina, with his military hardware, stolen treasure, and potentially, the components of an atomic weapon."

A black-and-white film beamed on the screen, giving a much clearer picture of several nondescript buildings with large lorries parked in front. Captain Morely continued.

"Nearly thirty years later, in 1975, we received information from one of Clarke's informants as to the possible locations of the hidden inventory and even Klaus. This film is early surveillance of what we believed to be the warehouse complex where Klaus stored the stolen items. We knew the Argentine government was aiding and perhaps in a partnership with Klaus. An atomic weapon would certainly embolden the dictatorship and give Argentina a strategic advantage over the rest of South America and the South Atlantic. Klaus also understood the tenuous position of the military in Argentina and the instability of the government at the time, so it was agreed to secretly move the material, under the protection of the Secretariat of Intelligence, to an unidentified location. There are ten agents that we know of, seven of them CIA and three of them ours, who lost their lives whilst observing the move."

Even when Captain Morely was talking to the group, Nicollette kept thinking of those grainy pictures of General Klaus, still trying to figure out why he looked so familiar. The Captain talked about Geoffrey Clarke's suspicions that one of his own friends and neighbors, the Van Ghents, were somehow involved with Klaus.

"His suspicions cost him his life."

That last comment was the missing piece Nicollette needed to complete her puzzle. She ran and reran the evidence through her mind; the cyanide syringe in the Nazi case, the fancy artwork and lavish Van Ghent house, meeting Ellen Van Ghent's uncle, and how out of place he looked.

Suddenly, it all made sense and she couldn't contain herself any longer. She stood from the chair and interrupted Captain Morley.

"It's him, it's him! Klaus is Luke Claassen! Ellen Van Ghent's uncle! It all makes sense."

Nicollette looked over the group and then at Captain Morely and finally at Sir Harold, waiting for some sort of reaction to her gush of emotion. Then, after realizing what she had done, she slowly sat down in her seat and bent her head, embarrassed by her outburst.

Sir Harold broke the silence at the table and stood from his chair.

"That's right, Miss Beverley, that's precisely right and we have you and your group to thank for the success of the mission. Your investigations, suspicions, and analysis, Miss Beverley, were spot on. You followed your instincts. With the information you bravely uncovered and reported, we were able to place and confirm Klaus was at the Van Ghent ranch. Ellen Van Ghent is actually Klaus's step niece from her mother's side. Ellen's family is Dutch, Klaus is German. Family ties, valuable materials, money, and willing accomplices make terrific partners. Well done, Miss Beverley, well done."

Sir Harold held out his hand and shook Nicollette's limp wrist. One by one, Sir Harold circled the table and congratulated each individual involved with the mission and Group 226/157.

He returned to his chair, but before he sat down, he placed

his hands on the table and leaned forward.

"I knew Lieutenant Gerald Clarke. He was under my command during and after the war. It was under my leadership that his messages regarding the trains and General Klaus were initially set aside. Lieutenant Clarke was a gentle soul, firmly believing in the good in man. But what he witnessed at the liberation of Bergen-Belsen and later, the information from the German Squad surrender, was too much for him. He confided this with me when he left the service and asked for our support in his personal quest. He was going to find 'that Nazi bastard Klaus' no matter the cost or how long it took. What he started, you lot finished."

Sir Harold caught his breath and with a firmness in his voice, continued, "Geoffrey Clarke said he wanted to complete his last mission no matter what, and damn if he didn't!"

Sir Harold resumed his seat and Captain Morley continued to explain the involvement of the Argentine government in an elaborate scheme to facilitate the export of the stored uranium and bomb components hidden at Smythe's Farm to a third party for enrichment.

"We discovered that the third party involved was the North Koreans. The processing of the uranium was to be done in China. In return for the processing, China and North Korea would get food products, atomic material, future mining rights near Antarctica, and a working ally in the South Atlantic. In return, Argentina would get two or more working atomic bombs."

After a short pause, the briefing continued. Captain Morely spoke about the discussions and high-level consultations with the Americans. The Americans responded that they were "friends" with Argentina and wanted to remain "neutral" in any conflict between Argentina and the United Kingdom. He described how the Americans were in a dilemma as well. They did not want any more atomic material dispersed in the world, let alone in South America or with the Kim regime in North

Korea. Staying neutral, at least on the surface, would allow the Americans to be "peacemakers" should any conflict arise over the Falkland Islands.

"In the end, after reviewing our intelligence, including the discoveries Miss Beverley reported, we received 'backhanded support' for an operation to disrupt the distribution of the materials and secure Smythe Ranch. At the same time, intelligence noted additional Argentine Air Force and Army movements towards bases on the coast. Two large cargo ships that were ported in Buenos Aires suddenly were also leaving. Something was in the mix, so the timing of any mission would be crucial."

Captain Morely took his seat and a well-dressed man stood and introduced himself as James Wilcox, a specialist of the Mission Planning Group 7, working directly for Sir Harold.

"When we saw the intelligence out of Argentina, we knew time was of the utmost importance. Our group predicted we had about forty-eight hours to act. The mission would have to be done with the utmost discretion, no need to alert the Argentines, nor anyone else for that matter. In coordination with the Royal Navy and Air Force, we quickly and quietly evacuated our people from Port Stanley. HMS Invincible would be in range and available for support within the forty-eight hours. Using all the resources available, we reported our position to Sir Harold, who gave the mission a 'go.' We were fully functional in thirty-six hours and on the West Falklands six hours later. I'm pleased to announce that our mission, which we call 'Operation Recovery,' was a success. We secured Smythe Ranch and repatriated Miss Beverley from the Clarke Ranch. The Argentines suffered thirty-six casualties, including twelve killed. We suffered some bumps and bruises and fortunately no fatalities. Our submarines intercepted and captured several vessels and a large number of weapons. Militarily, the mission was a success, however, we are still dealing with the political implications. We'll leave that to the PM and Whitehall.

Overall, well done team."

The briefing went on. Nicollette was listening but not absorbing the information. After hearing about Joanne Clarke's ranch, her thoughts were focused on Jo. *Is Jo alright? What happened there?*

Sir Harold stood to make his final remarks. He reiterated the seriousness of the mission and thanked everyone for their efforts, concluding, "When the history books are written, the operation at Smythe Ranch won't be mentioned, but you can take comfort that whatever the future is in that part of the world, you did Her Majesty's Intelligence Services very proud! And so, I would like to present Colonels Hartwell and Major Blasingame an accommodation directly from the Minister of Defence for 'A mission accomplished with extraordinary skill and bravery in defense of the realm.'"

The well-dressed man handed the two colonels a framed document with a red wax seal. Colonel Hartwell thanked Sir Harold and the group and said a few words. When she was finished, Sir Harold rose from his chair and left the room followed by Captain Morely and the well-dressed man. When the door closed behind Sir Harold, Nicollette felt a numbness creep over her body. The mission was over. Nearly four months had passed since she started preparations and so much had happened, but now, it was finished. 'Mission accomplished' did not fill the emptiness.

Major Blasingame touched Nicollette's shoulder and handed her a folded document. Nicollette unfolded the paper and read an updated report from Joanne Clarke's place. *Joanne is alright. The ranch had little damage. The dogs were a little frightened but are doing well. They are going to use the ranch as an outpost, so Jo will have some company for a while.*

A smile crossed Nicollette's face as Major Blasingame asked if everything was alright.

"Yes ma'am. Everything is fine! Yes, everything is fine!"

The Journey Continues

"What's the first thing you're going to do when you get home, Val?" Sarah asked.

"Probably call my parents and then my boyfriend."

Val had been seeing her boyfriend for about three months before the assignment in the Falklands. Because of their unique positions within British Intelligence, any "dates" the women had would require a background check. Some of these checks could take up to two weeks to complete. The friends had a chuckle when Val related some of the excuses she would use. "Thank goodness he was persistent."

Sarah and Peg also replied to the question saying they would call their parents first. Nicollette expressed agreement with Sarah and Peg, and added, "I'm going to boil a pot of tea, kick off my shoes, and breathe."

The four of them spent the three-hour train ride from London to Cheltenham with each other. They had been through a lot, but despite working and living in the same group of flats with each other, there hadn't been a lot of time when they were all together. Recently, there always seemed to be an assignment away or in a secluded operation at work. But now, they could enjoy each other's company for the trip home and, according to Colonel Hartwell, there was no travel in the system for the "foreseeable future for our group."

The Colonel had taken the women as well as Peter Johnson, Charles Thompson, and Major Blasingame to a posh London restaurant the night before in celebration of the commendation the group received from the Minister of Defence.

At dinner, Colonel Hartwell raised a glass. "Today is a special day. We have worked hard and have come such a long way since Group 226/157 started six years ago! Today we were personally acknowledged by the Minister of Defence for our service. Think about that. It's almost hard to believe!"

Colonel Hartwell paused to let the words sink in, then continued.

"Today's award is recognition that as women, we have beaten the odds and climbed above seemingly impossible obstacles. When our group was first formed, there was more than a little scepticism. In fact, I understand there was even a wager poll to guess how long our group would actually last! Well it looks like some of our 'friends' have had to dig into their pockets! With determination and strength, instinct, skill, and character, we have proven the sceptics wrong, leaving no doubt that a woman can successfully do a man's job in our dangerous profession. We have, we can, and we will continue to operate at the highest level when we are called upon. I know I speak for Major Blasingame as well when I say how proud we are of you and all that this group has accomplished. It's a great day for you, a great day for Group 226/157, and an even greater day for women."

The Colonel then took a moment to add her deep gratitude for the men in the group, saying that they too were instrumental to the success of the group.

"We couldn't have done it without you!"

Later, Major Blasingame handed out train tickets and reviewed the cover story to be used when Nicollette, Val, Peg and Sarah were back home. Colonel Hartwell said to enjoy their trip on the train, purposely leaving out that she had arranged for a suite for their voyage. She left the restaurant.

"I will see you lot Monday morning, sharp!"

Nicollette entered her flat in Cheltenham for the first time since she left it nearly two months earlier. She was surprised to see that the flat had been cleaned. A fresh flower arrangement was on the table with the note, "Welcome home! From Colonel

Hartwell and Major Blasingame." There was even fresh milk in the refrigerator.

Nicollette kicked off her shoes and changed into a pair of jeans while the kettle was boiling. Remembering the large, thick envelope given to her by Joanne Clarke, she grabbed her tea, sat down on the sofa, and slowly emptied the contents.

Lying in front of her were about fifty photographs, most of them in black and white with a few colorized ones mixed in. Nicollette looked inside the envelope to see if it was empty and pulled out two folded up pages of lined paper. She immediately recognized Jo's handwriting as she unfolded them:

My dearest niece Nicky,

Here are some photographs I thought you might like to have. I think you will find them interesting and enjoyable. I was waiting for the right time to give them to you, but that didn't happen. Please share them with your parents and send them my regards. As you know, my health has been failing rather fast and Dr. Khan is coming next week to see if I need to move to Port Stanley. I have made arrangements with Cyril and his wife to move in with me and they will look after the ranch. Cyril tells me there is still a lot of activity around the Van Ghents' place. My guess is you already know about that. Monty is missing you and he has been sleeping in your bed almost every night. Please, Nicky, take care and thank you. I love you, my girl.

Auntie Jo

Nicollette put down the letter and tears started to well in her eyes. She understood that it might be the last time she would hear from Jo, *but I will never forget her!*

She took a sip of tea and then spent most of the evening looking through the stack. She knew there was a call she still needed to make.

Friday night was the men's night at the Cricket Club in Brockworth. Nicollette knew her father would normally get home around half-past ten. At 10:45, she took a breath and called. On the third ring, her mum answered in a groggy voice.

"Hello, who is calling so late?"

"It's me, Mum, Nicky! Sorry for calling so late, but I'm home in Cheltenham!"

There was silence on the phone.

"Mum! Mum! You alright!"

"Yes, Nicky! Just very happy to hear your voice and know you are home. When did you get home? How was the trip?"

Her mum rattled away with questions until her father came on the line.

"Nicky! Everything alright?"

"Yes, Dad. I just got back to Cheltenham and I wanted to let you know."

"I'm glad you called. It's been almost three months since we saw you or heard from you. We were getting worried. When can we see you?"

"I have some things to do tomorrow, but we could have dinner tomorrow night?"

"Sure, we have a roast for Sunday lunch, but we'll have that for dinner tomorrow."

The cab promptly picked Nicollette up at 3:30 Saturday afternoon. She had completed her errands and her body was slowly becoming acclimated to early March English weather. A nice chocolate cake sat beside her in the cab and the envelope with the pictures laid on her lap. Nicollette knew that tonight she would have to be a little more open about her job and the thought of that discussion made her legs quiver.

She was greeted by her mum at the door and the wonderful smell of her cooking permeated the house. Sunday lunch on Saturday! Her dad gave her a hug and they sat down in the sitting room. James had bought bottles of wine and suggested they open one.

As he sat down, he asked about her trip to America. Nicollette took a long sip of wine and started with her story. She explained that her job wasn't really involving visas, passports, international tours, and the like, but that she was involved with government communications throughout the world. She assured them she was always safe and apologized for deceiving her own parents.

"I love you both so much and this was the hardest thing I ever had to do. I'm so, so sorry," she said, her voice breaking up with that last remark.

James stood up and offered his daughter a comforting embrace and Alice did the same. When they sat back down, James turned to Alice and nodded his head.

"We have something to tell you Nicky," Alice whispered.

As if on cue, there was a knock on the front door. James left to open the front door. There was small talk in the little foyer and Nicollette just about hit her head on the ceiling when Peter Johnson and Colonel Hartwell walked into the room.

Nicollette was speechless. Alice kissed the colonel and Peter and everyone sat down with a fresh glass of wine.

"What the devil is going on here?" Nicollette questioned as her father poured wine for the guests.

He turned to her and responded.

"Nicky, you know that Peter and I knew each other a long time ago. After you brought us together at the pub, we decided to all get reacquainted. We were all very close at one time and your mum was a bridesmaid and I was the best man at Elizabeth's and Peter's wedding!"

"Here, here!" Peter added, raising his glass.

Nicollette had already been told in confidence that Peter was secretly married to the colonel, but now it was out in the open.

James continued his story. "When you accepted the position with the government, your Mum and I thought it was a job like you described, but when your brother and I dropped you off at Brize, well, we had our suspicions. Later, when you called about bringing Peter here for Sunday lunch, we both knew you were doing something rather 'hush hush.' After all, we knew Peter was in that sort of secret communications work, so we put it together that you were too. Your mum suspected all along, but refused to believe it. She didn't want to worry about you, so she just didn't accept the truth."

"Mum?"

"It's true, Nicky, I knew that you had more than a government job."

A wide range of emotions swept across Nicollette. On the one hand, she was greatly relieved that her parents had accepted her position. On the other hand, she still felt bad about not being able to fully tell them what her work really entailed. *They understand I am in some sort of secret communications job and are ok with that. I'm not happy about the deception, but I guess I'm going to have to live with that partial fib for a long time.*

Later that evening, Nicollette opened the envelope from Joanne Clarke and shared the photos with the group.

"Where did you get these, Nicky?" her father asked tersely.

"Joanne Clarke gave them to me," she responded.

"But Joanne and Geoffrey moved to the Falkland Islands years ago, Nicky. Were you in the Falklands? What's going on here?"

The feeling of relief after talking with her parents earlier had all but disappeared and was now being replaced with an unnerving anxiousness. Nicollette looked nervously at her father, then at Colonel Hartwell, then back at her parents. *Maybe bringing the photos wasn't such a good idea,* she thought.

However, what was done was done. She had to answer her father, but she also understood there was a line she could not cross no matter what. She took a swallow of wine and tried to formulate a response to her parents. Just as Nicollette opened her mouth to speak, Peter jumped in and responded to James.

"Nicollette has a particular set of skills and we needed her to do some work in Port Stanley. Nothing really, just tidying up some government programs, checking equipment, census, taxes and the like. While she was there, I reached out to Jo to see if she was interested in meeting your daughter. I mean, how often could that happen? To make a long story short, Jo agreed and they spent some time together."

Nicollette was asked about Joanne by her mum.

"Joanne was really nice to meet and I had a wonderful afternoon listening to her stories and looking at the photographs. I think she misses Mr. Clarke and you lot very much. I think she is lonely. Joanne looked well when we visited, but she did mention 'a bit of bother' with some health issues. 'Nothing to worry about,' she said. Joanne was insistent for me to pass on her regards when I saw you again."

After looking at the photos and reminiscing about the events thirty-five years ago, and nearly putting Nicollette to sleep, a final round of drinks was poured and Peter rose from his chair.

"As you know, Elizabeth and I have had to keep our marriage secret for a long time. We've just received permission to be open about it. In celebration, we're going to have a public ceremony to renew our vows, complete with a party afterwards! And, I would like you, James, to be my Best Man again."

"And you Alice, to be my Maid of Honor," Elizabeth added. "And you, Nicky, will you be my Bridesmaid, please?"

Nicollette looked at her parents and smiled. "Absolutely!"

Monday mornings always seemed to come around too fast, but this one was almost welcomed by Nicollette. There was a sense of stability in her life for now. It was the first time in over two months that she, Val, Peg and Sarah would march into work together.

The morning briefing felt like a welcome home reception at first, while the certificate from the Minister of Defence was shared with the rest of the group. But the festivities were short lived. Major Blasingame reminded the group there was still plenty of serious business at hand.

Nicollette was assigned to the European communications cluster along with Val. Peg resumed her role as Colonel Hartwell's assistant and Sarah was assigned to the South American/Argentine cluster. All seemed back to normal. It was March 8th, 1982.

The next few weeks, the communications rooms were busier than normal. There was increasing unrest behind the Iron Curtain and belligerent activity from Argentina.

Nicollette's days were spent communicating with agents, both British and American, in Poland and East Germany. She would occasionally look in on activities in the Balkans, especially Bulgaria, the arena of her first mission. But more often than not, she would find herself wandering to Sarah's area, listening in for news about the Falklands and, by default, Joanne Clarke.

Sarah would, with Major Blasingame's approval, share information with Nicollette occasionally. But on March 23rd, Sarah told Nicollette that a large Argentine taskforce was being assembled at ports along the Argentine coast. "Argentina is getting very aggressive towards us," Sarah said.

"But maybe the Americans can still calm this down," Nicollette responded.

"Maybe but it's getting very serious now and it might be too late."

Those last few words brought a sense of feeling helpless for her Auntie Jo. She thanked Sarah for the update and went back to her desk, calming herself with a cup of tea.

After the next morning's briefing, Nicollette was asked to join Colonel Hartwell in her office. At first, she thought this might be some news on the upcoming marriage celebration, but Nicollette knew that the Colonel never did personal business at work.

She walked into the office and saw Major Blasingame and Colonel Hartwell waiting for her. Peg was there of course, but so were two suited men that she had never seen before. Colonel Hartwell asked Nicollette to take a seat.

An uneasy feeling crept over her as Colonel Hartwell introduced the two men. One of the guests was from Sir Harold's office in London and the other was from Washington, D.C.

Colonel Hartwell opened an interoffice envelope and read the letter inside. The message was intended for Colonel Hartwell and Miss Nicollette Beverley and was directly from Sir Harold Stanley.

Nicollette listened intently as Colonel Hartwell read there was a new group forming between British Intelligence and the American CIA. The group was being put together to coordinate operations and communications between the two agencies. Unlike merely sharing intelligence, this group would be involved in the actual planning and execution of mutual activities for the two agencies. "And Sir Harold has nominated you, Miss Nicollette Beverley, to represent us in this organization."

Nicollette almost fell off her chair. Sir Harold was nominating her to go to Washington and work with the largest Intelligence Agency in the world. She also understood that "nominating" her meant "instructing." She was going to Washington!

The American in the room said he was a CIA Liaison Officer and interjected how excited they were to have her on board. "Sir Harold feels very strongly about you, Miss Beverley."

He described how all arrangements would be made for her, a fully furnished apartment, an on-call driver, and even a visiting chef, if she wanted. "But most importantly Miss Beverley, with you on board, we will build an organization that will further strengthen the safety and security of our nations and enhance our countries' 'special relationship.'"

Nicollette looked directly at the American, then at her superiors. "When would I be leaving? It seems like I just got home."

Colonel Hartwell responded, "In three weeks."

The men left the room and there was surreal quiet as the four women looked at each other, waiting for a reaction from Nicollette. Finally, Major Blasingame broke the tension and reviewed the details of her assignment.

"The appointment is for three years. There will be ten weeks of holiday time, but you will always be on call. All of your travel to and from America will be on special flights. You will still be assigned to Group 226/157 and your salary will be adjusted accordingly."

Major Blasingame removed her reading glasses and leaned forward towards Nicollette.

"Nicky, I know I speak for Colonel Hartwell and the rest of us, that we are going to miss you here in this office. You have grown so much since your days at Brize! We are so proud of you! This assignment along with the personal recommendation of you from Sir Harold is acknowledgement that Group 226/157 has broken through the segregation and prejudices under which we as women have been held back for far too long. We did it because of the determination and courage of our agents and the successes we've had in the field. And you, Nicollette, were more than a big part of that!"

Major Blasingame resumed her seat and Colonel Hartwell looked at Nicollette, "One hundred fold, I agree!"

Nicollette was numb. She felt like she had been just doing her job, not letting the fact she was a woman interfere with the mission at hand. She thanked her superiors for the opportunity. She knew there would be more planning and briefings before she left for America as well as the huge task of telling her mum and dad. But this assignment would be different, she thought. *They will know that I will really be stationed in Washington, at my own place, and I can call home anytime, and they may even be able to visit me!*

When Nicollette was leaving work that night, Colonel Hartwell called her back into the conference room.

"I know you have a lot going on inside, Nicky, but you really are the one for this assignment and I know Alice and James will be alright with this, in fact, they will be very proud of you like we are."

"But what about the wedding?"

Colonel Hartwell reached for Nicollette's hand.

"Don't you worry about that, young lady. You have more important work to do."

As she moved past the security desk and out into the cool Spring air, Nicollette turned to look back at the gray iron door. Her mind was racing with thoughts about her new assignment and all the work that needed to be done before she left for Washington. *Just three weeks!*

Then there was the call she would make later tonight to her parents. She thought about Carol and Ashley. It was nearly four months since she had seen them. So much to do, so little time!

Nicollette took a deep breath. *That gray door. So much of my life is behind that door!*

She turned away and walked briskly to catch up with Val, Sarah, and Peg. *Perhaps a pub night tonight with them, she thought.*

It was March 24th, 1982. Little did Nicollette know that in nine days, Britain would be at war with Argentina and everything would change.

A NICOLLETTE BEVERLEY SPY NOVEL

A NASTY BUSINESS

THE
JOURNEY
BEGINS

A.R. Goldsmith

THE FIRST NOVEL IN THE
NICOLLETTE BEVERLY SPY NOVEL SERIES

In the 1970's. a directive was issued by the British Ministry of Defence to employ more women in crucial roles. This is a story of a young woman living in a small English village that through a series of events, finds herself recruited to join a new group tied to British Intelligence. Nicollette Beverley is caught between the safe and secure life of the village or following her yearning to find something bigger in the outside world and within herself. She deals with the emotion and angst as she accepts the recruitment, leaves her village and begins her secret training, separating from the life she knows and entering into the shadowy world of espionage. We follow her journey and experiences form a Cold War prisoner exchange, to an operation in Bulgaria and finally, completing a mission in the Middle East as she grows into her role in British Intelligence.

www.ingramcontent.com/pod-product-compliance
Lightning Source LLC
Chambersburg PA
CBHW030343020726
47493CB00003B/656